Stranger in the Valley

Book One of the Stranger Series

Gregory Haley

ISBN-13: 979-8-9884071-3-3

Arches Publishing, LLC
www.archespublishing.com

Edited by Jennifer Munro

Cover design by harbinger design

PRINTED IN THE UNITED STATES OF AMERICA

First paperback edition, 2023
10 9 8 7 6 5 4 3 2

For Tricia
I love you more than words

SPECIAL THANKS

No project of this size is created in a vacuum. I wish to extend a special thanks to the early readers who gave me great feedback, advice and encouragement, and the many friends, fans, and others who helped bring this project to life.

Tricia Haley
Catherine Duncan
Amanda Guinn
Ciaran Cooper
Susan Milam
Bruce Findlay
Dorothy Roach
Eric Schimel
The entire staff of Studio One Cafe

Chapter One

Always Honor a Threat

A.J. shrugged to resettle his pack, and cold rain seeped between his rain shell and pants. It was near midnight as he trudged up a forest service road a few miles from his destination. Towering fir trees and rocky cliffs offered some protection from the worst of the storm, but the downpour flooded the narrow ditches and water swept past his feet on the dirt and gravel road, which made even walking treacherous.

Stopping meant freezing to death or drowning, probably both, so he kept his legs moving in a steady rhythm, his head lowered to create a pocket of water-free air to breathe. His headlamp reflected off the rain and made it difficult to see, but his eyes stayed glued to the edge of the road so he wouldn't step off it in the dark. Beyond the glow of his light lay an ocean of darkness devoid of sympathy or forgiveness. There were no cell phone towers this far from civilization, and there was little hope for survival if he got injured or lost. He cursed his misery, and he cursed himself for the thousandth time for making this promise. All his life, A.J. had felt a strangely compulsive need to fulfill any promise made, so he tried to never make them, but he couldn't deny Malcolm that day. So here he was – cold and alone and exhausted – a million miles from nowhere. An old mantra from his military days kept his feet moving forward: "Suck it up and drive on."

Lightening cracked the sky and lit the forest around him. A.J. reflexively squeezed his eyes shut against the inevitable visions of war he knew would accompany the thunder. His mind flooded with gruesome images of Malcolm, mangled and dying in his arms and begging for A.J. to finish him, but A.J. couldn't find the way. Humvees burned and shells exploded around them. The sounds of the .50 caliber machine gun from the forward APC, and the smells of sulfur and blood and burning flesh overwhelmed A.J.'s senses from a decade away. He stepped into a puddle of water halfway to his knee, and the icy coldness snapped him back to the present where he stood with one foot sunk in the roadside ditch.

"Fracking hell..." A.J grumbled. He shook the haunting memories out of his mind and pulled his boot from the muck and adjusted his pack again. The last of Malcolm's ashes weighed heavy on his back, so A.J. focused his mind on the task ahead and resumed his march in the rain.

He rounded the next turn and spotted tail lights ahead that gave him hope for a dry ride. "Finally, a break," he whispered and began jogging toward the lights lest they drive away before he could reach them. His hope faded to dread as the scene of an obvious accident came slowly into view. He approached an SUV rolled onto its passenger side in the narrow ditch coursing with water. The driver's side headlight and bumper were smashed, but a floodlight mounted in front of the driver's side mirror still shone bright enough to illuminate the road for several meters around the vehicle. At the edge of that light, A.J. spied a human body in the road, unmoving and twisted in the unmistakable agony of death.

His head flooded again with unwanted visions, and his heart pounded like a jackhammer against his ribs. He tried desperately to maintain his hold on the present and ignore that terrible nightmare from which he had never quite awakened. He crouched and focused on slowing his breathing and stared at the crumpled form on the road until all he could see or smell or hear was the falling rain. He took a deep breath, shrugged off his pack, and walked slowly toward the corpse.

A golden badge reflected the light, and the gun belt and uniform identified the dead man as law enforcement. A.J. knelt beside the body, and his headlamp showed a curved gash in the man's forehead that resembled the edge of a steering wheel. The rain had washed the wound clean, exposing the bright white skull, but that wound was not what killed him. A.J.'s attention was drawn to a hole the size of a soccer ball in the chest cavity half filled with rainwater. The splintered ribs were folded inward, and the heart was missing, along with a large chunk of the bone, muscle, and flesh of the front chest wall. The dead man's jaw was stretched open with his eyes rolled up in a stare of terminal terror, a look A.J. had seen too many times in a drier climate a long way from an Oregon mountain road.

A.J. examined the heavy badge that was still attached to the ripped shirt. "SHERIFF" was printed in a curved script with a county seal imprinted beneath.

"What the hell happened to you, sheriff?" A.J. whispered in the rain and almost instantly came a terrifying response. A piercing scream from the nearby trees filled him with terror and turned his blood to ice. It was a sound like nothing he had ever heard, not even in the war. It began as a high-pitched wail that lasted several seconds and then devolved into a low growl that slowly faded until only the sounds of the heavy rain on his jacket hood remained.

A.J.'s heart was pounding, and his senses sharpened as they always did when adrenaline flooded his body. He covered his headlamp with a hand and forced his breathing deep and slow while he studied the shadows of the tree line beyond the edge of his light. A.J. knew from experience that there is a place beyond panic where calm determination takes charge. He embraced that place like an old and intimate friend and waited for his turn to die.

That terrible scream wailed again from further away, and then it was gone. A.J. let out a long slow breath in relief. Whatever creature made that sound was moving off. He sat motionless and silent for a full minute before he took his hand off the headlamp and returned his attention to the corpse in front of him. Before he could take a closer look, the sound of breaking branches alerted him to something big crashing through the trees and headed straight at him. His sixth-sense reflexes took control of his body, and A.J. was already sprinting for the SUV before his mind could fully register what was happening. He heard a loud growl and heavy paws splashing through the water behind him, which drove A.J. to pump his legs harder, pulling against the ground with every step while shedding his raincoat as a distraction. Rain pelted his face and blurred his vision, but lightning struck a nearby tree with the booming crack of a howitzer firing, and it lit up the ground in front of him. His muscles screamed for relief from his exhaustion and his will to drive them harder. Safe cover was five steps away, then two. A.J. launched himself at the driver's side window facing the sky and brought a fist down with all his strength to shatter the window glass. It would also break his hand, no question, but he could only deal with one problem at a time. He hit nothing.

A.J.'s clenched fist sailed through the already open window and the momentum pulled his body headfirst toward the water below. He heard the screech of ripping steel behind him as the spotlight and mirror were torn from their anchors and searing pain in his calf as something cut into him on his way through the window. He landed crumpled inside the cab, head and shoulders under water. He scrambled to get his feet beneath him. As his head broke the surface and he gasped for air, an ear-splitting howl of frustration filled the air from somewhere close outside.

He immediately ripped off his headlamp and killed the light. The light from the spotlight outside was gone, but the remaining headlight of the SUV still glowed under the rising water of the ditch, casting a sickly glow through the rain-streaked windshield. He felt around for a weapon or a radio and found both. A pump-action shotgun was still locked in its cradle by the gearshift, and he popped the retaining ring and pulled it free, jacked in a shell, and clicked off the safety. A.J. crouched with the weapon at ready until he was sitting waist deep in the water, staring up into the rain falling through the open driver's side window. He willed himself to take a deep breath and with trembling hands traced the radio cord into the water until his fingers found the handset. It was dripping as he keyed the mic, but he was relieved by the comforting "squawk" that told him it was still working.

"Mayday, mayday!" he yelled. "Anyone on this frequency, please respond! Mayday, Mayday!"

He released the button and waited before repeating the call. Another terrifying howl sliced through the rain, and A.J. began to shake from fear and the cold. He pressed against the steel cage that separated the passenger's seat from the prisoners' bench behind it. He wished it weren't there, as the back seat might give him more distance from the open window, but this was the best it was going to get. He kept one hand on the shotgun pointed toward the falling rain and repeated his call.

"Mayday, mayday!" It was hard to keep the panic from his voice. He forced his fingers to let go of the button long enough to take another breath, and a woman's voice crackled back at him.

"Hello? Frank, is that you? Frank? What's going on?"

"Hey, lady!" A.J. yelled into the mic. "I need immediate assistance. Your sheriff is dead, and something out here is trying to kill me too. Send help!"

"What?" came the startled reply. "Dead? Who is this? Where's Frank? Put Frank on right now!"

"Lady, this is no joke!" A.J. screamed into the mic. "Your sheriff is dead, and I'm about to join him if you don't get some help out here." Another terrifying howl sounded just outside the car. He still had the mic button down. "Did you hear that? What the hell is out here?"

A few long seconds passed before the woman responded. "Give me your location. Do you know where you are?"

"About four miles up a forest service road, where it crosses a two-lane blacktop on the north side of the valley." A blast of lightning lit up the SUV and the land around it. The rain made it hard to see through the windshield, but something big moved in front of the vehicle. He keyed the mic again. "Please hurry!"

"I've got your location," said the woman. "That puts you up near Alice and David's place. Sit tight, I'll send help. Over."

"Copy that," he replied and dropped the mic.

Another lightning bolt cracked among the trees and lit up the mountain. He watched intensely through the windshield but saw nothing. The rain pounding on the side panels made it hard to hear anything beyond the sound of his own heartbeat hammering in his ears. He crouched in near freezing water and stared into the falling rain, waiting and shaking.

He heard the howl again, this time in clipped bursts coming from the trees beside the road, but the roof of the cruiser blocked his sight.

"Well," he said, gripping the shotgun tighter, "come and get me, you bast…"

A second, deeper howl sounded from farther away.

"Well, that's just fucking great. There's two of them." He clamped his jaw to keep his teeth from chattering. He felt an old familiar rush of adrenaline course through his body, and the smell of rusting iron reached his senses. He adjusted his feet and pain flared in his calf. He reached down and felt torn flesh and an oily slickness between his fingers. He was bleeding and badly.

He was in a good defensive position, but he needed to stop the bleeding, or he might pass out before help arrived. A.J. pressed his back into the corner of the roof and steel cage, so he could leverage his injured leg over the center console and out of the water. It was an awkward position with one knee on the passenger door and the other by his chin, but he managed to keep his face above water with the shotgun aimed at the sky.

He took a deep breath and tried to control the shaking in his hands. Keeping a finger on the trigger, he undid his belt with the other hand and worked it out through wet belt loops. It was challenging and slow with his near frozen fingers, but he kept at it and never took his eyes off the window.

He looped the belt just below his knee and pulled it tight enough to slow the bleeding but not enough to stop the blood flow completely. Then he wrapped it around and through itself and pulled tight. It wasn't much, but it would have to do.

A large shadow moved at the edge of the dim light in front of the vehicle. A.J. stared through the blurred windshield, trying to make out what he was seeing. It was like looking through the bottom of wet beer mug. Then the light went out.

The vehicle rocked as something heavy jumped onto it, and A.J. reflexively pulled the shotgun's trigger. The bright flare of the muzzle blinded him, and the blast of the 12-gauge left his ears ringing as the closed space of the cab amplified and reflected it back.

He reached up, feeling for the pump to reload. He was temporarily blinded by the bright light of the muzzle flash, but getting another shell ready was his only hope against whatever was coming in. He was breathing hard and blinking into the falling rain trying to get his sight back. The darkness was broken only by the sickly green glow of the radio, which slowly sharpened into focus. Whatever had jumped onto the SUV was gone. A.J. didn't know if he had hit it or if the sound had simply scared it away, but he didn't care so long as it stayed out there.

The sound of deep, resonant howling began from just outside and was picked up by other howls both close by and deeper in the forest. There weren't just two of these beasts around him. There were more, lots more. They joined in a near perfect, resounding harmony that surrounded and overwhelmed him with the dreadful feeling that this would be his end. It was both terrifying and strangely comforting for A.J., who had imagined a hundred different ways he would likely die, all of them violent, but none like this.

A.J. stared into the blackness, waiting for the attack. The howling stopped, and he heard claws on steel as the SUV rocked again under the weight of something heavy jumping onto the rear of the vehicle, but A.J. couldn't get a shot. The prisoner cage prevented him from aiming the gun in that direction, so he kept it trained on the driver's window and held his breath so his returning hearing might catch the sound of the beast coming in.

"Hello?" the radio startled him. "Are you there? Mister? Hello?" The voice seemed more panicked than before. "If you can still hear me, help is—"

The cab filled with bright light and the sound of a blaring horn. It came from a large truck with a bar full of floodlights speeding toward him, and its engine roared in the night. In the light, A.J. clearly saw the bottom of a wolf's paw the size of a catcher's mitt with claws longer than his own fingers pressed against the rear window glass, and then it was gone. The SUV rocked again as the giant wolf jumped away.

The truck stopped on the road outside. "Hello?" A man's deep voice called out. "Anyone in there?"

A.J. blinked the falling rain out of his eyes and scrambled to get his feet beneath him so he could peer carefully out of the driver's side window at the lights of the truck a few yards away.

"Here!" A.J. screamed back, laughing with relief. "I'm here!" He waved an arm frantically in the light.

"You can come out of there, it's safe now," the voice called back. "Keep your hands where I can see them and exit the vehicle unarmed!"

A.J. felt weak, and his body shook violently. He dropped the shotgun in the water and climbed out of the driver's window with more effort than he expected. He lowered himself to the road, and imagined what he must look like in the bright lights of the big truck. He was muddy, wet, unshaven, and in need of a few good meals. He showed his open hands to a tall shadow outlined by the lights and smiled as big as he knew how.

"Th-Thanks for the rescue," A.J. said through chattering teeth. "Th-Thought I was a go-gonner there. You c-came ju-ju-just in time."

The tall man grunted and looked warily at the SUV and the forest around them. The only sounds were the falling rain and the idling engine of the old Dodge pickup he was standing next to.

"This is a dangerous forest," the man said in a strong, gravelly voice. "It's not safe at night. Get in the truck, and I'll come back in the morning for the vehicle."

"What about the sheriff?" A.J. looked past the man to where the body lay, but the road was empty. The sheriff's body was gone.

"What about the sheriff?" The man pulled a large silver revolver from behind the truck's door and pointed it at A.J. The lights reflected off it like a lighthouse beacon. "Get in," he said.

A.J. considered his options and quickly decided a ride in a warm working truck at gunpoint was a significant improvement in his fortunes. He raised his hands, limped to the truck, and got in.

The tall man climbed into the driver's seat. He wore coveralls and leather boots, and thick white hair stuck out wildly from beneath an oiled leather cowboy hat. He held the big revolver in his left hand, resting on his right thigh and pointed at A.J.'s chest. He put the truck in gear and drove down the two-lane blacktop toward the bottom of the mountain, the windshield wipers click-clacking in the heavy rain.

"Name's Skinner," the man said. "You got a name, stranger?"

"A.J. They call me A.J."

"A.J., huh? That stand for something?"

"Honestly," A.J. answered, "I have no idea."

They rode the rest of the way down the mountain in silence.

Chapter Two

Miss Polly

A.J. kept his eyes on the big .357 Magnum pointed at his chest as Skinner drove slowly down the winding mountain road with the forest looming tall and dark on either side of them. After a few miles, the truck turned into a parking lot where the road met a wider two-lane that cut through the valley floor. Skinner pulled up to a large metal building with a large red fire station logo painted on the side. A smaller house sat across the parking lot. Two rolling doors big enough for fire trucks took up most of the building, but the only light shone through a single glass door on one end with the words FALIA FIRE STATION AND SHERIFF'S OFFICE printed on it.

Skinner killed the engine. It popped and sputtered and tried to restart once, then died. The sudden quiet left only the sound of rain on the truck's cab, lighter than before but still falling hard enough that Skinner had to speak up.

"Now, son," Skinner said in the way old men have when addressing younger guys. "I don't know what happened up there tonight, and I don't know what your part is in it, but Sheriff Standish is a friend of mine, and I damn sure aim to find out."

Skinner raised the big gun to emphasize his point. It wasn't the first time A.J. had stared down the business end of a weapon held by a man willing to use it, but it was the first time he had stared down one that big. A.J. knew his mouth had a bad habit of getting the rest of him into trouble. He decided keeping it shut was the prudent choice.

"The way I see it, you got two options," Skinner spoke calmly but with an edge that suggested he had no problem pulling the trigger if it came to that. "One is to get out nice and calm and walk into that office where Margaret has a warm fire and hot coffee, and we can talk about how your evening's been going so far." Skinner paused. A.J. didn't blink.

"The other," Skinner continued, "is to run and take your chances out there on your own. Now, you ain't from around here, and I know every inch of this valley by heart in case that's what you're thinking. I'm not a man who jumps to conclusions without all the facts, and right now I've got precious few of those and a whole barrel of questions. You might've done something to Frank, and then again you might not have, but the decision you make next will go a long way toward helping make up my mind. Understand?"

A.J. nodded slowly.

"Good. I'll just give you a second to think about it while I put Miss Polly away. No sense gettin' Margaret more worked up than she already is until we know what's what."

Skinner lowered the gun and took his thumb off the hammer, then slid it into a leather holster riveted to the inside of the driver's door. "Any questions before we go inside?"

A.J. couldn't help himself. "Miss Polly?"

Skinner chuckled grimly. "Well, I'm gettin' old and my aim ain't what it used to be. I might miss a little, but she's polly gonna kill you anyways."

"Miss. Polly." A.J. smiled. "Got it." Then he carefully got out and limped into the office.

The heat from a wood-fired stove hit him like a blast from a jet engine. After a long march in the rain, the nightmare on the mountain, and the drive back at gunpoint, A.J.'s adrenaline finally crashed. A wave of weakness washed over him, and his legs began to buckle. He grabbed the front counter to steady himself and dropped his head to keep from passing out. He took slow, deep breaths. It took enormous effort to prevent his shrinking tunnel of consciousness from closing into darkness, but the threat of fainting slowly dissipated, and he lifted his head to survey the room.

A bright orange light glowed through the glass panel of a wood-fired stove on one wall, with an audience of mix-matched chairs arranged in a semi-circle around the fireplace. A heavy woven rug covered the concrete floor.

Beyond the fireplace, a coffee maker, fax machine, computer, and other office necessities crowded a folding table. The back corner held a cage for prisoners. At first glance it looked like a standard-issue jail with painted gray bars, a steel door, and a stainless-steel bench welded to the length of one side. On closer examination, however, A.J. could see it was much more.

The bars of the heavy steel cage were much thicker than a simple holding cell called for, and they formed a cube, with bars on all four walls as well as the ceiling and floor. It was an odd set-up for a small-town sheriff.

To A.J.'s right, a window separated the main room from a small office with a single desk, two chairs, and the scared-looking woman A.J. had seen through the front door when they pulled up, and she wasn't alone. She stood with her arms wrapped around a second, much younger woman with jet black hair who looked like she'd been crying.

"Take a seat," Skinner motioned toward the chairs by the fireplace. "Leave your boots by the door. No need sloppin' up the place."

A.J. pulled off his boots and wet socks, one of them dripping blood.

"You're injured," Skinner noticed the belt-tourniquet as well as the torn pants. "Let's get you patched up."

A.J. tossed the socks into a trash can by the desk and limped barefoot to a wood-slat chair in front of the fire. It was the warmest he'd felt in three days. He sat and motioned to the women. "You can tell them to come out. I don't bite."

"At least you have that going for you." Skinner waved the two women into the room.

A.J. stood as they entered. The women paused before recognizing the move as one of politeness rather than aggression. Margaret forced a smile.

"This here is Margaret. She runs the place." Skinner motioned to the older woman. She didn't offer to shake hands, and A.J. didn't press the matter. He just smiled and nodded.

"And this is Darcy," Skinner said, adding, "Sheriff Frank Standish's daughter."

"Margaret, Darcy, this is A.J."

Darcy looked about sixteen or seventeen, and she was stunning, even with red puffy eyes and tear-smeared cheeks. He'd noticed her dark hair through the office window, but up close it was mesmerizing. It was a deep, oily black without another shade, split end, or stray hair. It seemed to possess a mind of its own, swirling and moving and falling in waves around her shoulders and face, and it glowed. It seemed as if the shine of her hair was produced by the hair itself. Her skin was pale but not translucent. She reminded A.J. of a marble statue he'd seen once in Rome.

Her eyes were the deepest green he had ever seen, almost black, but with a dark gold shimmer when they moved. She shifted uncomfortably under his gaze.

"Hello," A.J. said with as much kindness as he could. He skipped his usual "nice to meet ya" smile. Under the circumstances, it was definitely not nice to meet her. She glanced at Margaret and said nothing. Margaret pulled her closer, and Darcy laid her head on Margaret's shoulder and sobbed.

Margaret combed her fingers through Darcy's hair. "She came running in here just after I sent you word about the distress call. I haven't been able to get a straight answer from her for all the crying.

"There, there, honey," she rocked Darcy from side to side. The girl's sobs tapered off.

"He's dead," Darcy blurted out when she could catch her breath. It wasn't a question. She looked at A.J. and then at Skinner. "My father is dead." Even through the grief in her voice, an odd vibration in her tone reminded A.J. of music.

"Now, we don't know anything yet, Darcy," Skinner assured her. "We just—"

"I know," she said firmly. "I saw it in my mind and felt it in my heart, and I know. He's gone." She buried her face in Margaret's shoulder and started sobbing again.

Skinner gave A.J. a grim look that had "keep your mouth shut" written all over it. A.J. turned to face the fire and sat with his back to the small group.

"Margaret, why don't you walk Darcy back to the house and make her some tea? I'll cover things until Connor gets in," said Skinner. "Let me talk to our guest here and find out what's happened."

"I want to stay," Darcy said. "I want to hear."

"I'm sorry, Darcy. You can't be here. If we need to start an investigation, we can't have the interview biased by your presence. We've got to do this by the book." Skinner helped them both with their raincoats. Darcy looked back at A.J. with a mix of hatred, accusation, and fear, as dreadful to behold as it was tragically beautiful. An image of the sun exploding flashed in his mind, and then she ducked into the night and was gone. A.J. felt a sudden emptiness inside and a longing for something he didn't understand, like a flicker of memory inspired by a smell that drifts by in the wind and then is gone. The harder he tried to concentrate on that memory, the further it slipped from his grasp. He shook his head in exhaustion and went back to staring at the fire.

He really was too tired, he thought. He had already been walking all day and half the night when he came on the Sheriff's body. Almost nothing is as tiring as marching in the rain, and nearly every moment since had been filled with adrenaline-fueled fear. His hands shook, and he was having trouble staying focused. He began to question how much of the last hour was the effect of fatigue-induced hallucinations: The sheriff's body? The monsters in the woods? Darcy's unique appearance? He hadn't felt this sick feeling in the pit of his stomach for years, not since the war and the drug-fueled benders he once used to endure it.

A.J. took a deep breath, shook the cobwebs out of his head, and centered his mind on the orange glow of the fireplace. It was an old technique he used to focus his thoughts when operating on too little rest. He was out of practice, but it helped. By the time Skinner handed A.J. a cup of fresh coffee, his hands were no longer shaking, and he felt mostly in control of his body, if only barely. He shut his eyes and took a careful sip of the opaque brew. It burned the tip of his tongue, but he didn't care. Anything warm felt good, and the pain provided a focal point for his concentration.

Skinner sat on a stool in front of A.J. and opened a steel first-aid kit. He lifted A.J.'s leg and used a pair of scissors to cut the pants so he could examine the wound. The calf had a pair of deep gashes from front to back, and a third shallower wound beneath them. Skinner wiped the dirt and crust away until blood flowed again. He opened a jar of thick white salve that smelled of antiseptic and rosemary and rubbed it into the wounds. The salve burned like fire, but then the pain in A.J.'s leg eased tremendously. Skinner taped the cuts closed, wrapped the calf in a bandage, and removed the belt from below A.J.'s knee. A.J. clenched his teeth against the intensity of pins and needles in his foot as blood rushed back through his leg.

"Why don't you start at the beginning," Skinner said as A.J. caught his breath. "Help me understand how you came to be crouching in the sheriff's wrecked vehicle in the middle of the night with him nowhere to be seen. Did he pick you up someplace?"

"No." A.J leaned back in his chair and cradled the warm cup against his chest. His leg throbbed, but Skinner had dressed it well. "I walked up on the wreck just like you saw it."

"Walked? In this storm?"

"Better than not walking and freezing to death," quipped A.J., then realized it sounded glib and spoke more kindly. "I was headed for the national forest. The weather was clear when I turned off the highway onto that old service road. I decided to push on a few more hours around dusk, but the skies opened up an hour later. In a situation like that, the choices are to find shelter and hole up for the night or just keep walking."

"Well, there ain't much in the way of shelter on that road till you get up near my place," Skinner said. "Okay, so you're headed camping. You camp without gear? Where's your tent? Your pack?"

A.J's heart jumped, and he looked around in panic. Where was his pack? It was the first time in ten years he'd been without it. It was everything he owned, but the stuff wasn't what he worried about. It was the ashes inside that made his guts clench and body tremble. He couldn't complete his promise without them, and it was an effort of will to control his fear and anxiety about its loss. He took a deep breath to calm his nerves and a vague memory filtered into his mind of setting it down when he saw the body, but everything after that was a blur of fear and survival.

"It's back where you found me," he stammered. "I need it."

Skinner watched A.J. carefully and spoke after a long pause. "Okay. I'll head back at first light and have a look. I'll bring it to you if I find it."

Skinner let the word "if" hang in the air before moving on. Then he smiled reassuringly and sat back in his chair. Skinner had a comforting way about him, like a loving father who wanted to hear about all your troubles. A.J. had seen trained interrogators use the same technique with such skill they could convince a captive he actually wanted to tell the nice man where he planted all those bombs. The memory set off A.J.'s internal caution sirens, and he looked carefully into Skinner's eyes.

Skinner didn't blink. His facial expression was kind, and he asked without a hint of judgment, "are you homeless, A.J.? Is there a reason you don't want to tell me your full name?"

It was a classic interrogation technique. Get the suspect to start a story, find a way to question its credibility and make the suspect uncomfortable, and then ask a question to get him thinking of something else, usually personal. The personal questions were throwaways. They only mattered if they proved relevant, but the point was to get the suspect off the story for a moment. When the interrogator goes back to the story, a suspect who is lying will be more likely to screw up the details. If the story is coming from actual memory, the interruptions won't matter. The overall story won't change.

A.J.'s mind was not nearly as sharp as he wished it were under the circumstances, especially facing a disarming but obviously well-trained investigator. Then his slow-moving thoughts caught up to something Skinner said to Darcy on her way out the door.

"You said something about 'doing this by the book.'" A.J. returned the warm smile with as much sincerity and non-hostility as a penitent monk. He was well trained, too.

"Are you an officer yourself? That would make me feel so much safer after the night I just had." A.J. took a slow sip of his coffee, watching Skinner over the edge of the mug.

The two men stared at one another, neither blinking, and then Skinner dropped the act and sat back in his chair. He rubbed the scruff on his chin. "Well, you ain't an idiot," he grumbled. "I'll give ya that."

"Neither are you, sir." A.J. used the clipped and practiced formality of a junior officer addressing brass. "If you don't mind my asking, where did you receive your training?"

"Well, first off, I'm no 'sir,' so just cut that shit out. I worked for a living. Twenty years in the Corps CID. I'm retired now, though I'm also a sworn deputy here. I fill in from time to time when Frank needs an extra hand or wants to go fishing, which is...was often." Skinner looked suddenly sad and shocked at the possibility of his friend's death.

A.J. picked up the conversation to distract Skinner from the dark thoughts he knew from experience were running through the older man's head.

"Marine CID?" A.J. raised his eyebrows and mug in a friendly salute. "Semper Fi, Gunny." He had run into a few of these guys in the sandbox. CID was military code for Criminal Investigation Division, and the Marine units were staffed with non-commissioned officers who had a reputation for cunning and tenacity. They were the only enlisted men A.J. ever saw make an army colonel nervous.

"You know something about the military?" asked Skinner. "Did you grow up in it? I can tell by looking at you that you're no Marine. Army?"

A.J. answered solemnly, staring into his mug. "I grew up in the foster system in Baltimore. Never knew my parents. Didn't even have a name. They told me I was found outside a police station wrapped in a blanket with the initials 'A.J.' stitched on it, so that's what they called me. I bounced around from home to home until I turned eighteen, then enlisted in the Army for a time. Airborne, 75th Regiment. Iraq."

Skinner gave A.J. an appraising look, and his demeanor softened.

"For a time?" Skinner asked after a pause.

"Four tours. Then another four with a private security outfit." A.J. waited for the inevitable sneer he got from career military types whenever they found out he'd turned Merc.

"Oh." Skinner leaned back in his chair. His expression lost its warmth, but there was no animosity in his face. He seemed more tired and sad than judgmental.

"Well, war is war, I guess. When the shooting starts, nobody's checking the tags on your gear so long as you're shootin' the same direction."

"Thanks," said A.J., grateful for Skinner's kindness.

"Don't thank me yet. I still want to know what happened up there, and you ain't told me nothin', so give me the run down."

A.J. took a deep breath. "Like I said, it was raining like hell, and I kept moving to stay warm, but I had my head down to keep the water out of my eyes. I saw the taillight on the SUV when I came up on the crossroads. I thought it might be a ride, but then saw it was on its side in the ditch. My next thought was someone had slid off in the rain, but the spotlight was still on, and I could see something in the road."

"Did you see anything else? Anything or anyone moving near the vehicle?"

A.J. shook his head. "No. Visibility was low." He closed his eyes, took another long breath, and visualized himself standing next to the wrecked SUV. He described the scene with as much detail as he could recall, leaving out the part where his own memories of war threatened to overwhelm him.

"The engine of the vehicle was still warm. There was steam coming off it, and I could see well enough to know there was a body in the road, so I sat my pack down to take a look."

The image of the dead sheriff hit A.J. harder than he expected in his current state of exhaustion. He took a sip of his coffee and opened his eyes. He had to hold the cup with both hands to keep them steady.

Skinner pulled a flask out of the pocket of his overalls and offered it to A.J., who gratefully extended his cup. Skinner poured a dark brown liquid into it that smelled like whiskey and tasted like heaven.

"Go on," Skinner urged. He took a long pull from the flask before dropping it back into his pocket.

A.J. told him everything that happened next, from the description of the corpse to finding the radio to the moment Skinner arrived. Skinner didn't flinch when A.J. told him about the animal sounds, nor did he react when A.J. described the giant paw on the back window. Skinner sat nodding and listening without judgment or scorn. Then he did what any good interrogator would do. He made A.J. tell it all over again while asking questions about specific details along the way.

"What do you do for money?" Skinner asked him at one point. It was A.J.'s least favorite question.

"The time I spent with the private outfit," said A.J. "I never quite felt right about it, so I didn't touch the money they paid me, and it was a lot of money. It's in a bank in Baltimore, and I sort of live off the interest now. It's not much, just a few thousand a year, but it's enough for food and camping fees. More than enough actually."

"I see."

By the time Skinner was satisfied, early morning light was beginning to fill the small space with a dull gray glow, and the last of A.J.'s tricks for staying sharp were failing him. His head felt like it was stuffed with cotton, and he couldn't stay focused. The eerie scream and the howls from the nightmare he had just lived kept playing over in his mind. Skinner stared into the glow of the wood stove and rubbed his chin stubble in thought.

A.J. yawned and rubbed his eyes. "So, you going to tell me what the hell lives in this valley with paws the size of dinner plates and sounds like that? And don't play dumb, I'm too tired for games."

Skinner grunted. "Lots of things live in this valley," he said coldly. "Some more dangerous than others. Could have been anything."

"Horse shit," growled A.J. "You showed up, horn blaring, with a gun in hand and haven't so much as raised an eyebrow at my story. You know what's out there."

"I don't know shit," Skinner growled back. "All I know is my friend is missing and an ex-merc transient was found crouched in his overturned vehicle. Whatever you think you heard or saw out there, all I have is your word, and I don't know you."

A.J. grudgingly admitted the older man had a point. "So, what now?"

"Now you're going to take a nap in that cage over there, and I'm going back up the mountain to have a look around."

The heavy cage and steel bench looked like the Four Seasons to A.J.'s exhausted mind. Skinner waited for him to use the bathroom and then handed him two blankets and a thin pillow. They weren't much, but A.J. was grateful.

"I'll be back soon." Skinner locked the cage door with a heavy steel key.

A.J. tossed the blankets and pillow on the bench and laid down in his dirty but now dry clothes.

Skinner turned back. "Just one question before I go."

"Yeah?" It took effort to focus on the words.

"You never did tell me why you're walking alone in a storm way out here in the first place."

"I made a promise to someone, a long time ago."

"A promise? Must have been one hell of a promise to have you out on a night like this."

"Aren't they all?" A.J. draped one arm across his eyes and took a deep breath.

Skinner paused as if considering something. "Get some rest," he said, then turned and walked out, locking the office door behind him. A.J. never heard him leave. He was already asleep.

Chapter Three

The Other Margaret

The sound of the steel door opening pulled A.J. out of a deep and dreamless sleep. His head pounded as he sat up, and it took him a few seconds to remember where he was. The smell of coffee being offered by Margaret helped clear his mind. His mouth was dry, and he sipped the hot liquid to unstick his tongue and croak out a hoarse "thanks."

Margaret smiled sadly and stepped back into the office, leaving the cell door open behind her. A man in a deputy's uniform sat at the computer, typing, and Skinner stood at the counter with another man in a sports coat and khakis. Standing alone in a corner, a pale woman in a black dress with dark black hair pulled up in a tight bun watched the two men talk. Margaret sat on a stool at the counter, put her head in her hands, and stared out the window at the gray morning. The rain had stopped.

Skinner looked at A.J., who stood up stiffly. The wound on his leg burned with pain, and his back felt like a rope full of knots. A crick in his neck hurt when he turned his head, but he was alive.

Everyone in the room stopped to stare at him. He felt like a tiger on display at the zoo, so he stepped out of the cage and nodded a greeting to Skinner.

"Everyone, this is A.J." Skinner waved in his direction.

A.J. smiled weakly, but no one returned it. A.J. looked down and saw that his already disheveled appearance hadn't improved much with sleep. He probably scared the hell out of them.

Skinner made introductions. "This here is Deputy Connor," he motioned to the thin, brown-haired young man at the computer who flashed a big dopey smile at A.J. and went back to typing. He had a long narrow face, a bad haircut, and his ill-fitting uniform looked at least three sizes too big.

Skinner ignored the woman in the corner, as did the others. She was attractive, with a strong jaw and intelligent eyes. A.J. nodded to her, and her eyes went wide for the briefest moment before narrowing and returning his stare in amusement. Her lips curved into a slight smile that seemed carefully applied and made A.J. feel like a fly invited into a web by its spider. A.J. broke the stare and instead concentrated his attention on Skinner and the other man.

"And this here is Mayor Bradley," added Skinner. "He owns the motel across the road."

The mayor nodded to A.J. with an easy smile and comforting charm that spoke more of naivety than cunning.

"Welcome to Falia," beamed the mayor in a practiced manner that seemed out of place under the circumstances. He took A.J.'s proffered hand and shook it like he was ringing a bell. "I'm sorry we have to meet this way. Frank was a good man and a great sheriff. His death is a huge loss for our valley."

A.J. raised his eyebrows in question toward Skinner. "So, you found his body?"

"Not exactly." Skinner shot a displeased look at the mayor. "I found a patch of Frank's, I mean the sheriff's, uniform and some other remains. The evidence suggests your description of the events last night is accurate. I also found this." Skinner handed A.J.'s pack to him. The zippers were half open, and Skinner made no effort to conceal that he had searched it.

"It was right where you said it would be."

"Thanks," A.J. frowned. He sat it on the ground and took a thorough inventory. He liked Skinner but didn't know him, and A.J. never trusted anyone he didn't know.

The pack was made of heavy-duty ballistic nylon, with a steel canteen hanging on one side and an all-purpose soup pan/skillet on the other. It held a change of clothes, a small towel, a K-bar survival knife, and a paperback copy of a Robert Heinlein novel. A couple of beef jerky packets and a bottle of water purification tablets were stuffed into one of the pockets, along with his toilet kit, a deck of playing cards, and a harmonica he couldn't play worth a damn. Strapped to the bottom was his camping hammock in a waterproof stuff sack and a tarp he slept under when it was raining, which seemed to be every night so far in the Pacific Northwest. It was everything he owned, and it was more than he needed. A.J. rummaged about in the bottom of the pack until his hand found the small remaining pouch of his friend Malcom's ashes, and he sighed in relief. He had a promise to keep.

"Well? Is at all there?" Skinner asked with an edge of annoyance.

"Seems to be." A.J. met Skinner's eyes. "Thanks for retrieving it. I was in such a hurry to leave last night..."

Skinner glanced sideways at the mayor, who wasn't paying much attention, and shot a look at A.J. that suggested Mayor Bradley was on a need-to-know basis about the previous evening's events, and Skinner didn't need him to know much.

A.J. smiled. He and Skinner were going to get along just fine. He slung the pack onto a shoulder and excused himself to the bathroom where he'd seen a small shower on his previous visit.

There was a dried-out bar of soap and a couple of travel-size shampoo bottles in the stall. A.J. took his time under the hot water, enjoying the feeling of warmth and cleanliness he hadn't had for weeks. He let the water soak the bandage off his leg and carefully washed around the painful wound, which seemed much less severe in the morning light. The cuts were clotted over but still raw and weeping. He dried off and re-wrapped the wound with gauze and tape from his own kit. When he wiped the steam from the bathroom mirror, he was startled by his reflection. His hair was longer than he ever remembered it growing, with straggly ends lying wet on his shoulders. His cheeks were hollow and eyes sunken from too many days walking on low rations, and he had two weeks of beard growth, with a few scarred bald patches on his jaw and neck courtesy of a mortar blast that nearly killed him in Iraq. He looked like a homeless bum, but then again, he *was* homeless and had been by choice for nearly a decade as he walked from national park to national park, spreading a bit of Malcolm's ashes in each one, just like he promised. Looking at the person in the mirror, A.J. would have pulled a gun on him, too, if he'd found him hiding out at the scene of a crime. He gave Skinner even more credit for the courtesies he'd been shown.

A.J. took his safety razor from his toilet kit, swapped in a new blade and added water to his lather brush, then set to work on the whiskers. When he was done, he combed his hair back into a tight ponytail and secured it with the rubber band he used to hold the playing cards together. He held up his clothes for inspection. They were torn, mud-covered, and pulled out of shape, so he rolled them up and stuffed them into the bathroom's small garbage can. He pulled out his last change of clean clothes and examined himself once more in the mirror after he dressed. It was a considerable improvement, though he could use another week's sleep and real food before he felt whole again.

When he stepped out of the bathroom, Skinner was stoking the fire, and Margaret still sat at the counter with her head in her hands staring solemnly into space. The others were gone. Skinner looked up at A.J. with a flash of surprise.

"Well, that's an improvement," Skinner mumbled gruffly before turning his attention back to the stove. He shoved the door closed with a stick of wood and latched it into place.

Margaret looked up and exclaimed, "Oh!" She blushed fiercely and hopped down off her stool. "Don't you look nice, all shaved and cleaned up? Are you hungry? There's leftover eggs and bacon from breakfast, and I just made a fresh pot of coffee."

A.J. smiled at her enthusiasm and accepted the food gratefully. He finished the plate in seconds while Skinner was pulling his coat on.

"Thanks, Margaret, but we've got to get moving. I want to take A.J. to the doc to check on his leg."

Margaret giggled and touched A.J.'s arm. This wasn't the first time he'd had this effect on a woman, or even the occasional man for that matter, but it had been a while. It occurred to him that maybe he'd spent too much time in the woods the past few years.

A blast of cold air carried the scent of the forest and rain into the office as the front door opened and two figures wrapped in rain gear, scarves, and knitted hats shuffled in. One pulled off her hat and coat to reveal the sheriff's daughter, Darcy. Her eyes were red, and her face was puffy as though she'd spent the entire night crying, but the mysterious glow was gone. Her hair was pulled back in a ponytail without a life of its own, and though she was quite pretty, there was nothing particularly remarkable about her. He chalked up the earlier visions to extreme exhaustion and smiled at her.

Darcy stopped in her tracks when she saw him and blushed despite her grief. A.J. thought he caught a glimpse of the glow, but it was gone so fast he dismissed it as wishful thinking. What happened next, however, seemed much weirder than Darcy's hair. The other visitor removed her hat to reveal an exact replica of the woman sitting behind the counter, right down to her carefully plucked eyebrows and tight bun drawn back on her head. The Margaret behind the counter wore a simple dark blue dress while the other wore a sweater and denim jeans, but otherwise the resemblance was uncanny. A.J had met a few twins in their late fifties before, but it was rare for them to look so perfectly alike at that age.

"Ah...hi," stammered A.J. as he reached out his hand to the new woman. "I'm A.J."

"Oh, we met last night, silly," replied the woman. "I'm Margaret."

"Oh. My apologies. Of course." A.J. turned to introduce himself to the woman behind the counter. "I mistook you for your sister. Hi, I'm A.J."

The two women shared a glance and giggled the same halting, high-pitched way. They returned to their previous frowns when Darcy wrapped her arms around Skinner and began to sob.

"That's okay," replied the woman behind the counter. "We're used to it. I'm Margaret, too."

A.J. stared at her in confusion and glanced at her sister suspiciously. "Are you putting me on?"

The two women grinned and shook their heads in unison.

"No, we're both Margaret," said the one in blue.

"Doesn't that get confusing?"

"Of course not," laughed the other one. "Why would it?" said the first.

A.J. felt like a bewildered schoolboy who'd just asked a stupid question.

"Don't let it fry your circuits," interrupted Skinner, who was tucking blankets around Darcy in a chair by the fire. "It does seem a bit strange at first, but folks around here don't mind. Doc can help explain a few things."

"That would be nice." A.J. felt very out of place. "I haven't had a checkup for some time." A.J. pulled on his boots while Skinner grabbed a heavy jacket off a hook.

"You're gonna need a coat. Here, use one of the sheriff's old ones. It's not like he's going to be needing it anymore." Skinner's face was sad, and he held it a moment too long before handing it over.

A.J. shrugged into the black leather jacket and nodded gratefully for the warmth. It was a bit too short in the sleeves and too tight in the shoulders, but it would serve. "Thanks. I'm really sorry about your friend. I hope you catch whoever the fuck did that to him last night."

The two Margarets gasped and their friendly smiles morphed simultaneously into identical scowls. The one in the blue dress raised her finger and shook it at A.J. while the other scolded him with a sharp toned, "Language!"

A.J. stepped back in surprise, Skinner snickered at him and headed toward the door. "Best watch your step around Margaret. She's a stickler for manners."

"Sorry, um…ladies?" A.J. touched his finger to his forelock like he'd seen in a British film once, and the two Margarets returned to their previously pleasant smiles.

"That's five dollars in the swear jar," said the second Margaret.

"Five dollars?" asked A.J. "Seems pretty steep."

"It's a sliding scale," replied the first Margaret, waving at the gallon-size jar on the counter. It was half-filled with bills and coins and taped to the side was a list of the more commonly used swear words and their associated fees. "Ass" was listed at fifty cents, and the fees rose to a bold and underlined "fuck," listed at five bucks.

"And you went straight for the grand prize!" The two Margarets giggled.

A.J. patted his empty pockets. "I think I'm gonna have to owe you. I'm a bit tapped at the moment, but I promise I won't forget."

The Margarets' smiles faded into a pair of thin lines while their eyes changed from shining sweetness to a cold hard glare.

"No," said the first Margaret. "You won't," finished the second. They blinked together, slowly and deliberately, which sent a cold chill up A.J.'s spine.

Skinner slapped him on the back. The two Margarets smiled sweetly again, and Darcy had fallen asleep in front of the fire. A deeply confused A.J. followed Skinner into the cold gray morning with a dozen questions in his head, but he only asked one as the two men climbed into the truck.

"Hey, Skinner? You got five bucks I can borrow?"

Chapter Four

The Mysterious Stranger

Only a few buildings made up the town of Falia. About a quarter mile from the sheriff's office along the main valley road were a couple of houses, a small café, a post office, and a general store that all shared one long gravel parking lot. Across the road was a small motel with about a dozen rooms extending off an old Victorian-style house that backed up to the small river than ran the length of the valley floor. "Vacancy" was lit up in neon under a hand painted sign that read "The Bradley Motel" in a fading cursive gold script.

Skinner turned between the café and the post-office onto a narrow road that wound into the trees behind the buildings and disappeared around a sharp bend. They rode in silence, and A.J. enjoyed the ancient forest that hemmed them in on both sides. Skinner took a pair of switchbacks, and the road dipped into a large clearing. A.J. was surprised to see a well-hidden village nestled among the trees with several modern glass buildings mixed in among much older wood frame homes. It seemed idyllic, with clean sidewalks and manicured lawns, and empty flower beds all tucked in from the cold under a layer of mulch. A.J. half-expected to see Mary Poppins float down from the sky.

"Well, isn't this place full of surprises?" A.J. said as they passed a small orchard still barren in winter. Skinner smiled but didn't respond. He clearly wasn't the chatty type. A.J. found his lack of engagement annoying and tried a different tactic.

"This doc of yours going to give me some answers, or am I gonna have to beat them out of him?" A.J. asked with an edge in his voice.

Skinner laughed. "I would love to see you try that. She would kick your ass before you even finished the thought."

"*She* would kick my ass?"

"In ways you cannot imagine. You may have noticed things around here aren't exactly what you're used to in the wider world."

"No kidding. I feel like I've stepped into an episode of the *Twilight Zone*."

"I know the feeling." Skinner pulled into the small parking lot of a flat-roofed, two-story office building covered in tinted glass. A single door was the only feature on the front, with no signs anywhere to indicate this was a medical building save for a lone ambulance that sat idle near a covered portico on the building's west side.

"The doc works here," said Skinner.

"How would anyone know?"

"Everyone knows." Skinner parked by the front entrance.

The interior was as sterile as the exterior. Padded white chairs lined the walls and a low rectangular table held the usual assortment of doctors' office magazines carefully arranged in neat rows and organized alphabetically by title. No pictures hung on the walls and no window opened onto a reception desk. A single door at the far end was the only other way out. A.J. felt like he was walking into an obsessive compulsive's wet dream of a waiting room.

"Should we knock?" A.J. nodded toward the door.

"The doc knows we're here." Skinner sat and picked up a copy of *Reader's Digest* from between a *People* and a *Saturday Evening Post*.

"My grandmother used to read those," A.J. teased him.

"Thought you were an orphan?" Skinner raised an eyebrow at A.J., who smiled broadly.

"Well, whoever she was, I bet she read them."

"I only read it for the articles." Skinner leaned back and flipped the pages. A.J. laughed.

Five minutes later, the door opened and a middle-aged woman with her hair in a bun waved for A.J. and Skinner to enter.

"The doctor will see you now," she said brusquely as they approached. A.J. stared at her in wonder. She looked almost exactly like the two Margarets from the sheriff's office, though a bit thinner with a bright blue streak in her hair. She winked at A.J. as he passed, and that same cold chill ran up his spine again. This place was too weird for words, he thought.

Behind the door was a brightly lit hallway with glass walls. On one side was the emergency room with its own small waiting area and exam tables separated by heavy curtains. The place was empty, but a desk lamp shone brightly above the reception desk, which held a computer and a steaming cup of coffee.

Opposite the clinic was another hallway with windows looking onto the forest across from several exam rooms. Margaret showed them into the first one and closed the door as she left. It looked like a typical doctor's exam room, and, like every other part of the facility, it was sparkling clean.

"A bit odd for a doctor's office." A.J. said as he slid onto the end of the exam table.

Skinner grinned. "'A bit odd' is pretty much the status quo around these parts."

"So, I've seen. What's up with the hidden village here? And what the hell is up with the multiple Margarets?"

Skinner rubbed his chin and considered his answer, but before he could speak, the door opened. Skinner's explanation would have to wait, and A.J. wouldn't have heard it anyway, because the woman who stepped through the door captured all his attention.

The doctor was breathtaking with high cheekbones and bright blonde hair that shimmered in the light similar to Darcy's the night before. It also appeared to generate its own glow rather than reflect the room's light.

She was tall, around five-foot-nine, but some of her height was from the heels of her very expensive leather boots. Her hands were fine, with a careful manicure, and her strong jaw gave her a determined and confident look. Above all, though, her eyes captured A.J.'s breath and held his unwavering stare. Once, during a three-day leave in Greece, following a night of binge drinking and cocaine, he had lain face down on a sailboat in the Mediterranean with his head hanging over the side and stared into the purest blue water he had ever seen. He never dreamed he would see a blue to surpass it. He was wrong.

The doctor smiled when A.J. didn't look away and then reached out her hand in greeting, but A.J.'s mind was too distracted by her beauty to react, and he sat on the table staring at it.

Skinner cleared his throat. "Hello, Brighed," he said politely. "This is A.J."

"Nice to meet you." Her voice also had that strange musical quality he'd heard in Darcy's.

A.J. blinked and nodded but didn't move until Skinner gave him a sharp elbow to the ribs. A.J. coughed and smiled. "Nice to meet you…er…Bridget?" he stammered.

"Bridg-id, with a 'D.'"

"That's pretty."

"I was named after a very great grandmother. She was a famous healer in her time." Brighed snapped on a pair of exam gloves and reached for A.J.'s leg.

"Mr. Skinner tells me you've been injured. May I examine the wound?"

A.J. scooted back on the table, removed his boot, and pulled up the pants leg to his knee to show her the bandage he'd wrapped on it after his shower. Some blood had seeped through.

"I think I caught it on a piece of metal last night." A.J. offered by way of explanation and glanced at Skinner.

"It's okay, she's been briefed," Skinner assured him. "I dropped off what evidence I could find with her this morning to analyze. She's not just the valley doctor, she's also our medical examiner."

Skinner looked at Brighed and spoke in a calm and direct voice without ridicule.

"A.J. here reports the presence of monsters on the north slope of the valley last night at the site where we recovered Frank's remains. Monsters with large paws and long claws like a wolf."

A.J. admired his cop skills again. Skinner new how to build rapport with a suspect.

"Monsters?" Brighed responded in an equally accepting tone. "How interesting." She continued cutting off the bandage without looking up.

It all sounded so crazy to A.J.'s ears now that it was being discussed in the open. "I can't tell if you're both fucking with me right now," he said. He hated being teased.

"Oh, I can assure you, I am not 'fucking' with you." Brighed looked up from her work to stare at him in earnest. "We take monsters in our valley very seriously." She returned her attention to A.J.'s bandage. When she spoke again, her voice was different. It was melodic and compelling, and it pulled A.J.'s attention away from his anger and suspicions and frustrations.

"I believe you, A.J., about the monsters. I want you to know that." Her voice washed over him and resonated with a power that vibrated through his body. It embraced him. It caressed him, and he found it calming and comforting like a warm blanket on a cold night.

"We've lost a very close friend in the death of our sheriff," she continued. "We are all in a bit of shock at the moment, and the most important thing to us right now is finding who, or what, killed him. I could really use your help with that. Will you help me?" She looked up again and trapped A.J.'s eyes with those incredible blue pools of light. He was lost in them, and his mind swam in those pools with an overwhelming desire for her. A.J. had never felt anything as loving, and compelling, as that look. He wanted to do everything possible to keep that feeling going. A small voice in the back of his mind shouted, "beware!" He ignored it.

Brighed smiled. "If it's all right with Mr. Skinner, I would very much like you to tell me everything that happened last night, and remember, details are important. You never know when one will lead to a vital discovery."

A.J. felt as though he might give his own liver to her if she asked. The warning voice in the back of his mind yelled louder, but he was enraptured. A.J. found himself telling the story of the previous evening, including details he now remembered clearly but hadn't recalled before. He remembered the sounds of something large and powerful splashing through the water, and the smells of wet fur and of blood. He also recalled more clearly the moment of sliding through the car window and feeling the sharp pain in his leg as something sliced into it on the way through. He shivered involuntarily in the crisp memory of cold rain and fear. The shivering pulled him back a little into his own mind.

A.J. became aware of a low hum in his head, but muted like a beautiful melody being played under a blanket. He tried hard to focus on it and heard a language he didn't understand, and a question buried inside like a cypher that slowly emerged in bits and pieces until he could make out a faint whisper… *"Did Dian send you? What is your purpose here? Did Dian send you…"* it repeated. He could feel tendrils of her thoughts touching his mind, exploring his memories, seeking… searching. His head began to ache with the effort of concentration.

The powerful sixth-sense instincts that had saved A.J. so many times in his life, whether he wanted them to or not, hammered against his determination to ignore them as he tried to focus on that whisper. It began to burn in the front of his mind, and he gradually became aware of a searing pain, just above and between his eyes. It finally distracted him from that whisper, and it broke the hold Brighed had on him for the briefest of moments, but a moment was all it took for his instincts to gain full control of his will and force the unwelcome intrusion from his mind.

Like a drowning man breaking the surface of the sea, A.J. took a sudden deep breath and nearly fell off the exam table as he jerked away from Brighed's touch. He squeezed his eyes shut against the splitting pain in his head that threatened to steal his consciousness away. He gripped the sides of the exam table and forced himself to exhale with a loud moan of pain. His heart beat rapidly, and it was a challenge to get control of his breathing, but after a few dozen heartbeats he felt it begin to slow as he concentrated on the moment. The pain subsided with each breath into a sharp throb that ranked somewhere between the worst hangover in the history of mankind and a rifle butt to the forehead, both of which he knew unfortunately from firsthand experience.

When he opened his eyes, he saw Skinner steadying Brighed against his shoulder as she leaned into his arms. The bandage on A.J.'s leg was almost off, and a pair of stainless-steel scissors lay on the floor.

"What in the hell was that?" A.J. pressed his palm to his forehead and spoke louder. "What did you do to me? Who the fuck are you people?"

The look on Skinner's face was a combination of confusion, anger, and fear. He held the doctor until she could steady herself. The glow about her was gone, and when she opened her eyes, they seemed less brilliant and confident than before. She was still the most beautiful woman A.J. had ever laid eyes on, but anger has a way of highlighting the bullshit the heart refuses to see. She was just another person after all, a strangely powerful, beautiful, and weird person, but a person who just invaded his mind in a way that confused and frightened him. Whatever it was, A.J. wanted no part of it.

Brighed opened her eyes and recovered her composure. She straightened her lab coat and retrieved the scissors from the floor. She tossed them into the sink, pulled a sterile pack from a drawer with another pair of scissors inside, and changed her gloves. She moved deliberately and efficiently and kept her head turned away from A.J., who glared at her in anger. Skinner's look of confusion turned to suspicion as he glanced back and forth between A.J. and Brighed, but he said nothing.

Brighed spoke first, facing A.J. with fresh scissors in hand and her eyes flashing bright once again. "You are a very interesting person, A.J., though I really think we must come up with a proper name for you. The initials simply will not do."

A.J. had reached his limit.

"Get the fuck off me," he snapped angrily and slid back on the exam table out of her reach. "Have I been drugged or something?" He pressed his palm into his forehead again and tried to clear the pain and fog from his mind, but he couldn't contain his temper. "Now, I've been damned patient waiting for some answers to what's going on around this place, and nobody is touching me until I get some. Who are you people? What in the hell were those things I ran into last night? Why does your hair glow? And who the fuck is Dian?"

"Now hold on…" Skinner jumped in to defend the doctor, but A.J.'s last question stopped him short and even Brighed lost her friendly smile. They both stared at A.J. as if seeing him for the first time.

"Who are you?" Brighed's melodic voice was commanding. It resonated power, and A.J. could feel again that strange pressure on his thoughts, but she lacked her previous effort's effect on his mind. A.J. wouldn't let her in his head again so easily. He saw surprise flash in her eyes before they turned cold again.

"Where are you from?" She demanded, but A.J. just stared at her in angry silence, which seemed to unsettle her. "What is your clan?" Her voice wavered. She seemed as confused as she was angry.

A.J. paused deliberately just to make clear to her that he was speaking on his own terms.

"My clan?" he asked in a low and steady voice despite the throbbing in his head. "Lady, I don't know who, or what, you think I am, but I have no fucking 'clan,' nor a family, nor friends, for that matter, and that's exactly how I intend to keep it. Trust me, everyone is better off that way." A.J. let his inner voice guide his words without filter, which very rarely ended well for him, but he was finished playing with these people.

Brighed narrowed her eyes and stepped back from A.J., and the tension in the room rose ominously. From the set of her jaw and the fire in her eyes, he could tell she didn't like being challenged and certainly wasn't accustomed to it. A.J. returned her stare without blinking and started calculating an exit strategy. The muscles in his shoulders tensed.

"How 'bout we all take a deep breath?" Skinner chimed in. He eased his body between them with his hands raised. "I'm fairly confident we're all on the same side here. A.J. tells me he grew up an orphan on the east coast. He never knew his parents."

A.J. and Brighed broke their gaze and looked at Skinner. A.J. was perturbed at Skinner for sharing that information, but the tension in the air eased perceptibly as Brighed's anger dissolved fully into confusion. A.J. relaxed his shoulders but not his suspicions. He noted the ease with which she slipped from one fully formed emotion to another. It was unsettling.

"This is impossible," she whispered to Skinner.

"Well, impossible seems to be sitting on your exam table," Skinner replied. "Believe me, I'm as surprised as you are."

"I doubt that very much," she replied and looked back at A.J. with intense curiosity. Then she spoke to him in the most beautiful language A.J. had never heard before, or rather, she *sang* it to him.

"*Na' luthu na'aha Avay?*"

The tones she used vibrated through him. He couldn't understand the words she was saying, but he felt a kind of sense of them, like something he heard in a dream and couldn't find the words to explain.

"*Ta'a eilu a'vay est Dha'Anam,*" she sang again. The sound mesmerized A.J., and he caught himself drifting off in search of its meaning. He could feel Brighed's mind pressing against his again. It still felt strange but not invasive this time. It was like a gentle, curious touch, as if she was asking for something politely, and he wanted her to have it, even if he had no idea what it was. A.J. pulled back from that mental caress lest he lose himself in it again and glared at Brighed suspiciously.

Brighed changed her demeanor yet again. She spoke in the confident voice of the doctor she had used when she first walked in.

"Please allow me to apologize for my rudeness." She removed and replaced her exam gloves again and stared at him appraisingly for a long moment. "I'm not quite sure where to begin explaining things. You see… well. You are a very unusual, umm…person, and I am caught a bit off guard." She peeled the last bits of blood-soaked bandage from A.J.'s leg and began cleaning the skin.

"You were an orphan?"

"I wasn't an orphan." A.J. replied without emotion. "Orphans had parents. I never had those. I did grow up in the system though."

"That must have been difficult," she replied. "Considering how different you must have felt from everyone around you?" Brighed watched A.J. carefully, but he kept his reactions to himself. She returned her attention to his leg. "I suspect you have always known that you are not like other people?"

"Doesn't everybody feel that way?"

"Well, yes, but not like this, and I think you know what I mean." Brighed glanced at him, and her eyes looked through him as easily as if he were made of glass. He shivered. He didn't like where this was heading.

"You're just like everyone else in most ways," she continued. "But you're better at everything, aren't you? You learn faster, you move faster, you're stronger, and you never get sick. Am I right?"

"Yeah, you're a regular psychic. You want to read my palms next?" He was trying to deflect from a topic he didn't like, even if what she said were true. His entire life he had indeed been faster, stronger, and smarter than everyone he met. He could read when he was three, and he could outrun the best varsity athletes by his freshman year in high school. His teachers called him 'gifted,' whatever the hell that means. He just knew it made him a target for every bully on the street and in the classroom, and that included most of the so-called adults. In his experience, that 'gift' was a curse that cost him everything he had ever cared about or wanted in this world. It was why he preferred to be alone.

Brighed carefully examined A.J.'s wound with a puzzled expression. "Do you heal faster, too?"

When he looked down, it appeared much less serious than it had the night before. It barely seemed bad enough to have bled so much.

"I've always been a fast healer," he said, astonished. "But never this fast."

"I see." Brighed glanced at Skinner with a knowing look. "Interesting," she said.

"I used some of your salve on it last night," Skinner added, rubbing his jaw. "But those wounds were bad. I've never seen anyone heal this fast, not even someone like you, Doc."

A.J. raised an eyebrow. He wanted to ask what "someone like you" meant, along with a dozen other questions, but Brighed changed the subject before he got the chance.

"How do you know the name Dian?" She asked. Her face was calm, but A.J. could sense the anxiety in her words.

"Do you usually ask questions you already know the answer to?" A.J. replied calmly, though he was still angry and wary and beginning to get a bit creeped out about the whole thing. "How did you do that by the way? Get inside my head like that? Is it some kind of hypnosis?"

Brighed's smile was kind. "Something like that," she said. "It's not as hard as it seems, at least not around here.

It wasn't an answer, but she didn't give A.J. a chance to object.

"And the glow you mention seeing around me," she said while putting a clean square bandage on his leg. "Have you ever seen this before?"

"Yes. Just now when you came in, and with the sheriff's daughter, Darcy, last night, but it wasn't there later." A.J. rubbed the back of his neck and added with a grin, "of course, there've been a few LSD trips where that sort of thing happened, but I probably wouldn't count those if I were you."

It was his turn to ask questions.

"What do you mean 'it's not hard around here'? What's so special about here?" He glanced at Skinner for support, but the old man was leaning against the wall and staring at A.J. through narrowed eyes as if trying to make up his mind whether A.J. was really the unlucky hiker he claimed to be. Skinner would be no help to him.

Brighed tossed her exam gloves in the trash and stared at A.J. curiously before answering. "Let's just say, this valley has a very 'magical' quality to it." She smiled at him with kind eyes, and that golden shimmer in her hair expanded, forming a halo about her head and a soft glow around the rest of her.

A.J. stared in wonder. "You're telling me I'm not hallucinating this right now?"

"No. You are not hallucinating."

Brighed placed a hand on A.J.'s shoulder, and the glow about her vanished. She smiled warmly, which calmed his rising anxiety but unsettled his mind. A.J. felt an intense desire to trust Brighed, even though he never trusted anyone. He felt unbalanced and confused and scared.

"I just have one more question." Brighed spoke with concern in her voice and a compassion that surprised him, but not as surprised as he was at what she asked. "Have you ever broken a promise?"

The question stunned A.J., and he pulled back from her touch and gasped. The look he gave her must have explained everything, because she broke her gaze and nodded as if she understood.

"How do you know about that?" A.J.'s voice was shaky. He resented that she knew such things about him when he knew nothing about her. He looked accusingly at Skinner, who merely shrugged.

"Words have power," said Brighed. "Especially those words, and especially for you. For…us."

A.J.'s head swam with questions, and he could feel an old familiar panic building inside him. Less than twenty-four hours earlier, his life had been simple. He was walking to the last stop on his long trek across the continent visiting every national park and scattering Malcolm's ashes a bit in each one. He remembered the night of heavy drinking and boasting when the two of them made a promise to hike across the lower United States together and camp in every national park, or to spread the other's ashes in each one should one of them not make it home. It was the kind of promise that had no real meaning to most people. It was a kind of boasting that comrades do to psych themselves for battle, but A.J. was not like most people.

He had learned early never to make promises to anyone, because, for some reason, he always felt obsessively compelled to fulfill them, but he couldn't deny Malcolm that one night. They had been through too much together, and, in truth, A.J. hadn't really minded, because he always assumed the one not making it home would be him.

Yet here he was, a hundred miles from nowhere with one last stop to make. Nine years and seven months had passed since he stepped off the transport from the Middle East. Nearly a decade of solitude and peace and penance, until last night when he found the sheriff's body on the cold and rain-drenched road. Now his life felt exponentially more complicated, and he still had no idea what the hell was going on in this gods' forsaken valley, but he knew he wanted out of it.

Brighed gently took A.J.'s hand in hers and spoke in a soothing voice that calmed his mind. "There is much I have to tell you, and a lot you will not understand," she said. "For now, it is enough to know that you are indeed very different from everyone you have ever met…*and now you are no longer alone in the world.*"

These last words overwhelmed him. She spoke without moving her lips or making a sound, but they were as clear to him as any words he had ever heard. All his life he'd been alone, except perhaps for a few years fighting with his unit in the desert, and those men were all dead now. The emptiness in his heart where family and love were supposed to live was a dark blanket that kept him warm in the cold and vicious world he had always known. Brighed's words, or perhaps her thoughts, touched gently upon that space, and A.J. reflexively pulled back.

"Who are you?" he whispered.

"I am Brighed of the First Clan, daughter of Elana of the line of Brighed. I provide healing and care for all the clans and people of the valley."

"Okay," he said, unfazed by her titles. "That tells me nothing. Maybe a better question is *what* the hell are you?"

"That is the better question," she smiled. "I am like you, and you are like me. We are Tuatha D'Anu. Then she sang again with that lyrical tone that sliced through his defenses and resonated in his soul. *"Nu a'Tuatha D'Anu. Loth a'a Tuatha De Danaan, toh Pan a'a Tuatha Mel'a a'dian,"* she sang. "I'm sorry, the words don't translate very well into modern English. Perhaps the simplest description is that we are descended of the First Ones, the first humans created by the gods to defeat chaos and bring order to the world. We are..." Brighed paused and considered her words, "somewhat unique among humans. It's how you could hear my thoughts before. I'm sorry about that. It wasn't very polite of me."

"No shit," A.J. agreed with her on that. "And what about those things I heard and saw last night?"

"They are the *Na'ahEEm*," she said. "They live in this valley. They are usually not dangerous to people. I refuse to believe they killed Sheriff Standish."

"Na-ah-what?" A.J. stared at her.

"We call them Shifters," Skinner butted in. "And the good doctor and I disagree about their relative danger to humans."

Brighed glanced at Skinner and pursed her lips in disapproval.

"Shifters?" A.J. stared at Skinner. You mean, like werewolves?" A.J. scoffed at the word, but Skinner's frown didn't change.

"Some of them, yeah." Skinner replied. "But what you've seen in the movies is not a very accurate depiction. They're not really what you think."

A.J. looked from one to the other. "Werewolves? You're out of your mind. What a load of horse shit. What are you people playing at?"

A.J. laughed and shook his head. "Nope. Sorry. I'm not buying whatever the hell you two are selling. I'm just a regular guy looking for a place to camp. I don't glow, and I don't sing, and I clearly am losing my fucking mind right now. I have no idea what the hell is going on around here, but I've had my fill. It's time to get off this crazy train." A.J. jumped off the table and laced up his boot.

"Thanks for the patch-up, Doc. I'm real sorry about your friend getting killed last night. You have my condolences. You've also just confirmed there was something else out there, whatever it was, and now you both know I had nothing do with his death. You have my statement. If it's all the same, I'd like to get on with my journey now."

A.J. motioned toward the door. "If you could just give me a ride to the edge of the valley closest to the national forest, I'll get out of your hair."

Skinner and Brighed looked at each other, but neither moved out of A.J.'s way.

"Oh, dear," Brighed said. "I can see that you are skeptical."

A.J. gave her his most polite "no shit" stare, then looked at Skinner. "Shall we?"

"Well," said Skinner slowly. "I can drive you there, but the walk out is harder than it looks."

"I can take it. I walked across this continent one step at a time. A few hard miles don't scare me." A.J. had the determined look of a person willing to dig through the mountain if that's what it took. Skinner stepped aside.

Brighed sighed and smiled sadly at A.J. "Thank you for sharing your story with me. I hope we get to meet again, so I can answer some of your questions."

"Thanks, but I've already heard enough," A.J. replied as courteously as he could.

She nodded and turned to Skinner. "Mr. Skinner, if you could please come back after your errand, I would like to review the autopsy results, at least what there are of them, from the evidence you brought by this morning."

She left the room without waiting for a response. Despite his desire to get away from the valley, A.J. felt a longing as the door closed behind her, like something he desperately needed had just been taken away. He shook the thought out of his head and followed Skinner back to the truck.

The drive out of the small village was silent save for the occasional rattle of Miss Polly against the driver's door. They turned west onto the two-lane that cut through the valley floor. It wasn't a busy road, but they passed a handful of cars and a couple of slow-moving lumber trucks laden with massive tree trunks on their way to the nearest mill. Falia was the kind of small town no one ever heard of. No one was ever from Falia, and no one was ever on their way here. Those who did find themselves on this lonely highway either lived here, or they were lost. Either way, it was the kind of place you might miss if you blinked at the wrong time, and no one driving through would know that a thriving modern village existed just over the next hill. A.J. was already trying to forget it.

The only buildings they passed were the fire station and sheriff's office and its accompanying residence. A.J. had seen people glowing with hair that moved on its own, had his mind invaded in a way that made him shudder, met three nearly identical women named Margaret who gave him the creeps, and been attacked by giant wolves on the side of a lonely mountain highway where the local sheriff had just been slain. A.J. had been to and through some mighty strange and dangerous places in his life, but this lonely valley was definitely the weirdest place so far. He'd be happy to be rid of it and never come back.

Skinner pulled the old Dodge onto the shoulder at the bottom of a hill. The air was dense with moisture and a heavy mist clung to the ground and licked the trees and thick undergrowth that hemmed them in on both sides. The popping and clicking of the truck's engine cooling were the only sounds in the stillness around them. Both men climbed out of the truck and met between the headlights to shake hands.

"Sorry about your friend." A.J. slung his pack onto his shoulders. "I hope you find out who, or what, killed him."

Skinner nodded his thanks and motioned toward the hill that disappeared into the mist. "That's the edge of the valley. The road's a bit steep and the mist gets thick, but make it through that and you'll be fine."

"You mean no more monsters to worry about in the dark of night?" asked A.J.

"Well, I wouldn't make a habit of walking alone at night through this forest if I were you. But I'm confident you'll have a safe place to sleep tonight."

A.J. let the subject drop. Whatever he would find, it would be somewhere away from here, and that was fine with him. Without looking back, he left Skinner standing in front of his truck and walked into the mist at the base of the hill. He breathed a sigh of relief when the cool wetness enveloped him. The sun dimly lit the haze, just bright enough to show the painted lines of the narrow road but not bright enough to see more than a few feet in any direction. Flashes from the previous night kept jumping into his mind. The sheriff's mutilated body and contorted face in the rain, the mad sprint to the wrecked SUV, the giant paw on the rear window, the glowing hair of Darcy and Brighed and her amazing blue eyes, all threatened to steal his attention from the white line that would take him away from this place of nightmares.

A.J. crested the hill between two sheer cliffs and felt the power of the ancient mountains around him. He walked the line on the road's edge in case a car sped past in the dense fog, but nothing came through. In the silence of the mist, he heard his own breathing and the slow, steady pace of his boots on the asphalt. His mind slipped into the easy meditative state of walking that he had perfected over many years.

That got him to thinking about things, like how long he had been walking and why he had taken nearly a decade to fulfill his promise to Malcolm. He thought about the doctor and how she had touched his mind with hers and how her singing words had struck him so deeply. What happened back there had scared him, and A.J. was not easily scared. Still, he wondered what it might feel like to not be alone in the world for a change. He wasn't prepared to believe such a thing was possible. It was a hope he had long since abandoned. He was breathing harder than usual for such an easy walk, and he felt lightheaded and dizzy. After a dozen more steps, he had to stop to catch his breath, leaning over with his hands on his knees.

"Too much blood loss, not enough rest," he muttered. He set his jaw and kept walking for several long minutes until the road turned downhill and he could breathe a little easier. The mist swirled and got thicker and wetter as he descended. He could barely see his own feet. He walked another few minutes when the mist thinned enough to reveal a pair of headlights emerge in the fog from a stationary vehicle. As he approached, the gray form took the shape of a pickup truck, and the man leaning against it seemed awfully familiar.

"Change your mind?" Skinner called out.

A.J. scratched his head in confusion. "I must be losing my mind. How did I get turned around? I was walking a straight line."

"That can happen in the mist sometimes," Skinner said with a sad smile. "You're welcome to try again. Just keep your eyes and feet on the white line headed out. I'll hang out here just in case you lose your way again."

A.J. narrowed his eyes at Skinner. Without another word, he spun on his heel and headed back into the mist. This time he wasn't taking chances. He locked his eyes on the white line and kept his boots marching along it. He picked up his pace to a fast march to keep his heart rate up and his mind sharp. The wound on his calf throbbed with each step, but his mind was focused as the road began to twist and climb and his breathing grew labored. At the crest of the hill between the two cliffs, he felt his mind fog again and the dizziness returned, but he dug a thumbnail into his palm and sucked quick deep breaths in through his nose. After a few more paces the feelings passed and A.J. practically sprinted down the hill.

He emerged from the mist in the trees that seemed so much a part of this region. Giant Fir trees mixed with occasional spruce and hemlock crowded in on both sides of the road like castle walls. The forest floor was thick with blackberry brambles and brush. The only way forward or back was this isolated two-lane blacktop. As the road levelled out again, A.J. squinted through the fog to assess his surroundings. After a few more steps, the same headlights appeared and an old Dodge pickup slowly came into view. Skinner sat in the driver's seat with his hat pulled down over his eyes.

A.J. marched straight toward the pickup, his anger rising with each step. He wanted to break something.

Skinner tipped up the brim of his hat. "Well," Skinner spoke slowly. His eyes were kind with a hint of sadness in them, "would you have believed me if I'd told you?"

A.J. ground his teeth, then marched to the passenger side and climbed in, slamming the door and staring through the windshield in silence.

"Hey," Skinner said, starting the engine. "It ain't the truck's fault!" He patted the old Dodge on the cracked dashboard and spoke soothingly as he put it in gear. "It's okay, darlin', he didn't mean it personal like."

The drive back to the doctor's office was as silent as the drive out but much less pleasant. A.J. stared out the passenger window. He hated feeling trapped or controlled, and right now he was feeling plenty of both. There had to be a way out of this damned valley, and the first step would be getting some answers about what was really going on.

Skinner broke the silence as they passed the post office and turned toward the peaceful little village over the hill. "For what it's worth, I'm sorry for all this. Of all the backwater roads you could have hiked down, you had to choose the one that leads through here."

"Wherever the hell 'here' is! What is up with this damned valley? Can you take me back out the way I came in?"

"Nope, sorry to say. You remember that winding switchback road you came down on the other end of the valley? Passes right through the same mist. The mist is always there. It keeps our somewhat 'unusual' residents safe, mostly by keeping them from leaving unless they have a pass. Can't really explain how it works, but that pretty much goes for most things around here."

A.J. shook his head in disbelief. "So, if I hadn't stumbled onto the sheriff's body —"

"You'd have walked back down the same road a few miles farther on. The mist wall goes all the way around the valley edge."

"Are you trapped here too?"

Skinner chuckled. "Nope. The mist don't care about Dredge like me."

"Dredge?" A.J. softened his tone.

"Regular humans."

"Regular… You saying I'm not human?"

"No. Well, not exactly. You are human." Skinner seemed to be looking for the right words. "You're just 'more' human than I am."

"That makes zero sense."

"Yeah, it's complicated."

"Sure. Complicated," A.J. growled. He had other questions, so he shoved his rising anger down and kept his voice steady. "You're telling me you can leave whenever you want? Why the hell are you still here then?"

"Here? Well, here ain't so bad," Skinner smiled. "I've been all over the world during my stint in the service, and most places are either dull, hot, or full of assholes. Usually, all three. Here, things are different. Hell, most days, it's actually kinda interestin'."

"Interesting isn't exactly how I'd describe it. You grow up around here?"

"Me?" laughed Skinner. "Nah. Not many Dredge from here, but there's plenty of us work or live here anyways. Usually, folks find their way here by travelling through and falling in love with the place, so they stay. I first stumbled into this valley almost forty years ago chasing a perp down from Whidbey Island. A young corporal got drunk at on off-base bar and smashed a townie in the face with a beer mug. Killed the poor kid. The corporal ran. He was sticking to back roads and heading south when I chased him into this valley. I caught up to him over by the lake when he ran out of gas, and he chose to take his chances in the woods with me about 100 meters behind him."

"Did you catch him?"

"Not exactly," said Skinner. "It was getting dark and starting to rain. Nothing like last night, mind you, but enough to make the ground slick. I was climbing past trees and scrambling around blackberry brambles looking for a way through when I heard a wolf howl somewhere up the hill that sent shivers down my spine. Then I heard another howl closer to me and decided the higher call of duty was back inside my car."

"Smart move," A.J. chuckled. "I take it your perp wasn't so bright."

"Apparently not. I sat there til first light, watching his car in case he returned, then I searched the whole area. There was a spot further up the hill that looked like a hell of fight had taken place, but other than some torn-up ground and a bit of blood, I didn't find a damned thing."

"So how do you know he didn't get away?"

"When I got back to my car, his bloody clothes were folded up on the hood, along with his boots, wallet, and dog tags. One of the tags had a hole through it about the size of a wolf fang. From the condition of his clothes and the amount of blood in his boots, I sincerely doubt he was the one who left them there."

A.J. let out a low whistle. "Damn. I'd say that's unbelievable, but the list of shit I don't believe has been getting awfully short today. What did you do?"

"What could I do? I reported back to my C.O. and turned over the evidence. I expected him to send me back with a squad and a helicopter, but it didn't happen. A few weeks later the report had been buried, and I was reassigned. I couldn't let it go, though, not a mystery like that. I had to know what the hell happened on the hill that night."

"That's a dangerous personality trait for the military," A.J. said, then added under his breath, "or any other outfit for that matter."

Skinner grunted. "Ain't that a truth? I started coming back every time I got a bit of leave. Poked my nose around a few times and damn near got my head blown off sticking it places I shouldn't have. That's how I first met Frank. Although he wasn't sheriff back then, just a wet-nosed deputy chasing drunks and handing out speeding tickets."

"So was your sheriff, Frank…was he a Dredge like you or was he one of these werewolves or whatever Brighed claims to be? What was it she called me? Tooth Ad…?"

"Tuatha D'Anu," Skinner corrected. "But no, he was a Dredge like me, but everybody liked him. He'd met a young D'Anu woman from here who was working in Seattle at the time. He followed her back when he was just a teenager and married her before joining the local law. He caught me trespassing on the mill owner's land while I was tracking that wolf pack. Frank tossed me in the cage, and eventually we got to talking, and by midnight we were into the whiskey. We were best friends by first light, though he got docked a week's pay for getting me drunk on duty."

"Sounds like my kind of guy." A.J. wanted to mention the irony of Skinner's friend being most likely killed by the same wolf pack that was the genesis of their meeting, but he saw in Skinner's face the shock of profound loss that A.J. himself knew only too well. He redirected the conversation.

"So, is Frank why you stayed? Must have been quite the 'bromance.'"

Skinner laughed again. "Nah. There was a pretty young gal named Alice who I met while cooling my heels in the cage. She delivered sandwiches twice a day. She had red hair and pale skin and freckles." This memory brought back Skinner's easy smile. "And the first time I kissed her, she glowed like an angel."

"It had to be a girl."

"Not just any girl. She was the one. Still is for that matter. Been married thirty-five years in April, and she still glows every time I kiss her."

The light in Skinner's eyes when he talked about his wife made A.J. sad in his own turn. Loneliness was an unfortunate side effect of his migrant life, though he usually felt a kind of pride in it as a self-imposed penance for his own dark past. Still, he'd never felt for anyone in a way that made his eyes shine like that. An image of the doctor flashed into his mind, and he quickly changed the subject.

"What about Darcy? Where's her mom?"

"Ingrid was killed by a drunk driver on this very road when Darcy was about two."

"Oh, damn. That's terrible. Poor kid." A.J. knew what growing up without parents felt like, and he felt sorry for the girl. He sighed and watched the towering trees pass them as Skinner wound his way back toward the hidden village. There were too many questions running through his mind, and he still couldn't accept the things he'd seen, heard, and felt in the past 24 hours. He thought of his military training courses on how to survive when caught in hostile territory. He felt like they applied to the moment. His first priorities were to gather intelligence and keep his head down while he assessed his next move.

"After you met Alice, you went back to CID?"

"I did. I put in my twenty while she went to university, and we spent all our spare time back here before we settled down for good when I retired."

"Are you telling me you purposefully chose to live in a valley full of werewolves?" This was his opportunity to pin

Skinner down on what A.J. felt was a crucially under-discussed topic of interest. The wound on his leg itched to the point of distraction. "Doesn't seem like a reasonable decision."

"Well, like I said, 'werewolf' is a fairly poor understanding of the situation, at least so far as Hollywood goes. There's some elements of truth there, of course, but there's a whole lot the outside world doesn't understand. It's—"

"If you say 'it's complicated,' I'm going to punch you in the nuts." A.J. was only half joking.

"Well, it ain't fuckin' simple!" Skinner glanced at A.J.'s leg. "I know what's on your mind, by the way, but you can't catch it."

"Catch it?" A.J. played dumb.

"Werewolf. Being a Shifter isn't a disease. It's not something you can get on accident from a bite or scratch. That's just some shit the storytellers made up to justify hunting 'em down. Shifters are all born that way, like any other species. The BS about people getting turned into werewolves is a myth."

"Well, that's a relief," A.J. said and meant it. He reached down and scratched until the itching subsided. "You know, you might've led with that information."

"Yeah, but what's the fun in that?" Skinner laughed and dropped the truck into lower gear to turn into the parking lot in front of the doctor's office. It was busier than it had been earlier with several more cars and a motor scooter leaning on its kickstand next to the front door. Skinner found a space and turned off the engine, which sputtered and tried to kick back on a couple of times before giving it up. The two men sat in the cab in silence staring at the front doors. A big man in a heavy coat with long hair and a thick beard shambled slowly inside. As he opened the door, a woman carrying a child in one arm and pulling another along by the hand walked out.

A.J. didn't relish the thought of going back in there. He knew from his days in the sand that individuals were rarely a threat, but crowds were both a threat and a target. The thought of going into a crowded building made his chest feel tight. It started getting hard to breathe, and he sniffed the tang of panic in his mind. He closed his eyes and took a long slow inhale.

"You okay?" Skinner asked.

"Fine," A.J. answered weakly, then repeated in a stronger voice, "I'm fine. Five by five." He sat up straight and took a few deep breaths to steady his hands. "So, what happens now?"

"Now we go find out what the doctor has to say about the remains I found this morning. We've still got a murder to solve."

"We?" A.J. stared at Skinner and shook his head. "Look, I'm sorry about your friend. Really, I am. But if you haven't noticed, I'm not exactly the 'getting involved' type. Not anymore, anyway. I abandoned that personality in the desert a long time ago. If it's all the same to you, I just want to figure out how to get the hell out of this crazy valley and be on my way."

"Well, it's not all the same to me," Skinner barked with the authority of a twenty-year veteran sergeant. "Frank was the best friend I ever had, and so far, you're the only witness to what the hell happened out there last night. So, I'll be damned if I let you out of my sight until I catch the son-of-a-bitch who killed him."

A.J. cracked a smile as he sat up at straight attention. It had been a long time since he'd felt the verbal lash of a sergeant, and coming from Skinner, it made him strangely homesick. Skinner glared at him for a moment, then sat back and frowned in sad resignation.

"Truth is, with Frank gone we're in a world of hurt. Frank was respected in this valley, and he somehow managed to keep most of the old feuds around here at a low simmer. If it really was the wolf clan that killed him, there's going to be hell to pay, and I'm just not prepared to handle that kind of trouble without some help."

"What about your deputy? What's his name? Connor?"

"Yeah, but he's just a kid. Don't get me wrong, Connor is a good deputy, but he lacks experience. I'm going to need a seasoned investigator on this case, and it's not like I can go to the state police for help with our 'werewolf' problem."

"But you hardly know me," protested A.J.

"On the contrary. I know three things about you. One, you were Airborne, which speaks highly of your fitness, character, and abilities if not necessarily your decision-making skills. Two, you worked security detail in a war zone for that merc outfit, which means you got police training and combat experience too. That's going to be helpful."

"You expecting a war?"

"If it turns out the wolf clan had something to do with Frank's death, especially in the particular place it happened, it's practically a declaration of war. That's why the only thing I've told anyone is that Frank died in a car crash. You, me, the doc, and her assistant are the only ones who know the rest so far, and we need to keep it that way until we have proof, or things are going to get very bad very fast around here."

"Your sales pitch could use a little work," A.J. said, but he didn't object to Skinner's argument. He wasn't wrong on any point. "So, what's the third thing?"

"You're one of them," said Skinner, motioning toward the building. "And that's going to help when it comes time to start asking questions."

"Oh, yeah? What makes you so damned sure?" His protest seemed foolish considering what he had experienced over the past few hours. Then it dawned on him. "The mist. That mist was a test, wasn't it?"

"It was the fastest way to be sure. Like I said, the mist don't care about Dredge like me."

A.J. shook his head in frustration, then a thought occurred to him. "If I help you catch this killer, then can I get out of this valley?"

"When we catch this bastard," replied Skinner. "I'll guarantee your safe passage out of here."

A.J. considered Skinner's offer. "You know, there's a very strong chance I'm actually dying from pneumonia in a ditch on that mountain right now, and this is all just a weird fever dream, right?"

"Well, then, it won't cost you nothin' to say yes, will it?"

"Fair point," A.J. laughed. "Okay, what the hell. Let's go catch some bad guys."

Chapter Five

Digger

In the clinic's waiting room, several chairs were occupied with patients waiting to be seen. What A.J. saw destroyed what remained of his grip on the reality he had always assumed. The shambling fellow sat with his head down and the coat's hood pulled low so A.J. couldn't see his eyes. Between the long beard and thick mane of dirty black dreads sticking out, he looked to be made almost completely out of hair, assuming it even was a fellow. A.J. couldn't actually tell.

A tired looking woman held a squirming and crying child whose skin was black as night and seemed to be, for all practical purposes, smoldering. A young girl of about twelve or thirteen sat alone, trying to hide her face behind a magazine she wasn't reading. She glanced up as A.J. passed and caught his eyes. He smiled, and she dropped the magazine a few inches to reveal her face half-transformed between human and cat. Black whiskers extended from one cheek covered in light brown fur and a lone fang stood in contrast to the human teeth next to it. A.J's eyebrows shot up in surprise. The poor girl covered her face again and slid down in her chair in obvious embarrassment.

Margaret with the blue streak in her hair was already holding the interior door open for Skinner and A.J. "Welcome back, gentlemen," Margaret beamed at them. She gestured toward the back of the building. "The doctor is waiting for you in the laboratory."

"She giving the scarecrow a new brain?" A.J. quipped, but Margaret ignored him.

Skinner laughed. "Better watch that," he warned A.J. "Humor is a complicated subject in these parts."

"Of course, it is," responded A.J. He looked Margaret in the eyes as they passed and saw the same shine and knowledge and strength he had seen in the other Margarets back at the station. He shivered.

There was more activity compared to the morning in this part of the clinic as well. It occurred to A.J. that Brighed had kept the clinic clear for his earlier visit. Now there were people and staff in blue scrubs moving about the hospital bay, and some of the curtains were drawn in the exam room. Instead of heading toward the treatment rooms as they had earlier, they continued straight through a set of automatic doors where two operating rooms sat on either side of a short hallway. A pair of doors at the far end stood open where he could see Brighed bent over a steel exam table looking intently into a specimen pan.

She looked up as the two men entered, and the sight of A.J. didn't seem to surprise her. She smiled warmly and, perhaps, a little sadly at him.

"So, it is true then," she said. "I suspected it, but I could not believe it. Yet here you are."

"Here I am," replied A.J. flatly. "A prisoner in your nightmare valley."

"Mystic Valley," Brighed corrected him.

"What?"

"It's called Mystic Valley."

"Whatever," A.J. replied. "I've agreed to help Deputy Skinner find out what happened to your sheriff, and then I'm leaving if I have to dig my way to China. That's the deal."

Brighed frowned but nodded. "That's very generous of you," she said kindly. A hint of the melodic tone to her voice made A.J.'s hands tingle, but at least she kept her mind out of his this time.

"I don't know about generous. It was that or sit in the truck handcuffed to the steering wheel."

A flush of color rose in Brighed's face, and she smiled uncomfortably. A.J. couldn't tell if she was upset or just blushing at the thought of him in handcuffs. He smiled in spite of his misgivings. He was still angry at her, and he didn't want to like her, but he couldn't help feeling excited by her presence. Her incredible blue eyes sparkled, and a bit of her glow showed through. A.J.'s heartbeat quickened.

Skinner cleared his throat. "You two need some privacy?"

Brighed glanced at Skinner and blushed, then she straightened her lab coat and returned her attention to the specimen tray. "The remains you brought by this morning appear to match Sheriff Standish. I'm running a more extensive test to be certain, but initial DNA results were positive."

"Don't those tests take a couple of days?" A.J. asked.

"My technology is a bit more…advanced," said Brighed without looking up from the tray. Then she added, looking at A.J., "Our technology, I should say."

"What else did you find?" asked Skinner before A.J. could object.

Brighed slid the specimen tray closer to him. "This is the lower half of Frank's sternum and xiphoid process." She indicated the bones on a round section of flesh about seven inches wide. "The costosternal articulations are still in place, along with portions of the third through seventh ribs, with their lateral aspects missing. Observe the terminal points on the ribs. They appear splintered rather than cut, indicating a sharp, powerful impact at the point of the breaks. I found particulate matter in the splintered bone. Digger is analyzing it now."

"Digger?" A.J. asked.

"Her assistant," said Skinner sharply, agitated at the interruption. "Anything else, Doc?"

"The skin and muscle tissue have a slightly red, hemorrhagic appearance, indicating the wound was antemortem and the likely cause of death, though I wasn't able to extract enough blood from the muscle tissue to determine if drugs or alcohol were in his system."

"There weren't," said Skinner. "Frank's been sober nearly twenty years now."

"Drugs in the system are not always voluntary," argued A.J.

"If you find his body, I can give you more information," said Brighed.

"*When* I find him," shot back Skinner. "I'll turn this damned valley inside out if I have to, but I'll find him. I've already got Connor searching the woods around the crash site with Mason's dogs."

"But you don't think they'll find him there, do you?" Brighed's question was more of a statement.

Skinner clenched his jaw and stared back at her in earnest. She seemed to understand something and shook her head in protest. "If you go charging into the den without proof—"

"Yeah, but it sure as hell looks like it, doesn't it," said Skinner.

"Looking like it is not enough," argued Brighed. "Tensions are already high. You could start a war we can neither afford nor likely win without help from the others, and allegiances are shifting."

"So, you guys do think it was this 'wolf clan' of yours, don't you?" said A.J. "I knew I saw a giant paw in that window last night!" He paused to consider how crazy that sounded, then shrugged and plowed ahead. "Okay, so why not confront them about it? Do what we used to do in the desert. Pick up a low-level guy and lean on him until he squeezes out a name, then start knocking over his bosses like dominos until we get what we want."

Brighed looked appalled. "That would be a very bad idea!"

"Wouldn't work, anyway," added Skinner. "Much as I enjoy the thought. Besides, something feels off about it. Subtlety and subterfuge aren't exactly strong traits of theirs. If the wolf clan decides to start a war, they'll do it publicly and loudly. There won't be any questions about their intentions. I believe it was them, but Brighed's right. I need more evidence than some broken ribs and the word of a stranger, no matter what you are."

"I think I can help you with that." A young woman wearing a white lab coat over tan overalls was suddenly standing right next to A.J. as if she'd appeared from thin air. A.J. jumped in surprise.

She stared at a computer tablet displaying what appeared to be strings of random numbers and an image of a molecule. The girl was short and barely reached the bottom of A.J.'s chest. She wore large dark goggles, but they were clear enough for the magnified lenses to give her a strange bug-eyed look. She was quite pretty, with a fine jawline and pale, almost white skin under short auburn hair.

"Hi, I'm Digger." She spoke with a slight German accent and had a broad smile. She also had a deep dimple on one side of her face, giving her a cute, lopsided look. She didn't offer a hand to shake, so he smiled back and said simply, "A.J."

"What do you have, Digger?" Skinner asked.

"I analyzed the particulates that Doc gave me." She placed her fingers on the tablet. The room lights dimmed to half their previous brightness. She swept her hand toward the end of the room and the contents of her tablet appeared floating in the air between the exam table and the wall. A.J. saw a tiny light being emitted from a device mounted to the ceiling that was the source of the floating screen.

"Neat!" He looked back at Digger, who was removing her goggles.

A.J. was surprised to see that the goggles weren't actually magnifying her eyes. They were really that large, easily twice the size they should be, and bulged slightly from their sockets, with pupils the size of quarters and a fine ring of bright green. They also had a faint glow to them, similar to what he had seen around Brighed's head. As she pulled off the goggles, her hair was pulled back, revealing pointed ears that were also large for her head.

A.J. stared at her in wonder.

Digger stared back, not moving. In fact, she stood so completely still, he couldn't tell if she was alive or a statue.

"What...?" A.J. stammered and glanced back at Brighed and Skinner, who seemed amused. A.J. looked back at Digger, and she was gone. She had vanished. He'd only glanced away for half a second. "What?" he repeated and reached toward the place where the perfectly motionless girl had been a heartbeat before.

A strange hand reached into his front pocket and A.J. jumped, looking behind him. Digger stood there, reaching for his other pockets. He tried to swat her hands away, with little success.

"Digger, be nice," admonished Brighed, who was smiling at the smaller but surprisingly quick girl.

"Me? He was the one being rude."

A.J. began to protest but Digger took advantage of his open mouth, grabbing hold of his lower jaw, sticking her thumb in, and prying it open with a surprisingly strong grip.

"Heeyth!" A.J. complained as she pulled him down and peered inside.

"Hrumph!" She let him go. "No gold. Not even an old silver filling!" She turned away from him, crossing her arms in disappointment.

A.J. stepped back, rubbing his jaw. "Sorry to disappoint," he said sharply. "I'm glad I've never had a cavity."

"Never?" Digger studied him. "Interesting—"

"Can we please stick to the matter at hand?" asked Skinner, exasperated.

Digger turned her attention back to the floating image. "There wasn't much to go on. The rain washed the specimen pretty clean, but I did find microscopic samples of keratin embedded in the splintered ends of the bones." She enlarged the image of the molecule by waving her fingers in the air. It began slowly spinning in three dimensions.

"Keratin?" asked Skinner.

"It's the fibrous protein that claws, hair, horns, hooves, and the external layer of human skin are made of," explained Brighed.

"Well, that doesn't exactly narrow it down," complained Skinner. "Is that all you've got?"

"Well, there is this." Digger cleared the screen. Up popped an image of a tiny black hook, like the very tip of a sharp claw. "I pulled this from the surrounding tissue."

"That looks like a wolf claw to me," exclaimed Skinner.

"That, or possibly eagle," said Digger. "But at night in the rain? I wouldn't bet on the bird." She giggled a little too hard at her own odd joke until Skinner shot her a dark look.

"I'm attempting to extract a DNA sample from it, but it's unlikely I can get anything," Digger added.

"It's enough for me." Skinner slapped Digger on the shoulder. "Thanks!"

"Mr. Skinner," interjected Brighed, "please proceed with caution. Don't make any accusations that—"

"Questions only, yeah, I know my job, Doc."

She was put off by his demeanor and glowed briefly in a deep red color. Skinner didn't seem to notice, but A.J. did. Brighed saw A.J. staring at the space around her. She blushed, and the glow disappeared. She spoke again in that lilting musical tone that seemed to cut straight to A.J.'s core.

"We have much to discuss," she said pleasantly, but underneath her tone was another message she delivered with a power that vibrated through the whole of A.J.'s being. *"Tell no one what you are."*

Then it was gone, and A.J. felt that deep and sudden loss he'd felt that morning when she walked out of the exam room. He cleared his throat and managed, "agreed."

"Do you have a place to stay tonight?" Brighed asked.

"Well, there's a steel cot in a cage with my name on it," A.J. replied. "And that little motel looks kind of nice, unless you've got a better option?"

"A pile of rotting hay in a wet barn is a better option than that old place," quipped Digger.

"He can bunk down with me and Alice, on the couch," offered Skinner.

"That's kind of you," replied Brighed. "Perhaps you could bring him by my house for dinner this evening, so we can speak privately."

"Sure thing, Doc," said Skinner. "I'll drop him off after our visit across the valley. I'll let you know how it goes."

"If you both return alive, I'll assume it went well," said Brighed in a matter-of-fact tone that A.J. found disconcerting.

"You're joking, right?" A.J. asked, offering a feeble laugh.

Brighed offered no reply.

Skinner smiled. "Come on, kid." He put his hand on A.J.'s shoulder. "It's time to earn your keep." He steered A.J. toward the door.

A.J. turned back to say goodbye to Brighed and Digger, but Brighed was the only one there. Digger had disappeared again.

"How does she do that?" asked A.J. "And what the hell is she?"

"Digger's a Dwarf," answered Skinner. "They're pretty quick on their feet when they want to be. A Dwarf that doesn't want to be seen, will not be seen."

"Dwarfs?" A.J.'s eyebrows shot up. "You mean like the short dudes with long beards and double blade axes Snow White kind of Dwarfs?"

"Ha!" laughed Skinner. "You watch too many movies, and they prefer to be called by their profession, if you're going to call them anything, but it's probably better not to, generally speaking. Dwarfs a bit touchy about, well, everything really. Damned clever though."

"She didn't look all that short, or dumpy, or bearded," noted A.J. "She was actually kinda pretty in a big-eyed sort of way."

"Dwarfs are generally smaller in size, but not by as much as some stories would have you believe," said Skinner. "But don't let it fool you. They're stronger than they look."

"I'll say!" A.J. rubbed his jaw.

"They don't grow beards until they've mastered a trade," added Skinner. "And that can take a while."

"How long?"

"About a hundred years, I've been told. Though who really knows with the Dwarfs. They're fairly secretive by nature. Now, let's go have a little chat with some wolves."

A.J.'s mind filled with questions, but he was learning to let them go. Besides, he was eager to learn more about these wolves. "Just how dangerous is this wolf clan?"

"Danger is a relative concept around here." Skinner started up the engine of the old Dodge. He revved it a couple of times to warm it up before putting it in gear. "But I'll radio Connor to meet us there as backup just in case."

"That skinny kid? I hope he's good with a gun, because I don't think he could back up a wheelbarrow full of feathers."

Skinner laughed and kept laughing as they drove away.

Chapter Six

The Wolf Den

Skinner drove in the direction A.J. had entered the valley from the day before, which already felt like a lifetime ago. Heavy trees crowded both sides of the road, interspersed with occasional small clearings where houses nestled behind the thickets. A few small side roads led off toward both valley edges, and an occasional cluster of buildings and small orchards of apple, pear, and nut trees appeared.

"Is everyone around here..." A.J. looked for the right word.

"Different?" Skinner filled in for him.

"Yeah. And Margaret. Is everyone here one of these Tuatha D'Anu?"

"No," answered Skinner. "You and the doc are, and Darcy is half. Shifters and their like are metamorphs, technically. Theirs and the Ubadian histories are connected. Digger's a Dwarf. The Dwarfs have their own story, they sort of hold themselves separate from all the others. Margaret's special even among them. It's..."

"Let me guess," A.J. interrupted him. "It's complicated?"

"Now yer gettin' it." Skinner laughed and slapped A.J. on the knee.

"Are those all of them?" A.J. asked hopefully.

"There are a few others," said Skinner. "Like the Drow and the Utukku, but you'll get to meet them all in time, I'm sure. The doc can explain it all much better than me."

A.J. wanted to know more, much more, and he was desperate to ask questions, but he held his tongue with effort and sat back to consider Skinner's words. He still didn't believe he was special, and certainly not one of these so-called Tuatha D'Anu, but he couldn't deny Brighed's words either, or the things he saw and felt her do. A.J. had always been different in so many ways from the people around him that it was a relief to think there could actually be a reason for his lifetime of feeling alone in the world. The very possibility that he wasn't alone, though, scared him more than the thought of being some faery tale story brought to life. He shivered.

Skinner dropped the gears on the Dodge as they turned down a narrow two-lane cut through densely packed woods. A mile later, they approached a small town in a large open area among the trees. They entered at a slow pace, moving cautiously past the rows of small buildings. A hand-painted sign that read, "Liquor, Beer, Cigarettes," hung on a squat, white corner store with peeling paint. A gas station with old-fashioned pumps straight out of the 1930s looked busy, with several trucks lined up waiting for fuel.

The older wooden buildings gave way to red brick ones that housed a hardware store, a small grocer, and a bank. The people in front of the stores all stopped to stare suspiciously at Skinner's truck as it rolled by. Most were dressed in heavy and often dirty clothing over muck boots. A few stood huddled in small groups, shoulders hunched as they passed around cigarettes, or possibly joints. It was hard to tell.

"Nice welcoming committee they got here," said A.J. "This the wolf clan?"

"These people? Nah. These are just workin' folks. Some Dredge, some not. All suspicious of outsiders. Must be getting near shift change."

"Shift change?"

Before Skinner could respond, A.J. had his answer. They passed a two-story, red brick building on the right to reveal a massive lumber mill. Behind a twelve-foot fence topped with razor wire, rose mountains of huge tree trunks stacked forty feet high or more. The trunks themselves were forty feet long and up to four feet across at their bases, stripped of branches and bark and waiting to be processed. A.J. felt as much as heard the steady low rumble of the massive machines moving and sawing the giant trees. A bank of white lights stood high above the yard along the back fence, shining brightly in the twilight and illuminating the busy mill like a professional football stadium. To A.J., the whole place felt like death and power.

"The yard runs 24/7," said Skinner. "The lights never turn off."

"It's always daytime at the mill, huh?"

A large man in a blue uniform with an assault rifle strapped to his shoulder stood in front of a guard shack as they rolled past the front gates. The guard tracked the passing of their truck with a similar scowl A.J. was getting from everyone else in town.

"They really don't like visitors, do they?" A.J. asked.

"Visitors means strangers. And strangers mean either trouble or competition for a job in a mill town like this. That whistle blows every eight hours loud enough for half the valley to hear. Between that and the lights, they don't get a lot of tourist trade."

"Charming," A.J. said. "This hellhole got a name?"

"Rome."

"You're shitting me. Romulus and Remus? Suckled by a wolf? Seems kind of obvious, don't you think?"

"Like I said," Skinner smiled, "subtlety and subterfuge are not exactly their strong suits."

As if proving his point, a blaring horn sounded from the lumber yard as they passed the last stack of felled trees. It was a low sound rather than a high-pitched one, but it was everywhere, invading the air around them and making the truck itself vibrate. A.J. could feel it in his bones. It stopped after a few seconds, but echoes bounced off the surrounding trees, hills, and valley walls for several more heartbeats.

"Wow," was all A.J. could say when it finished.

"Three times every day." Skinner turned onto a side street that wound its way up the low eastern foothills toward the valley edge. The brick buildings and low-slung wooden houses gave way to small acreages with more modern, two-story homes interspersed with the occasional trailer set back into the trees. They crested a small rise, revealing a large clearing among the towering fir trees with a gravel parking lot surrounded by several businesses. A convenience store, a small hardware store, and a nail and hair salon took up three slots of a short strip mall. A chain-link fence surrounded another building set farther back, with a dozen cars in various states of repair and a stack of tires next to a single bay door that told A.J. this was the local mechanic.

None of these caught A.J.'s interest, however, as much as the next and largest building, a massive log-cabin style with a steel roof, surrounding porch, and neon beer signs hanging in all of the tinted plate-glass windows. About a dozen Harleys parked in a line leaned on their kickstands next to several new trucks with extra-large wheels. Skinner parked between the last truck and a large sculpture of three giant wolves, carved with a chainsaw from a single, massive block of wood. A painted sign hanging between a pair of totem poles read "The Den."

"Nice place," said A.J. "Not subtle."

Skinner chuckled. "Nope."

A.J. reached for his door handle, but Skinner sat staring at the building's front doors.

"We going in?" A.J. asked.

"We wait for Connor."

"Really? Seems like a friendly enough place."

"If we were passing through and stopped for lunch, we'd get good service and a smile. But that's not why we're here, and it's likely to get tense when we start asking questions, so we wait."

They sat listening to the truck engine cool and pop. The place was getting busier as workers from the mill's previous shift began to arrive. One truck, then another pulled into the gravel parking lot. The people heading into The Den all had the tired but expectant look of hard work followed by a beer and good food.

Connor pulled up in his cruiser. The lanky young man in his ill-fitting uniform climbed out of the car and put on his wide-brimmed hat. He flashed a toothy grin as he walked to the truck.

"He looks like one of those little umbrellas you stick in island drinks," A.J. said. "You sure about this kid?"

"He can hold his own." Skinner climbed out of the truck to shake hands with the deputy. A.J. joined them.

"Anything?" asked Skinner. His tone wasn't hopeful.

"Not much," answered Connor in a much deeper voice than A.J. expected, almost resonant like a bassoon. "Whatever happened out there, the rain washed it clean. The dogs couldn't get a trail on Frank's body."

"Not much ain't nothin' though," said Skinner, one eyebrow raised in expectation.

"Well, there was one thing that was kinda weird."

A.J. leaned in closer as Connor dropped his voice to a near whisper. "One of the dogs hit on something under a big fallen tree where the roots made a sort of cave. It wasn't wet in there."

"And?" Skinner asked.

"The dogs are trained to bark and circle when they catch a scent, and the other dogs join in and look for a trail, but that's not what happened. A couple of Mason's dogs nosed up under that tree and started growling something fierce. I thought maybe they'd cornered a bear at first, but there was nothing in there. Just some matted leaves with a bit of blood on them. They refused to get called off, and their hackles were standing straight up."

"Wolves?" suggested A.J., but both Skinner and Connor shook their heads.

"They know what wolves smell like," said Skinner. "They don't like 'em, but they wouldn't act like that. What else?"

"The rest of the pack. They wouldn't go near the place. As soon as the other dogs got a whiff, they backed off, whimpering with their heads down and tails tucked. Those are the best dogs west of Montana, and I've never seen anything like it. It's got Mason spooked too. He took those dogs straight home, and they weren't hesitating to go."

Skinner rubbed the stubble on his jaw and stared at the ground. "Some unknown Shifter maybe?"

Connor shook his head. "What could it be that those dogs haven't smelled before? No, something very strange was in that hole last night…strange and dangerous. I took samples of the blood and leaves and dropped them off with Digger on the way here."

"Good work." Skinner looked at the front doors of The Den. "Let's go see what old man Fergus knows about it."

"Fergus? You think he's got something to do with Frank's death?" Connor seemed unnerved by the idea.

"I don't know what to think yet. The wolf clan is involved in some way, but I'm not going to jump to conclusions until I talk to Fergus." Skinner headed toward the door, and Connor straightened his shoulders and hiked up his pants before following.

They entered the building, and A.J. was immediately struck by the noise of the place. The sounds of conversation, music, and general raucousness made the place feel like one big party. There were more customers inside than the parking lot suggested. A loud crack of a cue ball slammed into a fresh rack across the room, and a group of heavy, bearded men in leather biker vests were laughing. A small stage with a microphone and speakers stood otherwise empty in the far corner and about half the tables were occupied with mill workers. In the center of the hall was a massive, round fireplace full of flames under a steel chimney.

When they stepped into the room, there was a noticeable reduction in noise as first a few heads near them turned to watch them and then more joined in, spreading across the room like a virus of silence. Deputy Connor took off his hat and leaned against a wooden pillar near the front door. He nodded toward a few men at a nearby table, who nodded back. Despite his uniform, they seemed more comfortable with Connor's presence than Skinner's and A.J.'s.

Skinner led A.J. to the bar and some conversation in the room returned, though in muted tones and whispers. Four heavy-set lumberjacks in overalls leaning against the bar parted and stared at the two men as they stepped up. An attractive Asian bartender with streaks of bright red in her long black hair, piercings, and tattoos covering both arms leaned toward them with eyebrows raised.

"I need to speak with him," was all Skinner said.

The bartender laughed. "He's not taking visitors." Her voice had a low rasping tone to it. "Aengus can answer any questions you have."

Skinner frowned. "Scarlett, you and I both know the boy can barely tie his own damned shoes." She frowned but didn't disagree. "I'm not here to complain about the food," he said. "This is official police business. I need to see Fergus."

Scarlett frowned and nodded. "Oh yeah? What's it about?"

Before Skinner could answer, a commotion from the end of the bar took their attention. A heavy-set man with long blond hair in an oversized sports jersey was moving toward them. He jerked his head at her in dismissal, and she glowered at him before backing away. The others around the bar backed away as well, creating space around A.J. and Skinner as the large fellow approached. He wasn't pleased to see them.

A.J. felt the tingling in the back of his neck that signaled danger, and his muscles tensed. The man was big, about six-one, an inch shorter than A.J., but more than twice as heavy. His long hair was the only tidy thing about him, hanging in carefully brushed waves almost to his ample waist. From the way he moved, A.J. could tell he was as much muscle as he was fat, and he was plenty fat. His eyes were small and narrow above broad cheekbones, and he breathed heavily and rapidly through his mouth, almost panting.

"What do you want, Skinner?" He spat out the older man's name. He looked A.J. up and down and his nostrils flared as if he was sniffing the air around A.J. and didn't like what he smelled. "Who the hell is this?" he demanded.

"Good to see you too, Aengus. How's the knee?" Skinner smiled. This made Aengus angrier, and his shoulders heaved with the effort of taking bigger breaths. A.J. caught a smell from Aengus that flashed overwhelmingly strong in his memory, like stale smoke from an illegal bar in the basement of an old hotel in Baghdad. The room around A.J. was overwhelmed with the memory of another place in another time, filled with the scent of stale opium, smoked from hookahs and mixed with a kind of desperate, pathetic longing for something just out of his reach that he was convinced he once had, and could have again if only he could get a little more —

"—and this is A.J.," said Skinner. The sound of his name snapped A.J.'s awareness back to the present and he focused on Aengus, whose full attention remained on Skinner. A.J. could sense Aengus wasn't as dumb as he looked, and he made a mental note to always keep his guard up around the man.

Skinner seemed relaxed, though. He smiled easily despite the tension rising in Aengus, who seemed to be getting redder in the face by the second.

"You look like you're about to shift, Aengus." Skinner spoke with the calm assurance of a man petting his favorite dog. "Right here, in front of all these Dredge?" Skinner waved his arm toward the room of people. Those at the nearby tables were watching the exchange with great interest. Skinner's friendly smile transformed into cold assurance. "You know the law, Aengus, and you know how much I would love it if you just let go and showed all these fine people what you really are."

A.J. saw a vein throb in Aengus's left temple, and then a ripple emanated from the spot, and the flesh of Aengus's face rolled and rippled with it. A.J. took a small step back, but Skinner stood his ground.

Connor stepped away from his post and moved toward them, but one of the men who had nodded at him earlier beat him to Aengus's side.

"Hey, Aengus, my brother! My friend. Take it easy, dude, you know this Dredge is only pushing your buttons. Don't give him the satisfaction, no need for violence." The interloper was tall and thin and bounced as he walked. His skin was covered in powder white make-up, but there was a blue tinge beneath, and his long white hair hung in ropes past his shoulders. A jagged scar cut across his neck, but his skin was otherwise unblemished. He looked albino, but his eyes were dark brown, almost black.

"Hello, Blue Jean," said Skinner. "Should have known you wouldn't be too far away if Aengus is here." Blue Jean ignored him and placed his hands on Aengus's shoulders. "Take a deep breath, my brother. This Dredge ain't no reason to go back to jail. Especially not right now, right?" This last comment had a noticeable effect on Aengus. His face stopped rippling, and he took a step backward and straightened his jersey. Then he cracked a grin and said, "I was just fooling around, Skinner. Can't you take a joke, old man?"

The tension in the room eased, and the customers at the nearest tables let out their breaths in a collective sigh.

Blue Jean patted Aengus on the back and cackled like a jester leading the crowd to laugh at a dull king's joke. A few of the tables joined in uncomfortably.

"See, he's just jokin', Skinner. No harm done." Blue Jean smiled broadly, showing perfect white teeth. A.J. thought he looked like a sun-bleached caricature of a handsome person.

Skinner frowned and shook his head in disappointment. "A.J., meet Blue Jean and Aengus, the Laurel and Hardy of Mystic Valley. I had the pleasure of putting Aengus in prison a few years back. He was moving drugs for some of his buddies in Florida, weren't you, Aengus?" Skinner was obviously trying to rile up Aengus again, but the big man wasn't biting. "Aengus tried to shift right as we were putting the cuffs on him and Frank had to shoot him in the knee to get his attention. I bet that aches when it rains, don't it?"

"I did my time, old man," was all Aengus said, though he flexed his knee as he said it. "I'm just a manager at a restaurant now."

"Horse shit," said Skinner. "You ain't 'just' anything. Being a crook's in your blood. It's who you are." The fat man easily outweighed Skinner by fifty pounds, but the power all belonged to Skinner. "Your pal Blue Jean here escaped only because you wouldn't roll on him. That kind of sacrifice builds loyalty, and loyalty breeds greed and a lust for power that you can't resist. I'm just biding my time, Aengus. I'll be here when you screw up again."

"We'll see about that," barked Aengus.

Skinner stood straighter and took a bold step forward.

Blue Jean jumped between them again and motioned toward the bartender. "Hey, Scarlett, why don't you get everybody a round of drinks? Put it on Skinner's tab." He smiled a big showman's smile.

"Gentlemen, what's the problem here?" The voice behind the question was smooth as silk, a woman's voice that spoke with the quiet confidence of a wolf stepping into her own den.

Everyone turned toward the source. A tall woman stepped around Aengus and locked eyes with A.J. He felt captured by her gaze. Her pupils were large in auburn eyes, and her jet black hair hung straight, almost to her waist. She wore black lipstick and a long black jacket over embroidered and perfectly tailored clothes that emphasized her breasts and muscular body. She was as neatly dressed as Aengus was slovenly. She placed a hand on Aengus's shoulder.

"I hope my brother is taking good care of our guest's needs." She reached a carefully manicured hand toward A.J. "I see we have a new customer. Welcome. My name is Morgan." A.J. stuck his hand out and the touch of her skin sent a powerful shiver through his midsection. She smiled seductively at him, and he smiled back. She felt dangerous and powerful and beautiful to A.J., who admired those qualities in a woman. Morgan was the kind of woman A.J. would normally pursue with reckless abandon, but he couldn't find the desire he might have expected. Thoughts of Brighed and her sparkling blue eyes crowded out all other interests. Brighed had touched on a raw hunger in him that A.J. had long since put away, but she made him want to set it free again. He nodded politely and pulled back from her touch. Morgan stared at him intently before turning away.

"Blue Jean, be a dear and get the sound system and lights going for open mic night, will you? Aengus can help." She spoke dismissively, and the two men shrugged and moved toward the corner stage.

"Hello, Morgan." Skinner spoke with a friendly, though wary, tone. "This here is A.J. He's helping us with an investigation."

"An investigation?" she said with surprise and interest. "How intriguing! What's it about?"

"That's why I need to speak with Fergus," Skinner said. "Official business, you know."

"Ah, of course. Official business. I understand." She smiled warmly at Skinner but shot a quick glance at A.J. that was filled with lust. He wasn't sure if her attempted seduction was a ruse or real, but he didn't much care, and that felt strange to him. He had never turned down a free beer or a beautiful woman in his life.

"Follow me. I'll take you to him." She led Skinner around the right side of the bar toward the office doors in the back. A.J. started to follow, but Scarlett blocked his progress with a full beer mug.

"Just him," she said. Her gaze was hard and final. Skinner waved at him to stay where he was, so A.J. sat on a barstool. Connor had resumed his casual lean against the post by the front door. The crowd turned back to their dinners and the low hum of conversation filled the room once more.

"At least I still want the beer," he muttered under his breath.

"Excuse me?" Scarlett looked puzzled.

"Never mind," smiled A.J.

"You're not from around here," Scarlett said as a matter of fact, but it came out as a question.

"That obvious, am I?" replied A.J. "Well, don't mind me, I'm just passing through." He took a sip of the beer and felt it spread into his limbs. It was a good beer.

"Don't get many of those here, either," said Scarlett. "Where you from?"

A.J. liked Scarlett. She was friendly and disarming with a tough girl's kindness about her.

"Lots of different places," he replied. It was a favorite line from an old movie that the girl was probably too young to remember. He noticed the heavily muscled men, and some of the women, standing around the bar staring at him. He raised his beer in salute.

"Don't mind them," said Scarlett. "They're not used to strangers."

"So I've been told. We're either trouble or competition, right?"

"Usually both." She wiped down the bar. "How do you know Skinner?" She smiled sweetly, and A.J. realized the unassuming girl was pumping him for information. She was good at it.

"He was in the service with my dad. I was passing through and stopped for a visit," A.J. lied.

"I thought he said you were helping him with an investigation?"

"I am," said A.J., kicking himself for walking so easily into her trap. "I have…specialized skills."

"Specialized?" She raised her eyebrows. "How specialized?"

"Very." He used his best pick-up smile. He could play that game too.

Scarlett giggled. A.J. glanced at the lumberjacks. His innocent flirtation with Scarlett clearly agitated them, so he pushed it harder. He giggled with her and touched her wrist lightly to order another beer. That really pissed them off.

The largest of the men moved toward A.J. just as the lights dimmed and a spotlight shone on the stage. All heads turned toward the light, including A.J.'s, but he watched out of the corner of his eye, and the big lumberjack stopped moving toward him, though he still stared at him in anger. A.J. leaned casually against the bar with his mug of beer in hand and laughed to himself.

Blue Jean jumped on stage and warmed the crowd with his big smile and jester's antics. He told a few bad jokes and even performed a little soft-shoe to get everyone in a common rhythm. A.J. had to admit the guy was good at playing the fool, but there was definitely more to the strange man than met the eye.

"…and now, to set the mood for an amazing show," Blue Jean elongated the word "amazing" for dramatic effect, "here's our very own Morgan! Give it up, everybody!"

Morgan sauntered onstage with grace. Something about the way she moved reminded A.J. of a predator circling its prey. When he turned his head, his peripheral vision caught sight of a massive black phantom wolf that seemed almost superimposed over her body, but he couldn't get a full view of it, no matter how hard he tried, and that disturbed him.

Morgan grasped the microphone in her long-fingered and manicured hand and leaned forward to peer hungrily at the crowd from under sharp black brows. The room clapped and cheered and then fell into collective silence as she took a deep inhale, paused for effect, and began to speak in a low, poetic voice that drew every breath from the room.

"I have come to inform you,
In this world that once bore you,
That you are no longer the top of the chain;
For the die is cast;
I'm a Werewolf. At last,
This is the end of humanity's reign."

About half the crowd let out a low rumble of approval and quite a few banged their beer mugs on the tables. They seemed to know this performance already and approved hungrily. Morgan paused until the silence returned. A.J. sat forward.

"For it's humans I crave,
As Luna's dark slave,
Thirteen nights every year.
A baker's dozen,
As Satan's cousin,
When I become a WERE!"

Another round of cheers let forth and a couple of soft howls escaped from the crowd. She silenced them with a look.

"When the full moon is born,
My body transforms.
Sharp teeth stretch past peeled lips.
I shift between these worlds unseen
Where the two halves of our souls exist.

As I shed the remains of my human domain,
I am no longer the social demure…
Now a wolf from the body
Of a woman is born,
Adorned in dark black fur."

Morgan rubbed her hands sensually down the length of her body, but her eyes were locked on A.J.'s while she did it. He normally would have enjoyed such play, but he couldn't get his mind off Brighed, and that annoyed him. He usually took pride in his determined solidarity. He shook his head to try and clear his mind of her as Morgan continued.

"It began on a night
When the stars were alight,
And I howled a wolf prayer to the moon.
Then my nostrils flared
As I caught on the air
The scent of humanity's boon.

My feast lay east,
So off I ran,
A shadow in the night.

My muscles flexed
As I caressed
The ground beneath my flight.

As I crested a hill,
My senses reeled
And I caught sight of my quarry at last.
They were roasting swine,
But that was just fine,
For it was long pig that would sate my fast..."

The crowd stood and cheered, momentarily blocking
A.J.'s view of the stage. He stood to get a better view and
felt something wet on his knee. He looked down to see he'd
tipped his own beer mug toward the floor.

"Like what you see, Dredge?" A.J. felt hot breath on his
cheek that stank of stale beer and cigarettes. The lumberjack
had moved quietly next to him. A.J. stepped back
reflexively and raised his hands in seeming supplication,
but it was a position better suited for defense should things
get physical. He realized Connor could no longer see him
through the crowd, and Morgan's poem kept all eyes turned
toward her. A.J. was isolated with the big bruiser. He could
still hear the performance, but his attention was focused on
the big man in front of him. The crowd cheered on Morgan
as the lumberjack sneered and stepped toward A.J., who in
turn bumped into several people behind him. This got their
attention and they made room for the two men, with several
egging on the lumberjack. Their eyes flashed hungrily at the
possibility of violence.

"I'm not looking for trouble, friend," A.J. implored in his
kindest voice. "I'm just passing through." The quickest way
to end a fight, he knew, was never to get in one in the first
place, but the words only encouraged the bigger man.

The lumberjack flexed his massive biceps, and spittle flew from his over-sized lips. "I'm not your friend, Dredge! You don't belong here!"

A.J. knew from experience there are only two kinds of fighters, those who know how to fight, and those who start them. He smiled reassuringly and waved his hands in a seemingly eager display of submission, though it was also a way to distract his opponent's attention. A.J. felt adrenaline rush through his veins as a long-buried part of him stirred in anticipation of the fight. The phantom smell of blood and hot steel flooded his senses, and his heartbeat increased its speed and power. It had been a long time since he'd felt this dark and lustful blood rush, and he tried in vain to hold it back. He glanced toward Connor, but the deputy was still blocked from view by the standing crowd. A.J. kept a friendly, scared look on his face, but a hidden part of him craved violence the way a sailor craves a brothel.

A.J. took the slightest hop to the right and flashed a hungry smile at the bigger man, whose eyebrows rose in surprise at A.J.'s sudden shift from submission to aggression. A.J. had used the tactic many times in his life of violence to great effect, and it worked equally well now.

The lumberjack drove his massive fist toward A.J.'s cheek. This was a mistake. Big brawlers like the lumberjack were used to opponents who either duck or start throwing wild punches. A.J. did neither. He drove his weight into his right toes and lurched sideways from the coming blow, stepping out of the lumberjack's line of attack. As his weight shifted to his left foot, he twisted hard at the waist, driving his left hip forward and using the power of his muscled core to propel his left palm across his body like a bullwhip toward the extending arm of the bigger man, accelerating through the point of impact. A.J.'s hardened hand caught the lumberjack's overextended elbow at full force. The sickening crunch of the big man's arm folding backwards and the accompanying gasps and low screams of the people who saw it was as satisfying to A.J. as an orgasm. The rest of the crowd turned toward this new commotion and Morgan's poetry performance cut off mid-sentence.

A.J. knew what would happen next. The lumberjack recovered enough from his shock to throw a wild left hook toward A.J.'s head. This was also a mistake. A.J. dropped into a deep lunge under the punch, and he pushed hard against his right foot, powering his body upward, his left hand hooked under the armpit of his foe and caught the big man's extended chin in the palm of his hand, pushing his head up and back, exposing the lumberjack's throat. A.J. used the momentum to wrap his body around the back of the lumberjack and brought the point of his right elbow down hard, pulling against the weight and momentum of the bigger man's swing and delivering all his own weight and power through the tip of his elbow to a point just beneath the lumberjack's right ear. It was a dangerous move. If he missed, he could break his own elbow on the bigger man's iron jaw, so he aimed slightly left and delivered the blow to the trigeminal nerve that runs from the lower jaw directly to the brainstem. Boxers call it "The Button," because a hard blow to this nerve will turn the lights out on an opponent like flipping a switch. A.J.'s elbow drove home, and the big lumberjack collapsed to the floor like a sack of wet flour, unconscious and snoring.

The whole thing was over in seconds. A.J. stood over the man, breathing hard. He was filled with a violent energy he hadn't felt in years, and it was delicious. Its return both alarmed and excited him.

The sudden quiet of the room drew A.J.'s attention back to the crowd. The cheers and claps for Morgan's poem transformed into a dangerous silence as all eyes turned toward him.

Scarlett, eyes wide, backed quickly toward the door at the end of the bar. A.J. caught a smell like sulfur and wet fur as the lumberjack's friends moved toward him, but it wasn't the number of them, nor the threat of further violence that filled A.J.'s heart with fear. On the contrary, now that he had tasted the fight, he was hungry for more.

What scared him was watching two of the big man's friends suddenly shift from humans into a pair of massive gray wolves. They didn't so much *turn* into giant wolves as they overwhelmed reality in a sudden tide of fur and teeth and claws. In one moment, there were two men moving toward him, the air around them rippled, and then there were two huge wolves. The crowd half screamed, half cheered, as they fell back. The big beasts snarled and snapped at A.J. with saliva dripping from three-inch fangs and red tongues licking the air. They flexed their powerful muscles in preparation to launch themselves at him.

A.J. stepped back and brought his arms up in defense, but he stumbled over the prostrate form of the snoring lumberjack. He fell to the floor, eyes wide, and scrambled backwards from the oncoming beasts in a hopeless attempt to escape. The wolves sprang forward with power and speed and snarls, black eyes flashing, jaws open, and teeth bared for the kill. A.J. brought his arms up to protect his face in what he knew was a useless attempt at defense, when a giant, dark figure flashed above A.J. with a roar that shook the rafters.

The two wolves were met mid-leap by a pair of massive hands attached to forearms the size of tree trunks. They drove both beasts' heads hard into the wooden floor, smashing through the boards in a shower of splinters and yelps. The towering hulk above A.J. had to be seven feet tall, with bulging shoulders and long, powerful arms that reached nearly to the floor. Dark hair sprouted everywhere and shoved itself through overstretched seams and bulging gaps between the buttons of a deputy sheriff's uniform. The huge creature looked down at A.J. with the eyes of Deputy Connor, whose previously oversized uniform was now stretched to its maximum across the body of what appeared to be a giant black ape. The big beast snorted in satisfaction that A.J. was unharmed and returned its attention to the wolves yelping and struggling against its powerful grip. Connor picked them up and slammed them both back to the ground again. The wolves stopped resisting.

"What is going on here?" A deep male voice resonated in the sudden stillness of the room, and all heads turned toward the door behind the bar. A.J. scrambled to his feet. A figure stood silhouetted in the open doorway, backlit by the bright lights of the office behind him. Every sound in the restaurant ceased, and the crowd took a collective breath. First one and then the next person closest to the door backed away and bowed. Others quickly followed until the only ones left erect were the backlit figure, the giant ape that was Connor, and A.J., who bowed for no man.

The tall figure walked into the main room with the aid of a cane that hammered the floor with each step like a slow drumbeat. He moved slowly and purposefully, stepping into the light of the bar and revealing an older but still vibrantly powerful man, his oiled black hair hung in loose waves to his shoulders, and a thick streak of polar white ran down one side above an eye of brilliant blue-white next to another of deep ebony green. He walked with a slight limp against the cane, but there was no mistaking the ancient power that emanated from the old man, flowing from him in waves of anger and confidence. A.J. had no doubt who was the real leader of the wolf clan.

This must be Fergus, he thought, and the old man's eyes turned directly on A.J. as if he had heard the words out loud. The gaze was powerful, and it took all of A.J.'s adrenaline-fueled willpower to return the stare without looking away.

Fergus broke his gaze with A.J. and slowly surveyed the room. His eyes fell on Connor, and the ape-man released his grip on the two wolves and stepped back, shaking the floor with his steps. The stretched fabric of his clothes began to relax as Connor shrank in size, appearing to deflate rather than transform, with the thick black fur receding into his skin until the skinny, boyish-faced kid stood again in clothes that draped his body in loose folds. He grabbed the waistband of his pants to keep them from slipping down.

The two wolves moved slowly, rolling onto their backs in supplication and exposing their underbellies and throats to the cold look of Fergus standing over them. They changed form too, shifting back into their human selves just as they had been a few minutes before, clothes and all. They were left on their backs, panting and sweating, faces full of fear and dismay.

Another figure moved into the doorway of the office. Skinner stepped into the room, put his cowboy hat back on and stared angrily toward A.J. and Connor.

"Well, Deputy Skinner," Fergus spoke with an old Irish accent, each word crisp and resonant in the quiet room. "The law is the law. You want to lock up these two knuckleheads for shifting in public? You're welcome to them."

Skinner rubbed his chin before answering. "Seems like a waste of resources to me. I have a feeling you can sort them out better than we can down at the station."

Fergus's smile was frightening to behold. "That's very generous of you. Indeed, I think we can handle this infraction internally." He looked menacingly at the two Shifters, who cringed against the floor, shaking with fear.

"A month shoveling out the shredders is a good start, I think." The duo moaned briefly in complaint but quickly shut up. "Now get the hell out of my sight, and take this piece of garbage with you," Fergus growled.

The two practically knocked one another down in their desperate scramble to crawl away, dragging the still-snoring lumberjack out with them.

Blue Jean hurried to the broken floor and began sweeping up splinters and wiping up the sweat and spilled beer. Fergus frowned at the two holes in his floor, then glanced up at Connor, who smiled meekly and shrugged.

"Scarlett, break out the scotch and pour everyone a shot. We have a toast to make," said Fergus coldly. He turned and limped toward the stage. The crowd parted before him like peasants before a king. Scarlett began setting up shot glasses and pouring scotch, and Aengus hurried behind the bar to assist her. The small glasses disappeared from the bar as those closest to it began passing around the shots. Not a single person took a sip until every hand held a glass, and the whole crowd rose to stand at silent attention while Fergus stepped carefully onto the stage.

"Deputy Skinner has just informed me of a terrible tragedy." Fergus's commanding voice bounced off the walls though he used no microphone. "Our beloved Sheriff Standish was killed last night." There was a collective gasp, and more than a few patrons whispered in shocked undertones to one another. A.J. noticed that Aengus, Blue Jean, and Scarlett didn't react at all, but kept their heads down and focused on their work. Fergus cleared his throat and the room returned to silence. "It appears to have been a tragic automobile accident."

A.J. watched Aengus, who glanced toward Blue Jean, then returned to cleaning the bar top.

Fergus accepted a glass of scotch from a nearby patron and raised it toward the heavens. "So, let us raise a toast to a dear and brave old friend who has departed too soon from the mortal coil and left us all poorer for the loss." A few audience members cleared their throats in objection to the words of praise, but every one of them raised their glasses in unison and waited for Fergus to take his drink first. Fergus stared skyward for a few heartbeats, then drained his glass in one quick toss. The rest of the room followed suit.

"Deputy Skinner says a witness…" Fergus let the word hang in the air and shot a glance at A.J. "…reports hearing and seeing wolves in the forest last night near the accident site."

The crowd broke into a low murmur and some looked around the room, searching others' faces, but the noise died when Fergus spoke again.

"If anyone," he said pointedly, staring from face to face in the crowd, "*anyone*…has any information to share with the deputy, I encourage you to step forward now. It would be in your best interests to speak up sooner rather than later." The crowd took up its murmuring again, this time louder and with a nervous edge. Fergus glared out at them with a clenched jaw and watched their reactions. Then he stepped down slowly from the stage and made his way to Skinner, waiting at the back of the room. The two men pulled out chairs at a nearby table and sat down.

With a quick nod of his head, Fergus motioned for A.J. to join them. His adrenaline levels crashing, A.J. blinked and looked around at the crowd as if seeing it for the first time. What he had just witnessed and experienced was difficult to process. It was beyond anything he had ever encountered. The last vestiges of his cautious disbelief were shattered.

A.J.'s hands shook, and he took a deep breath to gather his wits enough to join them. He shoved his hands into his pockets and took an unsteady step forward. Connor, straightening and tucking his uniform, resumed his position at the entrance. The thinning crowd moved away from Fergus's table. Many returned to their meals and took up eating again, but almost as many left their beers unfinished and headed out the door.

A.J. dropped into the chair next to Skinner and across from Fergus, who had his back to the wall and could watch the whole room. It gave A.J. an uncomfortable itch between his shoulder blades whenever he sat with his back to a room, but knowing Connor was back there helped him let it go, though his brain was having trouble grasping the dissonance of Connor also being a giant ape.

"First time seeing Shifters in action?" Fergus spoke in the caring voice of an old Irish uncle. A.J. instantly wanted to please him, to be liked by the old man, and this raised a warning flag in the recesses of his exhausted mind. Fergus smiled warmly. "It can be quite unsettling if you aren't accustomed to it."

"It was…unusual, but very interesting," was all he managed to say.

"Interesting is one way to describe it," replied Fergus. "Technically speaking, your friend Connor there is a shape-changer rather than a Shifter. His actual body transforms while those like myself and my daughter Morgan exist as two distinct animals at once, both human and wolf, rather like two sides of a coin. You can only see one side at a time, but the other is always there, always aware. Changers versus Shifters is a distinction lost on most folks though, who just call the lot of us Shifters. Either way, changing to our animal forms feels like freedom to us. The moment when we change, whether wolf...or ape. We are liberated."

"So why change back?" A.J. was too tired for niceties. Skinner sat stiffly, scowling.

Fergus studied A.J., his one bright blue eye standing in sharp contrast to the dark green one, but both looking at A.J. like they were looking through him.

"You really don't know, do you?" Fergus sat forward, rubbing his chin with new interest in A.J.

Skinner filled in the details. "Some of them wouldn't change back if they could stay that way, but they can't."

"No, we can't," Fergus said. "Much as we'd like to. In another age, it would have been easy, but these days...we can only stay shifted through a determined strength of will, by concentrating on it. It's easier to maintain sometimes than others, but eventually the call of the wild defeats our human willpower, and when it does, our form reverts to our human appearance, whether we want it to or not."

A.J. squinted at him through tired eyes. "In another age? What the hell are you talking about?"

Fergus's eyes flashed, but he merely smiled a wicked smile and sat back in his chair. Aengus sidled up to the table with a tray of shot glasses and an ancient bottle made of thick, black glass with a waxed wooden stopper held on by a strip of old leather.

"It was this Dredge here who caused all the trouble." Aengus sneered at A.J. "He should pay."

The sharp rap of Fergus's cane on the barroom floor silenced Aengus, but his eyes flashed of defiance.

"Please excuse my youngest son's poor manners." Fergus glared at Aengus, who dropped his head and muttered under his breath. Fergus smiled warmly at A.J. "He forgets the old ways of treating guests with the proper respect at my table."

"In his defense, Father," said Morgan, joining them, "in the old days we would have eaten this Dredge for supper rather than invite him to sit down for a drink." She slid gracefully into a chair next to Fergus and sneered hungrily at A.J. Her dark eyes flashed like a predator about to eat its prey. She licked her teeth and glanced at her younger brother.

Fergus pulled the bottle's stopper and poured a thick amber liquid that smelled strongly of honey, anise, and alcohol.

"Gentlemen, I trust you have met my daughter, Morgan?" Fergus seemed pleased just to say her name. It was clear he favored her equally as much as he disdained Aengus.

"Morgan, that is no way to treat Deputy Skinner," added Fergus. "He has come all this way to share this tragic news with me before anyone else in the valley. He's showing us respect, dear daughter. Surely, we can return the honor."

Morgan glanced at Skinner and growled, "not him." She turned her gaze menacingly on A.J. "I meant him."

"Him?" Fergus laughed. "Ha!"

Morgan's expression changed to confusion. Aengus seemed equally bewildered. Fergus lifted his cane over the table and prodded A.J. gently in the chest. "He's no Dredge. Are you, boy?" The old man's blue eye twinkled, and he smiled a knowing smile.

A.J. said nothing, because nothing made sense anymore. Skinner grumbled under his breath. Morgan and Aengus glanced questioningly at each other and at A.J. Morgan no longer looked at him like he was a meal but as something strange, almost dangerous. He ignored them all and reached an unsteady hand for the shot glass filled to the brim with the thick golden drink that shined of its own accord, not unlike Brighed's hair had that morning.

Fergus, Skinner, and Morgan each lifted their own glasses in turn. Aengus stood aside like an obedient butler.

Fergus glanced at A.J. and said, "It appears we have an D'Anu stranger in the valley. That is a cause for celebration even in our moment of grief, wouldn't you say so, Deputy Skinner?"

Skinner nodded curtly, forcing a fake smile. Fergus raised his glass higher. "Well, then, gentlemen, lady, here's to our late Sheriff Standish and to our new mysterious friend here. Slàinte!"

They all drank at once. The thick liquid warmed A.J.'s throat and spread like a wave across his chest and arms. His mind cleared from its fog of exhaustion, and he felt strength and energy flow into his limbs. He took a deep breath and smelled and saw and heard a hundred things around him, from the sweet aroma of the honeyed drink to the oiled wooden tables to the stale sweat of the patrons. He smelled meat grilling in the kitchen and the lavender perfume worn by Scarlett twenty feet away. His shot glass's microfractures glinted in the light, and Fergus's dark green eye swirled with dozens of shades of green and black. He closed his eyes and heard the heartbeats of the others around him, and if he concentrated, he could distinguish each one from the others.

A.J.'s hands stopped shaking. He felt like he could run a marathon, and kind of wanted to.

He looked at Skinner and saw a man with many wrinkles and more than a few scars of his own, all fading as the skin tightened on his face and his gray beard turned darker. Skinner's eyes were bright, but he coughed a few times at the sting of the drink going down.

"It's got a hell of a kick, don't it?" Skinner's mood brightened, and his eyebrows began climbing his forehead as he stared at A.J.

"Well, there he is," said Fergus with a smile. The old man's eyes were also shining, and he appeared much younger and healthier than before the drink. Morgan took a deep breath and rolled her head back, taking in all the sounds and smells of the room. Her hair floated in the air around her, alive and glistening. She returned her gaze to A.J., her face filled with a hungry energy, but her eyes widened in surprise, and she blinked a few times. She blushed when A.J. stared back into her eyes with a strength of will and confidence he'd long since lost but had found again in this moment. He felt like he could conquer the world.

The hairs on A.J.'s arms tingled. He glanced down and saw that they glowed and moved in waves. A bright golden light emanated from his skin, and he felt energy and power moving in and out of himself in waves with every breath. He stared at the shot glass in disbelief.

"Nectar of the Gods," said Fergus. "Very rare. Some call it Brighid's Draft, others Ambrosia. Call it what you will, it surely packs a punch, especially for magical creatures like us." Fergus winked at A.J.

"I'll say." A.J. laughed out loud because he felt so good. "What is happening to me?"

"You're awakening, my boy!" Fergus smiled at A.J. with pride. "Welcome to the Queendom."

"Now, Deputy Skinner." Fergus pushed himself to his feet. "As you can see, no one in this establishment heard or saw anything last night. No one has stepped forward. Perhaps your, ah, 'witness' was hearing things in the storm."

Skinner frowned. He surveyed the thinning crowd; many were watching Fergus's table.

"Doesn't mean anything," Skinner argued. "Maybe a wolf or three have been stepping off the reservation without you knowing."

Fergus's smile vanished. "What makes you so certain wolves were there?" The tension around the table rose ominously.

"Evidence at the scene suggests a wolf was involved," replied Skinner.

Fergus laughed in relief. "Well, there you go, Deputy. There's your proof wolves didn't do it."

"How do you figure?" Skinner stood and put on his hat. He was much taller than A.J. remembered.

"Why, the 'evidence,' Deputy! Aside from a few folded clothes left on your car many years ago, have you ever found evidence of a wolf attack on any human, or other animal for that matter, anywhere in this valley? Even once?"

Skinner rubbed his whiskers and stared at Fergus without replying.

"It wasn't wolves who killed Frank." Fergus rapped his cane once on the wooden floor. "I'm sorry for your loss, David," he added softly. "I truly am. But you'll have to find your answers elsewhere."

Fergus nodded at A.J. "As for this other, more pleasant surprise, tell Brighed we need to talk. In fact, considering all the developments of the last twenty-four hours, I think it prudent to assemble a Council meeting. Don't you?" His tone suggested that no question had been asked.

Skinner grunted, "I'll give her the message." It appeared the meeting had come to an end.

Fergus nodded pointedly to Skinner and A.J. each in turn and walked toward his office, Morgan and Aengus in tow. "Aengus, fix the floor," Fergus said gruffly. Aengus glared at his father's back until the old man and Morgan closed the office door behind them.

Skinner, Connor, and A.J. stepped outside into the early evening fog. "Well?" Connor asked as they reached their vehicles. "What did you find out?"

Skinner glared at A.J. and Connor, clearly angry about the fight though he didn't say so. "Fergus makes a good point about the evidence. It's out of character for them to leave anything for anyone to find, but whether they killed Frank or not, one thing is certain. They definitely knew Frank was dead before we got here."

"How do you know?" asked A.J., "Did Fergus tell you that?"

"Hell, no. I barely had time to fill him in on Frank's death before we were...interrupted." He gave them a pointed look.

Connor asked, "So how do you know they knew Frank was dead?"

"Because they let me talk to Fergus in the first place. Remember, I'm just a part-time, retired deputy. Hell, technically speaking, Connor here is the next man in charge since he's the only other full-time officer besides Frank. If Morgan thought Frank was still alive, she would never have let me talk to Fergus about official business. He's not one for meeting with underlings."

"So, if Morgan didn't know, she'd have sent you away and told you to send back Frank?" A.J. asked.

"Exactly. They may or may not have killed him, but they surely know more than they're letting on." Skinner looked at Connor. "Get back to the office and write up a report of what you saw in the woods and what happened in the bar. Don't miss any details. The Council's gonna want 'em all."

Connor nodded and headed for his car. A.J. stared at the skinny kid and imagined him as a giant hairy ape.

Something sparked in the back of his mind about Oregon forests and giant apes. "Hey, is he a…you know…"

Skinner laughed. "You catch on quick. His kind were roaming these woods long before the rest of your kind moved into this valley. He's a native, strictly speaking."

"That might explain why nobody can find them."

"Damn fools keep searching the woods and forests for 'em, but don't realize they're probably buying supplies for their search while standing in line next to 'em at the Bi-Mart," said Skinner. "Sasquatches are gentle beings by nature. Hermits mostly, living in the deep thicket off the land, but they can sure be handy in a bar fight."

A.J. nodded agreement and felt gratitude for the young man backing them up. "Sorry I underestimated him."

Skinner nodded. "That can be fatal around these parts. Things here are rarely what they seem, but Brighed should probably be the one to explain a bit more about it. She won't be free for a few more hours, so you can help me clean up Frank's place and go through his effects. Darcy's got enough to deal with, and we might even find something useful."

"Sure thing, boss. Lead the way." A.J. felt better than he had in years, and his heightened senses from the drink highlighted and enhanced the beauty of the forested valley around them.

Skinner gave him an appraising look and frowned. He pulled a crushed and dirty trucker's cap from under his seat. "Here, put this on and slink down in the seat a little. You're glowing like a lightning bug stuck in the 'on' position."

A.J. stared at his arms and turned Skinner's rear-view mirror so he could see his reflection. He *was* glowing. A bright, golden light shone from him, and his hair moved and floated like Darcy's and Brighed's. He touched his face and smiled. His teeth were brilliant white.

"How do you turn it off?" he asked.

"How the fuck should I know?" Skinner put the truck in gear, and the old Dodge rattled as the gears dropped into place. A.J. pulled the cap down tight on his head and sank low in the passenger seat for the drive back into town.

Chapter Seven

Brighed's Tale

Brighed lived in a modest but stylish white shingle house about half a mile from the doctor's office. Every pillow was carefully arranged and not a speck of dust appeared on any of the small objets d'art adorning her shelves and tables. Her light blue gown of silk and lace danced on her body as she paced the polished wooden floors. She burned with a red light of fury.

"This is a fucking disaster!" she yelled at Skinner and A.J. "Don't make accusations! Keep the details of Frank's death to yourself! Don't tell anyone what you are!" She threw her hands in the air. "Simple fucking instructions that you both managed to screw up in less than a day! And now? Now Fergus has called for a meeting of the Council! This was exactly what I was trying to avoid. Do you know what this means?"

"No, actually. I don't." A.J.'s voice was hard and cold. He didn't like being yelled at.

Brighed's icy stare would have filled a common man with dread, but A.J. was no common man. "Why don't you fill me in?"

He stood his ground, waiting for answers. "In my defense," he added, provoking Brighed further, "I didn't say shit. Fergus knew me from the minute he saw me."

Skinner gripped his oiled cowboy hat in both hands and edged away from him.

"Of course, he did!" Brighed roared. "If I'd thought for one second you would actually come face to face with the Fallen King, I would never have let you go there."

"The who?" A.J. was learning a lot from Brighed's tirade.

"It doesn't matter," she said through clenched teeth. "What matters is that Fergus would never have entered the public room if you hadn't started brawling like a schoolboy!"

"Hey, I didn't start anything..." A.J. protested and looked to Skinner for backup.

Skinner only shrugged and nodded toward Brighed. "She's right. A dominance contest inside his own den? Fergus had to intervene. I told you; wolves are not subtle creatures. The only reason he announced Frank's death was he needed a good excuse to justify coming into the room in the first place. He would have looked weak otherwise, and any sign of weakness in the leader of the wolf clan is likely to spawn challengers. Fergus hasn't lived as long as he has by accident."

"Oh yeah? How long is that?" A.J. asked.

Skinner started to answer, but Brighed cut him off. "That doesn't matter! What matters now is what he said and did. Tell me what happened and the exact words he used. Leave no detail out."

A.J. and Skinner filled her in on what each remembered from their earlier encounter. "Then the old man gave me this crazy drink," said A.J.

"Brighed's Draft. It's named for my great grandmother," she waved a hand dismissively. "He was testing you. He wanted to confirm what you are, and you walked right into his trap."

"Beats a long walk in a cold mist," A.J. fired back.

This caught Brighed off guard, and she calmed a bit and nodded with a look of guilt.

"For what it's worth, I still feel great and it's been nearly six hours," added A.J. "I don't know what this stuff is, but I like it."

"Wait till it wears off," said Skinner.

Brighed gave Skinner a disapproving look, then said in a loving voice, "David, why don't you go home to Alice? It's been a long day, and I'm sure she's worried. A.J. can sleep on my couch tonight. You can pick him up in the morning. Get some rest. You're going to need it."

Skinner smiled tiredly and pulled his hat onto his head. She patted him on the back and walked him to the door. When she closed it, she turned on A.J., the red fury of energy and light pouring off her once again.

"All you had to do was not get into a bar fight. How hard is that?" Her blue eyes flashed white.

"You'd be surprised." A.J. deadpanned. He wasn't going to let her anger drive his. As far as A.J. was concerned, the whole damn valley could burn to the ground if it meant getting out of there.

Brighed fumed and paced. A.J. casually unlaced his boots and left them by his pack, and then dropped onto her sofa and propped his feet on her coffee table. She stopped pacing to stare angrily at his stocking feet, but he didn't budge. Instead, he wiggled his toes at her and flashed his most disarming and charming smile, one that had often served to keep him out of trouble with women and senior officers alike. It had the opposite effect this time.

Brighed seethed. Her eyes turned black and the color of her glow changed from red to a deep pulsing purple. Her body lifted into the air on a wave of anger and power, and a crackle of lightning sparked from the ends of her floating hair. She was both magnificent and terrifying in her fury.

A.J. dropped his smile, sat up straight, and put his feet on the floor. He suddenly wished he were back to just facing a pair of werewolves.

A.J. shrugged apologetically and sighed. "Honestly, I really don't understand what the hell is going on, and no one around here seems interested in explaining it to me. So, if it's all the same to you, why don't you get me past that wall of mist out there, and I'll stop being your problem."

The sadness in his voice pierced Brighed's anger. Her color softened and the energy around her calmed until she appeared her normal self again.

"You are not a problem." Her voice was caring, even if her body language was still cold. "If anything, you are a miracle. I still have trouble accepting that you are even real, but here you sit. At any other time, your arrival would be celebrated across the realm, a cause for excitement. But now? Well, let's just say your timing could have been better." She looked at A.J. with pity and sat next to him on the sofa.

"You mentioned that before. What's so bad about the timing?"

Brighed frowned. "I won't bore you with the details, but let's just say our Queendom's politics are perilous at the moment, and some very long negotiations over significant and emotionally charged issues are nearing a conclusion. They could still go either way, with terrible consequences for us all should they fail. It's been nearly two centuries since an unknown Tuatha D'Anu has appeared, and your arrival on the same night as Frank's murder is disturbing. I don't know what it means."

"Probably just a coincidence," said A.J. "They happen."

"Not here they don't," Brighed pursed her lips and stared into A.J.'s eyes as if trying to ascertain if he were a threat or truly as ignorant as he seemed to be. A.J. kept his face expressionless, but inside him raged a tempest of uncertainty, and anger.

Brighed sighed. "There are much larger forces at play here that you have no idea about, and your sudden appearance, right at this moment, will look very suspicious to all the wrong players. The surprise of your arrival could undo decades of work at a time when we cannot afford a delay. It's why I hoped to keep your ancestry secret for now, but that's all out the window if Fergus knows."

A.J. nodded. "I take it Fergus has his own agenda?"

"He always does," Brighed replied, but she had a far-away look in her eyes as she said it. Over the course of one day, A.J. had witnessed Brighed's mood change from suspicion to anger to laughter and even sadness, but what he saw now in her eyes was genuine fear. The door in A.J.'s heart cracked open a little wider for her.

Brighed read the look of pity on his face and changed the subject.

"All the things that you have missed," she said. "So much you do not know. I can't imagine the challenges you faced as a D'Anu child growing up in the Incog world. It must have felt terribly lonely."

Brighed was like no one A.J. had ever met, and he felt a longing to hold her that he couldn't let go. No one had ever affected him that way, except perhaps for Malcolm, and that's why it scared him. He forced himself to lean away from her touch.

"I grew up just fine," he lied. Her words had struck a chord that he didn't like touched, and he had more pressing questions. "What's an Incog?"

"The Incognizant. It what we call the rest of humankind who don't have our connection to magic, and can't really understand it. Save for a few like Skinner and...Frank..." A moment of grief washed over her face before she regained control. "Virtually all of them are unaware of our existence or don't believe we are real. It's better for everyone that way."

"Spoken like a true aristocrat, you deciding what's 'better' for everyone else."

Brighed's eyes flashed, but she shrugged. "You are not wrong. Nevertheless, it is a policy that has kept us safe for centuries, but that could all change soon." The look of fear returned to her eyes.

A.J. plowed ahead with questions. He didn't want to lose this opportunity to gain information that might prove helpful for getting out of the valley.

"Just who exactly is 'us'? What is a Tuatha D'Anu?" He had so many questions. Why couldn't he get through that damned mist? How could Shifters be real? How the hell was any of what he had experienced even possible? He could feel the Brighed's Draft wearing off and his shoulders drooped. He held his spinning head in his hands.

Brighed watched him with concern as he struggled to make sense of it all. "It's clear we have much to discuss, though, honestly, I'm not sure where to begin." She placed a hand on his chest and her touch sent chills through his body but also calmed his anxiety.

"Perhaps we should just start with you," she said. "You know you have always been different from everyone around you." It wasn't a question. "You know in your heart this is true."

A.J. looked up into Brighed's eyes. "Always," he whispered. "As confused as I feel about what I've encountered in this weird ass valley, I also feel strangely relieved, like someone is finally telling me I haven't been the crazy one all my life. I just can't believe any of it, and yet I watched two people turn into wolves right in front of me today, and Connor! He's a fucking Sasquatch? Really? I'm just too stunned to think straight. Then there's Darcy, and you, and Digger and, and Margaret! What the hell is up with all the Margarets?"

Brighed lowered her head and put a hand over her mouth, but it was obvious she was laughing. Her blue eyes sparkled brilliantly when she looked up at him again. A.J. tried to appear indignant at her mockery but broke into laughter himself. It all sounded so crazy to him, but he was feeling a kind of vindicating relief that he couldn't deny. A wave of exhaustion washed over him, and the golden glow on his arms faded a bit more. He turned his hands over and back again and looked at Brighed half in astonishment and half pleading, and he spoke aloud the secret question that had plagued him all his life.

"What the hell am I?"

Brighed's eyes filled with tears, and she spoke with a quiet kindness that cut straight to his heart. "You are human, A.J., and you are D'Anu, which means you are also more than human. You are a member of the tribe of Anu, a very rare breed whose lineage traces directly to the creation of humankind."

"Creation?" A.J. rolled his eyes and sighed in disappointment. "I've got no use for religious claptrap," he said. "Trust me, after what I've seen and experienced in this world, I don't accept there is a God."

"Perhaps you need to alter your concept of god," Brighed replied. "There is no rule in this universe that says a god has to be 'good.' In fact, most of them aren't."

A.J. stared skeptically, but he didn't object. An evil god was something he might be able to accept.

"Think about it," Brighed continued. "Virtually every major religion, today or in the past, involves a god creating, or mating with a human who gives birth to a magical superhuman. From the Greek god Zeus turning himself into a swan to the god of Abraham mating with an unwed woman, it is a common thread of their mythologies upon which many dogmas rest."

A.J. had never considered her point before, and he found it strangely comforting, even if he didn't believe any of it. "You may be correct on that point, but if it's all the same to you, I'll stick with Darwin."

"Of course," Brighed smiled. "You should. Charles was such a sweet, kind, and gentle soul. I miss him terribly."

A.J.'s stunned look made Brighed laugh. "I'm older than I look. You know, Charles waited decades to publish his work on evolution because he knew how society would react, but he was generous enough to share it with me. I offered some guidance and recommendations and encouraged him to publish it. Most importantly, Charles recognized that, in addition to natural selection, there exists artificial selection. Farmers have been breeding animals since the dawn of time to achieve specific traits. Is it so far-fetched then to accept that a being of great magical power might breed with a human to achieve similar results?"

"I suppose not," A.J. conceded. "If you accept these so-called 'beings of great power' actually exist."

"Trust me, they do," Brighed replied with a weary look that suggested personal experience. "At the dawn of time there were tens of thousands of them that roamed the world in a variety of forms wreaking havoc and sowing chaos wherever they went. Anu, among a few others, recognized the threat to reality that such chaos represented, so she chose a clever, tool-using hominid to create the first modern humans, our ancestors."

"I see," A.J. shook his head in disbelief. "So, this Anu, is she the reason I can't break a promise?"

"Yes. When Anu completed the creation of the first humans, it occurred to her that since they were capable of challenging the other gods and their creations, someday these first humans might challenge her. So, she wove into their DNA a simple curse, that they will be compelled to always keep a promise. Then she made them promise never to attack her."

"Clever," A.J. chuckled.

"That's one word to describe it," Brighed smiled. "While languages may change over time, the intent of a promise triggers a response in our chromosomes, and we are compelled to fulfill it. I could go into the details of how specific genes can be switched on to drive obsessive and compulsive behaviors, but it is enough to know that a D'Anu who is unable to fulfill a promise can be driven mad over time. It's one of the many reasons I am surprised you have survived as long as you have among the Incogs."

"I learned early not to make promises," A.J. glanced at his pack on the floor. "Though sometimes it can't be avoided."

"Indeed," Brighed nodded.

They sat in silence together for several minutes while A.J. digested this information. He was finding it difficult to keep his thoughts together.

"If I'm supposed to be D'Anu like you, why can't I do magic?"

"One doesn't 'do' magic, A.J. We *are* magical creatures. You are young, and it takes many years of study and practice to purposefully direct celestial energies to your will, but I suspect it's already showed itself in your life in some way. I'm sure there something you can do that surprises you or others. Something unexpected?"

The look on A.J.'s face must have told her everything. His body always seemed to know when he was in danger, even before his mind realized it. It made him remember the moment of anguish when he held Malcolm's mangled body in his arms and wished desperately for Death to take him too, but his cursed reflexes stole that from him and made him do the thing for which he would always consider himself a monster.

Brighed nodded slowly without having to ask. "It can sometimes feel like a curse at first."

"Or always..." A.J. replied. He shook his head to knock the flashback out of his mind and tried to concentrate on the next question, but his mind was getting foggy and he struggled to find the words. "Why here? What's so special about this valley?"

Brighed leaned against A.J.'s chest and looked up into his eyes. Her mouth was close to his, and he could feel the warmth of her sweet breath on his lips. His heart skipped a beat.

"This valley is one of a few places on earth with a high concentration of luminiferous aether."

"The lumin-what?" A.J. raised an eyebrow.

"The luminiferous aether. The insubstantial medium in which all matter floats and connects all things to one another."

"Oh, yeah." A.J. recalled reading something about that a few years back. "That's how they used to think light moved through space, right? But I thought they proved it doesn't exist."

"Ha!" Brighed Scoffed. "No. The only thing science has proven is that the luminiferous aethers have no direct physical influence on light, which is obvious to anyone who has studied magic. Trying to measure the aethers with light is like trying to measure your feelings with a ruler."

"Writing about music is like dancing about architecture," A.J. quoted the famous axiom.

"Indeed! You get it," she laughed. "Incog scientists rely too much on physical science for observing the universe, when the vast majority of it exists outside of the physical plane. The aethers have no mass and exist outside of time, yet all space and energy and time float through them in all directions. The gods are creatures of the aethers, and they created the physical plane and all the life that inhabits it. Magical creatures, however, such as ourselves and the Shifters, Drow, Utukku, and others, can influence and manipulate the aethers in ways that concentrate the energies within it. That is the nature of magic. For many, like the Shifters, their magic is limited to their shifting abilities, but the D'Anu can wield those energies for our own purposes, such as a weapon, or for healing, as I do."

"Why do you…or we, I guess… get such special privileges?" A.J. asked.

"Perhaps because we are made from a part of Anu herself, or perhaps because it was our purpose to be this way." Brighed caressed his glowing hands in demonstration.

"The aethers filled the void before the Big Bang, and will fill the void long after this universe has faded to little more than dust in the aethereal wind. Magic is the manipulation of these aethers, and it is similar in force to gravity."

"Imagine a heavy ball resting on stretched fabric." Brighed pressed her fingertip into the palm of his hand. "Where the ball sits, it forms an indent. The heavier the ball, the bigger the indent until the ball becomes so heavy that it rips a hole in the fabric, which is how gravity works and how black holes are created. It is the same with the aethers. The greater the concentration of magic in one place, the greater the concentration of aethers, until the forces that float within it begin to interact with each other, and that interaction can be manipulated and directed. There is danger, however. Should the aether concentration become too great, it will rip a hole in the fabric of existence, but instead of gravity flowing in as it does with a black hole, magic flows in. It is how the First Age came to an abrupt end."

"This valley, however, is one of a few places in the world where our link to magic is still strong," she said. "It's why Shifters and other magical creatures choose to live here. In most of the Incog world, magic is suppressed."

"Suppressed?" That peaked A.J.'s curiosity, but with Brighed's body pressed close to his and his rapid descent into exhaustion, the thread of conversation was fraying.

"Yes… it's…"

"Complicated?" A.J. mumbled in frustration.

Brighed laughed. "It is, but perhaps this will help." She laid her head against A.J.'s chest and closed her eyes. She began to sing in that magical, enchanting voice that he could feel vibrating in every cell of his body. Her song resonated with his own thoughts and carried them away from the small living room to form images of people and places he had never seen. Though he had no understanding of the words, he still had a clear sense of them as they wove a story in his mind, and his emotions moved through sadness and anger and joy and pride in turns with the rhythm. Whatever the song meant, A.J.'s connection to it felt like home, a feeling he had never known, and until that moment had never known how much he wanted.

"What was that? What did I just see?" he whispered when the last note faded from the room.

"That is our story, of where we come from and how we came to be here. The creation of the tribe of Anu launched the First Age of Humankind. It was an age of heroes and monsters when some of the first humans could wield magic to rival the gods, and as they did so, the chaos of the before times was quelled. Many of the early gods were vanquished or imprisoned in other realms, and those that weren't were forced to submit to the rule of Anu. These gods became known as the Anu'nakki, and for the first time in the history of the gods, there was peace on Earth, for a time at least.

"Peace never lasts," A.J. grumbled.

"It is true," Brighed sighed. "Though this peace lasted for more than a Millennia, and in that time, four great city-states emerged: Gorias, Murias, Finias, and Falias. They were majestic cities filled with wonders beyond imagination. They held great libraries and universities and centers for magic and the arts. Artists and craftsmen and wizards worked side by side to create great monuments worthy of the Anu'nakki."

"Power, as we know, is corrupting, and the Anu'nakki were eventually corrupted by this worship to became petty and greedy overlords, teaching human wizards to build great and terrible armies of unnatural creatures genetically spliced together from all manner of beasts and humans alike to wage war against one another and against the D'Anu. This is where Shifters, Dwarfs and other magical creatures of our Queendom originated."

"You were all enemies?" A.J.'s eyebrows shot up. "But now you're allies?"

Brighed sat up and looked A.J. in the eyes. "Allies is much too strong a word for what we are," she replied, emphasizing the word 'we.' "Let's just say a tenuous peace exists for the sake of all of us."

Brighed settled back into A.J.'s arms and continued. "Every child of the Queendom is taught this history to help hold that peace in place. At the end of the First Age, a terrible and ferocious war broke out between the cities and the Anu'nakki and raged for many years, with the greatest of human wizards from the four cities joining together against the power of the gods and their demon armies. Dragon riders filled the skies with fire and charged upon the Anu'nakki with their lightning lances, slaying many, but the Anu'nakki were too strong. They ripped the world apart, sinking the beautiful Murias and its powerful navy into the ocean, and burying Glorias, the shining city of steel and glass, in molten lava. They caused great earthquakes that shook the ancient Finias, a city carved from the very mountains of granite and marble, until nothing remained but pebbles in the sand. The last to fall was Falias, the first and most majestic of the four great cities. It was a forest city of magic and medicine and music that was grown and carved over centuries from the giant Ollmhór trees that grew 300 meters tall and whose bark was strong as iron. Falias, our home that had stood so long and created so much, was burned to ashes by spirit fire, which consumes all that it touches, until nothing of the city or those majestic trees remained."

A.J. looked at Brighed critically. "You know, it was probably a natural cataclysm that destroyed those cities, or the war, or both. Gods usually get the blame for such things."

"That is true," Brighed frowned. "Yet our ancestors survived, according to our history, because Anu sacrificed herself to save them. Many ships from each of the cities carried refugees of all kinds away from the war, but the Anu'nakki were relentless and attacked these vessels in their fury to wipe out all the first humans and other creatures alike. To save the Tuatha D'Anu and many other creatures of that age, Anu transformed herself into a thick mist and surrounded these ships, obscuring them from the other gods and transporting them through time, to this third age of humankind. My ancestor, Brighed, for whom I am named, arrived in the land called Erin with hundreds of other D'Anu and Shifters, where we were called De Danann by the modern humans there. Others of our ancestors landed in the Middle East and were called Ubaidians. In Central Africa we were called Chwezi. In South Asia we were called Silla, and in ancient China we were called Sanxingdui. There are a few others as well, but what all these D'Anu had in common was advanced technology and the gift of magic that modern humans had long since lost or could only access in very limited ways by a handful of their wisest women and men."

"I see," A.J. tried to absorb this new information but was having trouble focusing with his fading energy and Brighed's body pressed to his. All he could think of was the warmth of her skin, so he focused on the one question he most wanted answered. "So, this 'mist'..." A.J. whispered "It's magic? Is there a way to get through it without being turned around?"

"Of course," replied Brighed. "One need merely ask the Anu for safe passage in the language of our ancestors. It is the first language from the First Age, and it is sung. Translating it into the modern tongue loses much of its meaning."

A.J. lowered his face closer to hers until their lips were almost brushing. He inhaled her scent. "Tongues are nice," he whispered.

She smiled seductively at him. "*Yes, they are...*"

Her words appeared only in A.J.'s mind, but he didn't resist them. He let her thoughts and feelings wash through him, overwhelming his last threads of resistance. He pressed his lips to hers, drawing in his breath as if he could inhale her very essence. In that moment, A.J. knew these were the lips he wanted to kiss forever, and in that same moment, the last vestiges of the Brighed's Draft left his body, and A.J. collapsed into the deepest, sweetest unconsciousness he had ever known.

Chapter Eight

Sayah

A.J. slowly became aware of a high-pitched whine invading his deep slumber. His groggy consciousness tried to locate the source and beg it to stop making that terrible noise, which amplified the pain of his pounding head. He tried to open his eyes, but the bright light drove them shut again. He tried to sit up, but he had trouble finding the "up" position. Then, most mercifully, the terrible sound stopped, and the words "vacuum cleaner" slid like wet sludge through his mind.

He shielded his eyes and managed to pry them wide enough to see a shadowy outline of a plump woman standing over him. As his eyes slowly focused, the figure transformed into the pleasant face of Margaret. She wore overalls under a white apron and looked like the Margaret who cared for Darcy, but it was hard to be certain. A.J. tried his best to smile back, but his best effort was just short of a painful grimace.

"Good morning, sleepyhead!" Margaret spoke with much more enthusiasm than the moment called for in A.J.'s opinion. He moaned a response.

"Brighed said you might be feeling under the weather, so she made this for you to drink when you woke up." She handed A.J. a small glass of warm liquid. He managed to focus one eye on its contents and saw gold and blue swirls in a cloudy base. It smelled awful.

A.J.'s head snapped away from the concoction, and his eyes popped open. "My gods, this stuff would knock the stink off a five-day-old corpse!"

"It'll cure what ails ya. Brighed's never wrong about her medicine. Now drink up!"

A.J. hesitated but decided death would feel better than he did right then, so he tossed it back in one quick gulp and grimaced. The taste was worse than the smell.

The relief, however, was instant. The throbbing in his head dropped to a dull beat, and the painful brightness of the room faded to a manageable glare. A.J. shook the sleep out of his head and was immediately, terribly thirsty and starving. Margaret traded the empty glass for a larger one filled with water, which he quickly downed.

"I'll get you some breakfast." Margaret giggled as she scurried off to the kitchen. A.J. took stock of his surroundings. The room that was so carefully arranged and compulsively cleaned the night before was now half in shambles. Picture frames were crooked on the walls and books and pillow cushions were strewn everywhere. The vacuum sat upright in the corner next to a plant that leaned haphazardly in its pot.

When he took stock of himself, A.J. was even more bewildered. He was naked save for a light silk blanket that barely covered his midsection, and he had an erection. Margaret swept back into the room beaming at A.J., who grabbed a cushion to cover his lap. Margaret giggled again.

"Ah, that will make a nice tray." She sat a plate filled to the edges with scrambled eggs, avocado, and steamed kale. She added a cup of aromatic coffee and a large glass of cold orange juice. "Now you eat that, and I'll bring more. You must be starving after your recent, um, exertions." She winked and went back to straightening the living room, humming a happy tune.

A.J. would have been embarrassed if he weren't so hungry. He dug into the eggs and found both the coffee and the orange juice to be the best he ever tasted. He was halfway through his second plate of eggs and third cup of coffee when Margaret abruptly stopped putting books away and walked purposefully toward the front door.

"Where are you going?" A.J. asked.

"Nowhere, dear, I'm just opening the door for Mr. Skinner. Did I forget to mention he was on his way to pick you up?" Margaret couldn't hide a smile. "Silly me, I must have been distracted."

"What?" A.J. desperately tried to put the plate down, stand up, hold the pillow in place, and finish chewing all at the same time. The result was only more mess for Margaret to clean, and A.J. half crouching, holding a pillow over his crotch with one hand and a fork raised in the air with the other when Margaret pulled open the door. Skinner stared into the living room. Both men looked at each other in surprise, then Skinner glanced around the room.

"Mornin'," was all he said, but his crooked smile spoke volumes. A.J. dropped the fork and turned in the direction of what he hoped was the shower.

"I'll just get myself a cup of coffee while you freshen up." Skinner laughed on his way toward the kitchen, but Margaret stopped him.

"Digger says she needs to see you at her lab right away. She says it's urgent!" She ushered Skinner toward the hallway.

"What do you mean "Digger says?" A.J. asked. "You haven't left the room!"

"Margaret has her ways," said Skinner. "It's best to do what she says. Well, come on! You can get dressed in the elevator."

"What elevator?" yelled A.J. He was flummoxed by the chaos and confusion of the morning, and he didn't even know where his clothes were. He looked desperately around the room. Margaret stepped past him into a bathroom and out again holding freshly laundered and pressed pants, shirt, and socks in one hand and his cleaned boots in the other.

"Now get moving," Margaret urged them into an office at the end of the hall, and A.J. saw a sleek steel elevator door on the opposite wall. "Digger asked if you know where Alice is this morning. She needs her too."

"Alice?" Skinner looked surprised. "Why would Digger need Alice?"

"I don't know. That girl never explains anything to me."

"I left her at the house," said Skinner looking as confused as A.J. for once.

The elevator door slid open soundlessly and Margaret shoved both men inside. "I'll go and fetch her. Digger says to hurry."

The elevator had no buttons but started down instantly. Skinner was quiet, so A.J. shrugged in frustration and began pulling his pants on. Just as he got one leg in, the elevator stopped moving down and began moving sideways at an accelerating speed. Skinner was prepared for the sudden change in direction, but A.J. bounced off the wall and landed hard on his butt.

"Hey! You could have warned me!" A.J. barked, struggling to stand with one leg in his pants.

"Yep, could have," Skinner suppressed a chuckle.

A.J. fumed as he finished dressing. He had one boot on when the elevator stopped moving and the door opened.

Standing in the hallway was Margaret with the white streak in her hair.

"Digger is waiting for you in her lab. Come quickly."

Limping in one boot, A.J. followed the pair down a short hallway to a heavy steel door set in a solid rock wall. It swung open as the trio approached, and they entered a large cavern carved from bedrock. Rows of metal shelves were filled to overflowing with steel scraps, springs, boxes of electronics, wheels, odd parts, and assorted other junk. The room opened onto a workshop with racks of tools, welding equipment, torches, and steel tables. Beyond that was a white wall with large plate glass windows and a sliding door that led to a well-equipped laboratory.

The lights to the lab brightened as they entered. Digger stood before a large piece of equipment, reading the computer screen with her shaded goggles firmly in place. If A.J. thought she looked pale when they first met, he was startled by her ghostly appearance now.

"I've brought Skinner and A.J. like you wanted," Margaret said. "Alice is on her way. I'll get Brighed. Won't be a moment!" She disappeared through another set of doors that opened onto a polished white stone stairway.

A.J. looked up at the high ceiling and figured they were somewhere beneath the doctor's clinic. "That's one way to get around commuter traffic," he grumbled.

"Digger installed the elevator transport for the doc years ago," said Skinner. "It's how they met, I think. Right, Digger?" The young Dwarf didn't reply. She only nodded her head and bounced back and forth from one foot to the other in front of her equipment. She started pressing buttons on the screen and the machine whirred and clicked. The doors at the far end of the lab opened and Brighed and Margaret entered, walking fast.

A.J.'s bad mood melted as Brighed approached. She moved with grace and confidence, and a soft golden glow surrounded her, making her hair shine. He recalled the feeling of her breath on his neck and the touch of her skin against his own, and his face flushed with excitement. He was anxious though. He had no memory of what happened after their kiss, but he didn't want to look like an idiot for not knowing. He was failing.

"Okay, we're all here now," Skinner said. "What's the big emergency, Digger?"

Digger touched her computer tablet, and the lights in the lab dropped by half. An image appeared on a floating screen projected from the ceiling. Two sets of thin vertical lines, some colored in shades of red, blue, and yellow hovered side by side in the air. They looked almost identical.

Digger spoke in a language that was guttural and strange, like a mix between German and gravel bouncing around in a dryer. She stamped her foot and turned from ghostly white to a crimson red. Margaret frowned in disapproval.

"Cursing isn't going to help you find the words." Brighed placed her hand on the Dwarf's shoulder, and Digger noticeably calmed at her touch. She shook herself all over like a dog shaking off water, and when she stopped moving, her color was better and the shivering was gone. She took a deep breath and let it out slowly.

"Remember the sample Connor dropped off yesterday, you know, the leaves and soil?"

"Did you find something interesting?"

"Yes," Digger nodded vigorously. "I found blood, and a number of short white hairs." She touched her screen and an enlarged photograph of a hair appeared next to the other floating image. "I sequenced them and ran a region of their mitochondrial genes against all living creatures."

"Well, don't keep us in suspense," Skinner growled. "What did you find? What is it?"

Digger took off her goggles to rub her eyes. They were rimmed in red like she hadn't slept. "That's hard to explain. It's weird."

"What do you mean?" asked Brighed. "Did you get a match or not?"

"Yes, well, no. I mean, sort of, I guess."

"That about covers the range of possibilities," A.J. smirked. Skinner smacked his shoulder.

"Digger, please explain." Margaret frowned at the two men.

"I got four somethings," said Digger. "It makes no sense, but all the samples tested the same. Different sections of this DNA match fairly closely with apes, wolves, and reptiles."

"That is strange," Brighed nodded. "What could cause that?

Digger began to answer but Skinner interrupted. "What was the fourth? You said there were four."

Digger grimaced. "There is a sequence of chromosomes that don't match anything I can find on record. I can't even tell you for certain that it comes from the Animal Kingdom, but I think so." Digger threw her hands in the air in visible frustration.

Brighed's brow furrowed. "Digger, there must be a problem with the equipment. This makes no sense."

"That's what I thought, too!" exclaimed Digger. "Just to be thorough, I ran it against the other database..." Digger glanced guiltily at Brighed and twisted her fingers together.

Brighed's eyes narrowed. "You mean the one you're not supposed to have access to? Digger! There are reasons that information is restricted!"

"I know, I know! But I was stumped! I wanted to check it against every possibility, just to be sure."

Brighed put her hands on her hips and glared at Digger. "We will discuss this later. I am assuming you are only telling me now because you think you found something useful. That is highly improbable."

"I ran it eight times!" argued Digger. "I'm running a ninth right now. It comes out the same every time, see?" She pointed to the floating image of the nearly identical sequences. "I even took the sequencer apart and cleaned its sensors and updated the operating system and ran diagnostics on its code. I ran known samples to calibrate it. Everything is in perfect working order. It still comes out the same."

"Well, don't keep us in suspense, dear," Margaret jumped in. "What did you find?"

"This is what my DNA algorithm came up with." Digger looked at each of them in turn, then touched her screen. The lines disappeared and were replaced by a color drawing. The image was frightening. A long-armed creature with a wolf-like muzzle filled with fangs and sharp teeth extending from the face of a baboon. The creature was covered head to toe in thick white fur.

"What the hell is that thing?" Skinner squinted at the image.

"It's a Wendigo," Digger said. "The closest match to the DNA Connor found is a Wendigo!"

"Oh!" Brighed put her hand over her mouth, but she didn't seem disturbed by the news. In fact, A.J. thought she was stifling a laugh. The look on Margaret's face changed from frightened to amused as well, and she stared at Digger suspiciously.

"Is this one of your practical jokes?" asked Margaret. "You had us frightened to death!"

"Digger, please be serious," added Brighed. "Did you find anything useful?"

Digger looked angry. She glanced from Brighed to Margaret in growing frustration, then clenched her jaw and pulled her goggles back into place so the tinted lenses hid her eyes. "I am not joking!" She crossed her arms and stared up defiantly at Brighed. "Look for yourself! The two sequences are the closest match."

A.J. raised his hand before speaking. "Somebody want to fill me in on what a Wendigo is?"

"It's nothing," said Brighed. "This has to be a joke. It can't be a Wendigo, they're…"

"Faery Tales?" offered A.J.

"No. Not like that. I mean, yes, they supposedly existed during the First Age and there have been anecdotal accounts of them from very remote places in this age. But even if they did exist, there is no way a Wendigo could make its way to this valley to kill our sheriff without coming across other humans. A Wendigo can't encounter a human without attacking. It was bred into them as an instinct. I promise, we would have known about it before now."

"How so?" asked Skinner. "There's a lot of forest around here with plenty of remote spaces. I mean, isn't it possible?"

"These creatures were designed to infect their victims with a virus that rearranges DNA. Their victims literally become Wendigos as well. It would only take one of these creatures to infect and destroy an entire army or city. They don't stop until they run out of humans, and then they kill each other until there is only one left."

"I can see how that would be a useful weapon." A.J. stared at the monster on the screen. "In a zombie apocalypse sort of way."

"Exactly," said Brighed. "That's why this can't be a Wendigo. Digger, there must be some mistake."

A.J. turned to ask Digger a question, but she was gone. He had only glanced up at Brighed for a moment, but that's all the Dwarf seemed to need. "Where'd she go?" A.J. asked in surprise.

Brighed looked at where Digger had been standing and sighed. "Digger, please come back out. I am not questioning your science, just your conclusion. You know this is impossible." The Dwarf did not appear.

"Why isn't it possible?" Skinner asked. "You said the genetic blueprint is in that secret database of yours?" He seemed keen on that last topic, but she pretended not to notice.

"The Database of Proscribed Species," said Brighed. "It contains genetic records of creatures from the First Age that are strictly banned under Queendom law. Some of the genetic experiments of the First Age are best left buried in the rubble of the Four Cities."

"And these 'Wendigos' were one of these experiments?" Skinner asked.

"Yes," said Brighed. "The genetic engineers of the First Age spliced together different species, including humans, with the heads or bodies of other animals. Some were created for war, some for curiosity, and some for practicality, like horses with the torsos of humans smart enough to plow fields without guidance. Once these engineers gained the knowledge of how to manipulate genetics, there seemed no end to their imaginations. A handful of those creations were cast into this age with the D'Anu, Shifters, and other Queendom species, but those particular mutations are all extinct now."

Skinner looked skeptical. "As far as you know. But you're also saying this creature could exist if someone had access to their genetic design and the skills to create them? In my experience, when people find out they 'can' do a thing, someone inevitably 'tries' to do that thing."

Brighed sighed. "That is highly improbable. Even our own advanced technology could barely pull something like this off, and it would take years to achieve. It's one thing to clone or splice genes from existing creatures, it's an entirely different thing to take a theoretical genetic design and create a brand-new, full-grown version from scratch. It could be done, theoretically, but I don't know a single D'Anu geneticist who would agree to such a task. There are only a handful of us who could even attempt it. Ask Alice, she knows us all personally."

"That's why I called for her," came Digger's annoyed voice from behind them. Everyone turned to see Digger standing in the open space a few feet away.

"How did you—" A.J. began to ask, but Skinner interrupted him.

"Digger, you said this sequence only mostly matches the Wendigo. What does that mean? Is it the same creature or not?"

"Why is the non-D'Anu human the only one who asks the smart questions?" Digger was indignant. "That's what I've been trying to get at if you would all listen!"

"Sorry, Digger," said Margaret. "What is it you want to tell us?"

"This Wendigo is only mostly Wendigo. It's like a bad forgery that was painted too fast with the wrong materials. Whatever this thing is, it was made! And I can think of at least one D'Anu who might do something like that!" Digger finished her rant, staring hard at Brighed, whose face turned from amused to cold hard anger in a flash.

"Oh, Digger!" she fumed. "That's ridiculous. Don't you dare say—"

"Magnivald?" Digger defiantly cut her off. "Don't say the name Magnivald? I can't imagine why you wouldn't to hear the name Magni—"

"Enough!" yelled Brighed. She put her hands over her face and took a slow deep breath. "Digger, please. This is not a joke."

Margaret stepped between Digger and Brighed and raised her hands. "Let's not jump to conclusions. We have very little evidence to go on and supposition isn't helping. Alice will be here in a minute, and I'm sure she'll have some answers to these questions."

"Who the hell is Magnivald?" A.J. didn't care who the question upset. He wanted answers.

"It's the D'Anu version of the bogeyman," said Brighed. "It's a ridiculous myth from the First Age that gets the blame anytime some bizarre crime or tragedy happens that no one can explain. Magnivald doesn't exist in this age and probably didn't in the First Age either."

"Oh, yeah? Tell that to the Council," challenged Digger. "Tell that to your brother!"

"Leave him out of this!" barked Brighed, and the red-hot energy flared as her chest heaved in anger.

Margaret tried again to calm them down. "Now, now. Let's not make this personal. We don't know anything yet. Digger, let's get some real evidence before we make accusations."

Digger clacked her teeth together and crossed her arms in protest. A.J. crouched so he was looking directly into Digger's darkened goggles.

"Digger, two days ago I would have sworn on my life that you couldn't exist, nor any of the D'Anu or Shifters I've already met. Yet here we all are."

Digger uncrossed her arms and tilted her head as if considering his comment. A.J. took one of her small hands in his and was surprised at how strong yet soft it felt.

"If you can be real, then as far as I'm concerned, Wendigos and Magnivald can be real. The only thing I care about is how to catch or kill them."

Digger raised her goggles and looked A.J. in the eyes with her much larger ones. She placed her hand on his shoulder and squeezed. Her grip was like a steel vice, and he was grateful she didn't squeeze harder.

"Wendigos can regenerate lost limbs and heal quickly from injury," she said. "Their thick hides and hard bones make them extremely difficult to kill. The only way to be certain they're dead is significant brain injury, most easily achieved by cutting off their heads."

A.J. nodded. "Cut off the heads, got it. Thank you. That's helpful."

"No, thank you, human, for believing me," said Digger. "I like you. You're a good human, I think. Now we must cut off your head before you turn into a Wendigo and kill us all." She smiled, but she didn't let go of his shoulder.

A.J. tried to stand but couldn't budge. "Excuse me?" He tried to pull away from the small Dwarf, but her grip was unyielding.

"It's the only way to be certain." Digger's voice was calm but inflexible.

"Certain of what?" A.J. grabbed her wrist, but it was useless. He couldn't even lift her off the floor, and she was half his size.

"That you won't turn into a Wendigo. The wound on your leg—if you were injured by whatever killed Sheriff Standish, and if that was a Wendigo, then you're a danger to us all. We can't take that chance."

"You want to cut off my head?" A.J. heard panic in his voice. He tried to look at Skinner for help but couldn't turn that far.

"Would you prefer an axe or a guillotine? I have both."

"Neither!" yelled A.J. "I am not turning into a Wendigo! Now let me go!"

"Digger, I think he's safe for the time being." Brighed tried to sound angry, but A.J. could hear she was stifling a laugh. Digger grabbed his chin and lifted it as if examining his neck for a good place to cut. He couldn't stop her.

"I'll make you a deal, Digger," Skinner chuckled. "If A.J. starts looking shifty, I'll provide the brain trauma. How's that sound?"

Digger considered it, then let go of A.J.'s shoulder. He toppled backward and landed staring up into the other faces, which were all smiling down at him. A.J. rubbed his shoulder where the bruises would soon be showing and climbed to his feet.

"She was joking, right? This is one of Digger's jokes. She wasn't really going to cut off my head, right?"

Skinner, Margaret, and Brighed collectively shrugged.

"Honestly, it can be hard to tell with Digger," said Skinner. "But she's usually willing to negotiate, if she likes you."

A.J. rubbed his neck protectively and looked back at Digger, who was staring at him like a butcher eyes cuts of meat on a steer. "Thank goodness for that!" Then a second thought crowded out the others. "Hey, I'm not actually going to turn into one of those things, am I?"

Skinner shrugged. "Probably not. I tend to favor the doc's opinion on these matters, and if she says Wendigos aren't possible, that's good enough for me. Still, those white hairs are real, and Connor saw Mason's dogs acting mighty strange. There's something out there that we haven't seen before."

Brighed looked worried. "That database of First Age creatures is restricted, but clearly not *that* restricted. Our chief geneticists have access to it, along with some members of the Council. How did you get access to it, Digger?"

Digger smirked like a teenager explaining electronics to a grandparent. "Are you kidding? I built your computer system, remember? I left myself access, you know, for diagnostic purposes."

Brighed wasn't amused, but she didn't pursue it. She seemed more troubled by the idea that someone might be using the database to create a Wendigo. "We don't even know for certain if the blood and hair Connor found is the same thing that killed Frank. Maybe his death and whatever left those hairs are unrelated."

"Too much of a coincidence," said Skinner. "Personally, I still like the wolf clan for his murder."

"But why would they kill Frank?" asked Brighed. "The only real animosity between the wolf clan and the sheriff's office is between you and Aengus, but there is absolutely no chance that he could pull something like this off."

Skinner nodded. "You can say that again. Aengus lacks both the intelligence and the patience for such a scheme. No, there's something else going on here, but the answers still run through the wolf clan. They know something, I can feel it in my gut. Maybe it's time for you to leverage your relationship with Fergus to get some information."

"I'm afraid that's going to have to wait," Margaret interrupted. "Brighed, the mayor is headed to your office right now and seems quite upset."

"Terrific." Brighed rubbed her eyes. "This day is getting better and better. Did the mayor say what they want?"

"No," said Margaret. "Only to see you and Skinner right away, and…" she hesitated.

"Well?" Brighed snapped. "Out with it."

"The mayor contacted your brother. He's on his way here too."

"Dian?" Brighed gasped. "Dian is coming here?"

"Yes. He'll be here tomorrow. I've already begun making the arrangements."

Brighed leaned on a steel table. "I suppose it was inevitable. Fergus has been pushing for a Council meeting for years and now he's probably going to get it. Thank you, Margaret. Please let me know as soon as possible when Alice completes her analysis. Feel free to interrupt the meeting. In fact, please do interrupt in about twenty minutes."

"Of course." Margaret headed toward the elevator.

A.J. wanted to ask Brighed about Margaret's abilities, but Brighed had both hands to her face and appeared to be crying. He felt an overwhelming desire to comfort her, but he wasn't sure if a hug or a pat on the back were more appropriate. He couldn't remember the night before and had no idea what level of intimacy Brighed might be expecting. He shuffled awkwardly instead.

"What's up with you?" Skinner asked. "You need a bathroom?"

"It's nothing." A.J. changed the subject without meeting Skinner's glare. "So, do you think the mayor is bringing lunch or should we stop somewhere on the way?"

Brighed lowered her hands to stare at A.J. and his awkward smile. Her eyes were red, but their focus was sharp. She dropped her hands. "You know, two days ago the worst thing happening around here was a Chlamydia outbreak in the Incog nursing home. Then you walk into my valley and all hell breaks loose."

"Yeah, that happens," said A.J. "It's usually better for everyone if I stay far from civilization. Hell has a bad habit of following with me. You ready to let me through that mist yet?"

"I hate to interrupt a tender moment," Skinner said, "but we should intervene with the mayor before more council members are contacted. Your brother is one thing—"

"Of course," Brighed said. "Let's go have a chat with our beloved mayor." She squared her shoulders and straightened her lab coat. "A.J., you're coming too. There's no hiding you now."

The stairs went up three stories before opening into a hallway of Brighed's clinic. She led them through a heavy wooden door into an office as carefully organized as every other part of her life. Unlike the rest of the clinic, this room was filled with color and warmth. A vase full of daisies sat on the corner of a glass desk next to a laptop and an old-fashioned blotter pad. A bottle of ink, a glass fountain pen, a stick of wax, and a signet stamp were carefully arranged to one side. Several paintings covered the walls, including what appeared to be an original Van Gogh as well as an ornately framed portrait of a woman in 17th century clothing with a startling resemblance to Brighed. Standing in the middle of the room was a visibly agitated Mayor Bradley. Sitting in a chair in the darkest corner behind him was the raven-haired woman. Her bright red lips were pressed into a thin line under a brooding brow.

"Mayor Bradley, so nice of you to stop by," began Brighed. "What can—"

"Oh, shut it," the mayor cut her off. "Why don't we skip the usual dance where you pretend not to know why I'm here? We have a problem." The mayor's voice was different than before. In place of the affable country charm was a stronger, more direct personality, but the mayor himself had a faraway, unfocused look in his eyes. Brighed turned her attention to the woman.

"Oh, I see," said Brighed. "It's nice to speak directly again, Sayah. It's been a while."

"Clearly too long." It was the mayor who spoke the words, but Brighed wasn't facing him, and he didn't seem to care. Brighed spoke to the woman in the chair instead, who stared back but didn't speak.

"Morgan made a visit to my home last night," spoke the mayor. "She was very upset about a disturbance at The Den."

"That was my fault," A.J. butted in. He didn't know what the hell was happening, but he had never been one to let another catch blame for his actions. Sayah shot an angry look at him for the interruption.

"Imagine my surprise to learn that Frank Standish wasn't killed in an accident but was murdered," the mayor continued. "And that you suspect the wolves and confronted them without speaking to me first! What were you thinking?"

"Ah…that would be my fault, Mayor Bradley, begging your pardon," Skinner spoke directly to the mayor but not to Sayah. "Brighed was four-square against the idea, if it makes any difference." Neither the mayor nor Sayah acknowledged Skinner. Instead, Sayah's stare at A.J. sent a chill down his spine.

"And you!" The mayor barked. "Unregistered! Unknown! Where did you come from? Who sent you? What are you doing in my valley?"

A.J. felt his blood boil. It may have been the mayor's voice, but he had little doubt who was making him talk. He wanted to yell at her, but Brighed beat him to it.

"You forget yourself, Sayah!" Red waves of energy flowed from Brighed. A.J. was once again awestruck by her glorious ferocity but grateful it wasn't aimed at him this time. Sayah looked furious, but she lowered her gaze and bowed her head to Brighed, who brought her own fury under control until the red glow faded.

"Frank's murder has us all on edge," said Brighed. "Mr. Skinner and I are working to find who committed this atrocity, and A.J. has graciously offered to help."

Sayah began to protest through the mayor, but Brighed shut her down. "A.J. is not our primary concern. It is true, he is D'Anu. He is an unknown D'Anu, and his arrival is a shock to us all, but we will have time to investigate that later. For now, the mist is keeping him here, and we need his assistance to find Frank's killer."

Sayah turned her cold stare on A.J. once again. "What do you have to say for yourself, D'Anu? Who are your clan?"

"Clan? No thanks," he said. "I prefer to walk alone. The last club I belonged to got all my friends killed."

Sayah looked confused. He understood how she felt. "The truth is, until yesterday morning, I was just a guy looking for a place to hang my hammock. Now it turns out I'm some genetically engineered mutant, and I've accidentally wandered into this bizarre Roach Motel of a valley that I can't get out of, and, trust me, lady, I would if I could."

Sayah looked furious and disbelieving at the same time.

"He doesn't know what he is," said Brighed. "He was raised in an Incog orphanage."

"Foster home," A.J. corrected. Brighed ignored him.

"A.J. was raised Incog. He arrived here, apparently, by accident."

"Ridiculous!" said the mayor. "How could he not know? What did he think was happening when he passed eighty years and still looked as he does now? Or when he turned 100?"

"Sayah, A.J. is less than two score years in age." Sayah's jaw dropped open. Her mouth was filled with rows of needle-sharp teeth, curved inward. A long, tube-like tongue with a pair of tiny hooks on the tip briefly darted between them. She saw A.J.'s startled look and quickly shut her mouth, returning to the thin line of lips pressed together. A.J. forced himself to stand still despite an overwhelming desire to run. Brighed seemed unfazed, and Skinner was still looking at the mayor.

"But how can this be? A full blood D'Anu born in the last half-century? How could we not know?" The mayor's voice expressed Sayah's curiosity. A.J. knew she controlled him somehow, like a marionette with invisible strings. Whatever creature Sayah was, A.J. was certain he did not want to know her better.

"It is indeed a miracle, Sayah," Brighed said, "and one worth celebrating, but right now we have a much more urgent problem. Frank Standish was under the protection of the D'Anu, and was murdered in this valley, possibly by the wolf clan. If true, it is a violation of the Pact of Boru. We must solve his murder quickly before this information gets out, or there will be war between the D'Anu and the Shifters."

"I know what it means," snapped the mayor. "So do the Shifters. It is why Fergus is demanding a meeting of the Council, and I am inclined to agree. It is why I contacted your brother."

"For Anu's sake!" yelled Brighed. "Don't you understand that is exactly what Fergus wants? If the wolf clan are behind this murder, then he is creating the excuse he needs to justify a Council meeting and push for a vote to interfere in Incog affairs. He would only be fighting so hard for the meeting if he knows he has the votes to win."

The mayor paced in front of Brighed, shaking his head and frowning. Sayah stared at her coldly. "Dian is the Chief Counselor, and it will be his decision whether to assemble the Council if it is warranted. Brighed, I might have held off contacting him if it were only about a dead human Sheriff, but murder and this…" Sayah looked hard at A.J. "An unknown D'Anu who stumbles into our valley on the same night? That is too much to keep under wraps. You know how Dian would react if I had not contacted him immediately? I do not welcome Dian's presence in our valley, but I do not welcome Dian's wrath even more."

Brighed calmed considerably. "Yes. I know. On that point you are doing your duty. Perhaps I can still talk Dian out of calling the meeting. If the vote to interfere is successful, the D'Anu will lose the throne, and we can never let that happen. Two hundred million Incogs died last time. It would happen again, only on a far larger scale. It would expose us. It would be the end of us!"

"Or the salvation!" the mayor yelled back. Sayah had a determined, pleading expression.

"The law of non-interference in the Incog world is only relevant if there is an Incog world left to protect, and every year without action is another year closer to destruction."

"Yet interfering would only hasten such a fate. How close did we come to destroying the world the last time we interfered? Hours? Minutes?" Brighed threw her hands up in dismay.

"We were already exposed to them. They would have hunted us to extinction!" The mayor's and Sayah's faces were indignant, while Brighed's glow flashed red again then faded until she seemed a smaller, quieter version of herself.

"These are old and tired arguments," she sighed. "Whatever happens, we all will lose, and Margaret may not be there to save us next time. It is too great a risk."

On cue, Margaret walked into the meeting, smiling as usual. "Brighed, Alice has news. Also, Dian will arrive at noon tomorrow and will meet you at the gate."

"That wasn't a request, was it?" said an exasperated Brighed. "Tell him I'll be there, but I won't be alone. He is my brother, not my king."

"Shall I include that message as well?" Margaret's smile didn't falter.

"Perhaps it's better if you don't," Brighed smiled back. "He gets combative when he thinks I'm mocking him."

"Very well." Margaret stared at Brighed quietly for a few moments, then said, "He says that is acceptable, but requests Mr. Skinner not be among the party."

Brighed frowned and rubbed her temples. Sayah and the mayor seemed unsurprised, and Skinner stuck his hands in his pockets and shrugged as if saying, "What can you do?" A.J. was annoyed, however.

"Why block Skinner from going? Does your politician brother have a problem with a Dredge like him?"

Silence dropped across the room like a heavy blanket. The mayor and Sayah looked shocked and Brighed blurted out, "A.J.!" Margaret's eyes widened.

Skinner, however, laughed. "Well, I never said it was a nice word, but you do use it with authority." The old man slapped A.J. on the shoulder.

"Sorry, Margaret, this one's on me. He didn't know." Skinner handed her a bill from his wallet. Margaret snatched it from his hand. Her mood was suddenly bright again. She shot A.J. a warning look, then smiled and left the room.

Mayor Bradley straightened his coat and plucked a hat off the back of the chair where Sayah was sitting. "Please keep me informed of any further developments in Frank's case."

Brighed ignored him and nodded toward Sayah. "I will, Sayah. You have my word."

"Good!" said the mayor, and his mannerisms and relaxed friendliness returned. Once again, he stood in front of A.J. as a bright and affable mayor whose smile and handshake were both well practiced and empty of all sincerity. "It was good seeing you again, Brighed, as always. You too, Deputy Skinner, and Mr., ah…A.J., was it? How are you liking our little valley?"

"It's kinda creepy. And full of assholes," A.J. looked sideways at Skinner.

"Glad to hear it!" said the mayor. "Yes, it certainly is a wonderful place. Well, I hope to see you again soon! Ciao for now." He waved and headed out the door. Sayah stood without making a sound and followed. As the mayor pulled the door closed behind him, Sayah's physical form wavered and dissolved into a dark shadow that slipped under the door behind him.

"What the hell was that?" A.J. gasped. "Did you see those teeth?"

"Actually, no," Skinner replied. "I can't see her. No Dre…I mean, no Incog can, but I know she's there. I've only had her described to me, but the description is bad enough."

"I'll say," said A.J. "Is the mayor her husband or her slave?"

"Slave? No. Nothing like that," said Brighed. "Sayah is Utukku, a very ancient race. She and the mayor are *Sha'avelee*," she sang in her musical language. "They are…" Brighed searched for the right word in English, "Symbiote?" She looked at Skinner for help.

"I think A.J. might know the word 'vampire' best," offered Skinner.

"Ugh," said Bridged. "What a terrible fiction. Her kind may be the source of such drivel, but biting people's necks, indeed! Do you know how filthy the average human neck is? It's disgusting!"

A.J. was curious and frightened at the same time. "Vampires? Really? They exist? Now I know this is a fever dream. So? If she doesn't bite him on the neck, where does she bite him, then?"

Brighed started to answer but struggled to find the words.

"Well, it certainly ain't his neck," Skinner laughed. "Though, if it helps any, it's supposed to be extremely pleasurable for the human."

"Yes." Bridged regained her composure. "Sayah's saliva contains a chemical similar to heroin, only much more potent and addictive. In fact, it adds a chromosome pair to the human genome that makes his body produce the nutrition Sayah needs. If the human host goes more than a few days without the Utukku venom, he dies very painfully. It is a mutually beneficial relationship. Sayah needs him to survive, and he is completely devoted to her protection."

"Sounds horrifying," shuddered A.J. "Did the poor guy get a choice in the matter?"

"Choice?" laughed Skinner. "Hell, rumor is he beat two other men to death for the privilege. Hey, come on, I'll introduce you to Alice. Let's see what she and Digger have found out."

Skinner led the way and A.J. and Brighed followed at a short distance. It was the first chance A.J. had to speak with her alone.

"Um, about last night…" A.J. began.

"It's okay. You were very tired. That sort of thing happens."

"Excuse me?" A.J.'s response was louder than he intended.

"You fell asleep."

"Yeah, but not until…after, right?"

Brighed looked confused. "After what?"

"Look, I don't remember anything after we kissed on the couch. I'm sorry."

"Nothing happened." Brighed smiled. "I kissed you, you fell asleep, which is not the usual response, I can promise you."

A.J. tried to stammer an apology, but Brighed stopped him. "It's fine. I put a blanket on you and went to bed. I awoke this morning and came straight to the office. Did something happen?"

"Are you joking? I woke up naked, there was a mess everywhere!"

Brighed burst out laughing. "Oh, my goodness. Margaret can be something of a practical joker, I'm afraid. I'm sure she meant no harm."

Skinner started laughing too. A.J. cleared his throat and walked past him, his face burning. Skinner patted him on the shoulder as he passed. "Bet you'll pay the swear jar next time won't you, Army?"

Chapter Nine

Wendigo

"So, what's the deal with you and Brighed's brother?" A.J. asked Skinner as they stepped into Digger's lab. "Did you piss him off specific or does he just have the good sense to avoid old jarhead cops on general principle?"

Skinner stopped laughing, but not because of A.J.'s insult. His eyes shone, and he grinned like a lovestruck schoolboy at a young woman working at a computer next to Digger. At the sound of footsteps approaching, Digger snapped her head around so fast and far, A.J. thought her neck would break. The young woman also turned around, and A.J. nearly tripped over his feet. The only word that came to mind was "radiant," and shine she did. Her long red hair was awash with the golden glow of the D'Anu, and it danced across her shoulders like liquid fire. She was tall, too, nearly as tall as Skinner, with long limbs on an athletic body. Her skin was so pale it looked blue in Digger's half-lit lab, and a patch of round freckles crossed the square bridge of her nose to spread out across high cheekbones. Her large pupils were ringed by gold irises that faded to bright green at the edges.

"She kinda has that effect on ya the first time you meet her," Skinner broke A.J. from his dumbstruck trance.

"Huh?"

"A.J., I'd like you to meet Alice," said Brighed. "Hopefully, she can help us solve our Wendigo mystery."

Alice shook his hand with a firm grip. "Nice to meet ya!" She spoke in a simple and friendly voice that contrasted sharply with her exotic looks.

"David has told me all about you. I'm super glad you'll be staying with us a few days; maybe you can help my old man get some chores done around the place." She kissed Skinner firmly on the lips and swatted his backside like a football player. Skinner laughed and took her hand.

A.J. had never seen a man so obviously in love. It filled him equally with happiness and regret. Skinner said he was married thirty-five years, but Alice was easily thirty years younger than he. A.J. recalled the painting in Brighed's office. He had a lot to learn about how D'Anu age, or rather, don't age.

It also made him angry and sad. Only sheer luck and his own cursed reflexes had kept him alive so far. He never had any intention of living a long life, and the thought of living hundreds of years was more than he could bear.

Brighed noticed his drop in mood and placed her hand over his heart. He felt it beat against her palm and looked up into her startling blue eyes. Her mind pressed against his, not invasively but more as a caress. He let her thoughts slide over his sadness and felt it washed away by feelings of love and home and kindness, concepts foreign to him but desperately desired.

"Okay," he thought. "Maybe for her." A.J. covered her hand with his own.

"To answer your question," Skinner said, "this exquisite creature is the problem Dian has with me. He and Alice were kind of a thing when she met me."

Alice laughed. "Now there's an understatement. We weren't just a thing, we were betrothed. It was arranged when I was born and a pretty big deal around these parts, but then David turned up in Frank's cell one night, and my heart was lost forever. Why are we talking about Dian, anyway?" she asked in a much colder voice.

"He's arriving tomorrow," answered Skinner. "Between Frank's murder and A.J. here, the mayor felt it prudent to invite him."

Alice rolled her eyes. "Oh, won't that be fun?" She threw her arm around Skinner's shoulders. "Our very own Chief Counselor slumming with his country cousins. Oh, well, if he gets out of line, I'll just have to kick his ass again, won't I dear?"

"Now that I'd pay front row prices for," smiled Skinner. "Damned sorry I missed it the first time."

Digger clacked her teeth and frowned. "I'm not running a brothel here. Can we please get back on task? We have something important to share."

"What did you two find?" Skinner asked.

"Those samples the Sasquatch found are definitely homemade," Digger said. "I never would have seen it without Alice."

"They covered their tracks pretty well," added Alice. "Whoever did it tried to recreate the original genetic frame, though it clearly was a rush job, and they lacked some of the original parts. That might explain the need for the unknown sequence, but it doesn't tell us much else."

"How do you know it was homemade?" Skinner asked.

"What gives it away is the profile itself. You see this segment of chromosomes?" Alice touched the screen and something that looked like a blurry bar code appeared.

"This sequence matches *Canis Lupus Occidentalis*, a Northwestern wolf. It's a large subspecies of *Canis Lupis*, but it didn't exist in the First Age when Wendigos were created. There is no way this sample came from an actual Wendigo, but it definitely came from something with a genetic profile similar to one. I won't know more until I've done some digging, and I need to talk to some of my colleagues at Nalanda to be certain."

A glaring siren and flashing yellow lights interrupted the meeting. Digger turned quickly to her computer and hit a few keys. A live image from a security camera appeared with an external view of a loading bay. Slowly entering the frame was an unmarked white panel van backing down a ramp.

"Who on earth is that?" Brighed asked. "Digger, are you expecting anyone?"

"No!" Digger punched a few keys. The image changed to a view of the van's passenger window, which was being cranked down. A dark-haired figure with a familiar face glared into the camera and motioned to open the bay door. It was Fergus, and he didn't look happy.

"Digger, open the doors," said Brighed.

"They're not authorized!" Digger complained, but Brighed shot her a look that would freeze a candle flame. Digger cursed in her odd Dwarf language and pushed a keyboard key, killing the lights and siren.

They left Alice working on the database while Digger led the others down a hallway and up a short flight of steps to a heavy steel door with a glass porthole. Digger grabbed the handle and waited. A.J. heard a series of clicks as the door's internal locks slid back.

"Biometric locks?" he asked as they filed into the room beyond.

Digger laughed. "Biometric? Please. My kid sister could hack those. These suckers are molecular. Top of the line!"

They entered a room the size of a small gymnasium, with two black SUVs with tinted windows parked against the wall. A third vehicle sat atop a mechanic's hydraulic lift. It was the sheriff's smashed SUV. Half-finished projects and overflowing shelves, like Digger's other workshop, packed the large garage, which also featured chains and lifts hanging from tracks for moving engines and other large parts around the bay.

Digger waited for the door behind them to lock before placing her hand on a panel set in the wall. A loud bang from the massive steel door at the other end of the room told A.J. the locks were disengaging, and it began rolling slowly sideways. The door was heavy, about four inches thick of layered steel, but it moved smoothly on tracks in the floor and ceiling. After the van entered, the big door reversed direction.

"Hell of a security system for a doctor's office," A.J. said to Skinner. "I've seen prisons with less steel."

"There's more to this place than meets the eye," Skinner replied. "You ain't seen nothin' yet."

The van's driver door opened to reveal a slender tattooed arm and long dark hair half dyed in bright red. Scarlett thrust out a mud-covered leather boot and jumped out. Her clothes were covered in blood. "We have wounded!" She ran toward the rear of the van.

Fergus limped into view on the other side. He looked exhausted and leaned heavily on his cane.

"Fergus," Brighed spoke the old man's name with a mixture of surprise and reverence. "What are you doing here?"

Fergus gave Brighed an affectionate smile, but it disappeared when Scarlett pulled open the rear doors and a large dead animal rolled out of the van, landing with a heavy thud on the concrete floor. "I think you'll agree," said Fergus, "this is worth making a house call."

"I told you! Wendigos!" Digger yelled. Brighed's face turned pale, and Skinner let out a low whistle. The dead beast was covered in thick white hair, and its long arms and short, powerful legs ended in sharp black claws. Half a dozen feathered bolts stuck out of its torso, but what was most noticeable was its complete lack of a head. Thick blood oozed like syrup from the empty space where its shoulders met.

"A little help here?" came Morgan's voice from inside the van as she helped another man toward the rear doors. He was in obvious pain, one leg wrapped in blood-soaked bandages with a tourniquet above the knee. On the blood-covered van floor was an unmoving body, its torso and head covered by a heavy raincoat.

Out of the way!" Brighed leapt the dead animal and rushed to help the injured man out of the van.

The sharp smell of iron unique to lots of fresh blood overwhelmed A.J., and he broke into a cold sweat as his legs went weak. His heart began beating fast, and an uncontrollable fear flooded his mind. He tried to take a deep breath and squeeze his eyes shut to regain control, but the heavy tang of blood rocked him, and the sounds of screaming and gunfire and the smell of smoke emerged from his memories like a runaway locomotive. The scars on his face and shoulder burned like fire, and he felt again the shrapnel and the bones of his best friend penetrating his body. A.J. began to shake, and Skinner placed a hand on his shoulder.

A.J. looked at Skinner with rising panic, but the old man's eyes were hard as steel. A.J. clung to their strength like a drowning man clings to a rope.

"What's my name, A.J.?" Skinner's voice was kind, calm, and clear.

A.J. tried hard to understand the meaning of the words and remember how to respond. The ghostly pops of gunfire and explosions sounded in his ears from a decade away and made it hard to comprehend what Skinner was asking. The world faded back and forth between the man in front of him and the smoke and blood and panic of the desert where A.J.'s dying friend lay in his lap.

"Look at my eyes, A.J.," Skinner soothed him. "Notice my eyes and tell me my name." Skinner's steel blue pools anchored A.J. in the moment, and from that anchor the rest of the world rushed back to him.

"Skinner," A.J. blurted out like a balloon bursting. "David Skinner."

A.J.'s reality snapped back into focus. His heart still hammered, but he closed his eyes and took control of his breathing and felt the blood and feeling return to his hands. He wanted to throw up, but he swallowed hard and concentrated on releasing the tension from his core. When he opened his eyes again, Skinner was looking at him with a compassion and understanding that spoke volumes about his own experiences with war. A.J.'s panic turned to embarrassment, but Skinner shook his head as if to say, "Don't you dare." It helped.

"Thanks," A.J. said.

"Digger! Open this door!" Brighed and Morgan supported the injured man between them at the steel door that led back to the lab. Brighed grabbed the handle and pulled, but it didn't budge.

"Why won't this door open for me? Digger! Open this door immediately! I have to get this man to my clinic! He needs help now!"

"Not a chance!" Digger's voice came from somewhere among the shelves. "He's been injured by a Wendigo! No way am I letting him through that door!"

"Digger!" Red energy flowed from Brighed. "I need my medical bag! Open this damned door!"

"First aid kit's in the closet," yelled Digger. "The door stays closed!"

"Damn it, Digger! Let's get him on that table at least." She and Morgan dragged the man to a steel workbench. Brighed swept the top clean with her free hand, sending parts and tools scattering across the floor.

"Hey!" Digger complained.

They laid the man on the table and Morgan ran for the first aid kit while Brighed set to work assessing the wounds. The man looked pale and clearly had lost a lot of blood. A.J. knew that look, and he shook his head sadly at what it meant. Chopper pilots in the sandbox called it "Death Eating a Cracker."

"Ever seen anything like this?" Fergus pulled A.J.'s attention back to the big dead animal on the ground. Skinner was examining its claws with the toe of his boot.

"Where's its head?" A.J. asked.

"Took it off as a precaution. Damn thing kept getting up every time we ran it through until Scarlett put a bolt through its eye."

Fergus pulled the grotesque skull of the dead Wendigo from the back of the van to reveal a head with the face of an ape and a long wolf's snout filled with teeth. A black bolt was buried up to its blue feathers in the left eye socket.

"Nice shot," said A.J.

"Thanks," said Scarlett. "I just wish I'd known sooner and maybe Mora would still be alive." She looked toward the body in the van and lowered her head.

Fergus placed a hand on her shoulder. "You couldn't have stopped it. It attacked her before any of us had time to react. Whatever the hell this thing is," he added.

"It looks like that thing Digger showed us," Skinner said.

"What thing?" Fergus asked.

"She called it a Wendigo," A.J. said. "Or at least a recently created imitation of one."

"A Wendigo?" Scarlett scoffed. "I thought those were a myth? That's crazy."

"Yeah? Well, crazy seems to be the new norm these days for things that aren't supposed to exist," said A.J.

"It's real enough to maul one of my pack and kill another!" Fergus snapped.

"Where'd you find it?" Skinner asked. "How did you find it?"

Fergus poked the dead Wendigo with the tip of his cane. "Actually, I wasn't entirely honest with you at The Den last night. We've been hunting this thing for a couple of weeks now. We didn't know what the hell it was, but we knew something was in our forest that didn't belong. We could smell it, but we couldn't find it, which is strange. Nothing hides from us for long. Certainly not fourteen days."

Skinner frowned. "You didn't feel this was important enough to report to Sheriff Standish?"

Fergus was defiant. "On the contrary, I told Frank about it right after we picked up its scent on last moon's hunt."

"Funny he didn't mention it," said Skinner. "Of course, there's no way to check now, is there?"

"Check with that daughter of his. She was there when I spoke to him."

"I'll be certain to. Right after we figure out where this thing came from. Where did you say you found it?"

"I didn't," said Fergus.

The two men squared off but neither spoke in anger. It seemed to A.J. like a well-rehearsed dance. They didn't seem to like each other, but there was a grudging respect, nonetheless.

"After you left last night, I took advantage of the drink to join the search with these four," continued Fergus. "We hadn't had much luck tracking it until it was injured, probably by the sheriff. We followed a blood trail to an old barn up near Bear's Hatchery, but I don't think it's been there long. The place was too clean."

"You knew about this when I was telling you about Frank's death last night but didn't bother to mention it?"

"You can write me a citation later. Besides, we didn't know what we were dealing with until this morning, and I needed proof it wasn't my pack who killed Frank, or you would never have believed me."

"Well, you got a point there," Skinner grunted.

"Where do you think it came from?" Scarlett asked. "It didn't just appear."

"Hold him still!" Brighed yelled from her place by the man she and Morgan were treating. The rest of them turned to look as the man began convulsing, his legs and arms drumming the steel table.

"Damn it!" Brighed yelled over the commotion. "I need my bag!"

A.J. sprinted toward her to help, but the man jerked even more wildly and knocked both Morgan and Brighed to the floor. His convulsions became so violent that his body practically hovered in the air, and the sound of bones breaking and tendons ripping set everyone in the room to yelling in panic and confusion. A.J. had almost reached the table when the man's arms lengthened and sprouted long black claws from the fingertips. His entire body doubled in size in an instant, sprouting thick white hair, while his head flattened, crunched in upon itself, and sprang forth a wolf's muzzle filled with fangs and blood and saliva.

"Get back!" A.J. screamed at Brighed, but she was already scrambling toward the rows of shelves behind her. She looked up and caught A.J.'s eyes, and her thoughts slammed into his like a freight train. There were no words that A.J. could understand, but the feelings of confusion, dismay, and abject terror nearly crippled him with their intensity. He had no chance of fending off the flood of emotion and panic projected into him by Brighed. He made a vain attempt at diverting that flood to a corner of his mind, so he could focus on the danger in front of him, but it was useless. He may as well have been pissing into a hurricane.

A.J. stumbled toward Morgan who had taken a hard blow to the side of her head when the man spasmed. She was laying dazed on the floor. The room spun around A.J. as his mind was flayed open by Brighed's panicked connection. Too many memories of war and terror and destruction flashed through his consciousness in the blink of an eye, and he had no grasp of which memories were his and which were Brighed's. It was like every PTSD flashback from his last decade rolled into a single moment, and it was too much. All the walls A.J. had built in his mind to help him deal with the tragedies and traumas of his life collapsed. He dropped to his knees next to Morgan, stunned and helpless.

The room faded to a dull haze around him. All he could see were shadows that flashed into detail and faded out again. He watched helplessly as the big white beast rolled off the table towards them, falling onto Morgan and sinking its claws and teeth into her body, and she screamed a scream to wake the dead.

"No!' A.J. screamed with her. "God's no!" He could have saved her, he thought, and that thought drove a spike of anger through his heart and his mind, and a cold determination took hold. The haze of the room was blown from his eyes in a wind of fury and rage, and A.J.'s head snapped up to see the Wendigo still flopping on the table, and Morgan stunned next to A.J. on the floor. Brighed's connection was gone, and A.J. regained control of his mind and muscles.

The transforming creature convulsed again and rolled off the table toward them, just as A.J. had seen it happen in his mind. He grabbed Morgan under the arms and pulled hard, flinging her back onto himself as the beast hit the floor in the spot where she had just been. A.J. landed on the concrete with Morgan's weight on top of him, knocking his breath away and hitting his head. The hard landing pulled Morgan from her daze, and she rolled off and helped drag him to his feet away from the Wendigo. A.J. gasped for air and tried to stop the room from spinning. The creature leapt to its feet, stumbled once, then raised its head and screamed that terrible scream A.J. remembered so vividly from the night he arrived.

"Look out!" Skinner yelled as the Wendigo lowered its head and charged. It was fast for such a big creature, and it screamed as it came. Morgan shoved A.J. with enough force to throw him ten feet through the air to collide with the wall. She propelled herself into a back handspring just as the Wendigo swiped at the spot where they had been. Its momentum carried it past, screaming in frustration.

Adrenaline flooded A.J.'s muscles, and he shoved the pains in his body into a dark corner of his troubled mind. He didn't have the luxury of thinking about what had just happened. His heart beat faster, and the world around him slowed to a crawl. His mind sharpened into a detailed situational awareness he hadn't experienced since the war, and his muscles tightened in anticipation of the fight ahead. A.J. had no idea how this world he'd found himself in could exist, but fighting was something he knew how to do. It was an anchor in this storm of impossibility, and a skill that had kept him alive too many times when his friends were dying around him.

The Wendigo screamed in rage. Scarlett pulled a rifle-length crossbow from the cab and pressed a button under its stock that cocked the heavy steel bow with a click and hiss of pressurized gas. The beast spun toward the sound, dug its front claws into the concrete, and launched itself in her direction.

Scarlett was standing in the corner of the open door and the cab, which cut off her retreat, and her eyes widened with the sudden awareness that death was upon her. A.J. caught a flash of the great white beast disemboweling Scarlett as its jaws closed on her throat, and a searing pain in the center of his forehead sent a shock down his spine and lit his nerves on fire. It was like touching a live wire, and then it was past, and the Wendigo was still charging Scarlett who stood frozen with fear. A.J.'s instincts drove him forward on an intercept path to the creature.

The Wendigo was fast, but so was A.J., who lowered a shoulder and aimed for the Wendigo's center mass. The beast lunged for Scarlett, giving A.J. a clear shot of its ribs, and the two met just feet from where Scarlett stood, the crossbow raised like a shield in front of her. He hit the monster with every ounce of energy he could drive into its body, accelerating up and through the impact. It was like charging into a fur covered wall. The Wendigo outweighed A.J. by a hundred pounds at least, but A.J. hit it hard enough to knock over a racehorse. The Wendigo slammed into the van, rocking it, while a sharp pain deep in A.J.'s shoulder told him something had given way there, too, because physics always wins.

Scarlett dropped neatly to the floor as the driver's door slammed shut an inch above her head, and A.J. fell to the ground next to her, not as neatly, more like a sack of potatoes. His face smacked the cold concrete and he tasted blood, but he had no time to complain. He rolled away and bounced to his feet but stumbled and dropped again as if the world had pulled the floor out from under him. Before he could clear his head, Scarlett sprang past, moving from the floor to full sprint in a single, smooth motion.

The Wendigo took two tries to get itself up. Scarlett's movement caught its attention, and it scrambled after her. Scarlett's head start put her halfway to the rows of shelves, and she was fast, but the Wendigo took two leaps and cut the difference in half, screaming all the way. It would have her in its next lunge, but Scarlett dove for a steel table, shifting mid-air into a giant white leopard. The Wendigo's claws sliced through empty air behind her.

Scarlett leapt from the table to the top of the nearest shelving unit, twenty feet away and twenty feet high. She cleared it with room to spare, landing among the steel parts stacked haphazardly on top and sending many of them clattering to floor below.

The Wendigo's momentum carried it full force into the edge of the steel table, bolted to the concrete floor. The Wendigo's body doubled around it, and the beast's long left arm broke cleanly on the table edge. It flopped back to the floor, screaming, writhing, and snapping at the air. The crushing force at that speed would have killed most creatures, but this one recovered fast, bones crunching against one another as its body healed near fatal wounds while it thrashed about.

A blue feathered crossbow bolt buried itself in the Wendigo's neck with a sound like a baseball bat hitting a heavy rug. The creature twisted and howled a blood-spewing scream and clawed at the bolt. Scarlett stood on the top shelf, loading another bolt into the crossbow from a clip on its side. It looked like her last one.

"Hold still!" She tried desperately to get a bead on its head.

A.J. looked for a way to help. He saw the van and sprinted toward it, yanking open the driver's door just as the Wendigo tore the bolt from its neck. A.J. slammed the accelerator down and turned the key at the same time. The engine roared almost as loud as the animal screamed behind him. He forced the gears into reverse and the van lurched backward, its wheels spinning on the concrete and bouncing over the legs of the dead Wendigo on the ground, tossing A.J. around the cab. He turned to look over his shoulder through the rear window as he backed toward the monster, but what he saw froze his blood. Another Wendigo, or almost one, was in its final throes of transformation inside the van. The dead body of the woman in the van had come back to life and was turning into one of these beasts, too. It looked up at A.J. and screamed its blood chilling scream.

The world stretched in front of A.J. like a retreating tunnel. Four feet away was a new Wendigo threat, and farther down the tunnel, the van hurtled backward toward the first one.

"One problem at a time," he thought and looked past the Wendigo in the van to his original target. He cranked the wheel hard to his left as the beast outside tried to dodge the van. The Wendigo inside was thrown sideways as the van collided with the Wendigo outside, driving it up onto the bolted steel table and pinning the beast under the rear bumper. A.J. bounced into the top of the cab and off the steering wheel, bruising his ribs and jaw. He didn't hesitate, though, no matter the pain. He shoved the door open and rolled out of the cab to land hard once again on the concrete. He wanted to yell a warning but couldn't make a sound come out. He rolled over just in time to see the Wendigo he had crushed against the table take a bolt directly into its right eye socket with such force that the steel tip broke through the skull and pinned its head to the steel table beneath. The Wendigo went limp.

A.J. slapped his palm on the concrete to get Scarlett's attention and pointed frantically at the van.

"What?" Scarlett yelled from her perch just as the windshield exploded outward and the second Wendigo followed with it, rolling onto the floor and coming to its feet, looking for prey.

A.J.'s adrenaline got him up, and his breath returned in short gasps of agony. The new creature saw him, and A.J. knew he would never make it to safety.

The Wendigo screamed and tensed its muscles to spring at him when the largest wolf A.J. had ever seen darted at the Wendigo's blind side, growling and biting and jumping clear of its swiping claws. The wolf had a gray muzzle and ears, and it limped on a hind leg. One blue eye shone like a diamond with a fierceness and confidence that made A.J. shiver. Here was Fergus in wolf form, and he was terrifying to behold. Despite his age, he was remarkably fast, darting in and out of the Wendigo's reach, driving it into a rage.

The Wendigo lost interest in A.J. and tracked Fergus around the room, preparing to launch itself at this new threat just as a second wolf darted in from the Wendigo's right. It was Morgan, solid black and smaller than Fergus, but not by much. Morgan was fast, too, almost too fast to follow as she circled and leapt and harried the beast from its blind side whenever it looked away.

Morgan closed in to sink her jaws into its back, making the beast scream. Then she bounded off as it turned to strike her, but Fergus darted in and bit into its calf before sprinting away himself. They were bringing it down slowly and staying out of its reach, but they weren't killing it. It was a temporary strategy at best. Sooner or later, they would tire and the Wendigo would catch them. A.J. looked for a way to help, but the van was stuck on the table and there was nothing he could use as a weapon within reach.

The sound of chains and steel wheels drew A.J.'s attention to the ceiling where Digger was standing on a loop of heavy chain as she rolled across the garage thirty feet overhead. In her hand trailed a line of steel cable with a large loop in the end a few feet from the floor. A.J. saw her plan, but getting the steel noose around the flailing Wendigo wasn't going to be easy. The bleeding Wendigo was catching on to their tactics and spinning to face each wolf before it could dart in. Morgan leapt to get another bite, but the Wendigo spun and hit her with the back of its arm, eliciting a sharp yelp and sending her flying across the garage to land sliding into one of the SUVs.

The Wendigo raised its arms and screamed in bloody rage at its foes. It caught sight of the approaching cable and looked up at Digger with fangs bared. She wasn't going to catch it by surprise, and A.J. knew there was no way it would let itself get caught in the cable's noose now. He could only see one option, but it was suicide. He could grab the noose and launch himself into the arms of the Wendigo, wrapping them both in the cable to give Digger time to pull it taut and hang them. It was a strange comfort knowing he could count on Digger to take his head before he turned into one of these things too.

Fergus leapt forward and clamped his jaws on the Wendigo's calf. At nearly the same moment, a blur of black fur hit the Wendigo at full speed in the upper back, knocking it to the ground. Fergus pulled hard on the monster's flesh, keeping it from getting its footing while Morgan leapt on its back and grabbed hold with her sharp teeth.

A.J. saw his chance. With the Wendigo distracted and flailing at the pair of wolves, A.J. grabbed the loop and threw it around the creature's head. Digger pulled at the other end of the cable, which was looped through a link in the heavy chain hanging from the ceiling. She was much stronger than she looked, and the Wendigo was quickly dragged up, thrashing its legs and spinning in a futile attempt to escape.

Digger leapt from the chain to the top of the Sheriff's SUV on the automotive lift. She hauled on the cable and looped it around the metal skid. The hydraulics lift whined to life. Skinner stood at the far wall with his hand on the power button. The lift fell quickly, pulling the noose tighter and lifting the Wendigo higher. The big beast violently kicked several times, and A.J. heard a soft "pop" as the noose hit the thick chain link and pulled through, severing the head of the great beast and dropping its lifeless body to the concrete floor with a wet thud. The head bounced down a few feet away.

"Well, that was disgusting," A.J. grimaced.

Skinner stopped short of the pooling blood and stared down at the twitching body. The others soon joined them in a quiet circle around the Wendigo, looking from it to one another without speaking.

Skinner broke the silence. "You keep pulling stunts like that, and you won't live long enough to get out of this valley."

A.J. laughed, but a wave of pain and nausea overwhelmed him as his adrenaline began to fade and the last few minutes caught up to him. The color drained from his face.

Brighed stepped over to support him. "Let's have a look at you."

"You might want to chain this one down first," Fergus joked, but A.J. caught Digger squinting hard at his ankle.

"I'm not a Wendigo!" A.J. protested.

"You got slashed when the Sheriff got killed," said Digger. "On the ankle."

"Is that so?" Fergus looked sideways at A.J.

"That was two days ago," Brighed offered. "How long were your pack mates injured before you arrived today?"

"Less than two hours," said Morgan.

"See!" protested A.J. "I would have turned already. I'm not a Wendigo!"

"You are D'Anu," argued Digger. "You are different."

"Not that different," said Brighed. "Digger, really. Let it go."

"It was Aengus," said a soft voice. The group's attention turned to Scarlett, who looked at Fergus with frightened eyes.

"Excuse me?" Fergus spoke softly but with power.

"It was Aengus who slashed A.J.'s ankle." Scarlett set her shoulders and straightened her back. She met Fergus's gaze without challenge and spoke her truth with conviction. "I saw him."

Fergus's nostrils flared. "What are you talking about?"

"We've been tracking the Wendigo for a couple of weeks, but you cancelled the hunt the other night because of the storm."

"I remember. Go on."

"Aengus was more agitated than usual that night, and I heard him arguing with Blue Jean. He kept saying something about 'sticking to the plan.' Blue Jean left The Den angry. Aengus gathered his pack mates, but they didn't want to go out in the rain. He yelled and threatened them until they all went anyway."

"And you followed them?" Fergus seemed more curious than angry now.

"Yes. I knew he was up to no good."

"He usually is." Morgan's voice was kinder than her father's. "Scarlett, tell them what you told me."

Scarlett looked at Morgan for reassurance before speaking. "We've all been tracking the Wendigo at the east end of the valley near the old mill, but Aengus took his pack somewhere else the other night." Scarlett glanced guiltily at Brighed. "He took them up the D'Anu side of the valley, where Davis Mountain Road cuts through."

A.J. felt a wave of heat radiate from Brighed, but she stayed quiet.

Fergus shrugged apologetically at Brighed, then looked back at Scarlett with cold, hard eyes. "You should have come to me the moment they crossed that line."

"You're right, but I thought you would want to know what they were doing there, so I followed them. I'm sorry. I didn't know what else to do."

Brighed spoke kindly to Scarlett. "It's okay, thank you for telling me. You did the right thing. What were they doing there?"

"I didn't figure out why they went there, but I can tell you that Aengus didn't kill the sheriff. None of the pack did.

They came on the wreck, and the sheriff was already dead. They saw someone kneeling over him." She looked at A.J. "It looked like you had just killed him. I think that's why Aengus attacked you. He sliced your leg when you dove into the sheriff's vehicle, and then Skinner showed up and we all cleared out."

"And Frank?" Skinner sounded angry. "What happened to his body?"

"I don't know. I got out of there and headed back to The Den.

"Why didn't you come straight to me?" asked Fergus.

"It was late, and you were sleeping. I know how you hate being disturbed when you get to sleep, so I woke Morgan and told her instead."

Morgan nodded. "It's true. I told her I would take care of it," Morgan added. "I didn't expect things to move so quickly as they have."

Fergus assessed his daughter with a cold stare, then seemed to nod in approval before turning back to Scarlett. "What happened next?"

"Aengus came back a couple of hours later, so I confronted him about what I'd seen."

Fergus looked surprised. "That took courage. What did he say?"

"He said he already told you everything, and that you knew all about what they were doing. He told me to stay out of wolf business if I knew what was good for me. You know how hard it is for me," she pleaded. "I'm in the pack but I'm not wolf. I couldn't challenge his word. If I were wrong, I'd have to fight him, and his pack would tear me to pieces. So, I kept quiet, but he barely took his eyes off me until these two came in with Connor."

"Where is he now?" Skinner demanded.

"After you left last night, he took off with what was left of his pack, minus the three Connor and A.J. took down, of course. He hadn't returned when we left to hunt that Wendigo."

Pounding on the door and a muffled yelling interrupted Scarlett's confession. Alice's face was visible through the porthole, her eyes wide at what she could see.

"Alice!" Skinner ran to the door. "Digger, let her in."

Digger didn't move. She looked from the door back to Fergus and then at the Wendigo's body. "You said she was attacked two hours ago?"

"Less than," Fergus replied.

"Two hours it is then," said Digger. "The doors open in two hours, and not a minute sooner." She headed back toward the rows of shelves.

"Hey!" several in the group yelled.

"None of us were injured by the Wendigos," said Brighed. "I'm sure it's safe to open the door."

"Digger, it's Alice," protested Skinner.

"I'm not taking any chances," Digger called back without looking. Two hours!"

"Where are you going?" asked Morgan.

"Weapons!" said Digger. "I need to make weapons!" She passed into the shelves, grabbing odd parts and tossing them out onto the nearest workbench or the floor nearby, depending on how they bounced.

"What are we supposed to do while we wait?" Fergus yelled over the noise.

"Mops and buckets are in the closet by the door," called back Digger. "I'm not cleaning that mess up!"

The group looked at each other with a mix of annoyance and resignation. Skinner used an intercom to tell Alice what was happening, and Scarlett helped Brighed move A.J. to one of the black SUVs where Brighed finished assessing his shoulder. He could barely breathe, but at least he wasn't dying.

A.J. locked eyes with Brighed with a question about the things he had seen before they happened, but Brighed touched his mind with hers... *"wait,"* she whispered into his thoughts. *"Not here, it isn't safe..."* and glanced furtively toward Scarlett.

"I don't think any bones are broken," Brighed said aloud, "but you didn't do your body any favors, either. Dislocated ribs, dislocated scapula, possible labral tear..."

"You should see the other guy," A.J. tried to joke, but laughing hurt worse than breathing, and that hurt plenty.

"Or gal, in this case." Scarlett looked at the dead Wendigo on the floor. "Her name was Mora. She was tough and smart, and she was my friend."

"I'm sorry," said A.J. "I didn't mean to offend."

"It's okay. She always said she didn't want to die in her bed but wanted to go down fighting like in the old stories. She would have appreciated this one."

"And the other?" A.J. motioned toward the Wendigo behind the van.

"Him? He was an asshole, but he didn't deserve this."

"You going to lend a hand or just lie around all day?" Skinner yelled, uncoiling a water hose attached to the wall.

Morgan was attaching an engine chain to the foot of the Wendigo on the floor. Fergus was staring at the van and considering how best to get it back on four wheels.

"Can't you see I'm injured?" A.J. smiled weakly. "I need my rest. Doctor's orders." He laid his head down in Brighed's lap, looking pitiful.

"Typical Army," said Skinner. "Make a big mess and call the Marines in to clean it up!"

"Semper Fi, Gunny." A.J. raised his good arm in salute. "Semper Fi."

Chapter Ten

Das Nebeltor (The Mist Gate)

A.J. woke in pain, gasping for air in the dark. His shoulder was on fire, and his ribs sent bolts of agony through his body with every inhale. He groaned and closed his eyes and took a slow, deep breath. It helped calm his panic, but it hurt like hell.

A light came on, and A.J. blinked to adjust his eyes to the brightness.

"Here, this will help with the pain." Brighed sat on the edge of his bed and lifted his head to help him drink a small cup of thick liquid. He groaned again at the movement and the sour medicine, though it didn't taste or smell as bad as the brew she'd given him for the hangover.

"Where am I?" he asked. The bed was soft, and the pillow smelled of lavender. A compression bandage around his chest and shoulder immobilized his right arm.

"At my house. It's four in the morning."

Brighed wore a thin silk gown that did little to hide her full breasts. He stared at them and felt a stirring in his groin despite the pain.

"Well, you don't seem too worse for wear," she grinned.

"I'm broken, not dead," replied A.J., which made him laugh, which made him cry.

"That's what you get," scolded Brighed. "Now get some rest. You have a big day ahead of you. I'll tell you all about it when you wake up. That potion is kicking in and will speed the healing. You'll feel better in a few hours."

Her beauty overwhelmed him. A soft golden glow permeated her skin, and her hair moved gently around her face, dancing in the energy of her light. She kissed his forehead, and warmth spread from the spot where her lips touched, filling him with a soothing calmness that eased the pain. His breathing felt easier too.

"That's some special magic you have." He felt drowsy. There was a question he wanted to ask her, needed to ask, but he couldn't remember, and it slipped away into the fog of drugs.

"That's D'Anu magic." Brighed's voice was in his mind again, and he let it flow into and wash over him like a warm blanket. She placed her palm on his injured shoulder. *"You'll learn it too, when you're ready,"* she thought. She began singing softly in the language of their ancestors. The music filled the room and rolled through his body. Every cell vibrated in harmony with her voice, aligning and healing and strengthening inside him. His pain and breathing eased further, and his consciousness drifted away to a restful sleep filled with dreams of giant trees and a city in the sky.

Hours later, sunlight flooded the room and pulled A.J. into the waking world. The ache in his shoulder and ribs washed the dreams away and snapped him back to a harsh reality. Though still bad, the pain was better. He could almost breathe without grimacing if he took it slowly. Whether Brighed's healing skills were magic or science, he didn't much care. They were impressive either way.

"So much for the indestructible hero," came a voice from the shadows. A short figure in welder's goggles stepped into the light. Digger had abandoned her overalls in favor of German lederhosen and a heavy leather apron. A bright red pick and shovel crossed the front in meticulous embossing. "It's time to get ready." She spoke as if he should know what she was talking about.

"What?" A.J. grumbled and blocked the sunlight with his forearm. "What's going on?"

"You're still asleep, and it's after ten. You need to get ready. Brighed's brother is arriving at noon and you're not even dressed!"

A.J. rubbed his face and managed to sit on the edge of the bed with some grunting and groaning. He was naked except for the compression wrap on his shoulder, so he pulled the sheets around his waist and waited for the dizziness to stop.

"Quickly now," Digger scolded. "Dian, head of the House of Erin in the First Clan and Chief Counselor to the Queen, is coming and you are to be…" she rubbed her chin, trying to find the right word. "Presented."

"Excuse me?" A.J. stammered. "What are you talking about? Where's Brighed? Where's Margaret?"

"Busy. Very busy. It takes much work to prepare for the arrival of a council member, especially with such short notice. I am here to get you ready and escort you to Das Nebeltor, the Mist Gate. Come now, human, we do not have much time." She walked to the closet and removed a garment bag.

"Human? I thought I was a D'Anu now, or whatever?"

Digger shook her head. "Only humans are so foolish as to divide yourselves by such trivial differences. You are D'Anu. And you are human. You are —"

"Yeah, yeah, more than human, whatever the hell that means."

"You have a very negative attitude. Has anyone ever told you that?"

This made A.J. laugh and wince at the flare of pain. "Once or twice," he groaned.

Digger tossed the bag on the bed next to A.J. "Margaret had this made for you. You will need help dressing." She unzipped the bag to reveal a fine suit in rich black with dark purple accents.

"Had it made?" A.J. touched the sleeve and the fine fabric flowed through his fingers like silk. "For me? When? How?"

"You ask stupid questions too. Quickly now, there is not time for delay." She took his chin in her vice-like grip and turned his head from side to side. "You need shaving. Wait here."

"Why did they send you?" A.J. asked while Digger retrieved supplies from the bathroom and set to whipping up a lather with a small brush.

"Das Nebeltor is in the Dwarfhold. You must have a Dwarf stand for you to allow passage. I am your escort."

"Dwarfhold? I'm never going to get all this stuff straight. What the hell is a Dwarfhold?"

Digger spoke slowly as if addressing a child. "A Dwarfhold is a place that holds Dwarfs."

"Ah. That makes sense. Thanks for the escort, I guess."

"I was not given a choice. Now hold still." A pearl and silver handled straight razor appeared in her hand and light flashed off the blade. A.J. took a painful breath and tried to sit still while Digger set to work on his whiskers in quick, precise swipes. In thirty seconds, she was finished and wiped his face with the damp towel. He rubbed his silky-smooth cheek and nodded his approval.

Digger removed the compression bandage, freeing his right arm but making everything else hurt more. She helped

A.J. into a white silk shirt from the garment bag, threading his arms into the sleeves and fastening the buttons. It felt like a second skin, and every fold fit perfectly to the lines of his body. She held up a pair of black silk undershorts.

A.J. grabbed them and pulled the sheets tighter around his waist. "I can handle this part."

Digger frowned but turned to face away while he wrestled the shorts on with his good arm, grimacing at the pain of bending and pulling. He sat back on the bed, exhausted from the exertion, and Digger helped him with the rest of the suit. It had a Nehru collar and shining black buttons all the way to the neck. There was no tie, but there was a matching sling. Digger combed his hair with oil and laced the fine leather shoes.

"It will do." Digger straightened his cuffs and brushed the back of the jacket.

A.J. had to admit he looked sharp in the bedroom mirror. "I've never worn anything this nice before."

"You will get used to it. Now come. We must not be late!"

"What'll they do, put us in detention?"

"You are the official reason Dian has stated for his visit. If you are late, it will be viewed as an insult and a challenge to his authority. It would be very bad."

Digger led him to Brighed's office and into the steel lift. This time he braced himself for the elevator to change directions, but it kept going down instead. He hadn't seen Digger push any buttons, nor were there buttons inside the elevator to push.

A.J. studied the polished steel. "How does it know where to go?"

"It goes where it is expected to go, just like all lifts. Don't ask stupid questions."

A.J. began to protest when the doors opened onto a dimly lit corridor of white marble adorned with intricately woven rugs and tapestries.

"Stay quiet, follow me, and do as I say." Digger removed her goggles. "And make no jokes, human. They will not be well received by Dwarfs."

"Who me?"

Digger ignored him. She nodded toward a steel-reinforced door at the end of the corridor. "Past that door, Dwarf law reigns, not human law. You would do well to remember that."

"Let me guess, short jokes are a felony offense?"

Digger glared at him.

"Okay, okay. I'll keep my mouth shut."

Digger growled. "Do not think you are special in the halls of the Dwarfs. To us you are little more than shiny humans with longer lives, but you all die the same when an axe takes off your head."

"Believe me, special is the last thing I want to be." The pain in A.J.'s shoulder had risen to an annoying throb that shortened his temper. "Can we just get this over with, whatever the hell it is?"

"Gladly!" Digger stepped up to the steel door and grabbed it, waiting for the locks to slide back.

A.J.'s curiosity got the better of his temper. "How exactly do these molecular locks of yours work?"

"You wouldn't understand."

"Try me. I'm a pretty smart guy."

"What do you know about fluorescent molecular sensors and the translocation of metal ions in cyclic octapeptides?"

"Uh..."

"Told you." Digger led him through the door to a bank of elevators. One stood open next to a sign in a beautiful but odd script. As soon as the doors closed, the lift began to move. The pit of his stomach rising was A.J's only clue that they were going down, and they rode in silence for a dozen seconds or more before the doors finally opened.

They stepped into a massive cavern that shocked A.J. with its size. He couldn't see the far wall, due to its distance and the many buildings and other structures that filled the enormous underground hall, nor could he see the ceiling far overhead. What light there was came from the moss-covered ground, buildings, and walls. Everything simply glowed, and the glow provided enough illumination to see how truly gigantic the cavern must be. A.J. stared, dumbfounded.

"Welcome to the Great Western Hall of the Dwarfs," said Digger. "We call it Neuhallé."

"New? How long did this take to build?"

"Three thousand seven hundred years and counting," said Digger proudly.

"Three thou… You call that new?"

"Any place younger than ten thousand years is new to a Dwarf. We are the most ancient of all the races."

"That's not how Brighed tells the story."

Digger grunted in disapproval. "The Dwarf and the D'Anu disagree on key aspects of our histories. Topside you may believe what you wish. In a Dwarfhold, it is known the Dwarfs were forged by the gods from the flesh and bones of the giant Ymir at the creation of the world. The D'Anu came much later."

"It is known, huh?"

"It is known," she said with finality.

They crossed a swath of mossy ground to a swift-moving river with a low crenelated wall on the opposite bank. The water curved away on either side, forming a moat that encircled the entire cavern. A narrow, arched bridge of stone provided the only way across. Looking back, A.J.

could see that the open space would make a fine killing field for defenders behind the wall. Everything about this valley, from the hidden hamlet to the reinforced steel doors to this medieval fortress suggested the D'Anu, or the Dwarfs at least, were prepared for serious warfare.

"Has Neuhallé ever been attacked?"

"Are you joking?" Digger led him across the bridge toward a gate where a heavily armed Dwarf stood waiting their arrival. "Who would be foolish enough to attack a Dwarfhold? Can you not see our superb defenses?"

"Well, yeah. But if you've never been attacked, why go to so much effort to prepare for one?"

"You ask stupid questions, even for a human." Digger rolled her eyes. "This much effort is why we have never been attacked."

The Dwarf guard stood motionless in black iron armor intricately etched in silver. His axe rested on its handle and stood nearly as tall as the guard himself. Its ornate, double-sided, half-moon blades shone brightly, even in the low light of the cavern. The guard's eyes never wavered from their stare across the bridge.

"Greetings, Guard," Digger said as they passed, but the guard offered no reply.

The heavy wooden gate opened onto a narrow stone hallway fifty feet long with kill holes set into the sides and top. At the end, another pair of guards stood motionless in black armor on either side of a low wooden desk where two more Dwarfs sat. They were dressed much as Digger was, in lederhosen with leather aprons, but theirs had quills and scepters embossed on the fronts. One of the Dwarfs monitored a pair of computer screens and was clean shaven. The other was older, with fine lines around his eyes and a thick curly beard that framed his round face. A large leather-bound book sat open on the table in front of him.

"Master Administrator," Digger spoke with reverence, "it is a pleasant surprise to see you on gate duty. To what do we owe this great honor?"

The bearded Dwarf spoke in a deep baritone. "I am here to greet this unknown D'Anu on behalf of the Masters of Neuhallé." He stopped to stare at A.J. with cold and calculating eyes. A.J. got the distinct impression the old Dwarf was not happy that he was there.

"This is a most unusual situation and warrants direct attention," said the Dwarf.

"Your presence compliments our ancestors, Master Administrator. I will sing your praise to Ymir upon the moment of my death." Digger bowed deeply and tugged on A.J.'s sleeve to follow her example.

"Uh…yeah, thanks." A.J. nodded toward the older Dwarf and tried not to grunt in pain.

Master Administrator regarded A.J. with sharp, disapproving eyes. "What are you called, human?" The Dwarf dipped an ornate feather quill in a pot of ink and bent over the book.

"I am called A.J."

Master Administrator raised one eyebrow in suspicion. "An unusual trade for a human. What does an 'A.J.' do, exactly?"

"Oh, uh, as little as possible." A sharp growl from Digger cut his joke short. "But I used to be a soldier."

The old Dwarf gave A.J. an angry glare and marked the book carefully in the same odd script A.J. had seen in the hallway above.

"What is your clan?"

A.J. shrugged "I have none."

The master Dwarf made another mark in the ledger. "Very unusual. Who stands for this human?"

"I do," Digger responded, then exchanged a few words in their odd language.

The old Dwarf made another note in the ledger and frowned at A.J. "You are protected by the Hall of Diggers as a visitor in Neuhallé and the holdings over which it rules. You are restricted from the citadel and inner sanctum. Do you acknowledge these restrictions and agree to adhere to Dwarf law at all times?"

"I do," A.J. said with as much formality as he could muster.

"You are free to pass." The old Dwarf nodded again at Digger, and the two guards slammed their fists into their chests and pulled their axes apart to symbolize the opening of the gate.

Digger bowed again, and they walked past the guard station into Neuhallé proper. As they passed, one of the guards turned and marched in step behind A.J., watching his every move. They followed an intricately laid stone pathway between gardens of ferns, flowers, and lichens, and small, twisted trees growing in heavy planters.

"Well, that wasn't so hard," A.J. said to Digger. "Anything in particular I should know about Dwarf law?"

"Know that if you break it, I will stand trial with you. I have spoken for you, so your actions reflect upon my reputation and clan. Do not embarrass me, human."

"Oh," A.J. said in surprise. "I'll try my best."

"Just follow me and do as I say. Spend as little time as possible here and do not speak unless absolutely necessary. Your ignorance shines like a magnesium fire in the dark."

Digger seemed annoyed at her assignment escorting him, so A.J. stopped trying to engage. He turned to the guard walking behind them.

"Hi there," A.J. flashed a friendly smile, but the guard's face may as well have been made of stone. "It's 'Guard,' isn't it? Nice to meet ya'. Grow up around here?"

A.J. got nothing. He sighed and gave up.

Fortunately, there were plenty of interesting things to look at. Statues of finely crafted marble and shining steel bordered the street between column-fronted buildings carved in place from the original rock. The sculpted steel Dwarfs played instruments with cleverly controlled mechanics, or they danced or swung weapons in mock battles against one another. A pair of massive figures hammered on anvils, with half-formed Dwarfs standing around them.

"That one is called, The Birth of the World," said Digger proudly. "It shows the gods hammering the Dwarfs out of the bones of Ymir."

The detail of carvings on the buildings and the carefully crafted gardens were stunning, but no one else was in the underground city.

"Where is everyone?"

"At the gathering. The arrival of the Chief Counselor is auspicious under normal circumstances, but the suddenness of this visit along with rumors of your appearance have everyone excited. They will all be at das Nebeltor in the village square. It is just ahead."

A.J. noticed the Dwarfhold was laid out like a wheel, with the big boulevards forming spokes that reached out to the city walls in every direction. It made the entire structure extremely efficient and highly defensible.

Two blocks later, a thick crowd stood shoulder to shoulder along the edge of a large open space. The crowd of Dwarfs, D'Anu, and Shifters of varying sizes and shapes began to thicken as A.J. and Digger approached. Those in the back saw A.J. and nudged and poked others, who turned to stare. What had been a dull roar of voices and shuffling bodies began to quiet, and a pathway opened in the throng. A.J.'s anxiety ratcheted higher from both the size of the crowd and its collective attention focused on him. Some stood on tiptoe and peered around others to get a look at him as he passed.

"Nothing intimidating about this," A.J. said as he and Digger moved through the throng of onlookers crowded to either side.

"Shut up, human, and keep walking. Do not make eye contact." Digger nudged him forward with her shoulder.

A.J. felt like a fly pinned and wriggling on a wall. He had trouble breathing in the tight collar of the suit. His hands began shaking, and sweat broke out on his forehead. He hated crowds.

They passed into a cleared courtyard about 100 yards across. Dwarf guards in black and silver armor stood at intervals, defining the large circle with a massive stone arch in its center, nearly fifty feet tall. Bright blue light interlaced the arch's stones, emitting a low rhythmic hum that A.J. felt in his bones.

Past the guards stood a smaller group of Dwarfs, D'Anu, and Shifters, all in fine clothing, with a few wearing sashes and gold medallions. A handful of others stood in close conversation, including the mayor and his vampire wife, Sayah. Darcy stood with Alice, who was dressed in jeans and a sweater and carried a steel box sealed with biomedical stickers. The three Margarets were also there, busy forming the crowd into straight lines.

Another group wore dark gray uniforms with a black wolf's head emblazoned on the chests. Standing at their head was Fergus, leaning on a cane and wearing a bright purple sash and a heavy gold medallion.

"A.J., thank goodness you made it!" Brighed rushed to his side and kissed him on the cheek. His heart fluttered, and he felt instant relief from his anxiety at her touch. She wore a dress similar in style to A.J.'s suit, but with a form fitting bodice. "The ceremony is about to begin."

"I got him here, as promised, on time. He's your problem now," said Digger and disappeared into the crowd before Brighed could respond.

"Nice to see you too," A.J. said with an edge of annoyance. Brighed blushed.

"I'm sorry I wasn't there when you woke up this morning as I promised, but I got called away early. There's been a development—"

"Aengus!" A.J. interrupted her. Beside Fergus stood Morgan, her dark hair curled into flowing waves over her leather uniform, but the unmistakable pudginess and blond hair of Aengus standing behind his father captured A.J.'s attention. "What the hell is he doing here?"

"That's what I'm trying to tell you. Aengus brought Frank's body to the morgue early this morning. He claims he rescued the body the other night from a monster they chased across the valley. He said he waited to bring it in because Skinner is in charge, and he claims Skinner is harassing him. Aengus says he didn't want Skinner to blame him for the death and waited until Fergus was back from the hunt before bringing the body in."

"What? That's insane! What did Fergus have to say?"

"He backed Aengus's story of course. Aengus is his son and his pack. Plus, there are witnesses who say Skinner harassed Aengus at The Den the other night without provocation and you were there."

"Unbelievable." His eyes landed on Scarlett, standing stoically at the rear of the gathering. She caught his look and returned it without smiling, then looked toward Aengus with hard eyes.

"What does Scarlett have to say about it?"

"She is part of Fergus's pack. Even if she is feline, she's still bound by wolf pack hierarchy and rules. She won't cross Fergus."

"Yeah, what's up that? Why is she with them?"

"Being in Fergus's pack is a matter of allegiance, not genetics. Fergus cares nothing about purity, only loyalty. Fergus has great power, and being close to him has its advantages. Thanks to his patronage, Scarlett serves as a representative for felines of all sorts on the council, and there are others, but none so highly placed as her. She got there by keeping her mouth shut and doing as Fergus says. She will not cross him, no matter the truth."

"And the Wendigo? And the attack in the garage yesterday?"

"For now, we're keeping that quiet, officially anyway, but rumors are already flying across the valley, and the whole thing's got everyone pretty spooked. The official reason for Dian's visit is your sudden appearance, but too many already know about the Wendigo, and we're doing our best to keep that news from panicking the entire valley. We still need more answers before we say anything official."

"So, we're just going to ignore yesterday's dance with zombie shapeshifters?" A.J. was livid.

"Of course not! Skinner and Connor took Mason and his dogs to the barn where Fergus caught the Wendigo. They're going to try and track its movements. If there's something to find in this valley, those three can do it. Alice is taking samples from the Wendigo to the Academy in Nalanda to get help from her colleagues with the unknown genetics.

She's done as much as she can from here, but what she's found so far is very unusual."

"Everything about this place is very unusual."

"Unusual for us, then." Brighed tried to soothe him. "The head librarian there, Seshat, is very ancient and knowledgeable. She'll help us get to the bottom of this mystery."

"I hope she works fast." A.J. wanted to wipe off Aengus's smug smile with his fists. "I have a feeling I'll need to justify some violence very soon."

"Maybe you should wait until you can swing both fists. Aengus is a fool, but he isn't weak. Don't make the classic mistake of underestimating your opposition."

"Speaking of unusual," A.J. began. "What the hell happened in the garage yesterday? What I saw…"

"I know," Brighed interrupted him. Her eyes locked on his with an intensity that scared him. "We were connected, and I saw too. I apologize for that. I was frightened and lost control for a moment, but what you can do… your foresight, is extremely rare in the Queendom, even among the D'Anu. Whatever you do, if you value your life and your freedom, you must not…"

Her words were drowned by a deep, bone-rattling sound of a blowing horn that bounced off the cavern walls and echoed back at them. When the sound died down, everyone stood silent. A.J. began to ask what she said, but she silenced him with a look. He felt her mind brush his with an emphatic, *'trust no one!'*

The horn sounded again, lower and slower this time.

"Quickly, come with me," Brighed whispered. She led him toward the assembling crowd of D'Anu, Shifters, and Dwarfs all dressed in their richly detailed uniforms. The group made room for A.J. and Brighed at the front of the assembled procession. The mayor and Sayah joined him on his left, with Darcy on their far side. Brighed stood on his right.

Margaret hurried over to A.J. and brushed a bit of lint from his suit jacket that he was certain wasn't there. She smiled reassuringly, but A.J. could see the stress in her shoulders and busy hands. It looked like she hadn't slept since he last saw her.

"Everything is taken care of." She spoke like she was trying to convince herself more than him. "At least as much as could be managed in a day. There's nothing to worry about, you'll do fine."

"What would I have to worry about? I still don't know what the hel…heck is going on," A.J. caught himself. His mind was distracted by Brighed's warning.

"Well, you're the star of this show, but all you have to do is follow Brighed's lead." Margaret squeezed his hand, then hurried to join the other two Margarets at the edge of the crowd just as the clarion call of the Dwarf horn filled the cavern for a third time.

This time the echoes were amplified by the blue lines in the arch's stones glowing brighter with each reverberation, until A.J. felt waves of deep, rumbling baritone and bass vibrations pass through him. It felt like every cell in his body was responding to the frequency of the notes with their own song.

Brighed glowed brighter than A.J. had seen yet. Her hair floated and twisted in the air, and her eyes shone a brilliant blue. She looked at him and smiled gently, and he was overwhelmed with love for her. She took his hand, and he looked down to see his own skin shining in bright gold, the hairs on his head standing up as if he were surrounded by static electricity. His arm was still in a sling, but he felt no pain or discomfort from his injuries. It was the most fulfilling physical sensation of his life, until a moment later when the D'Anu began to sing.

As one, the voices rose in harmony with the horn's vibrations. They began to modulate and change the key, lifting it a half step and increasing the intensity of the frequencies in his body to a near orgasmic level. A.J. tried to dismiss a rising erection by thinking of war, but Brighed's hand in his kept drawing his mind to the present and her touch. He could only hope the quality of the suit would provide some camouflage.

The singers shone with a brightness that was difficult to look at. The golden glow about their heads was joined by tendrils of golden energy that extended up and back from their bodies in the semblance of golden wings. They resembled the depictions of angels A.J. had seen in churches, and the implications of what that meant added another layer of anxiety to A.J.'s already troubled mind. He had no time to contemplate it though, as he suddenly felt lighter, almost rising from the ground by the rhythmic wash of the music and magic around them. He felt an overwhelming desire to add his own voice to the song, and a glance to his right showed him Brighed was already singing, but he knew better than to try. Shrapnel from the war left scars in more places than just his face.

The tone dropped to a longer and deeper bass, and the bright blue lines that spider-webbed through the stones dimmed to almost black. A.J. felt dizzy, and the ground beneath him shifted, or rather, the gravity beneath him shifted, and he had a sudden, unmistakable feeling of standing on a wall looking down at the floor. He thought for certain he would fall toward the arch, whose center had changed from a clear opening to a blackness into which the light from the D'Anu began to pour.

The clarion horn of the Dwarfs sounded again, resonating with the low hum of the arch. Something deep inside A.J. let go. All the energy rising in his body and lifting him and flowing through him rushed together into his core and shot from him straight toward the center of the arch. The energy they had built with their voices flooded the arch's center to form a ball of light with the brilliance of a sun. With the next beat, the ball exploded into the blackness of the archway, pushing a blast of energy out from the center that nearly knocked A.J. off his feet. Before he could catch his breath, the wave reversed course back toward the archway, steadying him and leaving him feeling both empty and clean.

A thick mist came boiling from the archway and filled the open space of the clearing, rolling outward to stop about six feet from the edge of the circle defined by the Dwarf guards. A wall of fog with light tendrils of mist licking into the cavern obscured the stone archway and everything else on the far side of the clearing. A cheer went up from the crowd outside the circle, with light applause and a few random whistles.

"Wow," was all A.J. could manage.

Brighed squeezed his hand and laughed. She was radiant. "That never gets old. Now the general travelers will proceed through the gate before Dian and his entourage arrives."

A small group stepped away from the crowd on his left. Alice was among them with the box of tissue samples. She waved at Brighed, glanced over her shoulder at Fergus and the group of Shifters and frowned, then turned and followed the others through the mist. A few moments later, a different group of varying shapes and sizes began emerging, first as faint shadows and then as solid beings as they stepped into the clearing and disappeared into the crowd.

"Now the drums will signal the procession of the regional counselor and Chief Master of Neuhallé," Brighed whispered.

The first beat sounded. The low and steady rhythms of the drums seemed hollow compared to the song of the D'Anu. The assembled group opened a space so Fergus—flanked on his right by Morgan, resplendent in her wolf's head uniform—could walk over next to A.J.'s small group. Aengus stayed with the rest of the wolf clan, and many around him murmured in surprise. Aengus himself stared straightforward, his face red and jaw clenched. The smug smile was long gone, and A.J. felt a small sense of satisfaction at Aengus's apparent embarrassment.

Joining Fergus on his left, at the far end of the reception line, was the oldest Dwarf A.J. had seen so far, with a snow-white beard and long silver hair tied back in a braid. He was bedecked in platinum rings, chains, and earrings, and a bright purple sash stood out across his finely tooled leather apron embossed with a gold scepter.

The last echo died, leaving the cavern in total silence, and then a bell sounded, high and clear and hung in the air. A shadow slowly took shape in the mist, followed by three more right behind it.

The first to emerge was a tall man with dark hair cut short, about A.J.'s height, but thinner and wearing an expensively tailored suit with a gold chain and purple sash like Fergus. He had the unmistakable glow of the D'Anu and the same incredible blue eyes as Brighed.

"Dian." Brighed's voice was hard, and she tightened her grip on A.J.'s hand.

Three more figures emerged from the mist behind Dian. One was a very tall and heavily muscled man with a midnight black complexion, dressed in dark wool and wearing thick gold bracelets, chains, and a circlet on his brow. His ebony skin was unblemished and perfectly smooth, and his eyes were dark and narrow. Long braids of hair adorned with colorful beads and gold bands hung almost to his waist.

Next was a woman with light brown skin and long black hair that touched the floor. She wore white buckskin clothing decorated in colored porcupine quills and carried a fan made of sage leaves. A.J. had met several Native American women on his long journey across the country, but he had never met one whose eyes shone with such power and light.

A second woman stepped into the clearing. She was shorter and wore a simple tailored business suit. She had glasses, and her red hair was pulled back into a tight bun. It was Margaret, a bit thinner than the other three he had met, but it was definitely her. She hurried to join the other Margarets and fell in with them without a word.

A handful of staff in uniforms carried luggage and other bags through the mist and quickly veered off into the crowd. As the last of them stepped into the clearing, the deep thrumming of the arch changed pitch, went silent, and then, with one last deep thrum, shut down. The mist wall evaporated, revealing a clear opening through the arch once again.

Dian approached the old Dwarf first and bowed in greeting. The Dwarf returned a bow so exaggerated that even those watching from a distance could see it clearly.

"Chief Counselor," the old Dwarf's strong voice carried across the large crowd. "Welcome to Neuhallé. Your presence honors our Dwarfhold."

"The honor is surely mine." Dian's voice was kind, with a slight British accent. "We are grateful for your generous hospitality. May I present his highness Kiongozi Kane, ruler of the free clans of Africa, Pride Master of the Lion tribes of Ta Netjer, and a member of the Council." The Dwarf bowed to the tall ebony man, who bowed deeply in return.

"May I also present the Princess Ptesan-Wi of the Buffalo Nation and senior member of the Council." The woman with the glowing eyes raised her fan and swept it low and wide as she bowed.

Dian stopped in front of Fergus and repeated the ritual. Both men wore well-practiced smiles and greeted one another as friends, but A.J. could smell the tension between them.

"My dearest Darcy." Dian stepped over to the late sheriff's daughter. "Please accept my sincere condolences on the passing of your father in such a tragic accident."

A.J. tried to keep his face neutral at the emphasis on the word 'accident.'

"His dedication to the safety of all those in the valley are a testament to his service. He will be missed by us all." Dian bowed as he finished, and everyone in the great hall followed suit. Darcy smiled sadly and curtsied in reply, but when she looked up her eyes were hard as diamonds. Dian stepped over to Sayah and the mayor, addressing them both as one while he reintroduced the other two counselors.

When Dian reached A.J., Brighed stepped forward to speak first. "Chief Counselor Dian, welcome home. May I present to you A.J., a D'Anu of no clan."

"Pleased to meet you," A.J. offered first, unsure of protocol but not really caring. With his right arm still in a sling, he stuck his left hand out to shake, but he did not bow.

"And I am very pleased to meet you." Dian grasped A.J.'s hand in both of his. "An unknown D'Anu stranger. You have no idea what an unusual occurrence this is."

"Oh, I have some idea," said A.J. coldly. Brighed cleared her throat to admonish him.

Dian only chuckled. "Well, with all these folks watching our exchange, I think it prudent to give them what they came for."

Only A.J. and Brighed could hear Dian's conspiratorial tone. Dian turned to the crowd and raised his arms wide, then theatrically wrapped them around A.J. in the semblance of a bear hug, but A.J. barely felt the touch. Dian stepped back and swept his arm wide and high for all the crowd to see.

"My long lost brother!" Dian's voice boomed across the cavern. "Welcome home!"

A raucous cheer erupted from the crowd, filling the silent cavern with noise and bouncing echoes so loud it became impossible for A.J. to hear what Brighed was trying to tell him. He looked at her in confusion and could see her eyes were serious and she gripped his hand even tighter than before. A.J. wondered why she didn't reach out to him with her thoughts as she had before, and he tried to open his mind to her, but a quick shake of her head and glance at Dian's back warned him to stop.

Dian turned back from the crowd and Brighed turned quickly away from A.J. lest Dian catch them talking. Dian smiled at them both, but A.J. could sense the wheels turning behind those piercing blue eyes as Dian looked back and forth between them.

A band started playing, and the crowd began dispersing back into the Dwarfhold, with more than a few sticking around to stare at A.J. in wonder. He felt intensely awkward.

"Come now," said Dian. "There is much to discuss. I've arranged for an immediate meeting about this terrible Wendigo debacle, and I've brought along some help," he nodded toward his two companions. "Margaret informed us of the terrible tragedy of Sheriff Standish's death and the miracle of your arrival. She has kept us apprised of the situation here, and when we heard news of the Wendigo discovery, we immediately prepared for travel. Fortunately for us, Ptesan-Wi is something of an authority on the subject."

A.J. was surprised at how much he wanted to like Dian. The man was charming and kind, with a friendly smile and way of making A.J. feel like the only person in the crowd. But A.J.'s gut told him to be cautious, and Brighed's discomfort with her brother only added to A.J.'s wariness. A.J. found her behavior concerning, and he decided to beware of her brother until he knew more about the situation. Still, it was hard not to smile back when Dian's attention was on him.

The Margaret who travelled with Dian hurried over to join them. "The conference room is ready. I'm rounding up the others."

The other Margarets led a small group toward a building with carved stone roses on its columns at the edge of the clearing. Dian placed his hand on A.J.s back and walked with him. Brighed stayed silent but didn't leave his side the entire way.

Chapter Eleven

Revelation

They entered the building and proceeded down a marble-lined hallway to heavy wood doors carved with scenes of Dwarfs engaged in mortal combat against twisted and deformed creatures of myth and imagination. They opened onto a well-appointed conference room with a long table of polished marble surrounded by leather chairs. Tapestries adorned the walls, and a soft red carpet cushioned their feet. The lights matched the brightness of the topside world, which hurt A.J.'s eyes at first. He had grown accustomed to the soft glow of the Dwarfhold.

Everyone from A.J.'s greeting line, save for Chief Master Administrator, was there, talking in small groups. Fergus and a small pack of his wolf clan stood at the far end of the table, including Morgan and Aengus, but Scarlett was not included.

"Brighed, may I have a word before we get started?" Dian asked. "If you'll excuse us, A.J.? It's been quite some time since I've seen my sister, and I want to say hello."

Brighed nodded stiffly and followed Dian out of the room.

A.J. turned to survey the room, and spied a thin, pale-skinned figure lurking in a corner. It had white dreads, pointed ears, and a large forehead with almond-shaped eyes of solid black. It was Aengus's sycophantic sidekick, Blue Jean, trying his best not to be noticed by anyone else in the room. He looked up with relief as Aengus approached with Morgan by his side, watching Aengus like a disapproving mother. Blue Jean scurried over to stand behind his big friend.

"We may have gotten off on the wrong foot the other day," Aengus mumbled without meeting A.J.'s eyes. "I would like to apologize for my poor behavior."

Morgan practically mouthed the words along with him and nodded approval at his performance. From the other end of the room, Fergus also kept a wary eye on them all.

A.J. frowned at the obviousness of the fake apology but nodded to Fergus out of respect first before turning back to Aengus and replying with a curt, "Thank you."

"Can everyone please take a seat?" Margaret began circling the room and settling people in. Everyone moved toward the table from their small discussion groups, which distracted Morgan for a moment as she looked back toward Fergus. Aengus took advantage of the opportunity to lean in close, sneering, "I don't care who you are, D'Anu trash. I should have killed you on that road when I had the chance." His breath smelled like stale marijuana smoke.

"Yeah." A.J. stared down the big man with a hardness that dwarfed Aengus's petty glare. "You should have."

Aengus drew back in surprise, and his eyes filled with fear for a flash, but A.J. saw it, and Aengus knew he saw it too.

"C'mon, Blue Jean," Aengus growled. "Let's sit down so we can get this stupid meeting over with and out of this Dwarf-infested shithole."

A low growl drew A.J.'s attention to Digger, standing next to him in her shaded goggles, nostril's flared and teeth bared at the retreating backs of Aengus and Blue Jean.

"Easy, Digger. Your anger is what he wants. A confrontation that you start only strengthens his hand. If you don't play his game, he can't win. Just let it go."

"You humans have a very odd way of fighting." Digger's voice dripped with fury. "If he were Dwarf, he would already be dead."

"Well, we can't have everything now, can we?"

Everyone stood as Dian entered the room with his travelling companions, Kane and Ptesan-Wi, followed by Brighed. The tall black man had changed into a loose shirt and slacks, and his eyes had lost their darkness. He was friendly, with a kind face, and he smiled at the group as he took a seat next to Dian. The Lakota woman had also changed from her intricately patterned white buckskin into a simple white dress that clung to her slender form. Her long black hair was tied in a ponytail and her eyes had lost their glow. If A.J. had met the pair on the street in a random city, he would assume they were perfectly normal humans, if more beautiful than most.

Digger and A.J. found a pair of chairs opposite Fergus. Brighed took the empty chair between A.J. and the mayor. A wave of anger flowed from her, but she kept her jaw clenched and eyes straight ahead. In the corner behind the group stood Sayah, hiding between two tapestries where the shadows were darkest.

"Thank you all for joining us," said Dian. The rest of the table went silent. "I thought it prudent to meet as soon as possible with everyone who has encountered this Wendigo creature, or whatever it is, so we can get to the bottom of this mystery."

"Not everyone," A.J. said, thinking of Skinner and Scarlett. Digger chuckled and Brighed nudged him under the table.

Dian ignored the remark and continued, "I've asked Ptesan-Wi to join us. She knows more about the Wendigo than anyone, and Kane will serve as an objective witness in the event the rest of the Council wants an investigation, which I predict they will."

Kane nodded to the crowd but said nothing. Ptesan-Wi spoke, "Please, everyone, call me Mina."

"Let's begin," said Dian. "I would like to hear firsthand from each of you, what you have seen, heard, or smelled about this creature since it first arrived. Fergus, I believe your pack was the first to catch wind of it?"

"Yes." Fergus cleared his throat and repeated the story A.J. heard in the garage. "The pack first picked up the scent about two weeks ago and tracked it, but we couldn't find anything, which, as I've said before, is very strange. However, after Sheriff Standish wounded the creature earlier this week, we were able to track it to an abandoned barn up near Bear Creek. We fought it, and the thing killed two of our own. It turned them into Wendigos, and I think everyone knows the rest."

"Thank you, Fergus," said Dian. "Aengus, what happened the night the sheriff was killed? I understand you were at the scene of the crash?"

Aengus looked at his father before speaking, and when he did his voice was weak and faltering. "I took my pack hunting for the Wendigo that night."

"Despite your father ordering the hunt cancelled?" Dian interrupted him. Aengus turned red around the collar but kept his eyes down. "I thought if I could catch the thing, he would reward me, so we went out hunting. I know we're not supposed to cross the valley floor in wolf form, but we picked up its scent real strong in the trees near the old mill and followed it all the way to the crash site. After I saw what happened to the sheriff, I thought it best to protect his body, so I took it and told my dad about it the next morning," he lied.

A.J. leaned forward to call him on it, but a sharp kick from Brighed's boot cut him short. He rubbed his shin and cursed under his breath, which caught Dian's eye.

"A.J., please tell us about the night you arrived."

A.J. noticed both Kane and Mina were paying careful attention. Mina smiled at him reassuringly, and A.J. ignored the rest of the room and spoke directly to her. He recounted his long walk, the heavy rain, and the sheriff's wrecked SUV. When he began describing the body in the road, he glanced at Darcy, who was sitting quietly with her head bowed next to Margaret, and he decided to skip those details. The rest of the tale, from the animal screams and howling wolves to the giant wolf paw on the rear window to Skinner's rescue, he told as he remembered, including the disappearance of the body. What frustrated him most was how much his own experience corroborated Aengus's bullshit story. Then a question occurred to him that no one else had asked.

"What was Sheriff Standish doing out there in the first place? Was he on a call? It was pouring that night. What reason would he have for going out?" A.J. looked at Margaret. "You were the dispatcher that night. Did a call come in for the sheriff?"

"No," said Margaret. "I was on duty all night in the office, and I was also with Darcy and Frank. Nothing came in by radio or phone. When I went to bed, the two of them were sitting in their living room in front of the fire. It wasn't until I heard Darcy scream later that I realized Frank had left."

A general murmur went around the table. A couple of suggestions about checking on flooding and nightly patrolling were dismissed as Connor's duties and the basic fact that no one in their right minds would be out on a night like that, which prompted Digger to poke A.J. with an elbow.

A stifled sob from A.J.'s left caught everyone's attention. Darcy's head was lowered and her shoulders shook. "There, there dear," Margaret hugged the girl against her breast. "Perhaps this is too much for you so soon. We should go."

"It was me." Darcy shook off Margaret's embrace and looked around the room with tears in her eyes. "I sent him out that night."

There was a collective gasp of surprise from the table. Even Dian looked dumbstruck by the revelation.

"For goodness' sakes why?" asked Margaret in surprise.

"I had a vision," said Darcy, "a vision of something horrible. Dad and I were sitting by the fire, and I sort of lost myself in its flames, and then I saw it. Millions upon millions, dead…so much screaming, so much grief, so much destruction! They were all dead. They were all dead…" Darcy stared at the table and rocked back and forth. Tears streamed down her face. Margaret tried to comfort her again, but Darcy shied away from her touch. She looked up and her eyes were red but determined in their conviction.

"Then I saw Mr. Skinner and Alice in the flames, and they were screaming and the flesh melted from their bones and I knew…I knew they were in terrible danger! I woke from the vision with my dad holding me and asking what was wrong, and so I told him. I told him he had to go and save them. I told him to go, and he went. I told him to go, and I sent my father to his death!"

Darcy broke down, and this time Margaret's hug was welcomed. Darcy buried her face in Margaret's sweater and cried hard as Margaret told her over and again it was not her fault and she mustn't blame herself.

"Come on, love, let's get you home. Some nice tea will calm you down. There, there, you did nothing wrong. It's not your fault." She helped the crying girl stand and led her from the room.

"The young witch's powers grow strong," came a hissing whisper from behind Aengus that carried across the room in a moment of unexpected silence.

"Quiet!" snapped Aengus, but it was too late.

"And you, Drow," Dian addressed Blue Jean for the first time. His voice was hard, and his eyes flashed deep red at the grey elf. "What is your role in all of this?" He made no attempt to hide his disgust for Aengus's skinny friend. Blue Jean tried to smile apologetically, but it only made him appear more sinister. He looked at Aengus before speaking, and when he did his voice was shaking.

"It all happened just as Aengus said. He wanted to hunt the creature the night of the storm, but his pack was afraid. He made them go. Later, he brought me the sheriff's body for safekeeping, until we could deliver it…him, to the good doctor this morning." Blue Jean shrunk behind Aengus's shoulder to spare himself Dian's penetrating stare.

One by one, the rest added their experiences with the Wendigo, from days of tracking it without luck, to the fight in the shed when Fergus's pack members were killed, to the battle in Digger's garage. Digger told what she and Alice uncovered in the database, including Alice's discovery of the Northern Gray Wolf genes, and her trip to the university at Nalanda to research the unknown section of the genetic profile. Brighed confirmed that her initial observations of the sheriff's body matched A.J.'s report, and that she would be completing a full autopsy after the meeting.

When everyone finished speaking, A.J. felt that little new was learned beyond Darcy's confession, but he didn't see how that would help find the culprits. The best they could piece together was that Sheriff Standish hit the creature with his SUV. His vehicle ended on its side in the ditch, and he climbed out through the driver's window with his head bleeding from the gash caused by the steering wheel. When the sheriff went to check on what he assumed was a dead animal, it came back to life and killed him with a swipe that ripped out his heart. He would have died instantly, and without a heart to pump the venom through his body, it prevented him from changing into a Wendigo himself. A.J. arrived soon after, at about the same time, apparently, as Aengus and his pack. A.J. didn't believe in coincidences, but he was having a hard time explaining that one.

Mina sat quietly considering all their stories. She spoke with a soft but powerful voice. "The Algonquin people tell stories of the Wendigo as a creature that lives in the dark woods and is only seen in winter when the snows are deep, and the air is bitter cold. The Wendigo is a malevolent creature that craves the taste of humans. It is said that humans who commit cannibalism are transformed into these giant monsters and become obsessed with eating human flesh. They transform and multiply, consuming all in their path. When the transformed Wendigos run out of human prey, they turn upon one another until only one remains. Many stories recount entire tribes disappearing overnight from villages left otherwise undisturbed. It is said this is the fate that befell the English settlement of Roanoke, though that may only be legend. That being said, I concur that this creature is not an actual Wendigo."

"I don't know," Fergus said. "Sounds like a good match to me."

Mina's eyes took on their powerful glow, and she raised one hand, palm up, toward the center of the table. A.J. felt the hairs on his arms stand on end, and the smell of ozone filled the air. Dust particles floated together in the center of the table to form a swirling cloud that transformed into a fearsome creature with white hair and long arms.

"This is a Wendigo," said Mina.

It looked like almost the monster they fought in Digger's garage, but with key differences. This creature had the same powerful arms and sharp claws, but it also had a second set of arms and was much thinner. Mina added another figure next to the first that looked like A.J., which made it clear the Wendigo of legend stood nearly fifteen feet high, twice as tall as the one that killed Fergus's pack mates.

Brighed spoke next. "Our analysis suggests this creature is a genetically engineered monster created from multiple species, including one we can't yet identify, in a crude attempt at creating a Wendigo."

"That is enough reason in itself for an investigation," said Kane. "That sort of genetic manipulation has been banned for four thousand years. To violate it would break every treaty among the D'Anu nations and is punishable by permanent imprisonment. The more important question than why, is who would do such a thing?"

The mayor leaned forward. "This level of technology isn't easy," he spoke in the calm and measured tone of Sayah's control. "In fact, there is only one person in this valley with both the knowledge and the facilities capable of producing such a creature, and that person is in this room."

"That is a good point." Fergus looked from Brighed to Dian. "If I wanted to create a creature like this—and I don't—Brighed is who I would go to. Well, you and Alice, anyway."

"Preposterous!" Brighed had to yell over the suddenly erupting table. "I would never debase my grandmothers' arts in this way. It's absurd!"

Blue Jean laughed and Aengus sat back with a satisfied grin while Fergus's face was impassive in the chaos. Digger ground her teeth while the Margarets tried in vain to restore order.

"Enough!" rang out a booming voice that rocked everyone back in their chairs. Kane stared down the table with a golden glow around his body. Everyone went silent.

Dian spoke. "While it may be accurate that my sister has the skills to commit this crime, it is inconceivable that she would be involved in such a scheme. She is not the only D'Anu in the world with this knowledge. It makes no sense for her to create this beast and then reveal it in her own valley, and she has zero motive. My sister and I may not agree on many things, but one thing is certain, she is not a murderer."

"Of course, you would take her side," whined Aengus. "The D'Anu always cover for D'Anu crimes."

Dian's eyes blazed red, and a wave of crimson energy rolled off his body. Brighed's own anger was building like a volcano.

"I will vouch for Brighed," interjected Morgan. "She did not do this."

The room went suddenly silent. It was Aengus's turn to go red in the face, and Fergus showed genuine surprise at his daughter's statement. "Is that so? What makes you so certain?"

"It is no secret there is no love lost between Brighed and myself. We have our history," said Morgan. "But yesterday in the garage, Brighed and I both treated Alfred's injuries from the Wendigo. Brighed fought hard to save his life. If she knew what he was about to become, she would not have been so close to him, trying to save him, when he turned."

This answer seemed to satisfy the room, though with grumbling acceptance. Brighed nodded thanks to Morgan, who nodded back. The table was silent as those gathered digested the information.

"There is one other possibility," said Digger, "It could be him. It could be…Magnivald." She whispered the name ominously.

Half the table chuckled at Digger's suggestion, while the other half erupted with indignation.

"Ridiculous!" yelled Brighed.

Aengus and Blue Jean laughed openly and pounded the table with their fists.

"Oh dear…" said both Margarets at once.

"Can we keep the suggestions serious?" complained Dian.

"Even if Magnivald is real, why on earth release this creature in our little backwoods valley?" protested Morgan. "Why not drop it in the middle of Times Square?"

"For the last time, Magnivald is not real!" yelled an exasperated Brighed.

Digger glared at everyone with her arms crossed.

"Such speculation gets us nowhere," interjected Dian. "I have made a decision. A crime has clearly been committed here, not just the murder of your sheriff but the emergence of this genetically designed creature, whomever did it," he nodded to a frustrated Digger, which calmed her somewhat. "The surprise arrival of a D'Anu stranger is also of grave importance and suspiciously coincidental. We have not even begun to investigate where you came from, my new friend." Dian stared at A.J. from beneath his brows.

The mayor and the wolves leaned forward expectantly, waiting on Dian's next words.

"However," he continued, "I think it is premature to assemble the Council."

This time angry shouts from Fergus, Aengus, and the mayor, drowned out Dian's voice before he could regain control. "At this time," he said as the shouting died down. "Until we have more information about who or why this creature was created, it would be a waste of effort and time to gather the full council. I will, however, with Fergus's support, ask the council to conduct a full investigation, and I recommend Kiongozi Kane to lead it. If the other counselors at this table have no objections, of course."

Fergus's eyes narrowed, and he sat back in his chair and rubbed his chin. "When we find out who is behind this crime, we will still need a trial by the Council."

"Agreed," said Dian.

"Then agreed." Fergus nodded down the table at Dian, Mina, and Kane, who all nodded back.

"That's settled then," Dian sighed. "Mina, thank you for sharing your knowledge with us. Please enjoy our hospitality while we await word from the rest of the counselors. Margaret, please deliver the message to the counselors and inform me of their answers."

"Of course," said Margaret.

"Then we are adjourned," said Dian. "Brighed, please proceed with the autopsy. A.J., join me for lunch."

A.J. felt Brighed stiffen next to him, her eyes fixed on Dian. When Dian turned away to speak with Kane, Brighed touched A.J.'s thoughts with her mind, *"Be cautious, A.J. Dian is more dangerous than he seems."* She squeezed his hand as Dian turned back toward them. He raised a questioning eyebrow at Brighed and glanced at A.J. as if he'd just heard Brighed too.

"Come," Dian smiled at A.J. and motioned toward the door with an open hand. "Margaret has offered us the use of her office. Lunch has been prepared. It will give us a chance to get to know one another."

"Sure thing," A.J. headed toward the door, "brother," he added as he passed Dian, who laughed pleasantly.

"Oh, yes, sorry about that, dear boy. There is much speculation among the D'Anu about your origins, and too much speculation without direction can lead to unrest. It is better to give the masses gossip of one's own making rather than let them invent their own."

"Spoken like a true politician. What happens when they find out I'm not your long, lost brother?" A.J. walked into the dimly lit cavern and waited for his eyes to adjust. A low-slung electric cart with wide tires was waiting with a Dwarf at the controls.

"My understanding is you were found in a basket on the doorstep of a police station in Baltimore, which may be the most cliché thing I've ever heard, but my people have checked it out and your records do match your story."

A.J. was perturbed by Dian checking his background, but it's what he would have done if he were in Dian's position. "What's your point?"

"Well, how do you know you're not my long, lost brother, then? Hmmm?"

Chapter Twelve

Truth and Consequences

The elevator rose, slid sideways, and then rose again to open on a small suite with large plate glass windows facing west. Margaret's office had a view of tall fir trees bordered by the wall of protective mist in the distance. A.J. realized the doctor's office was only a small part of a much greater complex that honeycombed under the north slope of the valley and sat atop the great Dwarfhold far below.

"Are you hungry?" Dian led the way into a conference room where a number of photos in both color and black and white decorated the walls. "Lunch will be along shortly. I'm positively famished."

There was something that bothered A.J. about Dian that he couldn't put his finger on. Dian was pleasant enough, and his demeanor seemed genuine, but everyone he'd met so far was either wary of the man or outright hostile toward him. A.J. wondered if their animosity was related to Skinner and Alice's storied romance or whether Dian's outward-facing personality was really a disturbingly perfect mask hiding a darker soul. Perhaps what disturbed A.J. most was how much he could identify with the latter.

A.J. pondered these thoughts while he studied the photographs on the walls. They were all of famous politicians, scientists, and inventors from American history. Henry Ford and Thomas Edison smiled together on a factory floor. Dwight Eisenhower in his uniform stood surrounded by typists in a war office. A group of scientists examined a large bomb, with Robert Oppenheimer's trademark fedora over his thin face chief among them. Then A.J. recognized a figure standing just behind Oppenheimer and almost out of the shot. She wore a close-fitting hat and cat's-eye glasses, but her pleasantly plump face was unmistakable. It was Margaret.

A.J. re-examined the other photographs more carefully and identified Margaret among the factory workers behind Ford and Edison, and one of the women hard at work typing field reports for Eisenhower bore a striking resemblance to her as well.

"Observe, the ubiquitous secretary." Dian stepped next to A.J. and looked at an old color photograph of President Johnson among his White House staff. "There she is, hard at work keeping the businesses running, the staff organized, and the projects on schedule but always going unnoticed and unrewarded for her successes while others take all the credit. It is a role perfectly positioned to offer advice, direct research, or even correct mathematical errors that help solve vital problems. In the course of human civilization, there is perhaps no one on the planet more vital to its ongoing success than the secretary, or whatever they're called these days."

"So, she's your spy in the Incog world?" A.J. marveled at the many pivotal moments in history Margaret must have witnessed. "Hiding in plain sight?"

"Spy?" Dian seemed surprised by the notion but then nodded. "Yes, I suppose so in her own way, but don't make the mistake of assuming Margaret reports to anyone. She provides communication among the Queendom's leaders and serves as a counselor for the most valued members of our community, but she does so of her own volition and shares what she chooses. No one is Margaret's boss, and we are fortunate to have her blessing."

"What is she?"

"Margaret is a truly unique creature among all magical creatures, the very last of her kind, and invaluable to our Queendom's survival. Surely, you've guessed her special quality by now?"

"There's only one Margaret isn't there?"

"One and many, yes," replied Dian. "You see, Margaret is the last Echo."

"Echo? You mean like the Greek goddess?"

"An Oread, technically, but yes. One in the same."

"I thought the story was the Satyrs tore her to pieces and spread her around the world."

"Not exactly. Such metaphors translate poorly across language, culture, and time," said Dian. "As you can see, Margaret is clearly very much alive."

"How many of her are there?"

"Ah, that is the right question, but only Margaret knows the answer, and she's not telling. Ask her sometime, see how far you get."

"No thanks," laughed A.J. "She's already taught me a lesson about paying the swear jar."

Dian laughed with him. "Yes, she is a stickler for politeness. I imagine if I had to listen to a thousand conversations at once then foul language would annoy me as well."

A.J. contemplated a photograph of Margaret with Albert Einstein hanging next to the one with Oppenheimer and a thought slammed into his mind. "My gods, Margaret helped build the atom bomb." It wasn't a question.

"Helped? She was instrumental," replied Dian.

A.J.'s jaw dropped. He wasn't certain how he felt about that news. "Brighed said Margaret saved the world. Is this what she was talking about?"

"One of many times, yes," said Dian. "And not the last."

"So much for non-interference," A.J. grumbled.

"Ah… yes. The crux of the matter." Dian stroked his chin in thought. "What has my sister told you about the Council of Elders?"

"Not much. Just that it's another group of politicians nobody trusts. No offense."

"None taken. It's an accurate description. Politics are the same the world over, I'm afraid. They all…what is it the kids say these days? They all suck?"

"They do indeed," said A.J. "So why is everyone so uptight about this Council getting together?"

"Ah, that might take some explaining. Let's see…first you must understand that D'Anu politics are divided among two factions, those who favor non-interference and those who think we should be more heavily involved in helping guide Incog technological and political development." began Dian.

"I see," said A.J. "It's a two-party system, then?"

"Eventually, they all are," replied Dian. "But yes, that's a simplified way of looking at it. The Isolationists consist mostly of D'Anu and Dwarfs and about half the Shifter species. Their position is for strict non-interference, mostly for religious reasons, but there is a certain logic to it. They are convinced the First Age was destroyed by gods who were angry over the genetic manipulation of the human species. Consequently, they believe mankind is meant to evolve at its own pace, and it is our job to simply stay out of the way and damn the consequences. On the other side are the Activists, consisting of the rest of the Shifters, like the wolves, plus the Utukku, the Drow, and a few others. They dismiss the Isolationists' religious philosophy and view Incogs as little more than a food source that should be ruled over to protect them from themselves."

"There's a certain logic to that, I have to admit," said A.J. "I take it the Isolationists control the Council then, since Incogs aren't being lined up in slaughterhouses."

"For now, yes," replied Dian. "That's why there is so much resistance to a new Council meeting. Every time a meeting is held, about once a century, the twelve members of the council hold votes on Queendom policies. Currently, the Council is divided equally between the two factions, with Queen Severa being the tie-breaking vote. So, the non-interference policy remains intact, for now. However, it only takes one of the six isolationists to alter their vote and change the policy, but that would likely be political suicide, so it's very rare."

"For the last four hundred years, this balance has kept us safe and unknown by the Incog world, but these long alliances are shifting. There is growing concern over the current affairs of the Incog world and the dangers they pose to the health of our planet. Many in the Queendom are now advocating interference again. It is likely that the next meeting will see a new policy adopted, and likely a new ruler since Queen Severa would never support the change. Fergus is the most obvious choice for the role. He's had the job before, a very long time ago."

"Experience has its benefits," said A.J. "What's so bad about having Fergus in charge?"

"Well, the last time a Shifter ruled the Queendom was in the fourteenth century, and her solution for the perceived threat to our people from the rapidly expanding Incog civilization was biological warfare. She wiped out half the population of Western Europe with a monster equally as deadly as this mutant Wendigo creation but microscopic in size."

"Are you telling me the Plague was a Shifter plot against humanity?"

"Yes, and an effective one too," replied Dian. "Many of us fear a similar outcome should Fergus take the throne, and I cannot dismiss the possibility that this genetically designed Wendigo is an audition for his cause. When word gets out, it could force a meeting and a new vote by the Council, and that would almost assuredly go Fergus's way."

"But the Wendigo killed Fergus's own pack mates!" protested A.J. "He fought it himself and almost died."

"Did he? Or did it only appear that way for his audience? If I had to guess, I'd say he was not the first one to the fight, was he? It makes perfect sense. What better way to showcase the creature and throw off suspicion than sacrificing some of his own? It wouldn't be the first time Fergus has played that exact trick. It's practically his signature move."

"But that's insane."

"That's Queendom politics. Whatever the outcome of the vote, our experience tells us interfering in Incog affairs usually leads to worse catastrophes than simply staying out of their way. The religious ones among the Queendom demand non-interference, while the rest fall somewhere between offering gentle guidance to outright enslavement. Queen Severa's loyalties usually lay with the religious faction, and the Council maintains a non-interference policy in support of her position. Unfortunately, interference is still sometimes unavoidable."

"Such is the justification for every war ever fought."

"Indeed," said Dian. "That was certainly the case when the rise of Nazi Germany threatened to expose the

Queendom's existence to the world because of some unknown D'Anu, we think, who was using the name Magnivald."

"Ah!" said A.J. "So, Magnivald is not a myth after all?"

"Yes, and no," replied Dian. "Technically speaking, Magnivald is an archetype, if you will, a legend that dates to the First Age of Mankind. The Isolationist religion tells the story of the first humans created by the goddess Anu with the power to challenge the gods of chaos and bring order to the world. They were, in effect, demigods, and they were successful in their quest. However, the first and greatest magic wielder of these demigods was called Magnivald, and after defeating the gods of chaos, Magnivald sought to use the power of magic to consolidate power over all the world and rule all its creatures to end war and suffering once and for all.

"Of course," A.J. frowned. "That's what they all say."

"True," Dian smiled. "It is ironic that the only path to lasting peace is total domination of all those who disagree with you."

"But you don't buy the Magnivald story?"

"About the end of the First Age? I have no idea. The Isolationists claim the Anu'nakki waged war against Magnivald and his army of magical creatures, causing the end of that world. According to those who believe, Magnivald was the 'First of the First,' as in the first creation of Anu, the prototype human with the immortality of a god and unrestrained powers capable of manipulating the forces of nature by his will alone. Others, like myself, think if Magnivald really did exist, it was merely a person, or persons, whose power was great enough to attempt to seize control of the natural forces of magic, and it blew up in their faces."

"Of course, there is no evidence Magnivald ever actually existed or still does," added Dian. "For Activists, Magnivald is nothing but a bogeyman that children and superstitious adults of the Queendom blame for any and all manner of unexplained events."

"You won't convince Digger of that."

"No, and a great many others as well, it seems. While the name, Magnivald, is old as time, there was one incident last century in which someone, some D'Anu, we believe, violated the Queendom's non-interference policy and attempted to manipulate world events. Magnivald is a myth that, for a short time last century, was indeed very real and very dangerous."

"I see," said A.J. "You don't know who it was?"

"We do not, though there is much speculation, as you have seen."

"So, what's got everyone so upset about it these days?"

Dian clasped his hands behind his back and paced as he spoke. "This modern story of Magnivald begins with a young German infantry soldier in World War I who escaped the slaughter of his entire brigade in Belgium by hiding in a cave."

"You're talking about Hitler, aren't you? All stories that begin with a World War I German infantry soldier are about Hitler."

"Yes," Dian chuckled. "And this one is no different. Of course, he wasn't a genocidal maniac at the time, just a scared and hungry kid looking for a place to hide. The story goes that in this cave he encountered a D'Anu using the name Magnivald. What little information we have is mostly secondhand rumor, but it suggests he, or she, made a deal with this young soldier in exchange for saving his life. Magnivald offered to provide technology and knowledge from the First Age for the benefit of the German 'master race' in exchange for the German army's help in locating some powerful First Age artifacts that would grant Magnivald the power to control and direct the forces of magic across the entire world. Among the many German innovations Magnivald influenced were rocketry, munitions, and nuclear fission."

"Oh, that's great," said A.J. "What could possibly go wrong with that knowledge in Nazi hands?"

"Precisely. Magnivald also provided more than weapons technology. Magnivald helped groom the young soldier into a national leader, and with Magnivald's guidance the Nazi party navigated German politics until it ruled all things. It wasn't until Germany advanced so rapidly in these technological discoveries that the Queendom Council became aware of D'Anu interference in Incog affairs, and by then it was almost too late."

"They chose interference because Magnivald was helping the Nazis get a nuclear bomb?" The thought stunned A.J. "That would have changed the outcome of the war. That would have changed everything!"

"It would have, and that is why the Council held an emergency meeting in 1939 to discuss whether to step in or let things take their course. With a D'Anu already interfering and the German High Command aware of the D'Anu presence in the world, the majority felt it necessary to interfere."

"The majority," said A.J. "Not everyone? I'm guessing since Brighed is the religious one, she would have voted against helping the Allies defeat the Nazis?" That thought made his stomach churn.

"Would have? My dear boy, she did vote against it. My sister was the Chief Counselor to the throne. She was outvoted and resigned in protest. That's how I came to take her place, reluctant as I was to get into politics. Seems odd she didn't tell you that, either."

A.J. fumed at the realization he actually knew nothing about Brighed. Maybe she only saw him as an easy to manipulate fool.

"Oh, don't be too hard on her," said Dian. "It's easy to see the outcome after the fact, but in 1939 no one knew what the Nazi Party would become. Everyone was still expecting rational minds to prevail over their insanity, and we thought we were only providing insurance against them, never imagining the Incogs would willingly destroy our very planet over such trifles as pride and greed. Alas, perhaps Brighed had the right of it. Civilizations have always risen and fallen on the slaughter of innocents and the oppression of others. Perhaps we should have just stayed out of the way."

A.J. shook his head in disbelief. "But if the Nazis had won..." He thought of the death camps and the millions of innocent people the Nazis slaughtered out of hate, and he shuddered at the idea of them winning the war. "What did the Council do? How did they stop the Nazis?"

"Well, in deference to the Isolationist's position of non-interference, the Council chose to act but not overtly. We asked for Margaret's help instead."

"Margaret?"

"Yes. Margaret was already positioned in the German government, as she is in many governments, to keep an eye on things and help us stay informed. Of course, she couldn't behave as though she knew about Magnivald and his patronage of the Nazi party without risking exposure, so she found a way to slow down German nuclear development while simultaneously helping the Americans advance their Manhattan Project."

"How?"

Dian smiled at the memory. "She took a position in the conscription office for the German war effort and kept drafting Germany's nuclear physicists into infantry divisions."

"That's fucking brilliant!" A.J. laughed. Then he thought about the practical joke played on him the morning before and made a mental note never to mess with Margaret. Then another thought struck him about Margaret's caretaking of Darcy.

"What is a woman who helped save the world from Nazi rule doing glued to the hip of a teenage girl in Oregon? What's so valuable about the sheriff's daughter?"

Dian considered his answer carefully. "Darcy is indeed extremely valuable. It is rare, but occasionally, over the centuries, a child is born who is half D'Anu and half Incog. Darcy's mother was D'Anu, but she died tragically in a vehicle collision when Darcy was very young. Her father, as you know, is, or was, an Incog human."

"Okay," shrugged A.J. "But why the special attention?"

"The simplest explanation is that these rare children almost always possess extremely powerful magic, much greater than any of the D'Anu. Some of them I'm sure you have heard of. Merlin, perhaps? Or King Arthur's sister, Morgan?"

"You're telling me Darcy is like Merlin?"

"Potentially," said Dian. "But not all these children achieve such fame. Sadly, some are unable to maintain mental stability as they grow into their full powers in adulthood. Does the name Rasputin ring a bell?"

"Oh!" said A.J. "That actually explains a lot."

"Yes, and there have been others you've never heard of who turned out equally as evil. You've already witnessed what a terrible burden such power and magical sight can bring. Poor Darcy's vision of Alice and Mr. Skinner's deaths has led directly to the slaying of her own father instead. You can see why the guiding hand of someone as ancient and wise as Margaret is important to her mental development."

"Yeah. Poor thing." A.J. stared at picture of Margaret standing over an early design of the integrated circuit as he contemplated all he'd heard. "So, whatever became of Magnivald, then?"

"No one knows. When the war turned against the Nazis, Magnivald abandoned them to their fate and disappeared. We sought Magnivald's identity by every means possible. We have our suspicions of who it might have been, but the truth is still a mystery about which many D'Anu disagree. That is why the appearance of this imitation Wendigo creature is of such concern."

"You think the Magnivald pretender could be in this valley?"

"It is a possibility one must consider," said Dian. "Among others."

"Like Fergus?"

"Yes," said Dian. "I also must consider Fergus's point that it could be my sister as well. Like I said, it would go against her nature, and my sister is nothing if not consistent in her convictions. As her brother, I do not think she would be involved in the creation of such a monstrous creature as this Wendigo. As Chief Counselor, however, I must admit that only she has both the knowledge and facilities in this valley to produce such a thing, and thus I cannot rule out her possible involvement."

Something clicked in A.J.'s mind as all the pieces suddenly fit together. "You think Brighed could be Magnivald, don't you?"

"Me? No, but I am in the minority on that position. Brighed tutored Machiavelli himself in politics, so she certainly has the skills to help a young German soldier rise to the rank of Fuhrer. She knows more about D'Anu artifacts and their powers than anyone in the D'Anu Queendom. She's practically obsessed with them, and her fierce resistance to the Council's actions to stop Magnivald's Nazi plot only adds to the suspicions."

"Many in the D'Anu Queendom are convinced Brighed is the false Magnivald, and that is why she insists, of course, that Magnivald is not real. In truth, she is safe in this valley only because she is under Fergus's protection. She cannot leave so long as this false Magnivald's identity remains a mystery, and if it is true that Magnivald does not actually exist…"

"Then she will always be suspect," A.J. finished Dian's sentence for him.

"Exactly. Now this Wendigo mess shows up on her doorstep in a valley where she is the only one capable of creating it. Either my sister is extremely unlucky, or I must consider that maybe she truly has gone mad. Sadly, that is not uncommon among the long lived. I fear for my sister's sanity."

A.J. began piecing the information together until it formed a trail. "That's why Kane is here, isn't it? He's not just witnessing a meeting; he's also assessing your sister."

"Precisely. You know, you really are very bright for such a young D'Anu." He smiled at A.J. with approval.

A.J.'s first instinct was to feel pride in Dian's praise, and that set off alarm bells all over his internal systems. It became clear why Dian was such an effective politician, and A.J. stiffened his resolve to be wary of him.

"The rest of the Council is demanding answers," Dian continued. "And they want an unbiased investigator. They didn't feel that I, as her brother, could remain objective, and it's probably true. Fortunately, Kane's honor and reputation are unimpeachable. I am confident he will find the truth of the matter, whatever that may be."

A pair of Dwarfs with knives and forks embossed on their aprons wheeled in a table loaded with food and drinks. There were fresh prawns, baked salmon, and several cuts of meat, along with cheeses, steamed vegetables, bowls of fresh cut fruit, and pitchers of cold tea and lemonade. There was enough food to feed at least twenty, but only two plates were set.

"Don't worry, it won't go to waste." Dian began adding small morsels of everything to his plate. "The Dwarfs will distribute the rest when we are finished. Eat up!"

A.J. didn't wait to be told twice. He eased his right arm from the sling and piled his own plate high with generous helpings. He breathed with discomfort but far less pain than he should have just a day after his injuries.

"Brighed's greatest talent has always been in the healing arts," said Dian as they sat across from one another at the table. "Though she does have many other talents as well. You're in good hands there. I'm sure you'll be feeling right as rain in a day or two. Here, try the roasted beets. They're delicious and good for the libido."

"My libido is just fine," replied A.J. through a mouthful of tender beef. "And, no, we haven't slept together, since you're asking."

Dian gave A.J. a sly look. "Well, you're not dumb at least. That's a start."

"Not dumb," replied A.J. coldly. "You're the second person this week who's said that to me. I don't think it's the compliment you people think it is."

"You people?" Dian shook his head. "We are your people, A.J., even if you don't understand what that means just yet, and if I know my sister, I suspect you know very little. How much has she told you about who and what you are?"

"She's told me nothing, or at least nothing useful. She sold me a similar tale about a First Age and gods at war and time travelling refugees, but I'm still having trouble believing any of this is real."

"Oh, it's quite real, I can assure you. Though to be fair, that's probably what a figment of your imagination would tell you."

"The pain is real enough." A.J. slid his right arm back into its sling.

"Well, that's one thing at least," Dian answered. "You are having difficulty accepting how different reality is from the reality you have always assumed. That's to be expected, and it's a perfectly normal reaction for a healthy mind under the circumstances."

"I don't know that 'healthy' is how I would describe my mind. I can barely function half the time these days."

"Ah, yes. The 'elephant in the attic,' so to speak," said Dian. "Post-traumatic stress does not discriminate among species, no matter how far evolved, I'm afraid. I've read your military service report, as well as field reports of your time in private combat employment. You're a true hero, A.J."

A.J. stopped chewing. "Don't use that fucking word," he scowled. "You don't know what you're talking about. Besides, that information is supposed to be classified." A.J. found it easier not to like this guy, who knew more about him than A.J. wanted anyone in the world to know.

"Classified?" Dian laughed. "Please. The Incog world fools itself into thinking secrets can exist. There are no secrets from us, dear boy."

"You keep calling me that. I haven't been a 'boy' since the first bullet hit the dirt next to me nearly twenty years ago."

"Please forgive my impertinence," said Dian. "It's merely a colloquial holdover from my days at Oxford."

"When were you at Oxford?"

"Originally? The 1650s," said Dian. "And on several other occasions the past few hundred years. I do love the smell of old books."

A.J. stared across the table with a fork halfway to his mouth. It was too much for his mind to grasp.

Dian looked at A.J. with a mixture of pity and surprise. "Didn't Brighed even tell you that much? Oh, dear," he shook his head. "How shocking this all must be to you. The D'Anu, like you and me, are a genetically engineered race of humans, whether by science or magic, it is the truth. We D'Anu are the most advanced of the human species. We don't get sick, and we don't grow old."

"Are you telling me I'm immortal? Horseshit. I've got the scars to prove it."

"For goodness' sakes, no. We die just like all humans can, whether by accident, natural disaster, or some foul deed. It's a tragedy always, but it happens. Others, though, with an abundance of caution and a bit of good luck, live a very long time indeed. I, for one, am nearly eight hundred years old, though I don't look a day over forty, don't you think?" Dian smiled and dramatically sucked in his gut.

A.J. laughed. He wanted to ask Brighed's age but decided he may not like the answer. He asked, instead, "Why is my arrival such a big deal? I'm no one, and I like it that way. Everyone around here, though, either treats me like a villain or the second coming of Christ, but I don't see why. I'm just a regular guy on a long walk."

"Oh, you are much more than that," said Dian. "I suspect you have always known that, but you still have no idea what you are or of what you are capable, though our magical potential often shows in some way when we are young. Has it not?"

A.J. remembered Brighed's warning and kept his mouth shut. He tried his best to keep his face expressionless and continued to eat.

Dian stared carefully at him until A.J. began to feel uncomfortable under his gaze.

"I see," Dian returned his attention to his plate. "My sister has given you some warning at least. Perhaps it is wisest for you to keep that information to yourself until you learn to control it lest it be manipulated by those whose interests may not align with your own. Speaking of which, how much do you know about my sister?"

Something in A.J.'s reaction made Dian chuckle as he shoved his now empty plate away from him. A.J. felt his face turn red.

"My sister has a long and troubled history you know nothing about," Dian spoke kindly but directly. "Whatever your feelings toward Brighed, have caution there. She is more dangerous than she seems."

"Funny, she said the same thing about you."

"She wasn't wrong," replied Dian with a cold smile. "Has she told you she lives in exile in this valley under Fergus' protection?"

A.J. remained silent.

"Hmmm, I thought not. Has she informed you she is under threat of execution if she ever steps outside this valley? No? Of course, she hasn't."

Dian looked at A.J. with concern. "A.J., there is a reason my sister, once the most powerful of the Queendom's Counselors, now lives alone in a backwater valley handing out potions to pubescent Shifters. She has fallen a very long way, politically speaking. Brighed is many things, but humble is not one of them. She may pretend otherwise, but she would do almost anything to regain her freedom and position in the Queendom, and that makes me question her motives for everything, including you."

A.J. felt sick at the thought of Brighed manipulating him. "Why me?"

"Two reasons, I can think of," answered Dian. "First, you must come from somewhere. You are full D'Anu, which means both your parents were D'Anu, yet your DNA doesn't match any we have on file, nor can we find familial matches. We thought we knew every living D'Anu in this world and yet here you are, the product of at least two more unknowns. Who are they, and how have they remained hidden all these centuries? Are there more than those two? The possibility of an unknown D'Anu clan is the most exciting topic in the Queendom in decades. Everyone is talking about it, and if Brighed can keep you under her influence, then you present a compelling opportunity for her benefit."

A.J.'s blood turned cold. No wonder Brighed was flirting with him. He cursed his own gullibility, but his mind caught on a key point of Dian's.

"What do you mean my DNA doesn't match?"

"Brighed tested it, of course," said Dian with a dismissive wave. "It was the first thing she checked. I would have expected no less."

"Guess that proves we are not related at all then," A.J. snapped. He was getting tired of the constant invasions into his privacy.

"Not genetically, no," replied Dian.

"And the second reason?" A.J. demanded, not really wanting to hear the answer.

"You are unattached and unspoken for. That makes you about the most valuable property in all the D'Anu Queendom."

"For gods' sakes why?"

"In a species that doesn't age, the potential for overpopulation is severe, so our creators built in a failsafe to help keep our numbers in check. D'Anu women are fertile for only a few days every few years. Between our limited birth rate and occasional deaths, the D'Anu population numbers only a few thousand the world over, and there are slightly more D'Anu women than D'Anu men. Consequently, the birth of a D'Anu male is widely celebrated, and most have arranged marriages before their first birthday. I've no doubt Brighed is already trading on favors, lining up your potential suitors from the highest bidders. Unless, of course, she is planning to keep you for herself, which wouldn't surprise me. She could as easily trade on the value of your fame as on your betrothal to improve her position."

A.J. didn't want to believe Brighed would do that, and Brighed's warning about Dian made him skeptical.

"She wouldn't do something like that," A.J. growled. "I'd know if she were just playing me." He didn't finish the sentence before Dian was laughing sympathetically.

"Oh, dear boy, please don't feel bad. My sister has seduced kings and princes for centuries. She was Machiavelli's tutor, for gods' sakes. Let me guess. Since you were raised an orphan in a world where you were ostracized for being unique, Brighed offered kindness and love but gave just enough information to keep you curious. She offered warmth and comfort and invited you into her home. She soothed your pains and made you feel for the first time in your life that you are not alone in the world, yet she didn't push it. She created a safe opening and let you step right in. But you're no fool, not you, dear boy! You're not that easily won, so I'm betting there was some anger on her part? Like a bully pushing your shoulders. You couldn't help but push back, and then she had you. Am I getting close?"

A.J. narrowed his eyes at Dian, annoyed at the accuracy of his assessment, but it was still just speculation. He wasn't ready to dismiss the kindness and affection Brighed had shown him based only on the words of her brother. Then Dian reached out with his thoughts and touched A.J.'s mind.

"Perhaps this was her weapon then?"

The words appeared in A.J. thoughts, and he felt a warmth from them, a sense of comradery and compassion. It wasn't invasive as Brighed's had been that first time, it was soothing. A.J felt suddenly confused by his feelings.

"You have a kind heart, A.J., I can sense that. It is buried beneath a mountain of pain and tragedy, but it's there, and it's worthy of protection, especially from my sister."

A.J. felt drawn by an overwhelming sense of connection to Dian in that moment. There was not a hint of animosity or manipulation in Dian's thoughts. It felt like genuine concern, and it awakened a feeling he had only ever known with Malcolm, a sense of brotherhood and love and trust. A.J. wanted to weep over the desperate longing for that feeling again. His wariness of Dian was at war with his feelings for Brighed and her warning against him. He could feel Dian watching his thoughts.

"Brighed has certainly done a number on you, that's for certain." Dian's voice was filled with empathy and concern. "She is beautiful, and she is wise, but she is also much more than that too. Please, allow me to show you."

A.J. felt Dian's mind press gently against his own, and those feeling of connection were very hard to resist. He didn't want to admit to himself how much he missed them. He carefully relaxed his concentration and felt Dian's thoughts infiltrate the contours of his mind until the conference room faded around them. Flashes of Dian's memories mingled with his own until he found himself standing in a large room surrounded by the sights and sounds of battle. A.J. was shocked at how real it felt, as if he were living it in the moment. Every detail was sharp. Every feeling felt real. The high ceiling was blackened with soot and tapestries burned on the walls. The marble floor was slick with blood and viscera. Bodies littered the floor around him and the sounds of steel on steel and the screams of men fighting and dying overwhelmed his senses.

A.J. looked down at his hands, adorned in leather gloves and covered in blood. His heavy woolen clothes were soaked through with sweat, and feelings of rage and fear and dismay washed through him. He was holding a rapier in his right hand and a dagger in his left, both stained brown and red and dripping.

A half dozen men, yelling in French, ran past him toward a line of guards holding off a group of knights wearing steel breastplates and helms over leather and chain. Their broadswords banged against the rotellas and bucklers of the defenders who were falling back under the onslaught.

"Monseigneur!" A dark-haired fighter in a capitano hat grabbed his shoulder. "Nous devons fuir! La batielle est perdue!"

Lost… yes… we must flee… The thoughts weren't A.J.'s, they were Dian's, and they were more concept than words. The fighter stepped in front of Dian and pushed him toward a doorway just as a bolt from a crossbow suddenly emerged from the fighter's throat. His eyes went wide, and he coughed blood onto Dian's chest before collapsing in his arms.

As the fighter fell, Dian saw a tall figure standing at the far entrance to the great hall reloading a crossbow. The pale hands and white hair hanging from the helm told Dian that bolt had been meant for him.

Kristoff… thought Dian. *The Drow Chieftain is fighting with the English! So that's how they got through…*

Dian fled down the hallway; the sounds of fighting and screaming following behind him. Women in powder-white wigs and bright woolen dresses with embroidery and lace ran through the halls chased by soldiers who had breached the castle, while a handful of guards fought desperately to hold them back. A blond-bearded English soldier in battle-scarred leather was ripping at the bodice of a young court maid who screamed in protest. Dian ran the man through with his rapier and pulled it free before the soldier even knew he was dead. Dian helped the maid to her feet and pushed her toward the nearest doorway.

For his part, Dian wasn't trying to escape. An image of a young man of about 14 years, with dark hair and bright blue eyes filled his thoughts. *Thomas! Where is Thomas?*

The name brought a flood of feelings into A.J.'s heart. Panic, devotion, fear, love… all nearly overwhelmed A.J.'s mind. He felt himself sob at the memory of a child that was not his.

He turned down a hallway where dead men lay in pools of their own blood and black smoke crawled along the ceiling like a demon searching for new souls. Thomas' rooms were this way.

He ran through the door to his personal apartments and saw a pair of poorly dressed English mercenaries dispatching the guard who protected his family. They saw Dian and turned their attention to him. The bigger man smiled at their sudden advantage, revealing a mouth half-filled with black and broken teeth and a scar where the end of his nose should be. He raised a dented short sword for an attack while his smaller partner in poorly mixed livery lunged at Dian with a rapier he'd taken from the dead guard.

Dian parried the lunge with his own rapier and sidestepped the swing from the bigger man's short sword. He plunged his dagger into the neck of the big man before he could recover, shoved the dying man into the path of his smaller partner, spun on his heel and neatly sliced the main artery of the smaller man's neck with the tip of his steel. He didn't take the time to watch either man die before he continued his race toward his son's chambers.

Dian stepped into the small corridor where his son's room lay, and saw Thomas running toward him, his favored flute in one hand and a broad smile on the young man's face at the sight of his father.

"Thomas!" Dian yelled. "Venez vite!" His relief at finding his son still alive nearly crippled him. He dropped his weapons and stumbled toward Thomas with his arms wide.

A woman's voice screamed at them both, "No!"

Dian looked behind Thomas and saw Brighed running toward them. Her ornate dress was ripped at one shoulder and blood ran down her arm. Her powdered hair was pulled free and soot stained her white makeup. But it was her eyes that froze Dian's blood. Her eyes were wild and crazed and filled with hatred. A deep black energy roiled about her head and dark bolts of electricity crackled in the air around her. She reached a hand toward Thomas and a bolt of electricity wrapped itself around the boy's body like a writhing whip of light, and Thomas went rigid as he froze in place, one foot raised in mid-run, his eyes wide with fear.

"Brighed?" Dian cried out. "Brighed! My God! No!" He screamed in anguish. He reached out for his son in a vain attempt to protect him, but Brighed's magic jerked the boy away from him and toward her clutching grasp. Brighed bared her teeth in rage, and with her free hand pulled a dagger from her waist coat and sliced the boy's throat.

Dian collapsed to the floor in horror as blood spewed from Thomas' neck, his young eyes wide with terror and his mouth open in a soundless scream. The favored flute clattered to the ground and rolled to a stop just inches from Dian's knees where he knelt, folded in despair and destroyed upon the ground.

The scene faded as A.J. wept nearly uncontrollably. He knew these feelings of betrayal and hatred and anguish too well, and despite his every attempt at avoiding them the past ten years, here they were again. As awful as they ever were.

"Thank you for indulging me, A.J. It is rare for me to share such tragedy, and sharing it with someone, even for a moment, helps soothe the pain. In my many years of life, I have had dozens of long and loving relationships, yet despite many attempts and a deep longing for more children, Thomas was my only child. I am deeply sorry to expose you to such atrocities in this way, but I felt it important for you to understand who you are dealing with, and of what she is truly capable."

A.J. fought to get his breathing under control. He wrapped his arms around himself and rocked in the chair until the emotional flood began to subside. He felt sick and had completely lost his appetite. He opened his eyes to the conference room and Dian sitting across the table from him with a look of pity and concern in his eyes, both of which A.J. despised.

"I thought you said Brighed wasn't a murderer," A.J. gasped in anger.

"I lied." Dian's face was impassive, but his eyes were filled with pain.

"How can you even look at her?" The thought of Brighed brought the feelings of rage back to the surface, and A.J. had to grind his teeth to keep them at bay. "How can you defend her? How can you be in the same room with her?"

Dian smiled sadly. "Alas, there is some truth to the axiom that time heals all wounds. Brighed and I will never be close again as we once were. There is simply too much between us now. However, when you have lived as long as I have and watched every love and every acquaintance and every partner eventually die or drift away, all that is left is family. Family is the only true permanence in this world, for better and for worse. At the end of the day, despite all the pain and tragedy family inflicts upon one another, it still has real value, and is, perhaps, the only thing truly worth protecting."

"I wouldn't know." A.J.'s voice was cold and hard.

"You wouldn't know...yet," smiled Dian. "Family can be found and chosen just as much as it can be born into. Perhaps that is the reason you are here in this valley."

"I thought you weren't the religious one."

"I'm not. Come, let's walk off that terrible memory together. I have something to show you that will explain things better than words ever could."

A.J. followed Dian from the conference room and into a long winding corridor that sloped downwards toward the heart of the mountain. He was grateful for the distraction from the turmoil of his feelings about Brighed. He kept seeing Thomas' face contorted with fear as Brighed, her eyes filled with rage, so effortlessly cut his throat. His own memories and tragedies of war threatened to steal his mind away, and he dug his nails into his palms to keep himself present.

"I can see my sister has had a great effect on you," Dian offered sympathetically. "I am disappointed in her behavior, but I'm not really surprised. Using people and crushing their hearts was once a regular hobby when she had power. Love is the cruelest of all torture, and it drives us all to madness from time to time. I should know."

"Yeah, I've met Alice." A.J.'s tone was harsh. He wasn't feeling much sympathy at that moment. "I can see why you'd hate Skinner over her."

"Ah, yes. Alice," Dian said with a sad smile. "Magnificent, isn't she? I must confess that I avoid coming to Falia if I can help it for fear of running into her again, but I bear no ill will toward Mr. Skinner. In fact, I quite admire the man for his integrity and honor. Such things are rare in the Incog world, and I'm quite certain they are why Alice loves him so dearly. It is just that I too love Alice. I have loved her since she was a child. She is an extraordinary and rare creature, even for the Queendom. You see, Alice is Margaret's daughter."

"Say what?" A.J.'s surprise overwhelmed his melancholy. "Her daughter?"

"Yes. As for Margaret, she is one consciousness but many bodies, each with its own animal needs and tendencies. The knowledge is all in one mind, but you'll notice differences in appearance and temperament for each one. She does take lovers and spouses from time to time, though it is a truly rare individual who can survive a relationship with a thousand women in one. As far as I know, Alice is Margaret's only child, but as I said, Margaret shares with us what she chooses and nothing more."

"Her daughter," A.J. repeated the news slowly, seeing their similarities in his mind. "Is she like Margaret?"

"No. She is more like Brighed or you or me, but she does have a mental connection to her birth mother. I suspect it is why Mr. Skinner was able to reach you so quickly that night in the storm. It sounds like he was just in time."

A.J. shuddered at the memory. "So, what is your deal with Skinner then?"

"It is an emotional weakness, I'm afraid to admit, but that is the truth of the matter. As Alice grew into womanhood. I fell in love with her as so many others did. She is kind and brilliant and funny. She made me laugh when I thought I had forgotten how. Our marriage was arranged, but I gave her my heart because she is magnificent. Unfortunately, she gave hers to an Incog marine in a jail cell. I was devastated, and I admit that I did not react with much grace for my loss at the time. For that I am forever ashamed. So, now I avoid seeing either of them, not because of ill will toward either, but because it is too hard for my heart to bear. I have so much responsibility in my position, you understand, and seeing them is too, well, distracting."

Dian's face looked like A.J. felt. He could identify with the desire to never again have to see Brighed. For some reason he wanted to make Dian feel better right then.

"You and Alice will both outlive Skinner by centuries. There is still plenty of time for you two, isn't there?"

"Thank you for the kind words. Unfortunately, Alice does not love me, and I doubt she ever will. We are too different, and while Queendom politics are subtle, they are also unrelenting. She chose an Incog human over me, and leaders of the Queendom are not rewarded for being second best, especially to an Incog. No, I think it will be a long time indeed before our two stars align, if ever."

Dian straightened his shoulders and shook off his melancholy look. "It doesn't do to dwell on such things. We must focus on our future."

They crossed a corridor where Dwarfs of various professions, some bearded, some not, moved with purpose toward their destinations. A cart selling sausages and beer was parked at the intersection, serving a long line of impatient patrons. A group of bearded Dwarfs in aprons with the image of an engineer's measuring gauge over a gear were arguing with a D'Anu woman with a glowing deep-red aura.

A.J. was awestruck by the marvel of engineering that it must take to maintain the massive Dwarfhold.

"How can all of this exist without the rest of the planet knowing about it? Is there some kind of magic spell you people have cast over the world?"

Dian laughed. "Magic spell? Oh, no. Nothing so fantastical as that. Besides, magic on that scale is no longer viable in this age. No, it is our seclusion that protects us, and our rules, but they are hardly necessary. It turns out the vast majority of Incogs don't want to know we exist. The truth of our existence, of our genetic differences, would undermine too many assumptions Incogs make about their own superiority, and their cognitive dissonance will never allow them to accept that we are here among them."

"Even when one or a few of us expose ourselves, Incogs will go to great lengths to explain away the experience as a hallucination or momentary delusion. Their occasional encounters with Shifters and other Queendom citizens become faery tales and myths. Consider your own skepticism even now, even after all you have seen and experienced these past few days. It is a curious evolutionary trait of modern humans that they will not see what their egos refuse to accept as possible. It's all very convenient for us."

"Convenient?" A.J. laughed. "An entire society hidden by convenience... I can't even use the word 'unbelievable' anymore. It's all just...incredible."

"There is more to this wild and mysterious world than is sold to you on television," Dian laughed. "Ah, here we are."

Dian stopped in front of a black steel door with the same kind of molecular lock A.J. had seen Digger use. Dian gripped the handle, waited for the lock to disengage, and then pulled it open. Beyond it, the smooth marble walls of the corridors gave way to a hallway of bare rock and low ceilings that sloped down and curved to the right, out of sight. The air was hot and dry, and A.J. felt it press against his skin in slow, rhythmic pulses like a heartbeat.

"What is this place?" A.J. had to speak up to be heard over the deep, thrumming sound.

"This is the answer to many of your questions," replied Dian.

They strolled down the sloping hallway and both the sound and pressure of the air pulsing against him slowly grew louder and stronger.

"The First Age of humankind was real, and it was an age of magic and science with technologies far different, and, in some cases, far advanced of what we have even now," said Dian. "We also know that the First Age came to a violent and abrupt ending."

"If you say so," A.J. replied. "I take it you don't buy the whole Magnivald story though, do you?"

"Brighed is the religious one in my family, I'm afraid. She is a true believer in the old stories that the Goddess Anu created humans who defeated the gods of chaos and brought order to the world, and then destroyed the world in a war against the Anu'nakki. I am much more pragmatic than my sister, however. I prefer science and evidence over faith. Our existence, our technology, and the artifacts we have from that time are simple evidence of the First Age, but all the greatest lies of history have some elements of truth to them. Such is the lifeblood of religion."

"That's a truth," A.J. nodded. "But you still buy the time travel part? Sounds ridiculous to me."

"What was it the famous author wrote? Any sufficient technology is indistinguishable from magic. You've witnessed the power of the Mist Gate yourself. It is one of the few technologies remaining from the First Age that we still employ on a regular basis, but time travel is not something it can do, and technically speaking is not what happened at the end of the First Age."

"Oh yeah? What really happened?" A.J. asked. They were descending in a long looping circle, and A.J. noticed a slight glow to his arms and hands and saw the same on Dian.

"The stories of exactly what happened are varied and conflicting. Some say a war between the gods unleashed chaotic magic upon the world. Others claim the wizard Magnivald had grown so powerful that the Dwarfs needed a magical weapon of equal power to defeat him. Whatever is true has long since lost its relevance. What we do know is the Dwarfs built a massive Mist Gate on the island of Murias in an attempt to gather the world's magic in one place and trap it there. Refugees from the four nations loaded onto every ship that could float and sailed to Murias to escape the war and be close to the magic gathered there. Some say the gate was too powerful and exploded, and the resulting cataclysm was great enough to end the First Age of Humankind in a storm of chaotic magic."

"It wasn't until this Third Age of Humankind that a curious side effect of that Mist Gate explosion was realized. Some of the ships filled with D'Anu, and Shifters, and Drow, and so many other species of our time began to reappear. The Mist Gate had ripped a hole in time and space and this age is where it drained into. A few ships, like those carrying the D'Anu and the Shifters, were still in the waters near where they had begun, while others appeared in other locations, and even at other times all over the planet. For the refugees, very little time passed before they emerged again in the physical world, but the world itself had aged more than a hundred thousand years."

"A hundred thousand?" A.J. was stunned at the thought.

"Apparently," said Dian. "And they did not emerge into an uninhabited world either. Many Dwarfs, humans, and other species of the First Age managed to survive whatever destroyed that civilization, and a Second Age of magic and dragons rose and fell in the time our ancestors were suspended in the mist. Those who survived arrived in this Third Age of humankind in damaged ships to find a civilization still using bronze and pulling carts with asses. The Dwarfs, however, had endured in their Holds with their knowledge of engineering and technology mostly intact. Once they became aware that Mist Gates could do more than trap magic but could serve as transportation devices, they set to work building a worldwide network of them on every continent. The Mist Gates serve a dual purpose. They provide quick transportation all over the planet, and they serve to suppress magic the world over by keeping it concentrated to the lands directly above each gate."

"Why would they want to suppress magic?" asked A.J.

"To keep humans from using it to destroy the world, again."

A.J. and Dian approached a second set of locked doors. This set had a pair of armed guards outside it whose eyes watched keenly as Dian and A.J. approached, but they otherwise showed no movement.

"Now it is my turn to ask you a question." Dian grasped the handle and waited for the lock to disengage. "Imagine leaving this world with all your knowledge of science and philosophy and landing in a world that has almost none of those things. What would you do? Would you abandon all you know and live a primitive life of struggle and face an early death, or would you attempt to share your knowledge with the emerging civilization and make your life more comfortable and likely save millions from needless suffering? I'm not talking about airplanes or televisions, mind you. I'm just talking about basic conveniences such as indoor plumbing and possibly penicillin. What would you do?"

"I guess I've never really thought about it. Though I've lived in a hammock in the woods for most of the last decade, so I may not be the best person to ask."

Dian laughed. "Even so, it's the question our ancestors faced when they arrived on the shores of Ireland nearly four thousand years ago, and it's the question that still divides the D'Anu Queendom to this day. What side do you think you would fall on?"

A.J. didn't have to think about it. He knew the answer. "I would share what I know if I thought it might help people. What others do with the information, whether good or bad, is not my responsibility."

"Ah, a pragmatic answer! That's good. It's also the conclusion the Council arrived at regarding nuclear technology to help the Allies win the world war. But what did they do with that technology? Two decades later they nearly destroyed everything over their petty politics and toxic masculinity. Fortunately, Margaret once again saved the day, but only barely. We came within minutes of the end of the world."

"Now these same Incogs are pouring carbon dioxide, methane, and petrochemicals into the atmosphere at an alarming rate and heating the entire planet, which threatens not only their own civilization but every Queendom refuge around the world as well. They've poisoned the oceans, driven thousands of species to extinction, and don't appear to be appropriately alarmed by the consequences of their greed, which brings us to our present dilemma."

They approached a third set of locked doors, unguarded but heavier than any A.J. had seen yet. He could feel heat radiating through the doors with the steady thrum vibrating the walls around them. Dian lifted a heat shield over a panel sunk into the wall and placed his hand there. A.J. heard the locks disengage on the doors, and they swung slowly toward them as if being controlled by hydraulics. The blast of hot air and near deafening beat of the cycling sound nearly knocked A.J. off his feet.

"What is this place?" A.J. had to yell to be heard over the sound. The heat on his skin reminded him of the desert sun in Iraq, and A.J. had to wrestle his mind to stay in the present. He focused on the anger he felt toward Brighed, and that pulled his thoughts away from the war.

"Quite possibly the solution to all our problems," Dian yelled back. The glow emanating from his skin at this point made him look like an angel. It was difficult for A.J. to stare at him.

Dian led A.J. through the doors onto a wide ledge with smooth stone walls on one side and sheer drop off the other. They approached the edge of the cliff, and A.J. saw they were standing on the edge of a large cavern that extended both below and above them. Fifty meters below them was a wide stone floor on which rested a massive concrete sphere the size of a two-story building, with dozens of long spikes spaced equally over its surface. Heavy cables were attached to the end of each spike, and both the heat and the deep resonant thrum emanated from its core. Dwarfs in heavy clothing and helmets worked on and around the sphere.

A.J. touched the stone wall nearest them, and it felt like glass, smelted over centuries into a smooth, hard surface from the constant heat. Dian waved for A.J. to follow, and they walked along the ledge to another heavy door and entered a much quieter, darker, and cooler hallway that sloped down toward another set of doors. Beyond those was a room filled with screens and meters and a dozen Dwarfs working at computer stations.

"Have a look." Dian motioned toward a window set low in the wall at the front of the room. It was made of thick black glass, and in its center was a bright light. It was like looking at a star through a telescope.

"It's about the size of a basketball up close," said Dian. "Isn't it beautiful?"

"What am I looking at?"

"A stable fusion reaction sparked and contained by Magic. Nearly unlimited energy in a twelve-inch ball of light. No more pollution. No more wars over oil. Clean energy for everyone, with the bonus that it consumes and suppresses magic for a thousand miles or more in all directions and prevents anyone, Incog or D'Anu, from abusing it."

"That's incredible," said A.J. "You guys really could save the planet with this thing. So, what's the problem?"

"What should we do?" asked Dian. "Should we give this power to the same people who nearly destroyed the world last time we offered help? We're talking about a culture that is willing to destroy its own habitat and all life on earth in exchange for such trifles as convenience and greed. Can you imagine what they would do with the knowledge of and access to magic? Do you really think those who have all that power and money invested in burning oil are going to give it up so easily? They will spend their last dime delaying or destroying this knowledge or starting new wars over who controls it. What's worse, such cheap and abundant energy means more population, more consumption, and faster destruction of the Earth's natural resources. The Incog world has yet to demonstrate it can live in sustainable balance with nature. Should we solve one problem only to create so many more that will lead to the same conclusion regardless?"

"I don't know," said A.J. "What's the alternative? You either save the planet or you let it burn."

"You have succinctly summed up the sticking point in current negotiations," replied Dian. "There are many interests to consider in releasing this technology to the Incogs, not least of which are the interests of the Dwarfs. They do control it after all, and they are the only ones with the knowledge of how to create one."

"What are they asking for?"

"A third option," said Dian. "Much more efficient and solves all the problems at once. We kill seventy percent of the Incog population and share this knowledge with the survivors."

A.J. started to chuckle but saw Dian wasn't smiling. "That's insane," he said slowly.

"That's the current offer on the table," said Dian. "Negotiations are fragile. The Isolationists would give the Incogs nothing and leave them to their fate, and the Queendom along with it. The Activists would save the planet and the Queendom, but only on the condition of mass genocide for the Incog population. The Dwarfs are playing both sides off one another to gain the most lucrative outcome for themselves. It is insane, but I don't have to tell you which side of the argument Fergus falls on. That's what is at stake."

A.J. stood stunned in the middle of the control room. The Dwarfs around him worked studiously at their stations and barely took notice of Dian and A.J.

In the maelstrom spinning inside A.J.'s head, an idea sparked and worked its way to the front of his consciousness. "That means Fergus has the strongest motive for the Wendigo to be discovered," A.J. said.

"It would seem so," said Dian. "It would create a panic, force the Council to a vote that he will likely win, and then, most assuredly, he would unleash a global catastrophe."

A.J. felt sick. His entire world had turned inside out more times than he could count in the space of a week. Now he stood next to the solution for many of the world's ills, but he knew Dian was right about what would happen when the world's powerbrokers got their hands on it.

"What are you going to do?"

Dian put a hand on A.J.'s shoulder and smiled broadly. "I think you mean, what are we going to do, dear brother? What are we going to do?"

Chapter Thirteen

Sacrifice

A.J. awoke to an orange and white cat sitting on his chest. The cat purred and kneaded its paws in the blankets, the silver bell on its blue collar jingled in rhythm with its movements. A wood-burning stove pushed the chill from the air in the early morning grayness while a steady rain tapped a rat-tat beat upon the windows.

"Hello, there," A.J. sat up on a long leather couch made into his bed. His stomach growled at the smell of bacon and coffee, and he took a deep breath and stretched without pain, which surprised him. He rotated his arm and felt his ribs for a tenderness no longer there.

Skinner walked in carrying a plate loaded with eggs and a cup of steaming coffee. "Feeling better?" Skinner handed him the plate.

"Yeah." A.J. elbowed the cat away as it tried to take a bite of his eggs. "It's amazing. Yesterday I could barely breathe and now there's no pain at all."

"Brighed certainly knows her magic. We're lucky to have her."

A.J. grunted to acknowledge Skinner's statement, but he didn't feel capable of showing Brighed gratitude at that moment. He changed the subject.

"What did you find at the barn? Anything useful?"

"In the barn? No. Fergus was right. The Wendigo must have holed up there after the accident. There was nothing to suggest it was living there, no spoor, no nest, no bones, nothing but a bit of blood and fur in one corner. It hadn't been there more than a couple of nights. Mason's dogs weren't much help either. They went haywire from the moment we got there. They whined and whimpered and chased a dozen different tracks around that place but got nothing useful. They didn't want to be out there and kept trying to get back in Mason's truck. It was strange."

"This whole valley is strange," said A.J.

"Well, it's strange even for here, but that's not the strangest or most worrisome part. We canvassed the houses and farms near there to ask if anyone had heard or seen anything, but no one was home."

"What, anywhere?"

"Anywhere," said Skinner. "They were all abandoned. We checked on the local general store and the houses around it, and they were empty too. Dozens of Shifters and Dredge alike are missing from that end of the valley, without a trace of where they've gone. The nearest occupied house was up at Bear Creek, and none of the bear clan had seen or heard anything. We gave up looking around midnight, but Connor and Mason are canvassing that whole end of the valley today to get an account of the missing. It's bad, A.J. Something terrible has happened up there."

"You think it's the Wendigo? It turned them all and they killed each other?"

"Where's the bodies? There was no sign of a struggle, much less of a slaughter. No, something else is going on here. I can feel it, I just can't figure it out yet."

"Maybe Alice will find something," said A.J. "Any word?"

"She emailed me last night. The university is on holiday, but she's already made progress in the archives with Seshat's help. Alice says she has news but wants to check it with some of the genetics professors if she can find them. That's about it. How was your meeting with Dian? Anything useful come out of that?"

"Lots, yeah," said A.J. "Just nothing that gets us closer to the killer. Turns out Darcy is the one who talked her dad into going out that night, to save you and Alice no less. She apparently had a vision of you and Alice being killed."

"Us?" Skinner looked shocked and turned paler than usual. "Damn. I guess that explains what he was doing up here. Thank the gods for Darcy and Frank. It's not the first time he's saved my ass. I'm truly sorry it was his last though." Skinner stared at the floor in thought for a moment, then shook his head. "That poor girl. She's had it hard with her mom's death and now Frank's. I should check on her. Anything else?"

"The Wendigo is a fake, but a dangerous one. Everyone thinks Brighed created it, except for Dian, who's betting on Fergus."

"No news there," said Skinner. "Dian would love to see Fergus take the fall for this, but I don't buy it. It's not Fergus's style."

"You think it's Brighed then?"

"Of course not. That makes even less sense. Don't get me wrong, she's capable if that's something she wanted to do, but she's been nothing but good to the people of this valley since the day I arrived here. I can't see her being involved in this. Besides, she nearly got it when that poor fellow changed into a Wendigo right under her nose."

"Morgan made that argument too," said A.J. "Much to the dismay of Aengus and Fergus."

"I would love to have seen the looks on their faces over that," Skinner chuckled. "That son-of-a-bitch Aengus is playing us all for fools though. That boy has something to do with all this, I can feel it in my gut. I thought I'd head back to The Den this morning and see if I can shake it out of him. Care to join me?"

A.J. smiled wide. "Gladly! Are we giving up on the diplomatic strategy?"

"Diplomacy can kiss my ass. I'm getting to the bottom of this today before anyone else goes missing."

"How do you plan on that?"

"Give him the toothpaste treatment. I'm gonna start at his toes and squeeze until I get every last word out of that worthless crook."

"That's the most sense anyone has made in a week." A.J. ran a hand through his greasy hair. "I got time for a quick shower?"

"Sure, I'll clean up. Your pack is by the door."

With one glance at his pack, A.J. felt a deep and painful cramp in his guts. His promise to Malcolm was calling.

"Hey, you okay?" asked Skinner.

"Yeah," A.J. lied. "Fuck the shower. I want this to be over, so I can get out of this valley. Let's go get that son-of-a-bitch."

"That's more like it. I'll get my hat."

They drove toward Rome, and A.J. told Skinner all that had transpired the day before, including his conversation with Dian, though he skipped over the bits about Brighed.

Skinner shook his head in disbelief. "At least Frank's body is safe in Brighed's hands. It makes me sick to know what's happened to him, and I'll be damned if I'm going to let whoever's behind this get away with it."

A.J. asked the question that was burning his stomach. "Could Brighed and Fergus be working together on this? She was awfully deferential to him when he showed up with the Wendigo in his van."

"That's got nothing to do with this. It's true Brighed was suspected of being Magnivald after she resigned from the Council, and there weren't many places she could go in the D'Anu Queendom after that. Fergus has never hidden his dislike for D'Anu politics, but he defended her, and he offered her a place in this valley under his protection. That's why she's here, but a conspiracy? I don't believe it."

"I wouldn't be so sure about that," A.J. mumbled and stared at the passing trees through the click-clack beat of the windshield wipers. No matter how hard he tried to let it go, though, A.J. kept coming to the same conclusion. Skinner's clenched jaw suggested he was having the same struggle.

"Belief's got nothing to do with it," A.J. finally said. "You know that. You also know the question you have to ask if Fergus takes the throne. What does she get out of it? Would it help Brighed get out of this valley? Maybe even back on the Council?"

Skinner clenched the steering wheel and let out a deep relenting sigh. "Yes. To both questions. A departing Counselor gets to nominate his or her successor. That's how Dian got his job, and if Fergus becomes King? He could name Brighed to replace him. They have motive and opportunity. Damn it all, but where's the evidence? Where are the missing people? Where did they create this damnable creature? It can't be in her lab over the Dwarfhold. Digger would have to be in on it, and I'll never buy that she has anything to do with this."

"Doesn't mean there's not another lab someplace. There's a lot more to this valley that meets the eye. You showed me that."

"You could be right, but damn it all to hell."

Skinner drove past Rome's little general store and gas station. The door was chained shut. A hastily painted sign stuck to the outside read, "Closed until further notice." A line of pick-ups loaded with household furnishings and several RVs passed them, headed toward the main highway.

"Looks like the Dredge are clearing out," Skinner said. "So much for keeping the Wendigo attack secret. Everybody knows about it now."

"What about the Shifters and D'Anu?" A.J. asked. "Doesn't the mist keep them in the valley? Where are they going to go?"

"Hunkered down in their dens and houses probably, though some might head into the mound and seek refuge with the Dwarfs, which will be a problem for the Shifters. Dwarfs and Shifters don't really get along."

By the time Skinner passed the lumber mill, he had unbuttoned the holster strap on Miss Polly. A pair of heavily loaded logging trucks were parked crossways at the entrance and a handful of men in heavy coats and assault rifles took cover behind them.

"This is not good. I really wish Frank were still here." Skinner pushed the accelerator to the floor and the old Dodge engine revved as they turned the corner toward The Den.

They saw smoke rising from half a mile away. Skinner pulled into the gravel parking lot as dark clouds billowed out of The Den's end where Fergus's offices were located. A dozen or more men and women fought the blaze with extinguishers and a fire hose stretched from a hydrant in the mechanic's shop.

Morgan moved rapidly among the firefighters, directing their efforts and lending a hand where she could. She saw Skinner and A.J. pull up and ran over.

"What happened?" asked Skinner.

"Aengus," said Morgan. "He's gone berserk. I was at the mill doing the books this morning when Scarlett called in a panic. She said something about Aengus attacking Fergus and a fight, and I could hear it in the background, and then Scarlett screamed and the line went dead. I left some of my guys to guard the mill and found this when I got here."

"Is anyone still inside?" A.J. asked.

"I don't know," she said, but A.J. was already out of the truck. He bolted through the front doors and pulled his shirt up around his nose and mouth in a makeshift mask. Inside the main room, thick black smoke rolled along the ceiling in waves seeking a way up. Heat came from the wall behind the bar. A.J. could see Fergus's office door was warped but still shut, keeping the fire isolated to that end of the building. Paint bubbled off the surfaces, and the wood and timbers at the edges smoldered.

Amongst the tables with chairs stacked on them from the previous night's cleaning, A.J. saw no bodies. He ran across the main room to the small office he'd seen Aengus use, finding it open and in disarray. The door to the office itself was broken and the desk was overturned, but the room was otherwise empty. The bathrooms were empty as well, and so was the kitchen. A.J. coughed from the smoke and headed back outside. That's when he saw the body lying on the floor behind the bar. A shock of red hair told him it was Scarlett, and she wasn't moving. Fergus's cane was clutched in her hands.

A.J. scooped her up, cane and all, and carried her into the rain outside. Wetness on his left arm told him she had a head wound, and her hair was matted with blood.

Skinner met him at the bottom of the steps. "Anyone else?"

A.J. shook his head and Skinner helped him carry Scarlett to the bed of his pickup.

Morgan jumped in and checked her pulse. "She's still alive, but just barely. She needs help right away."

"I'll get her to Brighed," Skinner opened the driver's door, but Morgan stopped him. "Let A.J. take her. I'm going after Aengus. I could use you, and Miss Polly too." Her eyes were hard and determined.

"Wouldn't miss it," growled Skinner. He pulled Miss Polly from her holster and A.J. jumped in the cab.

"Be careful," he said to Skinner as the truck's engine roared to life.

"Not to worry. I've been looking forward to taking this bastard down for a long time." Then he said, "Hold up." A.J. turned to see Morgan helping another man with a broad-brimmed hat and a burned arm wrapped in towels into the truck bed. He took a seat with his back to the cab and held Scarlett in his lap. Skinner slapped the side of the truck, and A.J. punched the accelerator, sending gravel flying.

He reached Brighed's clinic in half the usual time and carried Scarlett through the doors to an exam table. "Get Brighed!" A.J. yelled at Margaret as he passed her at her desk. The clinic was otherwise empty.

Seconds later Digger appeared by Scarlett's side. "What happened?" She checked Scarlett's pulse and shone a light into her eyes. She disappeared for a split second and reappeared next to a supply cart across the room, and then she was gone and suddenly standing on A.J.'s side of the table with a stethoscope. Watching Digger's fast hands examine Scarlett and begin addressing the head wound helped A.J. see that Digger wasn't disappearing and reappearing, she was just moving too fast to be seen.

"Well?" Digger's impatient prompt reminded A.J. of her question.

"Head injury, smoke inhalation, possibly more," A.J. responded. Digger was gone and back in a flash with an oxygen mask she put over Scarlett's face and a pair of clippers to shave the hair away from the wound. Brighed ran into the room, pulling on gloves, and A.J.'s heart burned at the sight of her. He tried to ignore his feelings while she and Digger worked on Scarlett. The images of Dian's memory echoed in his mind, and A.J. struggled with Brighed's own warnings about her brother. A.J. didn't know whom to believe, and his gut instincts were failing him. He watched Brighed work on Scarlett, and she was beautiful in her efficiency and focus. She and Digger didn't speak but worked fluidly together in a dance of hands and scissors and bandages.

Scarlett coughed weakly and opened her eyes. She looked at Digger and Brighed and scanned the room to get her bearings. She began coughing and Brighed pulled a flask from her bag.

"Drink this." Brighed pulled up the mask and tilted the flask to Scarlett's lips. Scarlett spluttered but managed to get a swallow or two down, and the impact was immediate. The color returned to her face, and she breathed easier. Scarlett reached a hand toward A.J., and he took a step closer to clasp it, but she waved at him to step aside. Behind A.J. stood the fellow with the big hat, holding Fergus's cane in his unburned hand. He stepped forward and handed it to her. She pulled it to her chest and tears ran down her cheeks. She tried to talk but her voice was weak.

"It's okay," Brighed soothed her. "Your throat and lungs are damaged from smoke. Don't try to speak."

Margaret led the man to another exam table and pulled the curtain closed between them.

Scarlett looked at Brighed with sad eyes and shook her head, then she managed to croak out a weak, "Fergus..."

Brighed stroked her hair. "Don't worry about that right now," but Scarlett pushed Brighed away and looked at A.J.

"Aengus shifted...attacked," she whispered. "Fergus..." she began crying again.

"Why did Aengus attack?" asked A.J. Brighed shot him a hard look but he ignored her. "Why, Scarlett?"

"Fergus told him..." she coughed again. "Resigning from the Council. Told him...not naming him to the Council. Naming..." A fit of coughing kept her from finishing, and this time blood sprayed from her mouth. Brighed quickly pulled up Scarlett's vest and shirt to reveal a blood-soaked bar towel shoved into a gaping wound from what appeared to be a large animal bite. Brighed pulled out the towel and then quickly replaced it. Her face went white.

"It's okay," Brighed said. "You need rest. Don't try to speak." She gave Scarlett an injection, and Scarlett's eyes fluttered and closed. Brighed shot A.J. a grim look and pulled him aside.

"It's not good." Brighed tried to place a hand on A.J.'s chest and look into his eyes, but A.J. stepped away from her touch. A flash of pain crossed Brighed's face, and then it was gone.

"Can you fix her?" A.J.'s voice was cold and hard. "Can you do your magic and make her better?"

"I'm afraid not. Her pancreas is gone, as is part of her liver and intestines. The towel clotted the blood, and it's the only reason she's still alive, and I'm surprised even at that. She should already be dead. It's just too much damage, even for me to fix. I'm sorry. All I can do is make her comfortable."

A.J. slammed his palm into the wall and tore back the curtains to the exam table across the way. The man he'd arrived with was sitting and holding his wide-brimmed hat crumpled in one hand while Margaret applied Brighed's salve to his burns.

"What happened?" A.J. demanded. "Who are you?"

The man cowered. "I'm…I'm Old Tom. I'm in Seline's clowder from down the crik'. I work the kitchen at The Den. Miss Scarlett got me the job." The whiskers on his face were cat-like, and his two eyes were different. One was brown and human, but the other was cloudy and slit like a cat's. A.J. realized Old Tom was blind on that side, the same side as his burned arm.

"I was gettin' ready for the mornin' breakfast, cuttin' taters and the like, when I heard a ruckus comin' from the main room, but it wasn't nuthin' unusual. Aengus is always a-yellin' and carryin' on, except this time I heard bangin' on the walls and a terrible crash like nuthin' I'd heard afore."

"Did you check on it?" A.J. demanded.

Old Tom just looked at the floor and shrugged. "I guess I shoulda. But I just hunkered down and kept workin'. It's usually best to stay outta Aengus's way when he's in a huff. Then I heard growling and yelpin', like they'd shifted and was fightin' something fierce, and then I heard a terrible scream, and then things got real quiet for a bit, so I stuck my head out the kitchen and saw smoke comin' from under Fergus's office door." Old Tom trembled.

Margaret put a hand on the old cat's face like a mother calming a frightened child.

"I ran over to the door and opened it to see if anyone was inside," Old Tom continued. "I burned my hand on the handle, and when I opened the door, fire shot out at me and

I put up my arm to block it. Then I pulled the door closed again and got outta there. I ran over to Willie's car shop to get help…and…is Miss Scarlett gonna be okay?"

Tears streamed down his cheeks and washed trails through the ash. "I didn't see anyone else when I ran out, but I didn't search neither. Oh gods, maybe if I'd looked harder…If Miss Scarlett dies because I ran…I'm so sorry." Old Tom broke down in sobs.

Old Tom's misery softened A.J.'s fury. A.J. had danced his own dance with death, smelled it, tasted it, and even caused it more times than he cared to recall. Death walked with A.J. like a shadow over his shoulder with a chain around his heart. He'd held friends who lay gasping with their life blood staining the desert sand, and in the darkness of his mind he knew Scarlett's death would be just another scar on his already tortured soul. But Old Tom knew nothing of that life. Here was a gentle fellow, grateful for the small kindnesses of a generous girl who helped him find pride in a simple job. He'd never known war nor experienced the dark panic of exploding mortar shells in the dead of night, killing those you cared for, or been forced to listen to their anguished screams or their mewling, desperate cries for their mothers as they lay dying.

Then A.J. did something he'd hadn't done in years, not since the desert heat had burned the last shreds of his sympathies to cinders. He stepped over to the sobbing man and held him in his arms, feeling the thinness of Old Tom's body as it shook against his chest. A.J. kissed the man on the top of his head where the thin gray hair had long since stopped growing.

"You could not have saved her." A.J. looked in Old Tom's good eye and spoke with the authority of a man who knew the truth of a thing. "She's already dead, her body just doesn't know it yet. You did the right thing, Old Tom, you got yourself to safety and you went and got help. That takes courage. You did everything right and nothing wrong, and as sure as I'm standing here holding you in my arms, I promise…"

"*A.J. No!*" Brighed's mind screamed out to A.J.'s, but he locked his thoughts down and shoved her out. A.J. had sworn he'd never make another promise, but even with Malcolm's promise still weighing on his heart, he knew it was right to make this one, not just to Old Tom, but to himself.

"I promise you," A.J. continued over Brighed's protests. He could feel her mind hammering against his own willpower keeping her out. "The wolf that killed her will lay dead at my feet. You have my word on that."

Brighed gasped. "A.J., what have you done?"

Old Tom lifted his head and looked A.J. in the eyes, then nodded and pushed A.J. away, letting Margaret resume her treatment of his arm. A.J. turned to see Brighed staring at him with a mix of astonishment and pain. He wanted to rage at her for her intrusion into his mind, for the way she used that connection to manipulate him. He wanted to tear at her soul for Thomas who was slaughtered at her own hand. He wanted to scream and pound his fists upon the walls at the fate of his life that brought him to this moment of anger and heartache and pain. He spent a decade walking alone in peace so that he never again would know such dark anguish, yet here it was, just as deep and dreadful as it ever was, and perhaps more. He could feel death's cold breath in his ear, laughing at him like a con man laughs at a fool.

A.J. embraced that coldness. He let it permeate his mind and body, driving the emotions into a closet in his heart where he sealed it with ice. There would be time to mourn Scarlett. There would be time to open that closet and deal with Brighed and his heartache and his anger, but for now,

A.J. had a mission again. Like putting on a favorite coat, he had a purpose. He was going to kill a werewolf. Everything else would wait.

"Wake her up." A.J. gave Brighed a cold stare.

Brighed frowned. "I don't think that's such a good—"

"Wake her!" He pushed past Brighed to stand next to Scarlett. Her face was peaceful, and A.J. hated himself for taking that from her. He gave Brighed another hard look, and Brighed hesitated before nodding to Digger, who took a syringe from a plastic wrap and a bottle from Brighed's bag to give Scarlett a shot.

In moments, Scarlett's eyes fluttered open, and her breathing became more labored in the oxygen mask. She looked around the room in brief panic, then seemed to remember something and laid her head back into the pillow, clenching her jaw in pain.

"Scarlett, do you know what happened to you?" A.J. asked softly. He picked up her hand and held it in both of his.

Scarlett nodded and tried to raise her head to look at her wounded side, but the effort was too much.

"Who bit you?" A.J. asked. "Was it Aengus?"

She nodded again.

"Did Aengus kill Fergus?" Scarlett still gripped the old wolf's cane, and she squeezed it against her chest and cried, but she only shrugged her shoulders in answer. She didn't know.

"Okay, it's okay," A.J. reassured her. "Just one more question, and it's really important." Scarlett nodded, and A.J. glanced at Brighed before he asked, "Scarlett, who did Fergus tell Aengus he would be naming to the Council?"

A.J. felt the room grow cold around him, and he knew without looking that it was coming from Brighed. He didn't look at her, and he wouldn't suggest her to Scarlett. He needed a clear answer without influence so he would know it was true. Scarlett looked from A.J. to Brighed and back again, and tried to speak, but the mask made it difficult to hear. A.J. pulled it off her face, making Scarlett breathe even harder, trying to get oxygen into her damaged lungs and body. He was torturing her, but he needed the truth.

"Who did he name, Scarlett? Please."

Scarlett forced herself to take a slow deep breath and said in a voice hoarse with pain. "Morgan. He is naming Morgan." The effort exhausted her, and she sank her head back into the pillow. A.J. put the mask back on her and looked at Brighed in surprise and remorse. She was glowing again, ice blue this time. She returned his gaze with cold anger and betrayal, and A.J. returned the same.

Scarlett pulled at the mask again, trying to speak. "Morgan…" she said in gasps. "Danger."

"It's okay," A.J. calmed her. "Morgan is safe. She's with Skinner and they've gone after Aengus for what he's done."

This panicked Scarlett. She began coughing and shaking her head, and A.J. held her hand tight until she could speak. "No! No…can't…It's…" but a new bout of coughing kept her from finishing. She looked at A.J. with fear in her eyes, gripped his hand and forced out the word, "Trap!"

A.J.'s blood went cold. "What do you mean? What kind of trap?" but Scarlett didn't answer. A.J. felt her hand go cold.

Scarlett took a final breath and looked at A.J. once more and her eyes went wide, as if seeing him for the first time. "Oh!" she managed to whisper in surprise, and she smiled. "You're…it's…you!" They were her final words in this world. Her grip tightened, and then she was gone. The light faded from her eyes and her chest stopped moving. A.J. placed her hand by her side and turned away.

Brighed's stare was hard, but she didn't speak. She stepped to Scarlett's side and closed the eyes with her fingers.

"I'm going after Skinner and Morgan," A.J. said, turning to leave.

Digger blocked his exit. "I'm coming with you. You'll need help and weapons. I have to go to my lab. I'll meet you in the truck." She was gone again in a flash, leaving him alone with Brighed.

A.J. didn't want to look back at her. He knew he was wrong about Fergus naming her to the Council, but that didn't mean she wasn't helping the old wolf in exchange for his continued protection. He also needed to keep his distance. His heart longed desperately for her touch again, but he could not unsee or un-feel what he had witnessed, and he needed time to think, time that he did not have at that moment. In truth, A.J. knew he was afraid of Brighed, not for what she had done to Thomas, but for what she had done to him. She had made him feel again, made him want to love again, made him want to care for someone besides himself again, and that path in his life was filled only with heartache and pain. Too many thoughts crowded his mind. Was he using her slaughter of Thomas as an excuse? Maybe. He'd killed before too, and in much the same way, but never a child. That didn't mean children didn't die in the wars he fought. Was he any better?

"A.J...." Brighed's thoughts sliced through the storm in his mind, but he refused to reach back. "A.J.," Brighed spoke softly. "A.J., look at me."

A.J. lowered his head but didn't turn around. He stared at the floor, waiting for her to speak.

"A.J.," she said again with pain in her voice. "Whatever Dian told you..."

"It's what he showed me,"

"Oh?" Brighed seemed surprised.

A.J. felt the now-familiar brush of her mind.

Show me…

A.J. let her in, and Brighed's thoughts mingled with his own. He thought he was prepared to handle that, so he could show her what he'd seen, to demand an explanation. What he wasn't prepared for was feeling her feelings of sadness and despair and anguish, so deeply powerful and pure, it was like standing next to the sun. It nearly destroyed him. He grunted from the shock as it dropped him to his knees. His hands found the cold hospital floor, and that coldness gave his reeling mind something to hold onto. It's the only thing that kept A.J. from passing out.

The flood of feelings eased considerably as Brighed quickly drew back, and he felt their connection weaken. A.J. summoned all the strength he could draw from the rage at the world he held in his heart and managed to refocus on Dian's memory. The details of the environment were lost to him, but the crazed look in Brighed's eyes and the shock in Thomas' as she drew her blade across his throat were seared into his mind's eye. All of A.J.'s anger and fury and sadness threatened to spill out through the crack he'd opened. He clenched his jaw until he thought his teeth might break and ignored the streams of tears running down his cheeks. He breathed heavily through his nose and focused on a single flake of glitter entombed in the epoxy floor as he fought to drive those feelings back into their cage like a lion tamer with a whip and chair.

A.J. felt Brighed's connection break like slamming a door on his mind, and it helped pull him back from the brink. He could feel a coldness falling on the room, and when he glanced up, Brighed was surrounded by a white-blue light that made her eyes shine like daggers of ice.

"Are you going to tell me that memory wasn't real, that it didn't happen?" A.J.'s voice was hoarse and showed more pain than he wanted it to. He climbed slowly to his feet and faced her.

"No," she whispered. "It happened just as he showed you."

The door closed in A.J.'s heart, and he sealed it with ice. He took a deep breath and squared his shoulders. So that was it, then. Now he knew who she was.

"Dian can only share what he has actually witnessed," she continued. "He doesn't have the ability to create false images and feelings in another's mind. He lacks…"

"What? The skill?" A.J. challenged her.

"The poetry," she replied. "But that's not the whole story either."

"It never is," he said sharply, ending the conversation. He had no interest in her justifications.

An uncomfortable silence hung between them. A.J. wanted to scream at her, and he also wanted to hold her, to comfort her and himself through their touch, and he could sense she wanted the same, on all counts, but neither of them spoke nor moved. The Dodge truck's horn blared from the parking lot. Digger was waiting.

"I have a job to do," A.J. said as he turned to walk away. "Don't get in my way," he whispered, but those words were directed at his own demons rather than her.

Chapter Fourteen

All Hell Breaks Loose

Digger was waiting for A.J. in Skinner's old Dodge. He climbed in beside her and the strangest rifle he had ever seen. It was nearly as long as Digger was tall, with open sights and an ebony black stock that was oddly short compared to the long steel barrel. It looked heavy. The weight of it pressed deep into the seat.

"That's for me," said Digger. "These are for you." Digger picked up a black bag from the floor of the truck and sat it on the seat between them. She unzipped it to reveal a pair of strange-looking weapons and a small glowing flask of Brighed's draft.

"What are they?" he asked.

"This one is a gas-powered tranquilizer pistol, in case you come across any non-Aengus wolves out there. It's still a crime to murder Shifters, even the evil ones. You have six darts. One will bring down a Shifter in a matter of seconds. Be careful not to shoot yourself. It will only put a Shifter to sleep, but I doubt a D'Anu would survive such a large dose."

A.J. picked up the one with a pistol grip beneath a small gas tank and long barrel. It was top heavy and cumbersome, but it felt good to have a weapon in his hands. "And that?"

He motioned toward the other one, which looked like a steel pipe with one end modified into a crude handle with a heavy looking spring trigger.

"A last resort," Digger said. "One shot, but big enough to take the head off a Wendigo at close range. It's not accurate beyond a few yards, so you'll have to wait until it gets close."

"Great."

Digger looked A.J. up and down critically. "And you probably want to use both hands."

"Well, let's hope it doesn't come to that." A.J. started the engine and headed toward The Den. He clicked on the police radio mounted under the old steel dash and grabbed the handset.

"Connor, it's A.J. Do you copy? Over." He paused a few seconds and then repeated it. "It's urgent. Over."

Connor responded, "Connor here, go ahead. Over."

A.J. breathed a sigh of relief. "Connor, we need back-up at The Den right away. Skinner and Morgan are in pursuit of Aengus for assault and arson. Over."

"Roger that. I'm fifteen minutes out. Over."

"Make it ten. All hell's breaking loose and Skinner may be headed into a trap. Over."

"Ten-four. En route. Over and Out."

A.J. hung the handset back on the radio and recalled the last time he'd used one, screaming for help in the pouring rain with no idea what was happening around him. He wished he'd chosen a different forest in a different state to spread Malcolm's ashes, but the thought of facing Aengus motivated him to drive faster. Confronting that murderous wolf was a cold pleasure he would not be denied, no matter how long it took.

Rome was deserted. The big trucks were still stationed at the entrance to the mill, but only one guard stood duty. No loaded pickups or RVs streamed past. The fire at The Den was out. Several scorched pieces of furniture had been dragged into the rain. One end of the building was little more than a black husk, but they'd saved the restaurant itself from further damage.

"Something is wrong here." Digger strained to see over the dashboard. "Where is everyone?"

Save for the sodden detritus of the fire dripping in the rain, there was no movement anywhere. None of the Shifters who were battling the blaze were around. The mechanic shop's bay door was open, but it was otherwise empty. A.J. killed the engine and an eerie silence descended on the parking lot.

"Maybe they're inside?" Digger asked hopefully.

A.J. rolled down the window so he could listen to the world. He smelled charred wood and fir trees and moss and rotting vegetation. The rain eased to a light mist, and the engine popped and sizzled as it cooled. Nothing else made a sound. A.J. wished Miss Polly were still strapped to the driver's door, but Digger's heavy revolver was better than nothing. He got out and walked cautiously toward The Den. The inside was as he had left it, empty, with the dank smell of heavy smoke. He walked around the end of the building and looked on the other side. There was no one.

A.J. turned back toward the truck and shrugged at Digger, who frantically pointed at the tree-line behind him. As he turned, the sounds of a large animal crashing through the trees made him step backward in fright, lifting the dart gun just as a brown Timberwolf sprang from the undergrowth almost on top of him. He yanked hard on the trigger, expecting the beast's jaws to sink into him, but no bite came. Instead, the wolf leapt over him, and A.J. saw why as he hit the ground. Another wolf, big and grey, leapt after the first, chasing it down and snarling.

A.J.'s dart had caught the Timberwolf on the inside of the back thigh, and it took three more long strides before its nose plowed into the mud and slid to a stop. A.J. rolled over to bring the tranquilizer pistol up on the big grey wolf, too, but it ignored him, rushing after its prey. The unconscious Timberwolf shifted back into human form, revealing a gray-bearded man lying in torn and muddy clothing on the wet ground. The grey wolf shifted too, and in its place a cinnamon-skinned, muscular woman stood over the Timberwolf, her heavy breath coming out as a cloud of mist in the cool wet air.

"Nice shot," she said as he got off the ground. "Saves me the trouble of chasing this one halfway across the valley. I'm Mayari, who are you?" She was broad faced and beautiful, with almond-shaped eyes and long dark hair. She stared critically at A.J. assessing whether he was friend or foe.

The sound of something much larger than the wolves crashed through the undergrowth in the trees behind them, and A.J. lifted the gun again, but Mayari put her hand on his arm to stop him. A large red bull loped out from the trees, blowing hard through its black nose. Its sharp horns curved forward, and its eyes were red as hot coals. When it saw Mayari standing with A.J., it shifted into human form, revealing a massive man in a t-shirt and jeans who loomed over them both. He was at least a half foot taller than A.J. with broad, muscular shoulders. His head was shaved, and he was as thick at the waist as he was in the chest. His large block frame rested on thighs the size of tree trunks, and it looked as though he could crush coal into diamonds with his bare hands.

"My partner, Bull," said Mayari. "And once again, you are?"

Mayari slid a long steel blade free of its scabbard. She looked skeptically at A.J. and glanced toward Skinner's truck, which looked empty.

"My name is A.J." He raised his hands defensively. "I'm no one, really."

Bull stepped between them facing Mayari. "I've seen him before. He's the stranger D'Anu who showed up here with Skinner the other night. He's the one who took down three of Aengus's trash-pack with Connor."

Mayari smiled and re-sheathed the sword. "Well done, then! Now you've taken down a fourth. You should be in pest control. Bull, please secure our friend there and see that he gets to the barn with the others."

The big Shifter picked the snoring man up by the waist and tossed him over his shoulder, then marched back into the woods the way they had come.

Mayari began combing out her long black hair with her fingers. "Call me May," she said.

A.J. looked around. "I was here earlier when the pack was fighting the fire, but now it's a ghost town. Where is everyone?"

"Word spread fast about the Wendigo attack, or whatever those things are, and we've heard about the disappearance of the Beaver clan and others down the valley. Add that news to what happened between Fergus and Aengus this morning and most folks have bugged out till things blow over. Aengus's crew has been pushing him to challenge Fergus for some time, and they're trying to take advantage of the evacuation to settle some scores with Fergus's allies, like us. Bull and I have a small farm down the road, and that fellow you just tranq'd and a few of his buddies showed up demanding allegiance to Aengus or else. We found their terms acceptable. We chose else."

"I can see that," A.J. nodded in respect. "This evacuation… Where is everyone going?"

"The Dredge have all loaded up and driven out, but the Shifters and D'Anu can't get out of the valley without going through the Dwarfhold. There's still plenty of us who would rather take our chances with Aengus and those monsters, though. I'd say half the town is hunkered down in their homes and dens. I should probably go check on Selena and her clowder. They'll be a target, for certain."

"Tell her Old Tom is with Brighed," said A.J. "He's hurt, but he's safe."

May looked relieved. "That's good. What about Scarlett? I heard she was injured too."

A.J. shook his head and stared at the ground trying to keep his emotions from rising again. May stopped combing and her eyes filled with tears.

"I'm sorry," A.J. whispered. "There was nothing we could do."

May cried out in despair, and shifted into her wolf and ran a short distance away. She raised her head and let out a long mournful howl that echoed off the surrounding forest and threatened to pull the sorrow from A.J.'s heart. He clenched his jaw to hold it down.

The sounds of May's howls were taken up by other wolves elsewhere in the forest. Some were solemn and sad like hers, but others, close by, sounded higher and challenging.

May shifted back and approached A.J. "Scarlett was my friend, and she was well liked in this valley. This will not go well for Aengus and his pack." Another challenging howl sounded closer, and May put her hand on A.J.'s shoulder and walked him toward the pickup. "It's not safe here. You'd best return to Falia. There will be war this night, and it will be dangerous for D'Anu and Dredge to be outdoors."

"Can't do that." A.J. pulled open the door. "Morgan and Skinner are in danger. I need to find them."

May stopped moving and stared into the cab at Digger.

"What, never seen a Dwarf before?" Digger cocked her head in defiance.

"Never topside," May answered. "The world is truly turning upside down today."

A.J. climbed into the truck and leaned out the window. "Where would Morgan and Skinner have gone to find Aengus? Before she died, Scarlett said they were headed into a trap. I need to find them."

"Aengus and his pack have turned the old mill into a second Den of sorts. It's not the kind of place a decent wolf would be caught dead, but it's where I'd start if I were you. Take the road about half a mile up the mountain and turn south. Follow it until it dead ends. You can't miss it." The sounds of howling grew closer. May looked over her shoulder and back at A.J. "Drive quickly, and whatever you do, don't get caught outside after dark. We'll get as many residents as we can to the Dwarfhold for evacuation. Maybe we'll see you there. Good luck." May turned and leapt, shifted in midair, and disappeared into the trees.

A.J. radioed Connor with their new destination and found the old mill road without trouble. It was narrow and wound between trees and around the hillsides as it snaked down the valley wall. The road was longer than A.J. expected, and the forest grew denser and closer the farther they drove. Between the overcast skies and towering trees, it was nearly dark along this stretch. The forest grew wild here, with large ferns blanketing the forest floor and fallen trees rotting where they lay.

Digger stared open-mouthed at the giant firs and ash and cedars that towered above them, and she stuck her head out of the window to see their tops.

"Don't get outside much?" A.J. kept a careful eye on the trees as well, but he was watching for danger while Digger seemed awestruck at their height.

"Everything worth finding is underground," she responded as if explaining it to a child. "Besides, open spaces make me nervous. They're hard to defend and the weather is inconsistent. I don't know how humans live up here without going crazy. It's pretty to visit, though."

"Most humans would say the same thing about caverns."

"That's because they are stupid. Well, most of them anyway," she nodded toward A.J. as if giving him a fine compliment.

They rounded another curve and the dense forest opened on a small valley. The trees were less dense here, but there were still plenty of them. The road curved toward an old timber mill on the valley floor, with a large open area around it where logs used to be stacked for milling. Now it looked like a junkyard and was filled with broken-down vehicles rusting in the rain, assorted trash, and a few ancient RVs rotting in place. A thin trail of smoke drifted out of a long narrow stack on the old mill building.

A.J. pulled off the road next to an open cliff face above them and killed the engine. He sat staring at the building and settled down in his seat to wait.

"What are we doing? Shouldn't we go in?" Digger asked.

"We're waiting for Connor. If it's a trap, then rushing in there with guns blazing is only going to get us caught in it too. We need back-up, so we wait, and we watch."

"I have a better idea." Digger climbed out of the truck and pulled the big rifle out with her. She slung it across her back and began climbing.

"What are you doing?" A.J. asked her.

"Getting a better view." She climbed the near vertical and wet cliff face as easily as if she were crawling along the ground. It was A.J.'s turn to crane his neck upward, watching Digger move with astonishing speed until she found a nook near the top where she settled in.

Connor pulled up a few minutes later and joined A.J. inside the pickup.

"Anything?" Connor asked. A.J. looked like a skinny kid in oversized clothing, but he was glad he was there. He thought Connor's other form would likely come in handy before the day was through. Unfortunately, he didn't have to wait that long.

They jumped as a rock bounced off the top of the cab. A.J. leaned out of the driver's window to look up at Digger, who was pointing toward the trees to the left of the old mill. A.J. stared hard in that direction but didn't see anything. Then a flash of movement caught his eye. A black speck emerged from the tree line. It was a wolf running hard toward the old mill, its head low in exhaustion.

"That's Morgan," said Connor. "What's she running—"

A thundering blast from Digger's rifle high above their heads made their ears ring. A.J. feared Digger was shooting at Morgan, but a half-second later a Wendigo emerged from the trees behind her, its powerful arms and legs propelling it forward, chasing her down. Even from the long distance A.J. saw its head explode as Digger's round caught it square in the face. A large brass shell clanged into the bed of the pick-up.

"Holy shi—"

Another blast from above obliterated all other sound. A second Wendigo emerged from the tree line, followed by a third. The one in front experienced the same fate as the first Wendigo, but the one behind it altered course back toward the tree line as a third shot rang out from Digger's perch. A tree exploded where the Wendigo's head would have been as it ducked back into cover.

Morgan heard the shots and saw the vehicles, and she found new energy to leap forward toward the truck. She would have to pass through the stacks of junk and old cars to reach them, but two more Wendigos emerged from the trees on an angle to cut off her path. Digger fired two more shots that missed them both as they used the rusted vehicles for cover.

Connor jumped out of the truck and ran toward Morgan, while A.J. yelled after him, "Don't let them scratch you!"

Connor raised a hand in acknowledgment and changed form. A.J. thought he looked comical in his stretched-out deputy uniform with black fur sticking out of the seams, but the speed with which Connor raced into battle was impressive. A.J. picked up the length of pipe with the handle on one end and felt its weight heavy in his hand. He left the tranq revolver on the seat. It would do him little good against these creatures. He stuck the pipe weapon under his belt and, as an afterthought, shoved the small flask of Brighed's draft in a pocket too. He climbed out of the cab, watching the trees for signs of more Wendigos, and saw a third rush into the junkyard from the left.

Connor swiftly closed the distance between himself and Morgan. The two closest Wendigos were almost on her, and Morgan darted to one side at the last moment to avoid their lunging grasps. The big gun fired again and the creature closest to Morgan lost its head.

Morgan altered course again and slid under the swiping arm of the nearest monster and got to her feet just as Connor reached her. In one motion, Connor ripped a steel axle from a rusting truck frame and swung it high overhead as easily as if he were swinging a feather. The steel hub on the end of the axle caught the pursuing Wendigo in the top of the head and drove it into the earth like a pile driver, crushing the monster's skull and sinking the hub into the dirt below.

Connor turned and ran back toward A.J., following Morgan and covering her retreat. The last Wendigo dove in and out of the piled junk and old cars, keeping cover between itself and Digger's rifle but still pursuing and gaining on its fleeing prey. A.J. ground his teeth, willing Connor and Morgan to move faster, but he could see that the Wendigo was on an intercept path, and there was no clear shot for Digger from her perch. His heart sank into his stomach, but all he could do was watch as it closed in for the kill.

Morgan had one more row of junk to clear, but the Wendigo was there, a flash of its white fur showing in the gaps of old rusted windows. Another blast from Digger's big gun surprised A.J. and caught the Wendigo in the side through a narrow gap between two old pickups, its impact knocking the monster off course as it leapt toward Morgan, missing her by inches, and then she was clear. The Wendigo rolled and flipped in anger from the round in its hip, but Connor was on it before it could get back up. Connor grabbed the Wendigo by one hind leg with both of his big Sasquatch hands and slung the monster in a wide arc, around and then up and over his head, bringing the Wendigo down with all his strength onto the edge of an old steel door sunk halfway in the mud. The force of the swing severed the Wendigo's neck at the point of impact on the top of the door in a kind of reverse-guillotine move.

Morgan made it the rest of the way up the hill to join A.J., shifting back to her human form and collapsing into his arms, gasping for breath as sweat and steam poured off her. Connor joined them a few seconds later, changing back as well. Morgan looked up at the cliff face and waved to Digger in thanks, and Digger responded by dropping another empty shell casing into the truck bed.

"Where's Skinner?" A.J. asked when her breathing had calmed a bit. He wasn't sure he wanted to hear the answer.

Morgan gulped down a couple of breaths before she could respond on the exhales. "Went after... Blue Jean... Don't know..." She took another deep breath. "We tracked Aengus from The Den toward the old mill. I figured that's where he was headed, but about a mile from here, up by the reservoir, his trail went cold. His and Fergus's scent just vanished in the middle of nowhere. Skinner and I circled and backtracked, but we couldn't find them, and that's when I caught the smell of Wendigos. There was at least a half dozen or more, and Blue Jean was right in the middle of them, laughing like he was expecting us."

"Those things didn't go after Blue Jean?" A.J. was confused.

"No! It was like he was controlling them. He pointed at me and said something in Drow, and then those things came after me. Blue Jean ran off, and Skinner took after him. I kept the Wendigos distracted and busy chasing me through the woods to give Skinner time to get clear. Then I made for the nearest cover I knew of at the old mill. I honestly didn't think I was going to make it. Damn, those things are fast." She looked back at the carnage in the junkyard and then at Connor. "Thank you." She hugged Connor's neck, making him blush and smile his giant-toothed grin.

"What happened to Aengus?" A.J. asked her. "Where's the rest of his pack?"

"Don't know. I never thought he would take on Fergus like that, and I know he wants control of the pack, but I never thought..."

A long deep steam whistle from the east reached their ears.

"Four p.m." Connor said. "Shift change."

That gave A.J. an idea. "Morgan, your pack still holds the mill. Can you get there and use the whistle to send out a warning to the valley? Send out an S.O.S?"

"Yes, I think so," she said.

"Connor, get her there fast, and get everyone you can to the Dwarfhold. They'll be safe inside the mound."

"What about you?" Morgan asked.

"I'm going to find Skinner. I'll meet you at the clinic."

"There's less than two hours' light left," Connor said as he and Morgan got into his car. "Don't get caught out here in the dark."

"Everybody's my mother today. Don't worry, I won't be late. Just make sure Rome gets evacuated, along with anyone else you can save." A.J. looked at Morgan. "Are you sure none of those things went after Skinner?" A gunshot sounded from the woods behind the old mill in answer to his question. Connor began to get out of the car, but A.J. shoved the door closed. "I've got Skinner. Now go. Save the rest!"

Connor fired up the cruiser and spun it in a circle to head back down the road. A.J. ran toward the woods where he'd heard Skinner's shot. Digger continued her watch from above.

A.J. was breathing hard by the time he hit the edge of the woods, and he slowed to a steady jog, waiting and listening and watching as he moved. He pulled the pipe weapon from his belt and held it ready. Once he passed the trees, he would no longer have Digger's covering fire, and he didn't want to stumble blindly into a Wendigo.

He pulled out the flask of Brighed's draft and took a heavy swig. He felt the effects flow through him instantly, warming his skin and filling his muscles with energy. The golden light of the D'Anu glowed from his every pore, and his sight and hearing got sharper in the late afternoon darkness of the trees. He took a deep breath and closed his eyes. The faint smell of human sweat and fear drifted across his mind from somewhere to his left, and A.J. sprinted in that direction. His feet barely touched the ground.

The sound of Miss Polly firing made A.J. stop to get his bearings. He listened carefully, his hearing heightened to an acuteness that made it difficult to filter the myriad thousands of sounds in the forest around him, from the bugs crunching through compost beneath his feet to the clacking of leaves in the branches of the trees. He closed his eyes and concentrated, reaching out with his senses for Skinner when the strange feeling he'd experienced in the garage overwhelmed him. In the fog of his mind, the biggest Wendigo A.J. had seen yet came crashing out of the brush, fangs bared and lunging. He felt the Wendigo's long sharp claws penetrate his body as its teeth closed on his throat, and A.J. screamed. The shock knocked him out of his trance, still screaming, and he reflexively swung Digger's pipe gun up in front of him and grabbed the heavy spring trigger with both hands as that huge beast of his vision leapt from the trees and bushes less than three feet from the end of the gun. A.J. squeezed the trigger with all his might.

The explosion was deafening. The powerful blast vaporized the left side of the Wendigo's head and split the steel pipe down the center. For his part, A.J. felt both his arms slam into his shoulders, propelling his body a dozen feet backward through the air to land sliding through the wet fir needles and mud. A.J. felt dizzy and his ears were ringing. It took a moment to get his bearings before he could climb back to his feet.

"Mother...fucker," he groaned, holding his head with numb hands, but the sound of another gunshot to his left cleared his mind and drove him forward at a stumbling run.

A.J. entered a small clearing and saw a dead Wendigo laying on the ground, face first with a large exit hole in the back of its head. Three more muffled gunshots told him Skinner was nearby. Then A.J. saw it. The legs of a Wendigo stuck out of a hole formed from the upturned roots of a big fallen cedar tree about twenty yards away.

A.J. ran to it and peered into the gloom of the rotted tree trunk, fearing the worst. He saw the wet, blood-matted fur of the Wendigo lying motionless on the ground, with one long arm reaching toward Skinner, who was pressed against the moss-covered muck at the back of the damp enclosure. Skinner's clothes were ripped in various places, and a small stream of blood from a cut in his forehead mixed with the rain running down his face, but those fierce blue eyes were shining strong as he raised Miss Polly in A.J.'s direction.

"Don't shoot!" A.J. called out. "Skinner, it's me."

Skinner lowered the gun and let out a chuckle of relief.

"It's good to see you, old man." A.J. handed him the flask of Brighed's draft. "How you feeling?"

Skinner took the flask in his mud-coated hand and pointed Miss Polly at the dead Wendigo with the other. He pulled the trigger, and the hammer raised and fell on nothing. Just a loud click announced that the gun was empty.

"Right now," replied Skinner, "I'm feeling pretty damned glad it was you who came through that hole. I'm assuming that explosion I heard a minute ago was you?"

"Yeah," A.J. took the empty gun from Skinner and reached his arm in to help him out of the dugout. "A little something Digger cooked up."

"Of course," said Skinner and stepped out with a limp. Blood seeped from a deep gash in his right calf. A.J. shook his head at the thought of what that meant, but he could only deal with one problem at a time.

"Think you can make it back to the road?" asked A.J.

"You gonna leave me behind if I can't?"

"Nope, but I'll be fairly annoyed if I have to carry your old ass all the way back to the truck." He slipped an arm under Skinner's shoulder, and they began the trek back through the trees. They only had to stop once for Skinner to catch his breath, next to where the Wendigo A.J. killed was sprawled on the ground with half its head missing.

"By the gods," exclaimed Skinner, staring at the carcass. "Was that what I heard?"

A.J. pointed toward the ruined pipe gun lying in the leaves. "Damn thing nearly ripped my arms off, but it worked."

"I'll say," Skinner whistled and got up. The sound of Digger's rifle firing twice bounced around the trees. "Let's not linger, shall we?"

They stumbled past the bodies of two more Wendigos about 300 yards from the road. Two perfectly placed headshots explained the gunfire. A.J. waved his arm, hoping Digger was looking. A whistle from the cliff face told him the sharp-eyed Dwarf saw them. Three more whistles followed with an urgency that suggested A.J. and Skinner pick up the pace, and the two men hobbled as quickly as possible toward the truck. In the distance, the shift horn at the mill began blowing in short and long bursts, sending out its SOS. Connor and Morgan had made it back.

An angry howl erupted from the trees behind them and was answered by another somewhere to their right. A.J. expected the Wendigos to drag them down at any moment as slowly as they were moving, but after a few dozen steps it became apparent the monsters were choosing to stay out of Digger's range. More howls and screams echoed through the forest, but A.J. and Skinner made it safely to the truck.

A.J. lifted Skinner into the passenger seat and ran around to the driver's door. He shoved the empty Miss Polly into her holster while the old Dodge engine roared to life. The truck rocked as Digger dropped into the bed from her perch. She threw herself against the back of the cab with her rifle against her shoulder, ready to fire. A.J. slammed on the accelerator as he pulled the clutch and the truck lurched backward, throwing up rock and dust around them. A.J. cut the wheel hard and spun the truck around, slamming it into first and accelerating forward in one smooth motion. The sound of Digger's heavy rifle sounded like a bomb exploding behind them, and the rear of the truck slid sideways from the impact of a dying Wendigo slamming into it from the side.

"Drive faster!" Digger yelled through the rear glass, and another boom came from her rifle. A.J. slammed the gears into second and stomped on the accelerator. They careened around the corners and over divots in the old mill road without slowing until the front tires hit pavement at the county road.

"Be a damned shame if you killed us all driving home from the rescue, don't ya think?" Skinner barked at him.

A.J. let out the breath he was holding with an unexpected laugh. Skinner started laughing too, then grimaced in pain.

"Don't laugh" grunted Skinner. "I've still got one good leg to kick your ass with."

This just made A.J. laugh harder. He looked down at Skinner's injured leg and shook his head. "Seems like a lifetime ago that we were sitting in opposite positions. Except that I'm not pointing a loaded Miss Polly at you."

"The evening's still young," Skinner said, looking down at his own leg. "Be careful what you wish for. Now keep your eyes peeled, but let's get to the doc. She needs to hear what I found before..." Skinner left the rest unsaid, and A.J. swallowed hard. He gripped the steering wheel and kept his foot heavy on the gas. Digger kept watch on their rear from the truck bed, but her rifle stayed silent the rest of the way into town.

Chapter Fifteen

Before You Go

As they drove into Rome, the mill's shift horn was still blaring its SOS. A handful of vehicles were parked in front of the two big logging trucks at the entrance, where Connor stood. A.J. pulled up and rolled down his window.

"Good to see you alive!" Connor yelled to be heard over the blaring horn. "I'm sending everyone to take refuge in the Dwarfhold, though Aengus's pack has done a good job of driving most folks away already. Morgan is inside the mill clearing the workers out and shutting things down." He noticed the blood-soaked pants below Skinner's knee and the color drained from his face.

"There's not much light left," said Skinner. "Those damned fake Wendigo creatures are headed this way. Don't stick around here long, and if you see 'em coming, clear out."

"Understood," Connor said glumly. "We're about done here anyway. We'll be right behind you."

"See you at the clinic," A.J. began rolling up his window, but Connor put his hand on the glass.

"Did you catch that bastard Drow, at least?" he asked Skinner.

"Slippery little son of a bitch got away," Skinner responded. "But if you see him, say hey for me, will ya?"

"Gladly!" Conner patted the side of truck to send them on their way.

When they reached the clinic, they found vehicles filling the clinic's parking lot; many were loaded down with their owners' possessions. A.J. pulled into the emergency entrance and Digger helped him move Skinner into the busy clinic, where two Margarets were directing people toward the lifts that would take them to the Dwarfhold below.

"Thank the gods!" Margaret ran over to help Skinner to an exam table, and Digger went to work dressing Skinner's wounds.

"It's a madhouse here," said Margaret. "We're sending everyone down to the Dwarfhold, but the Dwarfs are throwing a fit. They're protesting the evacuation. Dian and Kane are using their Council privileges to get them through, but it's getting pretty tense down there. Dian plans to open the Mist Gate and get everyone to safety as soon as he can coordinate with another Dwarfhold to arrange a direct mass travel." Margaret took one look at Skinner's leg and her face turned white. "Oh gods," she moaned and held Skinner's hand without looking up again. A.J. could see she was crying.

Skinner wasn't looking good either. His face was pale, and he shivered. "It's okay," he said. "Is there one of you in Nalanda right now? Can you talk to Alice? I want to tell her I love her before...."

The dam in A.J.'s heart was breaking. It was one thing to lose Scarlett this day, but losing Skinner too was more than he could bear.

"Tell her yourself," came the sweet voice of Alice stepping into the room. "A little birdie told me you were back, old man, and so am I. Hello, love." She kissed his forehead. "Oh, honey, you're burning up."

Skinner's eyes lit up at the sight of his wife, and he pulled her into his arms and held her tight. Then he broke down and began to cry.

"I'm so sorry, darlin'," Skinner sobbed. "I promised you more time, but this is it, the damned things got me." Alice tried to soothe her husband's grief, holding his head against her heart and kissing his white-haired scalp as tears streamed down her cheeks.

Skinner pulled back and looked at A.J. with grief in his eyes. "I'm gonna need a favor from you. I'm not gonna let her see me change into one of those mutant abominations. You know what you gotta do." He implored A.J. with a look A.J. had seen before, and the dam inside his heart finally burst.

The emotions flooding through him were crippling in their ferocity. Skinner seemed to slide away from him, as if the room suddenly extended into a long hallway, with sounds and sights around him replaced by a memory of another land far away. A.J. felt the fire of a burning Humvee hotter than the desert sun. The smell of blood overwhelmed the smells of burning flesh and steel. Gunfire popped in every direction, and A.J. sat on the blood-soaked ground holding Malcolm in his lap. The IED had been hidden on the side of the road. It exploded when his squad deployed from their Humvees to confront a band of insurgents that ambushed their convoy. RPGs hit the trucks, and smoke and screams and his commander yelling orders were all confusing noises in his head. Malcolm's right leg was missing below the knee, and his right arm ended in a burned stump where his hand should be. The right side of his face had melted too, and A.J. stared at bone and teeth and ragged flesh and into the one eye his best friend had left, imploring him, begging him, to end the pain. Malcolm's left hand scrabbled for A.J.'s sidearm, reaching for his own quick death.

Malcolm was the first person A.J. had ever trusted. He was raised in the system too, and they became best friends right away that first week at boot camp. They trained together and fought together and for the first time in his life, A.J. knew what it meant to love and be loved by another human being. Malcolm was the first man who ever hugged him and meant it, and A.J. sat motionless and stunned in the center of the firefight as Malcolm pleaded for A.J. to end him, but A.J. couldn't find the way. He sat staring at his dying friend without moving while Hell erupted around them. Then his unique prescient instincts warned him another shell was coming. Instead of yelling a warning, instead of diving away, A.J.'s body did the reflexive thing for which he would forever judge himself a monster. He used his dying best friend's mangled body for cover. The shell exploded ten feet away.

A.J. felt Malcolm take the brunt of the blast, but searing hot shrapnel and Malcolm's splintered bones penetrated A.J.'s body and face and neck. It burned with the heat of a thousand suns, and he screamed from the pain and the shock and the anger inside him. He screamed for days, it seemed, even after he'd been rescued, even after the surgery to repair his face and neck. The sound may not have been audible to those around him, but inside his mind and his heart and his soul, it felt like he would scream forever. So, he chose to walk away from a life where such heartache could exist. He wanted no part of a world where such pain and grief were delivered upon the souls of the innocent for no more reason than rich men sending others to kill and die for their greed. Yet here he was again, facing his new friend

Skinner, facing the same fate he faced in the desert that day, and he still lacked the courage to find a way.

"A.J.! Hey, A.J.!" Skinner's voice broke through the fog in A.J.'s mind. "Come here son, I have something to say." With his head bowed low, A.J. stepped to Skinner's side, and the old man took his hand. "I don't know what you're going through, and I wasn't there, whatever happened that sent you down this dark path that haunts your soul. But I know I've been where you're standing, trapped in your own heart and head with no way out. It's not your fault, you know, whatever happened, and I know you've heard that before, but here's what I want to say."

"A.J., you didn't survive whatever Hell you've been through because you're special, you didn't survive because you're D'Anu. There isn't a reason life has worked out this way. There is no fate, there is no luck, and there are no bad decisions in battle if you survived it to live another day. You could have died, but you didn't. You could have changed things, it could have been you, but why live with that torture? It is only yourself that you punish, and you tarnish the sacrifice others made by regretting it wasn't you. The only thing that truly matters in this world is what is right now, and that is you standing here today. Yesterday is a memory, and tomorrow is a dream, and the search for reasons why is a fantasy we chase to justify a trauma that can never be satisfied with reason. The only thing that 'is,' A.J., is now. Right here. Right now. And right now, son, I need you. You know what comes next for me, so I need you. Okay?"

Skinner's words washed over A.J. like a warm bath. "The only thing there is, is now," A.J. repeated. The sounds and smells of his memories faded slowly, and A.J. looked around at the sad faces of the others. Even Digger was staring at the floor and sniffling. A.J. understood it was the only way, and Skinner's words helped. A.J. knew he would never forgive himself for doing it, and even that would be okay. It's just what is. A.J. looked into the fierce blue eyes of his friend and nodded and squeezed the old man's hand. "I'll do it," he said.

"Thanks," Skinner said with relief in his eyes. "And after... after, I want you to have Miss Polly. I want you to take her, and I want you to kill the son-of-a-bitch who did this."

"I wouldn't go giving the family jewels away just yet," said Brighed, walking into the exam bay holding a cloth covered tray. "Alice, I think we're ready."

A.J. and Skinner exchanged confused glances and Alice turned to take something off the tray. When she turned back, she looked at Skinner and clutched his hand to her chest.

"My darling, my dearest. You know that I love you, right?" Alice asked.

"With every ounce of my soul," Skinner said.

"And you know that I would never harm you, right?"

"Of course," said Skinner. "But why—"

Alice swung her free hand with all her strength and plunged a three-inch steel hypodermic directly into his chest and pressed hard on the plunger. Skinner's eyes went wide in shock, and he stared at the syringe for a moment before Alice could pull it free. Then he convulsed.

Skinner's entire body stiffened, with his head thrown back and hips in the air before he doubled over and began to shake violently from head to toe. A dark black liquid oozed from his skin and out of his eyes, nose, and ears. Alice grabbed a steel pan for Skinner to retch into, expelling the same oily blackness that now covered his skin and soaked through his clothes. Brighed shone a UV light on the liquid, which evaporated completely wherever the light touched it.

"Holy mother of mercy, that fucking hurts!" Skinner's voice was loud and clear between his convulsions. "What the hell is happening?"

Alice rubbed his brow with a towel. "Just a little antidote Seshat the Librarian helped me cook up. It has a stimulant, some gene and cell repair serums, and something called liquid UV that Seshat created many years ago. She has quite an impressive laboratory down there, actually—"

"Antidote?" A.J. interrupted her. "What are you saying? Is Skinner going to be okay?"

"Well, I don't know about that, but he's not going to turn into a Wendigo today," replied Alice. "He should be fine in a couple of hours."

A.J. was stunned and delighted, and everyone else began laughing and cheering in relief.

"Will this antidote work on those creatures that have already turned? Can we save the rest of those people from the valley?" A.J. asked.

"I'm afraid not," said Alice. "Once the transformation is complete, it would kill the host completely. It must be delivered within the first two hours, before they change. Fortunately, you got my husband here in time." She gave A.J. a fierce hug. "He's going to be okay. Thanks to you."

"I feel fine," Skinner protested. "In fact, I feel kinda great." He began to sit up, but Alice put her hand on his chest and pushed him back onto the table.

"Not a chance, my dear," she said. "With the stimulants I gave you, you could probably lift a house right now, but I'm not letting you out of my sight until I know for sure this worked. Thanks for being the first test subject, by the way. You always did know how to be exactly what I needed at just the right time." She kissed him.

"How did you know what to use?" A.J. asked Brighed. "How did you make this so fast?"

"I didn't," said Brighed. "Seshat was able to help Alice identify the unknown genetics in the fake Wendigo, and you'll never guess what it is."

"Utukku," said Skinner. "The unknown genetics is Utukku."

It was Alice's turn for her eyes to go wide, and Brighed looked surprised as well. "I hate when you do that," Alice laughed and punched Skinner in the arm. "How did you know?"

"Blue Jean," answered Skinner. "I followed him through the woods after Morgan pulled those Wendigos the other way. He never saw me. I don't even think he was looking. He headed straight for the old mill, and I followed him into the basement. I heard him laughing and bragging about catching Morgan in a trap, but I couldn't see who he was talking to. The furnace was burning and the whole place smelled like death and rotten meat. I tried to get a better view and that's when I saw..."

"Saw what?" asked A.J.

"Mayor Bradley," said Skinner. "He was feeding dead animals to several more Wendigos. I must have made a sound because he looked up and saw me, and that's when I knew. Both Bradley and Blue Jean took on that stupid blank look Bradley gets when Sayah is speaking through him. Blue Jean and Bradley spoke at the same time, in the same voice, staring right at me. I can't see the Utukku, so I ran back toward the light."

"Smart move," said Brighed. "That was fast thinking."

"Not fast enough," said Skinner. "She was on me before I could make it out. I couldn't see her, but she scratched and pulled at me. Her sharp nails tore my clothes and dug into me. She was strong, but I was near the door. I managed to pull it open, and in the flash of daylight I saw her and those rows of needle-sharp teeth just inches from my face. The light drove her off me, and I made it outside. They sent those damn Wendigo things after me, and that's when I heard Digger's rifle. I tried to run toward it, but the Wendigos cut me off. I tried to go around them, and I killed a couple of 'em too, but one got past, and I crawled into that dugout and killed it too, but not before it ripped into my calf, and then A.J. showed up."

"Blue Jean is under the control of the Utukku, and that's how they're controlling the Wendigos. It has to be," said Alice.

"That explains the speed of the mutations too," added Brighed. "And why the dead woman came back to life as it changed. The Utukku's venom doesn't just put their victims under their control, it fundamentally alters their cellular structure to rely on steady doses of the venom but also produces the food that Utukkus need to survive. If someone were to genetically alter how the venom functions, they wouldn't need to create a new Wendigo from scratch. They would only need to inject the mutated venom and let it do the work for them, effectively weaponizing the Utukku venom to spread a virus-based genetic sequence from victim to victim with every new infection…my gods! They could destroy half the world in a matter of weeks if these creatures ever got free."

"I've never heard of an Utukku doing something like this though," said Margaret. "I wasn't even aware they have the knowledge to engineer the genetics like that, but it doesn't explain why she would do it, or why she would do it here. I mean, this isn't exactly a population center."

"I don't know why they chose this valley, but it's no secret the Utukku favor direct intervention in Incog affairs," said Brighed. "What Sayah has done here breaks every D'Anu law there is. Even for an Utukku, it's a bold gamble, and I still don't believe Fergus could be mixed up in something like this. It just doesn't fit his nature."

"He may not be," said A.J. "Aengus is making a play for control of the whole wolf pack and now Fergus is missing. It can't be a coincidence Aengus makes that move the same day the Wendigos are let loose in the valley."

They were interrupted by Conner walking into the exam room looking worried. "Is Skinner okay?"

"Never better," Skinner grinned back from where he lay on the table. "Thanks to a little help."

Connor's drawn face broke into a huge smile of relief. "How?" he stammered. "Thank the gods! I thought I saw—"

"It's okay, I was saved by this sweet bell here," Skinner kissed Alice's hands. "She found an antidote. Did you get everyone out of Rome okay?"

"We waited until the last moment we could. No more cars or people showed up, and Morgan got her crew clear of the mill, and just in time too. I saw one of those Wendigo things along the eastern fence as we were leaving. Morgan's taking the last group of Shifters down to the Dwarfhold to help with the evacuation."

"What about the rest of the valley?" asked A.J., then a thought struck him. "What if the Wendigos get out of the valley?"

"The mist wall will keep them in," assured Connor. "I radioed Mason on the west end and told him about the evacuation. He's sending folks there up to Bear Creek camp. They've got their own protected caves, but that's not what worries me. Mason went to every place out there and came up with a rough count of who's missing. It's more than sixty."

"Sixty?" a few of them exclaimed.

"We've accounted for fewer than ten of these things," A.J. said. "Where are the rest?"

"Wherever they are, they can't get out of the valley," said Brighed. "Connor's right. The mist will keep them in. The only way out would be through the Mist Gate, and they'd have to get into the Dwarfhold and past all the security check points for that. Plus, the gate would have to be activated when they got there, and the Dwarfs would never let that happen, so I really don't see how —"

A tray dropped on the floor with a loud clang. Digger had been examining the UV light and listening to their conversation, but now she stood with a look of terror rising in her face.

"Digger, what's wrong?" asked Brighed.

"The old mill," said Digger. "The old mill," she repeated. "You said they were using the basement of the old mill?"

"So?" asked Margaret. She put an arm around Digger, trying to calm the young Dwarf. "There are no entrances to the Dwarfhold on the far side of the valley —"

Digger cut her off and shoved her hand away. "That's not entirely accurate. I'm a Digger, and all Diggers know every inch of every tunnel and dig in the valley, including the old ones, and the abandoned ones."

"Abandoned?" asked Brighed. "What do you mean?"

"The old mill was built nearly two hundred years ago," said Digger.

"I remember, sort of," said Brighed. "I was there for the groundbreaking. The Shifters built it after the Council formed a treaty with the local indigenous people to sell timber to Incog settlers in the region, but it was just dirt and wild forest land even then."

"On top, yeah," said Digger. "But we've been digging under this valley since the D'Anu and Shifters first arrived 3,700 years ago. The deep caverns and bedrock under our feet are ideal for a Dwarfhold, but we also explored every fissure and cranny in this valley for precious metals. We pack old prospecting tunnels with backfill when we dig new ones, so it's not like they're open access, but…"

"But what?" Skinner demanded.

"Well…when they were digging the basement for the old mill, they broke through into an old tunnel that the Dwarfs had to fill with rock. My pap used to tell us about doing that work and the strange things he heard and saw being that close to the surface. He used to try and scare us from going topside with the stories, but they just made me want to go more."

Brighed sighed with relief. "Well, if it's all filled with rock, then they can't get through."

"But you said Sayah and her thralls, Mayor Bradley and Blue Jean, could control the Wendigos," Digger argued. "So, how strong are those things?"

Brighed's face went pale, and A.J. felt the pit of his stomach drop. "How long would it take to clear out one of those tunnels Digger, if Dwarfs were doing it?" he asked.

"About a week, maybe more," she said.

"So, two weeks for a platoon of giant creatures with long powerful arms?" A.J. put the pieces together in his mind. "When did Morgan say her pack first caught scent of the Wendigo in the forest?"

"About two weeks ago," said Skinner. "That's why they couldn't find it, or them. They were under their feet. They were underground!"

"Clearing the old tunnel," said Brighed.

"Behind the old mill, when I ran out," said Skinner. "I passed piles of rocks. I didn't think anything of it until now, but—"

"They would still need to get past a security door at some point, though," said Margaret. "No outside tunnels or entrances are completely open to the Dwarfhold, and Dwarf guards patrol every corridor and check all the access points. They could only get through if someone has access."

"Fergus has access," said Digger. "So does Dian. All members of the Council have access in every Dwarfhold. If either of them is involved…"

The room went silent as everyone stared at each other letting the reality of the situation sink in.

"My gods, the evacuation!" said Brighed.

"That's the plan," A.J. suddenly realized. "That's been the plan all along. The Wendigos in the valley would spark an evacuation through the Mist Gate, and the Wendigos will attack when it opens. They'll get through, along with dozens or hundreds of Shifters and D'Anu wounded by them. In two hours, we'll have the beginning of a pandemic. Digger! You have to warn…" but Digger was already gone.

"Margaret, is one of you with Dian?" asked Brighed. "We have to inform him about Sayah and the Wendigos."

"No," replied Margaret. "I haven't seen him all day. He was supposed to be meeting with Kane and Mina who have been in communication with the rest of the Council about Fergus's disappearance, but they haven't seen Dian either. I'm helping organize the evacuation down below while the Dwarf Masters recalibrate the Mist Gate. The countdown has already begun, and it will be open in about an hour."

"Can we stop it?" asked A.J.

"No," said Margaret. "Once the process begins, it runs through its cycle. Besides, there are over a thousand D'Anu down there, plus that many Dwarfs at least. If the Wendigos are loose in the Dwarfhold…" She rubbed her hands with worry.

Skinner got off the table, much to Alice's objections, and reached for his hat. "Let's get down there. They're going to need all the help they can get. How much of that antidote do you have?" he asked Brighed.

"A little," she said. "We have plenty of the other ingredients, but the liquid UV takes some time to create. Seshat sent Alice with enough for about a hundred doses and said she would make more, but it will take a few days before we can get it. So please, be careful!"

Skinner wrapped his arms around Alice and kissed her, holding her in a long embrace. Then he turned to Connor and grabbed the young man by both lapels and stuck his nose an inch from Connor's face.

"You stay by her side, you hear me?" Skinner growled. "Don't you dare let her out of your sight for even a moment, or it's your ass I'll be kicking from here to eternity!"

Connor nodded and swallowed hard, his Adam's apple bobbing up and down. Remembering what Connor had done to those Wendigos reminded A.J. just how much respect Skinner commanded.

A.J. looked at Brighed and they locked eyes, but neither moved toward one another. A.J. felt a mix of anger, regret, and longing for her touch. Brighed's face was emotionless and cold, but her eyes were filled with pain. She broke the stare and turned to Margaret.

"Please find Dian right away and inform him and the rest of the high counselors of what we've discovered. The Utukku member of the court will demand proof and deny all knowledge of the plot, I am certain. We will have to give it to them. Alice and I will get to work on the antidotes. There's no time to lose, let's get going."

Margaret nodded and turned to leave, but Brighed stopped her.

"Margaret, is Darcy safe?"

"We are together in the Dwarfhold administration building. We're waiting on the gate to open."

"Keep her safe," said Brighed. "Above all others, you must keep her safe."

Margaret nodded again and left. Brighed gave A.J. one more quick glance and walked out of the exam bay, with Alice and Connor following close behind, leaving A.J. and Skinner alone in the empty clinic. They stared at one another in embarrassment.

"The 'damned things got me'?" A.J. asked in a mocking impersonation of Skinner.

"Fuck you," said Skinner trying to hide a grin. "Were you really gonna shoot me?"

"The evening's young. I still might."

"Shut up," laughed Skinner. "And go get my gun. Don't forget the shells, they're in the glove box, and look behind the seat. You might find something useful."

"Don't you mean 'my' gun?" A.J. headed toward the door to retrieve Miss Polly from the old Dodge.

"I'm not dead yet!" protested Skinner.

"Like I said, the evening's still young." It was A.J.'s turn to laugh, and it felt good. He felt alive again like he hadn't remembered feeling in years, and the thought of what they faced made him realize the feeling may be a short-lived one, but he was okay with that. He'd found himself again, and he swore he'd never let go, even if never was only for a few minutes more.

Chapter Sixteen

End Game

A.J. and Skinner stepped out of the lift to find the outer ring of the Dwarfhold filled with D'Anu, Shifters, and Dwarfs. Everyone seemed agitated, with Shifters gathered in tight groups watching the Dwarfs warily, and the Dwarfs returning the stares with sneers. A dozen D'Anu were doing their best to keep the two separated and calm, but they were slowly losing the battle.

"We've got to get all these people on the other side of the wall right now," said A.J.

"I'll see what the hold-up is," said Skinner. "You try and find Digger and figure out what tunnel those Wendigos are about to climb out of. See if you can organize a defense!" Skinner shoved Miss Polly into his shoulder holster and headed for the bridge. A.J. slung the big Winchester rifle over his shoulder that Skinner kept behind the seat of the old Dodge. A.J. felt like an idiot for not looking back there when they were taking on the Wendigos at the old mill. Of course, Skinner would have another gun in the truck.

The nearest crowd of D'Anu and Dwarfs stopped scowling at each other as they all turned to watch A.J. move into their midst. The Dwarfs in particular seemed upset by something, and in the flash of an eye A.J. found himself surrounded by half a dozen of the fast-moving Dwarfs holding a variety of sharp knives, tools, and other weapons at A.J.

"Hey! Ho! What's going on?" asked A.J. in alarm, putting his hands in the air. "I'm in a hurry, it's an emergency!"

"What are you doing with a weapon in the Dwarfhold?" demanded a heavily bearded Dwarf. "You know it's forbidden!"

"Like I said," A.J. smiled with as much friendliness as he could with a butcher knife an inch from his groin. "It's an emergency. A horde of Wendigo knockoffs are about to invade the Dwarfhold, and we have to stop them."

The assembled Dwarfs looked at one another in confusion and broke out laughing.

"Is this one of your human jokes?" asked the Master Butcher. "Nobody would be stupid enough to attack a Dwarfhold."

"You be sure to tell them that while they're gnawing on your bones," said A.J. "I'm telling you, the Dwarfhold is coming under attack as soon as the Mist Gate opens."

More serious looks passed among the Dwarfs this time. An apprentice stonemason poked A.J. with a hammer. "No weapons! That's the law. Who vouches for you?"

"Digger!" said A.J. "It's who I'm looking for. Do you know where Digger is?"

"I'm Digger," said a gruff master in an apron with a shovel and pickaxe. "And I don't know ye."

"Aye, I'm Digger too, and I've never laid eyes on ye," said a Dwarf from behind A.J. that he couldn't see. The rest of the Dwarves pressed in even closer with their weapons.

"The Digger who works for Doc Brighed up top, I mean, topside," yelped A.J. as something sharp jabbed his back.

"Oh! You mean Digger!" The Master Digger backed off. "Why didn't ya say so?" He nodded to the other Dwarfs, who backed off with the weapons but didn't put them away. A.J. let out a frustrated sigh of relief.

"I saw her fly through here just a bit ago," said a cleanshaven Dwarf. "She grabbed Guard and ran into the Dwarfhold in a hurry. Didn't even take a moment to say hello. It was very rude, if you ask me." The others nodded in agreement.

"Gentlemen," said A.J. "Please. We really must hurry—"

"Who you calling Gentleman?" another bearded Dwarf, whose voice was as deep as the rest, cut him off. "I'm a proper lady I am." Several Dwarfs added their agreement in mutually offended looks.

"Ladies and gentlemen," A.J. amended quickly. "I apologize. But please, I must insist, we really must hurry." Before he could say another word, a deep, resonant horn sounded from the center of the Dwarfhold and echoed off the cavern walls.

"That's the battle horn!" said Master Butcher.

"Is this a drill?" asked an apprentice stonemason.

"No drill scheduled," said another Dwarf.

The horn sounded again, and the Dwarfs forgot about A.J. and all ran toward the bridge, joining the growing throng trying to get past the gates. A.J. lowered his hands and took a deep breath. The surging crowd looked around in panic and began pressing toward the bridge, turning it into a bottleneck no one could get through.

Skinner worked his way through the back of the crowd and jogged toward him. "The attack hasn't started yet, but it looks like Digger has convinced Chief Master Guard it's coming."

"What's the holdup at the bridge?" asked A.J. "Why aren't they letting these people inside?"

"Dwarf protocols," said Skinner. "Damned Administrators are insisting every D'Anu and Shifter be vouched for and walked through their identification system. It's taking a damned long time and they're only letting one through every few minutes. Mina is in there vouching for each one and negotiating with Master Administrator and Master Gatekeeper to speed up the process, but she may as well be arguing with one of those damned statues. Dwarfs don't dismiss a hundred millennia of protocols easily."

"If we don't get these people through that gate, it's going to be a slaughter," said A.J. "We can't defend them on open ground out here."

"I'm not sure it's going to make much difference," frowned Skinner. "The moat and walls are designed to repel human invaders. They won't be much of a challenge for these Wendigo knock-offs. They'll be over them in seconds and there's little we can do to stop them. I just hope the Dwarfs are as good at actual fighting as they like to brag they are."

The horn sounded a third time, and the waiting crowd seemed near rioting when a large section of the wall began lowering like a drawbridge across the moat with a slow grinding of rock against rock and the sound of old steel gears moving for the first time in centuries. The sound and motion quieted the crowd until the wall touched down across the moat. Kane stood on it, his black and gold armor shining like a beacon in the dim light of the Dwarfhold. He held a seven-foot spear with a long black blade in his right hand, and a tall shield with the image of the sun blazing in gold in his left.

The crowd didn't wait for an invitation. It surged toward the ramp into the Dwarfhold. A.J. and Skinner brought up the rear and found Kane, watching the crowd pass him.

"Well done," said A.J. "Things were about to turn ugly out here. This is David Skinner, the local deputy sheriff in charge these days. Skinner, meet Kiongozi Kane, a member of the Council with a bunch of titles I don't remember."

Kane laughed. "It is an honor," he said bending low to Skinner. "Your reputation is known among the Council, and I am pleased to meet you."

"Likewise." Skinner shook Kane's massive hand. "I'll be even more pleased to meet ya if you know how to use that pig sticker you got there. You're going to need it. Thanks for getting the wall open, by the way."

"Don't thank me, thank the young Dwarf, Digger, who knew it was there. She's the one who insisted it be lowered, much to the dismay of the Master Administrators. They will be filing a formal protest with the Council over it. There will be many lawyers. One has not truly experienced hell on this plane until one has faced off against Dwarf lawyers."

"Amen to that," said a familiar voice. Mina was dressed in white leather with her long black hair pulled back. Power flowed from her in waves.

"Looks like they're all in," said Skinner. "Let's get this wall up and figure out where the Wendigos will attack."

"The Northeast tunnels are most likely," said Digger, stepping out of a side building. The wall behind them began grinding and creaking again as it raised itself back upright. Centuries old gears whined from the strain of use. "The abandoned tunnel under the old mill intersects with an access corridor that connects to several other possible points of entry. Guards are monitoring security doors from the administration building's main computer room. We'll know which tunnel they're coming down as soon as they access it."

"Can't you turn off the access?" Skinner asked.

"Sure," said Digger. "But there are protocols and paperwork for that sort of thing."

"Paperwork?" exclaimed A.J. "You're saying the Dwarfs would let an army of mutant monsters in here over paperwork?"

Digger blinked at A.J. as if he'd just asked the dumbest question she'd ever heard. "I have told you before, Dwarf law is not human law."

"But this is crazy," said A.J. "You ignored it to lower this wall and get all these people in."

Digger shrugged. "Yes. I'm probably going to the mines for that, but Brighed says sometimes you have to do the right thing to save lives, even if it's the wrong thing on paper."

"They would send you to the mines for saving these people's lives?" Skinner asked.

"Beats the alternative," Digger said.

"What the hell is the alternative?" A.J. asked, but before Digger could answer, the war horn blew again, drowning out all sound, and the wall stopped moving before it was fully closed. Digger stared at it perplexed, then walked over and kicked it a few times.

"Something is wrong," she yelled over the echoes of the horn. It sounded again and Digger's head snapped all the way around toward the center of the Dwarfhold. "We must hurry," she said and disappeared. A.J. and Skinner followed Kane and Mina toward the taller buildings in the center of the giant cavern.

Others soon joined them, Dwarf, D'Anu, and Shifter alike. By the time they reached the first pillared building, the crowd was so dense they had difficulty moving through it together. A.J. felt the energy of the crowd evolving swiftly toward panic, and he knew from experience how fast an otherwise rational person can fall victim to mob energy. From a distance he saw a flash of bright blue lights that must be coming from the Mist Gate as it began its power cycle. The Wendigo attack would happen soon.

Digger appeared at A.J.'s side and grabbed his hand. "Come on, this way!" She led the four of them down a small path between buildings, turned right through a steel gate, down a flight of stone steps to an underground corridor, and up a flight of stairs directly into the main administration building about fifty yards farther on.

The glowing stones, plants, and tapestries throughout provided low level lighting for the building, but everything else was turned off. Computer screens were blank, and Dwarfs were milling about in consternation, discussing what might be going on. Digger found the nearest Master Administrator and spoke quickly in the odd Dwarf language. After a brief exchange, she returned to the group with a worried look.

"Power has been cut to the Dwarfhold everywhere except the Mist Gate." Through the windows facing the central square, the giant arch thrummed in vibration they felt through the stone floor. Digger glanced at it nervously. "This is impossible. The power for the Dwarfhold is wired directly from the reactor. Someone would have to take over the control room and redirect the energy, but..." She worked through the possibilities in her mind, and then the Mist Gate flashed a bright blue through the windows so brilliant that A.J. had to shut his eyes against the glare. When he opened them, all the Dwarfs were rubbing their eyes or pulling their goggles into place. Digger blinked and shook her head to clear it, then her eyes went wide and her already pale skin turned an even whiter shade. "By the gods, they're overcharging the Mist Gate! No!"

"They're what?" A.J. asked.

"The Mist Gate!" Digger exclaimed and pointed toward the pulsing ring outside. "They're sending it too much power!"

"Okay… and this is bad, because?"

"Because it will explode!" said Digger, chittering and rubbing her hands. "If they overcharge the gate, the quantum field will expand exponentially and then collapse in on itself. The gate will explode, scattering everyone and everything in the Dwarfhold across the globe and across time. The cavern itself will collapse and turn half the valley into a molten slagheap. If they complete the connection with Munich, the explosion could short out the entire Mist Gate matrix, unleashing chaotic magic around the world. Oh, gods! This is bad, this is very, very bad!"

"That means the mist wall around the valley would fall, too," added Mina. "The Wendigos outside would be unrestrained. Billions could die. We must do something!"

The Dwarfs inside the administration building were reaching the same conclusions, and a general state of panic began to set in; Dwarfs ran toward the doors or stared in shock through the windows at the pulsating Mist Gate. Kane climbed a flight of steps to a landing where all could see his giant frame. He spun his long spear once and brought the butt of it down hard onto the marble, sending out a shock wave and loud boom that quieted the rising chorus of panic and pulled all eyes toward him.

"I am Kiongozi Kane, and I declare this an emergency of the Council! We must send guards to secure the reactor and prepare to defend the walls against invaders! Where are Chief Master Guard and Chief Master Administrator?"

The old Dwarf A.J. had seen when he met Dian spoke up from a small crowd of Master Dwarfs gathered closely around him. His beard was long and ghostly white, and he wore gold wire spectacles under a thick and wrinkled brow.

"This is not your Dwarfhold!" he said with a strong but raspy voice. "The treaty requires three counselors to declare an emergency, and I see only one of you!"

All the Dwarfs nodded their heads or grunted in approval of the old Dwarf.

"Are you fucking kidding?" A.J. asked. Digger shushed him.

Mina stepped next to Kane, white light shining from her eyes. "I am Ptesan-Wi of the Buffalo Nation and member of the Council. I second the emergency declaration."

"That's two," said the old Dwarf in response. "Two is not three! We must hold a meeting to choose who will be in charge of this emergency! That is the protocol!" Many of the Dwarfs stamped their feet on the floor in approval.

Another Master Dwarf in a Scribe's apron spoke up next. "First we must hold a meeting to determine there actually is an emergency," he called out. "Protocol!"

"Protocol!" echoed the voices of virtually every Dwarf in the room. A.J. put his head in his hands and Digger grunted in frustration. The Mist Gate flashed a brilliant blue again that forced them all to shield their eyes. A.J. could see the large crowd through the window begin pushing back from the giant arch. Things were getting out of control.

"We're running out of time!" Digger yelled at the crowd. Chief Master Administrator wagged his finger at her.

"That's enough out of you, Digger! You've already broken protocol today by lowering the wall. There will be a hearing!" he yelled to general applause from the surrounding Dwarfs.

"We're all gonna die," moaned A.J. in disbelief.

"I am the third!" said a voice from the top of the stairs. Dian suddenly stepped out between a pair of plinth columns, with Darcy next to him looking frightened and

Margaret following behind, clasping her hands in worry. All heads turned toward Dian as he descended the stairs.

"This is an emergency declaration of the Council, and I name Kiongazi Kane as Chief General. Any objections?"

Chief Master Administrator stepped forward and bowed to Kane. "The law is the law! Send for Chief Master Guard at once! General Kane, what are your orders?"

"Assemble your guards and fighters!" Kane bellowed.

In response, Chief Master Administrator raised his cane in the air. "If the Dwarfhold is in danger, today, all Dwarfs are fighters!" A general cheer erupted and every weapon, hammer, pen, and fist available was raised. By the time he finished his statement, another heavily bearded Dwarf in the engraved black armor of the Guards stood in front of Kane. A gold chain hung around his neck.

Another vibration from the Mist Gate, powerful enough to shake the dust from the ancient stone walls, silenced the grumbling Dwarfs. A.J. recalled the dozens of glowing D'Anu singing in unison and the feeling of the light being pulled from his body when the gate opened.

"Hey, what about the singing?" A.J. asked Digger. "Don't the D'Anu have to sing to make the gate open?"

"That is only for rituals," Digger whispered back in annoyance. She was watching the exchange between Kane and Chief Master Guard intently. "The harmonics are built into the system so we can use it whenever we want. It's part of the..." and then Digger stood up with a shocked look in her eyes and a huge smile. "You're a genius! Of course! That's it!" She yelled loud enough to draw the attention of the room. Chief Master Administrator scowled at her again.

"If I can get to the control room, I can modulate the harmonic frequency to create a counter-propagating waveform! If I time it just right, I can zero out the energy wave. I just need to figure out where to drain all the power. I'll figure it out on the way!"

Kane smiled at Digger and turned to the Dwarf in front of him. "Chief Master Guard. Dispatch a squad to the reactor cavern and secure the control room. Take an engineer and Digger with you to restore power to the Dwarfhold and protect the Mist Gate!" Another blue flash, even brighter than the rest, punctuated the order, and at least a dozen Dwarfs in armor stepped forward. Digger moved to join them.

"I've been to the control room." A.J. started to follow her. "Dian showed it to me. I can help."

"No offense, human." Digger raised a hand to stop him. "But you'll only slow us down. This is a job for Dwarfs!" She yelled this last bit for the assembled Dwarfs to hear, and they joined her in a chorus of cheers. "There's not a moment to waste. Let's go!" And with that, the space where the group had assembled was suddenly empty, and A.J. felt a rush of air as they sped past him and through the door to the underground corridor.

Crowd noises from outside the administration building told A.J. things were deteriorating rapidly.

Kane began yelling orders. "Administrators, Scribes, and Crafters, secure the courtyard and organize the evacuation. Move the refugees into the main buildings and secure the doors. The rest of you, defend the walls! Concentrate forces to the Northeast!"

The remaining Dwarfs moved with speed. A.J. stood bewildered in the suddenly empty main room.

"Once you get them organized and moving, they're really quite efficient," said Dian, joining Kane and Mina on the landing.

"What now?" A.J. asked.

"We must get the counselors safely through the Mist Gate when it opens," said Dian. "It is too late to flee. If Digger fails and the gate is overcharged, our safest route is through it. The Main Mist Gate in Munich is set to match the opening of this one. It's the only way to move so many at once. If we move together at the moment it opens, we will all arrive there safely, even if this valley is destroyed. We must move quickly! Come!"

Dian turned toward the door with Darcy and Margaret in tow, but Kane and Mina did not follow. Dian stopped and looked at them expectantly.

"Take the young sorceress and save yourself," said Kane. "One of us must report what has happened here to the rest of the Council. I am the Chief General of this emergency, and I will not flee."

Dian frowned but acknowledged the point. Then he looked at Ptesan-Wi. "Et tu, Mina?"

The White Buffalo Woman stood tall and the shining light of power grew stronger around her. "I will stay and fight."

Dian looked at A.J. and Skinner, who both shrugged and stayed put. Dian wrapped his arm around Darcy. "Suit yourselves. I wish luck to you all," he said and headed for the door to the underground corridor with Margaret close behind.

"I really hate that guy," grumbled Skinner. Dian's exit was punctuated by another flash from the Mist Gate, but this time it did not fade and the deep vibrations began to oscillate in an ongoing rumble. The main doors to the building opened again and a large group of the refugees were ushered in by Dwarfs. Sounds of an unruly crowd flowed in from the outside.

"Let's get to the Northeast wall," Kane said, leading the way.

Outside was chaotic, with half the crowd pushing toward the gate, and those closest to it pushing away from it. Dwarfs and D'Anu were moving among them, encouraging the crowd to take shelter in the administration buildings. A group of Shifters were loudly facing off against one another in the middle of the broad boulevard. Morgan stood tall in the center, trying desperately to maintain order. A.J. and Skinner ran toward her.

"...not the time or place!" Morgan was yelling over the deepening rumble of the Mist Gate at a female Shifter who was hissing at a bearded man in suspenders on the opposite side of Morgan. For his part, the man was snarling back and pointing at his adversary.

"What the hell is going on here?" Skinner demanded. Morgan looked relieved to see him. Several of the Shifters began talking at once.

"The wolves killed Scarlett!" The angry woman yelled.

"Not these wolves," the snarling man yelled back.

"You're all savages!" A young woman with long dark hair screamed at them like a panther as she finished the words.

"Enough!" Skinner barked. "While the whole lot of you genetic malfunctions are busy sucking up the air the rest of us need to live, there's a gods' damned invasion of actual monsters headed this way!"

A.J. clenched his jaw to keep from smiling. Skinner was using an old drill sergeant's technique of problem-solving in the ranks. Giving a divided crowd a common enemy is the fastest way to build unity among them. His insult worked too, as every eye turned toward him, and every throat growled in his direction. It didn't faze him, and he pressed harder.

"Now if you want a mutant creation of Hell to chew the hairballs out of your throats, that's fine by me, but if you hope to walk away from this with your tails intact, you'll button your kibble holes and defend the gods' damned walls!"

A screaming howl from the end of the boulevard cut through the deep thrum of the Mist Gate and silenced the crowd as they all turned to look. White flashed in the distance as a pair of Wendigos cleared the far wall.

"They're over the wall to the south!" Skinner pulled Miss Polly from her holster. A.J. unslung the heavy rifle and jacked the bolt up and back to load a round. He put the scope to his eye and targeted the head of the nearest Wendigo, but its rocking gait made it hard to draw a bead. A.J. counted to three to get the rhythm of its movement through the crosshairs and fired on the four count. The ten-gram round hit the Wendigo in the forehead travelling 3,000 feet per second, and the result was highly effective, if not quite as spectacular as Digger's modified long gun. A.J. loaded another round and aimed at the second creature, but it darted between two buildings as he fired and missed.

The sound of the rifle was barely audible over the sound of the Mist Gate, and its bright blue light was making it harder to see. Kane yelled at the panicked crowd to take cover, and D'Anu and Dwarfs alike were trying their best to get everyone inside the stone buildings. Skinner tapped A.J. on the shoulder and pointed down the boulevard behind him.

Four more Wendigos looked like they were dancing at first, or maybe swatting at a swarm of bees. A.J. realized that Dwarfs were stopping for brief moments to slash at the creatures with axes before darting away again. One of the Wendigos went to the ground, and a Dwarf appeared long enough to sever its head. Within seconds the other three were dispatched in similar fashion, and a dozen Dwarfs stopped moving and leaned on one another, breathing hard.

The last of the refugees pushed their way into the big buildings near the Mist Gate, and the rest of the Dwarfs joined A.J. and Skinner's small crowd in the central hub of the Dwarfhold boulevards.

Skinner grabbed the nearest apprentice, a stonemason by the look of his apron. "Get to the Northeast wall and find General Kane. Tell him the south and southwest walls are breached."

"And the west!" A.J. pointed to where three more of the white beasts were running toward them, darting among the statues and topiary for cover from A.J.'s rifle. "They're communicating with each other somehow. Sayah must be in the Dwarfhold controlling them." It was hard to hear over the Mist Gate, and the ground shook with each pulse, making standing difficult.

"It may not matter much longer," yelled Skinner. "That thing's about to blow and send us all to hell!"

"Only if we're lucky," added Morgan. "We're just as likely to land thousands of years in the future anywhere from the middle of the Atlantic to the Middle East!"

"The Middle East?" A.J. groaned hopelessly. "I've already been there, and given a choice, I'll take Hell!" A.J. was shouting at the top of his lungs to be heard as the Mist Gate began broadcasting a sudden, intense note like the song of the D'Anu, but an instant later all sound suddenly ceased, leaving a moment of unexpected silence into which A.J.'s last three words were so yelled loud enough for everyone in the Dwarfhold to hear.

The Dwarfs around him stopped and stared in stunned silence for a heartbeat, and then as one raised their fists and cheered, "I'll take Hell!"

The giant arch had changed from the powerful vibrating force from the moment earlier into the lower intensity thrumming that A.J. remembered from the previous morning. The statues and fountains lining the boulevards, however, came back to life with a violence and speed that shocked everyone. Water shot a dozen stories straight up from some of the fountains, while others exploded in showers of water and concrete. The intricate dance of the automaton statues became blurs of flashing steel, grinding gears, and crunching metal as parts flew off them and several heated to red hot and began melting in place.

One of the approaching Wendigos was impaled on the suddenly fast-moving machines, and two others were knocked into the middle of the road. A.J. drew a bead and fired, hitting one in the shoulder as it scrambled to its feet. He jacked another round and fired again, hitting the wounded beast in its right ear and dropping it for good.

Skinner looked around at the crowd of Shifters. "Well? Are you going to stand there or are you going to fight?" He pointed down the southeast boulevard toward yet another group of Wendigos, and the Shifters howled and leapt forward, shifting into their animal forms and charging at their foes with Morgan's big black wolf in the lead.

"Looks like Digger made it to the control room," said Skinner.

"And figured out where to redirect the energy." A.J. dodged a large steel spring that came spinning across the street at their feet. The metal statues were still moving wildly and spinning out of control. Several were melting the ground in flowing slags of red hot steel.

The sound of the D'Anu vocal vibrations began emanating from the Mist Gate, growing in frequency and volume, making A.J.'s skin glow brighter and his body vibrate with the rhythm, and then the energy flowed and a white cloud of mist blasted forth from the arch, reaching nearly to the middle of the boulevard before pulling back to the central hub.

"The gate is open!" yelled Skinner. "Evacuate the Dwarfhold and protect the gate. If even one of those creatures gets through..." he grabbed a Dwarf apprentice rushing by. "Get to the main buildings and start moving people through the gate."

Kane and Mina ran toward them with Mayari, the Shifter A.J. had met at The Den, running with them. She was dressed in black from neck to toe and wielded a pair of swords curved down at the tips. The swords were covered in blood.

"We got your message," said Kane. "The Wendigos hit us hard at the northeast and eastern walls. Our defenders are holding them, but they won't last long. I ordered them to fall back to the Gate to protect the refugees. Those things are still coming out of the tunnels, too, and there are more than we thought. A lot more."

"Sayah used the power outage to blind us while the Wendigos circled around," added Mina. "We're surrounded, but we won't need to hold for long. As soon as we get the refugees through, they'll close the gate from the Munich side, and it will shut down here as well."

"Leaving the rest of us to our fates?" A.J. was incredulous.

Skinner only shrugged. "What's the matter, you want to live forever?"

"I'd like to make it through today," replied A.J.

"It's always complaints with you army boys."

"I guess Jarheads are just better at dying than we are."

"Damn straight, and don't you forget it," said Skinner.

One of the Wendigos broke free of the melee on the southern boulevard and bolted toward the gate. Skinner pulled the hammer back on Miss Polly. "Incoming," he said softly.

A.J. tried to get a shot at it, but the Wendigo was moving erratically and using the whirling statues and topiary for cover as it came. Another broke free behind it, and then a third. Yelling from the western boulevard told them another had gotten through there.

"Fall back!" Kane yelled. "Fall back to the center! Protect the gate!"

Down the boulevards, small groups of armored guards fought in retreat, trying to slow the advancing Wendigos while the rest of the Dwarfs, Shifters, and D'Anu rushed to assemble around the gate. Most were breathing heavily and more than a few sported injuries. A.J. hoped Alice's antidote worked on Dwarfs, and then he hoped enough of them lasted long enough to receive it.

The main doors of the administration building opened, and a stream of refugees ran out toward the mist. Many shifted to their animal forms as they fled beside a number of D'Anu and a great many Dwarfs. Dian and Darcy emerged from a side door without Margaret. Dian had a hand on Darcy's shoulder and the two of them walked quickly toward the Mist Gate, using the larger crowd of refugees for cover.

In the moment before they disappeared, Dian stopped to survey the battle and saw A.J. They locked eyes across the moss-covered ground, and Dian smiled a wicked smile. Darcy looked at Dian with frightened eyes, while Dian glanced down the broad boulevard at the advancing Wendigos. He smiled at A.J. again and then shoved Darcy ahead of him into the mist, disappearing with the rest of the refugees fleeing the Dwarfhold.

"Form a circle around the gate!" Kane's voice boomed. "Shields locked and forward!"

Dwarf guards and others with shields formed a half circle along the boulevard, from the corner of the administration building on the western point to the corner of another large stone building on the eastern point of the hub, protecting the path for refugees passing into the mist.

A dozen glowing D'Anu joined the remaining fighters behind the line and prepared to fight any creatures breaking through. The sounds of heavy fighting from the opposite side of the gate attracted Kane's attention.

"I'll take charge here. Go help them," Mina yelled over the din.

Kane nodded and ran in long powerful strides around the edge of the mist with Mayari following on his heels.

Mina's eyes glowed bright white and waves of power rolled off her shoulders. "Repel the beasts! Hold strong! Close the gaps and aim for their heads!"

A.J. fired at an approaching Wendigo closing on the Dwarfs. It went down and another leapt over it as more of the great monsters filled the boulevards in a rush toward the center. A.J. dropped the next closest one he saw. The skirmishing Dwarfs and Shifters in the boulevards had either pulled back to the central hub or had fallen, with a few small numbers cut off from retreat and holding their own in doorways and alleys along the way.

"On the right!" Skinner ran toward the end of the line, where the first Wendigo hit the shield wall. The creature tried to reach its long arms past the interlocked shields to pull them down and lost a hand in the attempt. The giant beast screamed, and blood flowed as more of the creatures crashed into the line behind it.

The scrape of claws on shields and the screams of the Wendigos and Dwarfs engaged in close battle drowned out all other sounds until the boom of Miss Polly split the air. The Wendigos towered over the Dwarfs on the line, but the skill and speed of the Dwarf fighters wielding axes and spears were more than a match for their fearsome foes. A.J.

himself stood a foot taller than most of the Dwarfs, giving him easy shots with plenty of clearance to fire the rifle, and he killed two more Wendigos in three shots. He pulled the extended clip off the bottom of the rifle and began reloading it from the box in his pocket as more of the monsters reached the hub of the Dwarfhold.

"Sixty my ass!" Skinner yelled. "There's got to be that many of these things on this side of the arch alone!" He fired Miss Polly again and joined A.J. at the shoulder as the two men crouched together, reloading their weapons.

"We could use a few more guns!" A.J. yelled.

"I'll be sure to leave a note in the suggestion box," Skinner said.

A.J. laughed. He felt his old blood lust again in a way that surprised and terrified him. For a decade he'd lived in fear of freezing up if faced with a life and death battle again, but Skinner's words played over in his mind, "All there is, is now." What he found in the now was power in his veins, and his skin glowed its own bright gold. His mind was sharp, and he felt the world around him slow down as he stepped into that zone that had saved him so many times before, but for the first time in his life, A.J. was glad to be there. He felt alive again.

He surveyed the battle. The fighting on the opposite side of the arch was obscured by the mist, but on his side at least, the line was holding. Behind the line were the Shifters, including the big black wolf that was Morgan. She led a pack of wolves, lions, panthers, and one sharp-horned bull on a running circle of the Mist Gate, passing behind A.J. and Skinner on their circuit, watching for breaks in the line.

Mina paced the perimeter of the mist, yelling encouragement and directing defenders to points of heavy fighting. The D'Anu standing behind the Dwarfs glowed intensely in various shades, from gold to deep red, but all of them moved swiftly, lending support where they could and pulling wounded Dwarfs out of the way so others could take their place. One of them was pushing the Wendigos back from the fight with what looked like concentrated balls of energy, giving the Dwarf guards a chance to link shields and regroup. Another threw what looked like daggers of fire at the giant beasts, burning and distracting them long enough for Dwarfs to take them down. A.J. thought he would have to learn that trick someday, if he survived.

At the gate, a steady stream of refugees disappeared into the mist. If they could hold for a few more minutes, they would be home safe, or at least those who got through the gate would be. He and the rest of the defenders would be left to fight the Wendigos with no way out. That bothered him a lot less than he expected.

The Wendigos also seemed to realize that time was running out, and the creatures stopped dancing and pecking at the shield wall and suddenly rushed it en masse. Many were repelled by the shields and weapons, but a few got past by climbing and leaping over the others. On the left end of the line, a Wendigo broke through and a pair of wolves and a black panther Shifter pulled it to the ground while a Dwarf chopped and stabbed at its head. A second raced past them toward the edge of the mist, and A.J. raised his rifle to kill it, but the beast's head disappeared from his field of view as Kane's spear completed a short arc with its razor-sharp edge decapitating the Wendigo easily.

Mayari sprinted past Kane to confront a third creature. The twin swords flew around her body, blocking the Wendigo's sharp claws every time it reached for her and taking chunks of flesh and fur out of the giant beast. It attempted to run around her to get to the mist, but Mayari flowed into her wolf form and caught the Wendigo by the heel in her teeth while Kane leapt over her to bury his spear in its throat and take it to the ground. As the Wendigo struggled to stand, Mayari shifted back to human form, turning in a tight arc with sword in hand to meet Kane's spear in the middle of the Wendigo's neck, slicing off its head like a pair of scissors.

Kane pulled his spear back and sprinted past, yelling, "Hold the line" and disappeared through the stream of refugees with Mayari following close behind him.

"Come for dinner…" prompted Skinner.

"Stay for the show!" finished A.J. "On your six!"

Skinner spun and raised Miss Polly into the face of an oncoming Wendigo with a Dwarf's axe buried in its back and a limp Dwarf clutched in its massive left claw. Skinner put a round in its eye and the monster fell at their feet. With the help of the Shifters and D'Anu fighters, the line recovered from the rush of Wendigos and reformed.

The number of refugees in Dwarf, human, and animal form running into the mist had dwindled. For a brief moment, A.J. believed they would make it. He raised his rifle toward another of the giant beasts, took aim, and as he squeezed the trigger with confidence in the shot, his body did the cursed thing that he hated, it moved on its own before his mind could register the danger. His hands pulled the butt of the rifle down as the gun fired and his shot disappeared toward the cavern ceiling. His body spun to the left and used the rifle like a staff to block the incoming blow from Sayah as she materialized into solid form, flying toward him with a blade in hand and her needle-sharp teeth bared in rage. The rifle caught the thrust of her blade and was ripped from his hands as he went to the ground, and both weapons slid, spinning away into the mist.

"Sayah! The Utukku is behind the line!" A.J. yelled, but his words were lost in the raging sounds of battle. Skinner's attention was focused on the line, and A.J. scrambled to his feet as Sayah pulled Skinner to the ground next. Before A.J. could reached her, she disappeared into a shadow. Skinner looked up in dazed confusion for what attacked him, and A.J. helped him to his feet.

"It's Sayah!" A.J. yelled again, and Skinner nodded in understanding.

There was no time to look for her though as the Wendigos all began fighting more fiercely, reflecting Sayah's own emotions in a panic to reach their objective. Several impaled themselves on spears, pulling the weapons from the hands of the defenders and then rushing again at the shields with the spears still sticking through their bodies. Sayah took form again, her face full of rage and fear as she grabbed defenders and threw them aside, then she was gone again. Ten feet further down the line, several more Dwarfs were taken to the ground as she reappeared, and even the speed and agility of the defenders were no match for the now rapidly failing line.

More Wendigos broke through gaps created by Sayah's attack. The line devolved into groups of Dwarfs fighting on all sides and doing their best to bring the attacking beasts to the ground before they could make it through the gate. Where the Wendigos and Dwarf defenders had been at a stalemate, now the Dwarfs were free to engage from multiple angles as the big white beasts fought their way past the chaos of battle. The Dwarfs were no longer moving too fast to see, but even in their exhaustion they were still twice as fast as any human could be.

Morgan led her pack into the path of the attackers. Every Shifter was covered in blood, whether Wendigo's or their own was impossible to tell. Gore dripped from the bull's sharp horns, and blood dripped down its hide. Several long gashes ran down its back, but its nostrils flared, and it lowered its head to charge the nearest beast. The Dwarfs and Shifters were killing the Wendigos swiftly, but there were just too many to stop them all.

Three Wendigos broke free and were almost into the mist when Mina stepped into their path. Her eyes shone brilliant white and she raised her fan of sage leaves, opening it fully and sweeping it across her body just as the creatures leapt at her, screaming, claws extended. A.J. wanted to yell for someone to help her, but he knew it was no use. All he could do was watch the White Buffalo Woman die as the Wendigos crushed her beneath them on their way into the gate, but that is not what happened.

The moment her fan came into contact with the charging monsters, the air around her wavered and distorted like a reflection on a bubble, and A.J. felt a blast of energy against his face as the three charging Wendigos disappeared, exploding into dozens of snakes of many sizes that fell at Mina's feet and hissed and writhed and slithered across the ground. Mina stepped backward from the impact, and her head drooped, but then she recovered and stood straight again, though with considerably less of the energy glow about her. She looked up with tired eyes no longer bright white, squared her shoulders, and strode forward toward the battles and skirmishes taking place all around them, yelling support and directing fighters.

"Well, that's fucking handy!" said Skinner.

"Yeah, but now there's snakes!" said A.J.

"Everybody's a critic," Skinner yelled, then, "Duck!"

A.J. curled down as Skinner raised and fired Miss Polly directly into the space where A.J.'s head had been. A Wendigo went down, sliding on its belly to stop inches from their feet.

"Don't suppose you have another gun hidden somewhere?" A.J. asked.

"What'd ya do with the last one I gave you?"

A.J. shrugged at the mist.

Skinner frowned. "No, and I'm down to my last three rounds, but I don't think it's going to matter. Look!"

A.J. turned as four Wendigos broke past the fighters. Two of them had spears sticking from their bodies and another was missing its right arm below the elbow, but no one stood between them and the mist.

A fair number of Dwarfs and Shifters, and several of the D'Anu fighters were on the ground unmoving. More were having wounds tended, while the rest fought tiredly, trying to take down their foes, but more of the creatures were getting by. Four Wendigos leapt a pair of Shifters and bounded toward the mist wall.

A.J. dropped his head in despair.

"All for naught," Skinner said quietly, and he placed a reassuring hand on A.J.'s shoulder.

"Why isn't it closed yet?" A.J. asked as the Wendigos disappeared into the fog. "We almost..." but he didn't finish the words. The four Wendigos flew backward from the mist with heavy steel bolts protruding from their chests. They tried to regain their feet, but more bolts appeared in their heads, and the big beasts stopped moving. Two more of the creatures were knocked back from the mist wall. A line of shadows emerged from the mist to reveal dozens of Dwarfs in black and red armor formed in three staggered lines, one behind the other. The front line would fire while the backlines used levers to re-cock their crossbows and load more bolts from quivers on their hips. Then they would shift places while the whole group advanced, the rotating front line firing in a near constant volley of heavy steel bolts.

They stepped into the clearing, and the Mist Gate closed behind them with a snap of air. In the middle of their lines stood Dian, directing the reinforcement Dwarfs toward new targets. A cheer went up from the remaining defenders, quickly drowned out by a piercing scream from the top of a nearby statue. Sayah stood there, eyes wide and mouth agape, arms and hands clawing the air in frustration at the scene below her.

Most of her Wendigo army had fallen, but many of the monsters, whether whole or injured, still fought savagely against the defenders who were newly emboldened by their crossbow-wielding brethren. Dian shone brilliantly. The golden light of the D'Anu enveloped his entire form. Mina joined him while Kane fought beside the Dwarf defenders, wielding his spear and shield with the skill of an ancient warrior king. Mayari defended his back. Sayah screamed again and pointed at Dian, and the Wendigos all turned and focused their attacks on his position, fighting with renewed rage.

Defend the center! Mina's voice was suddenly inside A.J.'s mind. Her eyes shone brilliant white again, and golden energy flowed out from her body and through A.J. and all others in the field. Her voice rode that wave to every defender.

Form a circle! Protect the wounded! With that last thought, the energy wave collapsed, and Mina crumpled, exhausted, to the ground behind Dian.

The remaining Dwarf, Shifter, and D'Anu defenders closed in from all sides. A.J. and Skinner helped pull the wounded into the center of the new defensive circle. Many of the Shifters were back in their human bodies, unable to maintain their animal forms due to exhaustion or injury, but Morgan was still a big black wolf leading a handful of her pack, including the big bull. The Dwarf fighters were tired and were falling back from the onslaught of remaining attackers. The intensity of the battle increased, and A.J. could see that even with the reinforcements, the renewed focus of the Wendigos would soon overwhelm their tightening circle of defense.

A.J. searched for a weapon and saw his lost rifle. He ran to pick it up, but most of the barrel was missing, the wooden stock sliced at a sharp angle as though sheared in half by a laser. Skinner fired his last three rounds and shoved Miss Polly in her holster.

"What now?" A.J. yelled.

Skinner frowned at the broken rifle. "Well, I guess you could beat 'em to death."

A Wendigo screamed as it leapt over the wall of fighters and rushed at Skinner, a giant claw raised for a killing blow. A.J. stepped between them and swung the rifle butt with all his might in a futile attempt to defend his friend, but the Wendigo's head exploded in front of him. The peal of a loud gunshot reached their ears. Down the boulevard, Digger stood on top of the partially melted statue depicting the birth of the world and loaded another round into her custom long rifle. Most of the Dwarf guards who had joined her in the fight for the control room were launching themselves into the battle as well.

"Here comes the cavalry!" yelled A.J., and another cheer erupted from the exhausted fighters. Three more people were sprinting down the boulevard behind the new arrivals. Two were glowing brightly in the golden light of the D'Anu. It was Brighed and Alice, carrying medical bags. Connor, his service weapon drawn, fired at the Wendigos as he ran. When the gun emptied, Connor changed into his Sasquatch form, ripped a Dwarf's axe from the body of a dead Wendigo, and waded into the fray where the great white beasts began dropping around him like wheat reaped by the scythe of death. Digger fired again from her statue, and another of the creatures fell. The tide had shifted again.

Sayah screamed and disappeared from her perch. A shadow rushed past A.J., and Sayah took form again near Dian, her mouth agape, eyes crazed. She grasped the back of Dian's coat and pulled him toward her mouth, intending to sink those needle-sharp teeth into his flesh, but a dark blur hit her broadside and knocked her to the ground. Morgan rolled off her, shifting back to her human form as the last of her energy and willpower fled. She struggled to stand but was knocked down again by Sayah, who leapt atop her screaming in a language A.J. didn't understand. Morgan fought against the Utukku's grip, but it was clear she wouldn't last long.

A.J. ran toward them. From the corner of his eye, he saw Skinner running too, holding a Dwarf spear in his hands.

"Give me something to aim at!" Skinner yelled.

A.J. increased his speed toward Sayah as she swiped wildly at Morgan's outstretched arms, her claws scraping bloody stripes into Morgan's flesh, and she bared her teeth to take a bite. A.J. spun the broken rifle, pointed the sliced end of the stock down, and drove it with all his strength into the center of Sayah's back.

Engaged as she was with Morgan, Sayah never saw him coming, and she didn't shift into shadow. The broken rifle penetrated Sayah's ancient flesh like a dull awl through heavy leather. A.J.'s hands vibrated as the wooden point slammed into the rock-hard heart of the ancient Utukku, but it penetrated nonetheless.

Sayah's scream was like nothing A.J. had ever heard, not even in the storm on the night he arrived. It ripped the air in a wail that filled the cavern and bounced off its walls. Many of the defenders covered their ears from the pain of the high-pitched noise. Sayah stood up, desperately clawing at the butt of the rifle protruding from her back. Skinner saw the rifle in the air and took aim just above it as he charged. Sayah tried to shift into smoke, and parts of her disappeared and reappeared, but her chest remained solid. She spun in a circle, trying to reach the source of her pain, just as Skinner reached her with the spear.

As Sayah spun toward him, the point of the Dwarf spear entered her wide-open mouth, full of those venomous needle teeth, and the wide blade cut through her cheeks and sliced the top half of her head clean off her body. The terrible scream stopped as Sayah stood motionless for a moment, then her body dropped to its knees and toppled forward onto the ground, spilling out a thick black ooze of blood. The ancient Utukku who had survived human and D'Anu civilizations for ten thousand years was dead.

The remaining Wendigos screamed in confusion and panic. Those that could, broke and ran, fleeing down the boulevards with a handful of Dwarfs in pursuit. The rest were cut down where they stood, unwilling or unable to keep up the fight. Digger's rifle boomed several more times, then it, too, went silent and the last echoes of her weapon bounced off the far walls, leaving only the cries of the wounded and the weak cheers of exhausted fighters.

A.J. helped Morgan to her feet, and she leaned on him weakly. A.J. pulled off his shirt and wrapped it around her badly bleeding arms, applying pressure. Sayah's body began to dissolve into the ground as if it were melting. Skinner's eyes were wide at the sight.

"You can see that?" A.J. asked.

"Unfortunately, yes," Skinner grimaced, then nodded toward the crowd of Dwarfs in front of him. "Well, don't that beat all?"

They lifted Dian onto their shoulders, and other Dwarfs and D'Anu and Shifters joined them in cheering for the chief counselor who had led the reinforcements through the Mist Gate.

A.J. shrugged. "Who cares who gets the glory? I'm just glad it's over."

"Is anything ever really over?" Skinner looked around at the wounded and the dead. "I thought I'd put this kind of shit behind me forever."

"Me too," said A.J.

He held Morgan against him and thought about her missing father and fugitive brother and the promise he made to kill Aengus. He looked at the dissolving Utukku lying on the ground, as well as the dead and headless Wendigos around the hub. Lying among them were the occasional Dwarf and Shifter, and at least two of the D'Anu fighters were dead as well. A small band of Dwarf guards with bloody axes walked among them, severing heads from the bodies to ensure none of them would get up again.

"It's going to take time to hunt the rest of those things down and clean this mess up," said A.J., "and there's still a lot about this whole thing we don't know. You're going to have your work cut out for you the next few weeks."

"Me?" Skinner laughed and patted A.J. on the back. "You're forgetting, my friend, I'm retired! If you two don't mind, I'm going to go kiss my wife now, and help her deliver that antidote. It's going to be a long night."

"Indeed," agreed A.J. He picked up Morgan and carried her to where Alice and Brighed were organizing first aid and delivering their antidotes. "All there is, is now."

Chapter Seventeen

The Road Less Travelled

A.J. knelt beside a bubbling brook that flowed lazily toward the lake in the national forest and scattered the last of Malcolm's ashes into the clear water.

"Goodbye," was all he said. Goodbye to Malcolm, goodbye to his burden, goodbye to the life he had lived for ten long years. Relief washed over him. The invisible yoke he had carried for so long lifted away, and A.J. stood tall and straight for the first time in as long as he could remember. It was finally over. His promise was fulfilled, but it was replaced by another, more ominous one. One he looked forward to finishing.

He walked back to the pickup parked at the top of hill where Skinner leaned back in the driver's seat, his oiled leather cowboy hat pulled down over his eyes.

"You done?" Skinner asked when A.J. climbed in.

"Yeah," said A.J., and that was all they had to say about it. A.J. was grateful.

"Well, let's get back. Some folks want to give you a proper sendoff to wherever you're going. Where did you say that was again?" Skinner raised a quizzical eyebrow.

"I didn't," A.J. shot back. They both laughed.

Skinner fired up the old Dodge and began the slow, winding drive over the mountain and back toward the valley floor. As a show of gratitude for A.J.'s efforts in the fight, the Dwarfs had granted him free passage through the mist to run his errand. A.J. didn't know how they did it, but the mist didn't turn them around on their way out, and now he was headed back in, voluntarily. He smiled at the irony.

"That poor bastard Mayor Bradley was brought into the clinic last night," said Skinner. "He was in pretty bad shape. Brighed gave the man enough morphine to kill an elephant, but the mayor's altered physiology is keeping him alive, at least for the moment. She said the withdrawal from the Utukku's venom would be excruciating, and she wasn't lying."

A.J. searched his heart for sympathy but was having trouble finding any. On the contrary, the darker part of his soul was finding a perverse kind of pleasure in the mayor's misery, and this is what bothered A.J. the most.

"Connor found him at the old mill, near the entrance to the tunnel they used to get to the Dwarfhold," Skinner added. "Said he was out of his mind and kept repeating the phrase, 'it is coming,' whatever that means."

"Nothing good, I'm sure," said A.J., but he's also insane, so I'll take it with a grain of salt.

You haven't heard what Connor found at the mayor's house yet."

"The mayor's dignity locked in Sayah's jewelry box?" A.J. asked.

Skinner chuckled, then his face turned grim. "Sadly, no. His basement has been turned into a genetics lab. There were cages with dead, misshapen creatures and other failed versions of their Wendigo creation. Worse, they found two of Alice's old genetics professors in there. Both had their throats cut, and it looked like they gave up without a fight.

It's why Alice couldn't find them when she visited Nalanda. They were here, under Sayah's control, creating the Wendigo."

"This story gets weirder by the day. What I don't understand is why? Why would she concoct such a crazy plan? And what do Fergus and Aengus have to do with it?"

"Like I said, none of the questions suggest positive conclusions, and there's definitely more here than meets the eye."

"On that, we can both agree. Any luck finding Blue Jean?"

"Nope. He's a slippery son-of-a-bitch. My guess is he either ran out with the refugees during the evacuation, or he's holed up in some pit someplace dying, but no one's seen him. I still don't know why he would even be part of Sayah's plan. The Utukku and the Drow are ancient enemies, but the truth is we may never know some of the answers."

"I'm surprisingly okay with that," said A.J. "Is it wrong that I don't even want to know?"

"Wrong?" said Skinner. "Hell, I don't know about right and wrong anymore. All we can do is live every day trying to be a better person than we were the day before."

"It's surprising how often I fail at that," A.J. grumbled.

"You and me both, my friend."

A.J. was shocked at how good Skinner looked after the previous day's battle and their week of adventure. Skinner's thick white hair was noticeably darker, and the skin around his neck and eyes was tighter. Skinner looked as though he'd gained twenty years of youth in the past twenty-four hours.

"You keep getting younger, you'll be calling me 'old man' by morning," said A.J.

"Yeah, ain't it somethin?" Skinner held up a hand and looked at it. "Alice says the cellular repair serum in that antidote has added some zip to my step. Unfortunately, it ain't gonna last. She says I'll be back to my cantankerous old self in a few weeks."

"Something tells me the cantankerous part won't take nearly that long."

Skinner laughed. Even his voice sounded younger.

"Did Digger tell you what they found at the power control room?"

"Yeah," replied Skinner. "A half dozen of those fake Wendigo creatures were guarding the door when they arrived, and after a tough fight they got inside to find all the Dwarf engineers torn apart, limb from limb. Sounds gruesome."

"What the hell could have done that? Not even those Wendigos could be that strong or fast," said A.J., remembering the fighting skills of the Dwarf defenders. "Plus, none of the computers or controls were damaged either. It doesn't make sense. There was just gore and dead bodies and that cursed name scrawled in blood across the control room wall."

"Magnivald," said Skinner. "Another unanswered question. As for what could have done it, there is one creature that has a reputation for tearing its victims apart, but they haven't been seen for going on 500 years."

"Oh yeah? What creature is that?"

"Satyrs," Skinner spat the name out.

"Satyrs?" A.J. scoffed. "You mean, like, little half-naked dudes with hooves for feet and pan pipes kind of satyrs? Why would they do that?"

"Those are the ones, but I don't think 'little' is an accurate description. Apparently, Satyrs were known for their insatiable appetites for, well, everything: Eating, fucking, fighting, killing. According to Brighed, they were created during the First Age as assassins. No one ever sees them coming until after the carnage is done."

"Brighed would know a thing or two about that herself," A.J. grumbled. The thought of Brighed made his stomach clench.

"What makes you say that?"

"It's not important, just something Dian shared with me."

"Dian?" scoffed Skinner. "You can trust that anything that son-of-a-bitch told you is a lie."

"It's what he showed me," snapped A.J., a bit more harshly than he intended. "Brighed practically admitted it! She murdered his son! Her own nephew!"

Skinner let out a low chuckle and shook his head in disgust. "Dian is playing you for a fool, boy. Brighed didn't kill his son, at least not according to how Margaret tells the story, and she should know. She was there, and she has her own dark history with satyrs."

"I know what he showed me," A.J. protested, but his heart dropped into his stomach. His head spun and he suddenly felt queasy. His trust of Skinner was at war with the memories and feelings he remembered from Dian's vision.

"Well, I trust Margaret, and as she tells that story, Brighed was very close with her nephew... I forget his name, now."

"Thomas," A.J. whispered the name, and his heart ached again for the boy who died.

"Thomas. Yeah, that was it. There was a feud between the D'Anu and the Drow, and Dian was right in the middle of it. One of the Drow chieftains contracted with a satyr to kill him and his whole family, including Brighed. The Drow used English mercenaries in an attack on Dian's estate in

France as a diversion for the satyr to slip in and kill them all. During the attack, Brighed went to protect Thomas and found one of those foul creatures standing in a pool of blood over the dismembered body of her nephew. It was eating the boy."

"Eating?" The blood drained from A.J.'s face, and he felt sick.

"Seems that satyrs can take the form of any person or creature they've fed upon. They use those damned flutes of theirs to hypnotize their victims, so they never see it coming. That satyr attacked Brighed too, but she was ready for it. Brighed may be dedicated to healing, but she can be a force to reckon with when she's angry."

"I'll say," A.J. gulped, recalling his own experience with Brighed's dark and powerful anger. He could suddenly see where the story was going, and he groaned at the embarrassment and guilt and shock he suddenly felt for how he had behaved toward Brighed.

"When that satyr heard Dian calling for Thomas, it changed into his son and went after its primary target. Brighed stopped it just in time. She saved Dian's life. I heard a song about it once a long time ago. It's kind of a famous story among the D'Anu and Shifter crowds, but there's no reason you'd have heard it, I suppose. According to that song, Brighed killed the last one of those things over four hundred years ago. She'll be particularly upset if they're actually back, but it's nothing to how Margaret will take the news."

A.J. sat stunned and silent. He felt like a fool, and now he understood why everyone hated Dian so much. His stomach was doing somersaults and he wanted to cry from the shame and embarrassment he felt for how he acted.

Skinner sighed and patted A.J.'s knee in sympathy. "That's the thing about lies," he said softly. "They're insidious. They sneak up on you and strangle your reason while you sleep. Truth though, will slap you in the face every time."

"Uh huh," was all A.J. could muster, but the truth of Skinner's words helped, and they reflected how he felt. They rode in silence the rest of the way to the clinic.

"There are too many unanswered questions about this whole damned affair," Skinner said as they pulled into a parking spot near the door. The clutter of vehicles from the evacuation had taken three days to clear out. "You know, we could really use your help to figure it all out."

A.J. lifted his pack off the floor of the truck and got out. "We found your sheriff's killer, and the two of us together put an end to her. That's where my obligation ends. That was the deal. The rest of this is not my fight."

"I'm afraid it could be everyone's fight before too long," Skinner repeated arguments he had already made. "We could use a new sheriff, too, and everyone thinks you'd be great at the job. Even Connor's voiced his support."

"I'm flattered. Really. Ten years ago, I would have jumped at the offer, but I'm clearly out of my depth here, and the valley needs someone who isn't so easily fooled. Besides, I've gotten used to a certain kind of freedom in my life."

"What good is freedom if you suffer it alone?" It was a new argument, and one Skinner had obviously been saving.

A.J. had to admit it was the best he'd heard yet, and he changed the subject. "Walk me to the Mist Gate? It'll be opening soon for the Chief Administrator and other Dwarfs to come back through. I plan to use it."

"Gladly." Skinner led A.J. through the empty clinic and down the corridor to the lift that would take them to the Dwarfhold. A.J. scanned the office for Brighed before they stepped in, but the place was deserted.

"Once we sweep up the last of those Wendigos, the rest of the valley can come back too," said Skinner. "The Dwarfs are scouring the tunnels around the Dwarfhold, and Morgan has her pack working through the woods. They found three of those things today. Sayah may not be controlling them, but they still put up a hell of a fight. Thank the gods we have some of the antidote left."

"Speaking of which, what's the final casualty count?" A.J. asked.

"Twenty-three dead, eighty-seven wounded. Some of those aren't going to make it."

"And how many Wendigos?"

"The Dwarfs count 133 so far. We know where half of them came from, but who knows where they got the rest? I suspect the mayor and Sayah have been turning some of the Incogs stopping at their place on the way through the valley."

"Glad I took the forest service road instead of coming through town," said A.J. "Sounds like they've been running a regular Motel Hell there. Guess you guys need a new mayor now too. Any interest in the position?"

The lift stopped moving at the Dwarfhold's door. "Fuck, no," he said as the doors opened. Margaret stood there, and her face turned sour at his words. "Sorry, Margaret." Skinner reached for his wallet. "Here you go."

Margaret shoved the bill in her pocket and smiled as the two men stepped out of the lift. "Right on time." She looped an arm with each of them and escorted them toward the bridge. "I was just coming to get you. The Mist Gate will be open soon."

"Any word on Darcy?" Skinner asked.

Margaret frowned. "Dian says she's someplace safe, and that she'll be enrolled at the university in Nalanda at the start of the next term. But I don't like it. Not a day of that girl's life has gone by that I haven't been by her side. I was with her and Dian when the gate opened yesterday, and he asked me to check upstairs on the progress of the evacuation. When I returned, they were gone. He says she's safe under the Council's protection, and I'll see her at the university this fall, but I don't like it. No, sir. I don't like it one bit."

A.J. glanced at Skinner, who looked back and shrugged. "I'm sure she's fine," Skinner reassured her. "Dian would never dare to harm her."

"I'm no longer certain what Dian would never dare to do," Margaret responded coldly. "But for today, he's the hero of the Dwarfhold. He's also called for a full meeting of the Council to take place here in six months. With Fergus missing and the Utukku under suspicion for this catastrophe, he has no choice, really. Mina and Kane agree. So, I have that to plan for now, too."

A.J. had come to like Margaret, and he would miss her. He leaned over and gave her a kiss on the cheek. "I'm sure you'll do great as always," he said. Margaret blushed.

"Here we are," said Skinner as they stepped off the bridge. Two Dwarf guards were waiting for them, and they both saluted and fell in step beside them.

"An escort?" asked A.J. "You guys afraid I might steal the silver on my way out?"

The two guards remained silent, but Skinner and Margaret laughed. More Dwarf guards joined them inside, and by the time they reached the hub where the Mist Gate stood, practically every guard in the Dwarfhold was marching along behind them, while every other Dwarf seemed to be drinking and singing.

A.J. and Skinner approached a small group of people huddled and talking on the platform where A.J. had greeted Dian a few days earlier. Alice stood with Mina and Kane.

Behind them stood Digger with another Dwarf guard, and next to her was Morgan with her bandaged forearms. They all smiled as A.J. stepped onto the platform to join them.

A.J. turned to thank the guards for their escort and was surprised at how large the procession had become. Not only the guards, but dozens of Dwarf apprentices and masters of every craft had joined them to say goodbye to A.J.

"Um...thank you for your generous hospitality," A.J. said in his loudest voice. "Please extend my heartfelt gratitude to Master Administrator and all other Dwarfs of Neuhállé, as well as my apologies for missing your celebrations this evening. May your tunnels run deep, and thick veins of gold lay beneath your feet," he finished with the sign-off Digger had suggested.

The Dwarfs let out a collective cheer, then as one raised their fists and yelled, "I'll take Hell!"

A.J. looked at Skinner in confusion.

"Apparently, it's a famous Dwarf battle cry from the second age," Skinner informed him. "They'll probably write a song about you now."

"Great. Glad I won't be around to hear it."

"Oh, you haven't lived until you've heard a Dwarf opera in their native language," added Margaret. "It sounds worse than a rock tumbler in a forest fire."

A.J. smiled and waved at the crowd of Dwarfs and turned back toward his group of friends. The Mist Gate was glowing blue and humming in preparation for its opening. A line of D'Anu singers walked out of the administration building, with more than one sporting visible bandages and slings. A.J. didn't see Brighed anywhere. He wasn't certain if he was disappointed or relieved.

"Quite the send-off," said A.J. to his group of new friends. "Not sure I'm worth all of this."

Alice approached A.J. first and kissed him on the cheek. "Well, you've made quite the impression around here. You are definitely worth it. The Dwarfs are grateful for all you've done for them, and so are we. Thank you for having my man's back and bringing him home to me. I'm forever grateful, and for us that's a very long time."

"I'm sorry to hear about your professors," he told her.

"Thank you." Alice smiled sadly. "Thank you for everything. You'll always have a home with us if you decide to come back. Mr. Snuggles misses you already."

A.J. raised an eyebrow at Skinner.

"It's the name of the cat," Skinner added.

"Sure it is," A.J. teased.

"Travel safely," Kane's deep voice vibrated the air around them. "You are a D'Anu warrior of the first class, and should you ever find yourself in Ta Netjer, you will be an honored guest."

A.J. shook the big man's hand, and his own was dwarfed by its size.

Mina stood on tip-toe to hug A.J.'s neck and kiss him lightly on the cheek. Then she stepped back, holding both his hands in hers. "Farewell, new friend. May you walk in peace on earth and may the rainbows always touch your shoulders."

"It has been a true honor to meet you, Ptesan-Wi," A.J. said. "I hope our paths cross again someday."

"Please. For you, I am always Mina."

"Dian extends his regrets he could not be here," added Kane. "As you can imagine, he is quite busy in the aftermath of this event. He sends his wishes for your safe travels."

A.J.'s anger flared in his heart and probably showed in his face as well. He merely nodded and kept his mouth shut. He didn't trust it when it came to speaking about Dian.

The Dwarf guard stepped forward next, and A.J. recognized the heavy gold medallion around his neck. "Chief Master Guard," A.J. bowed his head. "It was an honor to fight alongside your company of courageous brothers and sisters. They fought well."

"The honor is ours," responded Chief Master Guard. "You fought bravely, for a human. I extend to you the right of passage across the Dwarf realm." He handed A.J. a black card made of the same unusual metal as the guard armor. A.J. flipped it over but saw no writing on either side. "It only appears blank to your human eyes," added the bearded Dwarf. "To a Dwarf, the message is clear as day. It grants you access to all Dwarfholds and mines. Do not lose this, human, it is more valuable than you can know."

A.J. bowed deeply and slipped the black card into his pack. Chief Master Guard took a step back, and Digger stepped forward. A metal chain ran between the Master Dwarf's belt and a steel hoop that encircled Digger's waist.

"What's going on?" A.J. asked.

"I have been arrested," said Digger in a very matter-of-fact tone. "Lowering the wall broke protocol, and there is a debt to pay."

"This is outrageous!"

Digger raised her hand to stop his outburst. "I told you before. Dwarf laws are not human laws. I knew the consequences of my action when I took it. I do not regret it, as I saved many lives, but the law is the law. Considering the circumstances, however, I will likely only be sent to the mines. It could be much worse. Do not concern yourself in the affairs of Dwarfs, A.J. I will be fine. Chief Master Magistrate herself has offered to defend me, for a sizeable fee, of course."

"Of course," said A.J., then added, "Digger, you called me A.J."

Digger smiled a broad smile and leaned against him for a long heartfelt hug. When she pulled back, she lowered her goggles despite the dim light of the Dwarfhold. "I am glad I did not behead you," she said softly and then stepped away and pretended to examine her feet.

"Me, too, Digger," said A.J. "Me too. Take care of yourself."

The Mist Gate cycled to a low vibrating hum, and the D'Anu singers took up their song around it. A.J. felt his skin grow warm, and the golden light of the D'Anu welled up inside him until his every cell hummed in unison along with it. Then he felt it leap from his body and the Mist Gate opened in a rush of fog and wind. He didn't think he could ever get used to that.

Morgan touched his chest and pulled his attention away from the gate. He put a hand around her shoulders and hugged her gently, careful not to brush against her bandaged arms. She leaned her head back and looked up at him with those beautiful dark brown eyes and smiled.

"Any word on your father?" A.J asked. He didn't mention Aengus. He didn't think he should.

"Nothing yet," she said. "But I don't think he's dead. I'm not certain my father can be killed. He's lived a very long time, you know. He's the oldest among us."

"I've heard," said A.J. "Good luck with the pack."

"Thanks. I wish you would stay, but I understand the call of the wild better than most. The D'Anu and Shifters are both long-lived creatures, though, and I look forward to the day when we meet again, for surely that day will come."

A.J. hoisted his pack onto his shoulder and turned back toward the gate. "Thank you all," he said. "Now, I've got someplace I need to be."

Skinner walked A.J. to the edge of the platform where they could speak in private. Skinner grasped A.J.'s hand

and held it tight. "You know that thing in your head you've been running away from isn't gone," he said. "It doesn't go away that easy. One way or another, you'll have to face that demon if you want to...."

"Destroy it?" A.J. offered.

"Embrace it," replied Skinner. "Like it or not, that demon is part of you, and until you can learn to love and forgive that part, you will never know peace."

"Yeah..." A.J. nodded, a bit stunned by the revelation. "The truth slaps you in the face, huh?"

"Every time," smiled Skinner. Then he pulled A.J. into his arms and pressed their hearts together. "You can't do it alone," he whispered in A.J.'s ear. "You'll need help."

"I know that, now. Thanks to you. That's actually where I'm headed. The VA has a program at Bethesda. I'm going to check into it."

"That's good." The old man's eyes turned red, and he sniffed a little. "Don't be a stranger."

"I won't," said A.J. "Thanks. Thanks for everything."

He looked up and saw shadows emerging from the mist as several Master Dwarfs and a few dozen Shifters and D'Anu emerged.

"That's my cue," said A.J. He nodded one last time to Skinner and stepped off the platform. As he approached the mist, one of the D'Anu singers stepped in his way and pulled back her hood.

It was Brighed, shining bright as gold, and her blue eyes pierced straight through to A.J.'s soul. He faltered.

"Oh, no," he whispered and his heart raced. He didn't know what to say. "I'm... I'm sorry..." he stuttered.

"Please, don't be afraid." She spoke softly and smiled. "I wanted to apologize to you, before you go."

"Me?" A.J. was incredulous. "No! No...I should apologize to you. I didn't know...but Skinner explained..."

"It's okay," she soothed. "I know, and I'm sorry Dian did that to you. You didn't deserve that from him."

"Why didn't you say something?"

"At the time, you seemed to need the anger more than you needed an explanation. I knew there would be time, later. There is always time, for us."

"Why is he like that?" A.J. shook his head in disgust. "Why would he do that to me?"

"Honestly, I've long since stopped trying to guess why Dian does anything. My best answer is, he's bored. Dian can channel genius better than most, and historically speaking, boredom and genius rarely mix well for the benefit of others."

"I also want to apologize to you for my impatience with you this past week," she continued. "I'm nearly seven hundred years old, and sometimes I forget that others are not, no matter how much I want them to be. You have a great deal to learn and tremendous growth ahead of you in this world. When you are ready, you will know where to find me."

A.J. stepped forward and took Brighed in his arms and pressed his lips to hers. She did not resist, but rather leaned in and returned the kiss with equal passion. For a moment, they breathed as one. The crowd, the Mist Gate, and the Dwarfhold all ceased to exist around them. All that existed in the universe was the touch of her skin and the taste of her lips and her intoxicating scent. He felt as though he could disappear forever into that moment, and a big part of him wanted to. A.J. almost dropped his pack and changed his mind right then, but the wise part of his mind knew it would be a mistake. Brighed was right, as usual, that he needed time to heal and to grow before he could learn to love her with the authenticity and vulnerability she deserved.

"You'd better go," she finally whispered and placed her hand over his heart one last time. "The Dwarfs have even less patience than I do." Brighed's laughter was musical and free. It sounded like wind chimes in a forest playing notes among the trees. "And when you are ready, try to find your way to the library at Nalanda. Seshat is expecting you. Everything you want to know about being D'Anu, you can find there."

"You're the true miracle here, you know that?" A.J. said. "Thank you for healing me. I will definitely miss you the most."

He surveyed the Dwarfhold and the crowd on the platform, who were watching his exchange with Brighed with deep interest. For the first time in his life, A.J. knew what it would feel like to miss a place. He waved farewell to his new family, then turned and disappeared in the mist.

~~THE END~~
The beginning…

Learn more about the world of the D'Anu, read cut scenes, and find special content and stories about your favorite characters.

Visit:

www.GregoryHaley.com

Coming Soon!

Stranger in the Den

It was the stench that pulled A.J. back into the waking world. The sharp tang of rotting flesh competed with old urine and sweat, and A.J. rolled onto his side and retched. When he opened his eyes, there was only more darkness. He held a hand in front of his face and saw his fingers only because of the faint glow left from the Brighed's Draft. He groaned and sat up, feeling his body for broken bones and finding only bruises and soreness. He felt lucky for that considering the fall, but the ambrosia in his system likely protected him from worse injury.

"Thanks for dropping in," said a deep, hoarse voice from somewhere to A.J.'s left. He couldn't tell if it was across the cavern or right next to him. He felt the ground around himself and found the butt of Digger's shotgun. He pulled it to his shoulder and ran a hand over it. The barrel magazine was twisted and dented, limiting A.J. to the lone round in the chamber. He didn't even know if it would still fire or blow up in his face if he pulled the trigger, but it was his only weapon.

"Who's there?" A.J. tried to hide his fear but wasn't having much luck. The voice spoke again, this time from behind A.J.

"Well, if it isn't the stranger in the valley?" It sounded old but resonated power.

A.J. looked around, but it was no use. He couldn't see two feet in front of him, but he thought the voice sounded familiar. "Fergus?"

"In the flesh, so to speak," the voice came from a bit further away, and in front of him this time. A.J. strained to see in that direction.

"Cover your eyes," said Fergus.

"It's not like I can see you coming with them open," A.J. tensed himself for an attack, but Fergus laughed instead. A spark flared bright white a dozen feet away, and A.J. cried out from the intensity of the light on his wide open pupils. "Hey!"

"I warned you," said Fergus. He held the end of the blinding white fire to the wick of an oil lantern, and lowered its mantle. The white glare extinguished leaving a warm yellow glow that filled the space with light. "Magnesium match," Fergus said looking at a small steel rod in his hand. "Supposed to be good for a thousand strikes. Too bad it can't help me get more oil. I'm running low."

A.J. was shocked by the gaunt figure of Fergus. The old man was wearing sweat-stained and torn clothes that hung loose on his frame. A.J. remembered Fergus as a strong and square-jawed leader of the wolf pack, but standing in front of him now was a man half that size with sunken eyes and pale skin.

"You can put that down," Fergus waved a hand toward the shotgun A.J. was still holding. I'm not going to eat you...today."